THIS
GOLDEN
STATE

THIS
GOLDEN
STATE

MARIT
WEISENBERG

FLATIRON
BOOKS
NEW YORK

THIS GOLDEN STATE. Copyright © 2022 by Marit Weisenberg.
All rights reserved. Printed in the United States of America.
For information, address Flatiron Books,
120 Broadway, New York, NY 10271.

www.flatironbooks.com

Designed by Michelle McMillian

The Library of Congress Cataloging-in-Publication Data
is available upon request.

ISBN 978-1-250-78627-2 (hardcover)
ISBN 978-1-250-78626-5 (ebook)

Our books may be purchased in bulk for promotional, educational, or
business use. Please contact your local bookseller or the Macmillan Corporate
and Premium Sales Department at 1-800-221-7945, extension 5442,
or by email at MacmillanSpecialMarkets@macmillan.com.

First Edition: 2022

10 9 8 7 6 5 4 3 2 1

For the Weisenbergs and the Hageys,
my Lindenwood family

Oh, California, I'm coming home.
—JONI MITCHELL

THIS
GOLDEN
STATE

PROLOGUE

I n the dim pink light of the girls' high school bathroom, I took apart the DNA test kit. I quickly read the instructions before I lost my nerve.

I spit into the tube. I slipped it into the envelope. At the bottom of my backpack, I found a cracked pen and carefully printed an email address I didn't own but prayed was still available.

I refused to think. I left the bathroom and headed straight for the front of the school, then to an opening in the chain-link fence. Every day, I passed the pollen-coated blue mailbox just off school grounds.

I heard a cough behind me. Harrison Addison—Silicon Valley royalty, whom I sat next to in class but whom I had barely spoken to, whom the other kids never dared speak to—held an identical package in his hand. He reached in front of me and grasped the mailbox lever. It yawned open with a creak.

I glanced up at Harrison and gave him a questioning look. He gestured with his chin for me to go first. I wavered, unsure if this was a path I should go down and if it would lead me to the truth my parents said I could never know.

CHAPTER ONE

One Month Earlier

f I could pinpoint the moment things changed, it would be as simple as this: a high school library in Illinois, cozy, me working at a table with my science fair group.

Then it was time to go.

The library was closing, so we cleaned up our scraps of paper and left behind the pods of tables and chairs, collected our coats, and exited the warmth of the orange-and-brown-hued room.

"Katie! You forgot this."

The second I set foot outside the library, my science-fair partner, Alina, followed with the registration form in her hand. I let myself be mesmerized by the color of her nail polish. Just for a moment. A sparkling, electric blue. Once I met her eyes, I'd have to lie.

"Take it!" she urged. "Me and Ruthie are all set. You're about to miss the deadline, and we're not doing this without you." The last comment was nice and took the edge off her bullying tone. I gently took the paper from her hand. Alina was no longer trusting that I would register online. It seemed I was the last person at Lincoln West High School who didn't own a smartphone.

Full of intensity and promise—the competition and the future hers for the taking—Alina placed both of her hands firmly on my shoulders. "Repeat after me: *We will advance to state. We will advance to state.*"

Ruthie, our other partner, sidled up to Alina in the doorway. "*We will advance to state!*" she chimed in and affectionately nudged Alina with her shoulder. I took in their happy faces and wanted in. "Come on, Katie! You're too sweet. It's okay to want to crush everyone."

Maybe there was a way this time.

"Thanks," I said and looked over my shoulder, as if there were somewhere I needed to be. I had to think this through. Maybe I could form an argument to convince my parents. *No one knew who I was. They didn't have to come. This couldn't be traced back to them.*

I knew we'd advance. That was the problem.

"See you at seven forty-five tomorrow? We need to work on the presentation boards."

"See you then," I agreed.

As I walked softly through the nearly empty hallway, trying to lighten the thud of my thrift-store clogs, I glanced at the questions on the registration form.

I should be satisfied that I'd helped Alina and Ruthie come this far. That should be enough. For sure, the project wouldn't have been as good without my help. I knew that was an arrogant thought, but it was true. When I'd arrived in January, I'd lurked in the back of the science-fair meetup, where twelve kids worked on their entries after school. Then I couldn't stop myself when I overheard Alina's spark of an idea on desalination using UV light. If I hadn't jumped in, Alina and Ruthie would still be fixated on their rechargeable battery.

I exited through double doors at the end of the main hallway, where glass trophy cases lined both sides, chock-full of strictly sports accolades, so similar to the other six high schools I'd attended over the past three years. In Nebraska for 76 days, 108 in Missouri, 91 in Iowa . . .

In the horseshoe driveway outside the school, my PE teacher was juggling a Tupperware container under one arm while fishing her car keys from her purse. "Bye, Katie!"

"Bye!" I said, impressed she remembered my name. It made me feel a little bit at home and like maybe I could be Katie. A French bulldog tied up to the bike rack growled low in its throat, indignant. I bent down to scratch under his smooth, warm armpits.

It was May, and though the temperature was brisk, the sun was still high at 5 P.M., lifting my spirits. I stood next to a newly planted tree, its light pink blossoms cheerily defying its scrawny stature, and watched for my dad, who was usually waiting for me. He'd pull into the half circle, I'd leap into the passenger seat, and then we'd begin the long drive home on country roads, letting loose for once and loudly singing along with pop songs on the radio. It was odd my dad wasn't here yet. He had a military sense of time.

I froze. I had that familiar, spreading sense that I wasn't alone and I was being watched.

Then I saw them.

They were in a different car—a silver truck—parked across the street where no one would notice them observing the front doors of the school.

I knew what it meant.

The school behind me moved underwater.

Usually I saw it coming. A month, a week, definitely a couple of days in advance. This one I hadn't sensed at all. I thought for sure I'd get to finish the school year. Three more weeks with Alina and Ruthie and our project.

The wind whirled copper-colored hair in front of my eyes. I tucked it behind an ear, looked both ways, and made my way toward them, darting across the four-lane road. All around us was flat expanse, grasses waving in the wind. Half of the truck was on the road, the other half sagging into a ditch. All four windows were rolled down. I inhaled the fresh Illinois air and took a final glance at Lincoln West High. The bulldog was the only one watching.

At the car, I met three pairs of eyes, my baby sister's wide like saucers. Mine came to rest on my mom's beautiful gray ones. They were haunted.

"Poppy," she said. "It's time."

That my mom was driving should have been warning number one that things had shifted. In all my seventeen years on the run—and I could remember maybe thirteen of them—this was a first. After years of our well-oiled machine working flawlessly, a cog had broken loose.

I hesitated at my mom's open window. "What happened?" I asked. "Did someone recognize you?" I was shaking my head, a subtle no.

My mom remained quiet. She waited patiently for me to come to my senses, her eyes calmly holding mine until I remembered: there wasn't another choice except to leave. Right now.

There was no point arguing that it was impossible to be discovered in this tiny rural town. My parents constantly preached that privacy was a thing of the past; it was almost nonexistent now. We lived in its rapidly eroding margins. Times had changed over the past eighteen years since my dad and pregnant mom first went on the run. Now it was the hardest thing in the world to hide.

I had one last moment to myself as I walked around to the empty seat on the other side of the truck. I felt so embarrassed that I was close to tears. To distract myself, I noted the red wildflowers, some flattened by tires, others leaning toward the sun. Suddenly I had the sensation that I'd been here before—outside of a car, separated from my family inside. *Deja vu.*

It felt real enough that I quickened my movements. I yanked open the heavy door and slipped into the back seat of the strange truck. The air in the car was warm and smelled like honey. I relaxed once I shut the door, closing me in with my family. It was okay—we were still together. We hadn't been split up.

My sister held a box of graham crackers, and one cheek looked sticky. I waited for my strong dad, always our leader, to greet me.

"Dad?"

"Hi, Poppy," he said, but he didn't turn around. He stared out his window. He seemed preoccupied, deep in thought as he looked out into the fields.

My mom twisted around so she could see me. She looked chic in her vintage clothing: an ankle-length skirt, cowboy-style ankle boots, and a thin gray T-shirt under a mauve cardigan that fell past her hips. Her long hair hung in a sheet down her back. Seeing her outdoors always startled me, like she was an apparition from one of my dreams. She wasn't often out in the open. Even now, while we were parked, she positioned her back to the school. She faced front again, but wordlessly she reached behind her for my hand, then squeezed.

"Did you leave anything inside?" My mom tipped her head to the building.

Maybe she meant a jacket or a water bottle or a photograph of me pinned on a wall. But I thought of the science fair and Ruthie and Alina and how much I'd loved working with them. My joy when Alina said they couldn't do it without me.

"No," I said quietly. "Not a thing."

CHAPTER TWO

The truck barreled down highway bordered by acres of cornfields. I kept checking behind us, but I hadn't seen another car for miles.

I guessed we were close to the safe house where we'd lived for the past six months, where things hadn't seemed urgent. Over the years, my parents' worry seemed to ebb and flow—I was never sure why, exactly. But these past six months, it had ebbed and I'd relaxed.

If we were going home, the highway would eventually give way to a choice of gravel roads. We'd take a left and drive for another five minutes, past mailboxes marking other offshoot gravel roads. There was so much space between houses and farms that we had never even seen the neighbors.

On a regular day, my dad would have slowed the car to a stop at the end of our driveway, the crunch of gravel popping beneath the tires, and I'd have to get out of the car to open the gate; that had been the worst in the rain and snow. Yesterday, before I showed my profile to the small camera for my mother, I held my face to the sun and basked for a second. A kaleidoscope of light had sprinkled through my eyelids and I'd made a wish: *Please, can we stay.*

I liked that house. My mom would sit at the round, country-kitchen table with her much too expensive paints and ask me all about my day and the science project. I could picture her taking a brush from the bowl of murky, blue-tinged water and squeezing liquid from the bristles while I chatted with her after school, telling her funny stories about my new friends. The house was the closest my sister, Emma, and I had come to having a home. I'd stood at the kitchen sink and stared out the window at the changing fields during the end of fall, the snowy winter, and the recent spring. *Who could ever find us here?* I thought.

Just this morning, when I was leaving for school, my mom was happily painting, deep in concentration. The canvas was so big and she was so far from finishing it, I'd taken it as a comforting sign that we were nowhere close to moving. Now I assumed they'd destroyed that painting, the way they always destroyed her artwork before leaving.

"Next time, can I use my real name?" Emma asked, breaking the silence.

Before my parents had to respond, I jumped in. "No, there's no using your real name. Ever. What are the family rules?"

When Emma didn't immediately answer, my mom lifted her eyes to the rearview mirror. The truck drifted just over the yellow line, into the oncoming lane, as my mom waited for Emma to answer. I double-checked that my sister's seat belt was fastened.

Emma sighed heavily, slunk low in her seat, and talked to the roof of the car. "One: no using your real name." Emma blew upward into her bangs and flared her nostrils. "Two: no staying in one place too long. Three: if something's weird, take one thing and run to the meeting spot."

"Good," my mom murmured, straightening out the car. "What else?" A shaft of golden light hit her arm where she'd draped it over the back of my father's headrest.

Emma was only eight. My mom said it was a dangerous age. At seven, Emma had believed in time machines. But at eight, Emma was starting to get it, like her feet were fully planted in reality. She could grasp what we were doing now, but, at the same time, an eight-year-old was not totally reliable.

Emma couldn't seem to remember the final rules, so I broke in with, "Four: keeping our family together is everything." I wanted to end there, on a happy note.

"Five." My dad lifted his cheek from his palm and spoke clearly to the windshield. "Don't ask about the past. For your own safety. It's the smallest mistake that will get us caught."

I noticed he said *will*.

"I was never a Katie," I said, trying to lighten the mood. The smell of earth and cattle blew in through the vents.

"Yeah, well. I don't pick the names, babe," my mom said. Now that we were in an area with more cars, she held the steering wheel in a proper nine-and-three position as if she hadn't driven in years and was nervous.

So, who the hell did pick our names? We'd wait in hotel rooms until my dad got word to pick up a packet with new identification. Once, when my dad thought I was asleep in a dark, dingy motel room, I saw him take a brick of cash and papers from the packet and put them in a metal lockbox.

"Why are *you* driving?" Emma asked my mom.

"I just am," my mom replied. Something very weird was going on. My dad continued to stare out the window, like he was calculating our options in his head. Were we moments away from being surrounded?

There was an awkward silence in the small truck cab.

"Were they close this time?" I prodded again, not expecting an answer. Who were we evading? The police? The FBI?

My mom picked a strand of hair from the ChapStick coating her lips. She stubbornly didn't answer. They always insisted the less we knew the better, for our protection.

I didn't know my parents' true identities. Or what they'd done. I'd imagined every possible scenario, even entertaining the idea that I'd been kidnapped, that they weren't my real parents. But I looked so much like my mom and enough like my dad. What I kept coming back to: I couldn't imagine them hurting anyone.

They told me I knew who they were, I just didn't know the superficial parts: given names, families they'd been born into, where they'd grown up. And, according to my parents, I didn't need to. These labels were society's identifications, and identities could be shed like snakeskins once they were no longer useful. Said like true radical thinkers or like people who read a lot of books on Buddhism, which both of them did.

In some respects, my parents were free spirits, but there was also strict order in our family. That came from my dad, who had always been the leader in our fugitive lifestyle. So it was extremely odd that he wasn't driving and that he was barely speaking.

I settled back into the seat, the edge of cracked vinyl catching my pale-yellow sweater from Goodwill. I pulled at the loose thread, then stopped and tried to push it through to hide the snag. I had to take care of what I had.

My dad straightened and pressed his knuckles to his forehead, like he had a headache. He turned to look at me. "I need your phone," he said. I thought he'd forgotten.

I dug into my backpack and found my little black flip phone. There was a voice mail from Ruthie.

"Can I just listen to this last voice mail?"

"Pops," he said to me, reaching for it.

I hesitated. Then I reluctantly handed it over.

He quickly removed the SIM card. I closed my eyes so I didn't have to see him snap it in two.

Alina and Ruthie were gone now. I stared into the cornfields and ignored the pinch in my chest.

My dad placed the phone into the glove compartment, then slammed it shut in a rare show of emotion. He wasn't mad at my mom, though, because he allowed her to take his hand and tenderly kiss the back of it.

I surreptitiously studied him for another minute, trying to figure out if he was angry or scared or just busy calculating our next move. Watching him, I wondered, not for the first time, if my dad had some kind of military training. Outside of whatever day job he picked up that paid him under the table, he spent his life behaving like Special Forces. He always set up what we called "Dad's hole"—a room or an area where he sat in front of his aged laptop screen and watched the surveillance cameras. He could sit so still for hours, which wasn't something a regular human could do. I imagined he'd been trained for a war in a desert, unable to move a muscle because the enemy would see the movement of his camouflage.

I strained to see what was in the truck bed behind me. Suitcases. So this exit hadn't been an emergency.

When it was an emergency, we were allowed to grab one item. My dad's was his laptop. For Emma, it was whatever we took for her. Until recently. Now she could choose for herself, and it was always a stuffed animal of some sort. Unlike me at her age, she had no loyalties. She was never attached to just one.

My mother's item was a small, framed painting of a California landscape—the size of a postcard. It was a picture of rugged coastline and an inviting blue ocean, and I'd been obsessed with it since I was little. During icy winters and long, gray springs, I would dream of living inside of it.

For me, it was babyish, but my item was my pink blanket. It had pinpoint holes now if you held it up to the light, and some areas were worn so thin it scared me to think what would happen when the fabric wore through. When it was cold and we lived in motels or apartments with no heat, I draped the blanket over my head to stay warm, but these days I tried to be as gentle as I could when I handled it. My mom used to joke that when I was small and fell down, I wanted my blanket before I wanted her.

My mom took one hand off the steering wheel and pressed at buttons on the unfamiliar car stereo. "Did you remember my blanket?" I asked. I tore open a granola-bar wrapper with my teeth.

There was dead silence.

I glanced up.

My parents looked at each other.

I leaned forward, my chin touching the cold of my mother's vinyl seat. "Tell me you remembered my blanket."

"I'm sorry," my mom said.

I sat back. "I've had it this whole time. I've had it since I was born."

"I'm *so* sorry, Poppy," my mom said. She briefly squeezed her eyes shut and mouthed *Fuck.*

"Can we go back? I'll run into the house. It will just take one second. *Please.*" But I knew it was futile, even as I said it. We were already hours away.

"We can't," my mom finally said. My dad rested his head against the window.

I thought of the landlord eventually coming to the abandoned house, having it cleaned, and my blanket being dropped into a large, black trash bag. I shut my eyes tight.

"It was my one thing," I whispered. The statement felt like it came up from a deep well inside me.

"What, baby?"

"Never mind," I said.

Now it was time to do what I always did for them. I put the mental image of my blanket into a compartment and closed the panel.

CHAPTER THREE

We were traveling west.

Hours passed before my mom finally said, "Dan, I need to stop."

We pulled over at a good-sized Comfort Inn along a long stretch of nondescript highway. I hoped we would keep going west, far west to the edge, to the world of that painting. I always requested California and I always got shot down. I thought that was odd, because it was such a big state. So many places to blend in.

My mom flung open her car door and stretched, her fingertips reaching to the black sky. Tonight I was mad at her and observed her with remove. Sometimes I would search her for clues about who she really was. Or used to be. Ballerina was one guess. She was so tall and elegant.

"Let's go," my dad said. Our family of four walked through the shadows of the great American parking lot, and I wondered what this area used to look like before it was paved. What used to stand in this exact spot?

My dad checked us in, and once we were in the utilitarian hotel room, we spread out our meager belongings. My mother slid the privacy sign on the door handle, then locked us in with the dead bolt. My dad had the "go bag" and got to work collecting our used IDs.

"Come with me," my mom gestured to my sister. "You need to take a bath."

Emma looked at her belligerently.

"Go!" I said, nudging her off the bed. I wasn't in the mood for a tantrum tonight. I was the one who deserved to have one. Not that I ever had. Not that I ever would.

My sister scrambled off the queen-size bed and followed my mom to the bathroom like a small prisoner going to her cell.

I kicked off my shoes, lay back on the bed, and threw a wrist over my eyes.

"Poppy." I dropped my hand and rolled to face my dad, who sat in the straight-backed desk chair, his hands folded in his lap. "You did good," he said.

I nodded in response and squeezed my eyes shut again. I didn't know if he meant I'd done a good job not losing my mind about my blanket or obeying when they'd asked me to get in the truck and leave the place we'd lived the longest to date.

Or maybe I was good because I'd closed yet another chapter and once again, I'd kept everyone from knowing me.

My sister pushed out of the bathroom. Her eyes were all red and so was her face. My mom had made Emma wash her hair and then combed through the tangles in her beautiful silky-fine baby hair. You would have thought Emma was being tortured.

"Are you okay?" I whispered and touched a strand of her wet hair. She just shook her head away angrily and got under the covers.

"Can I take a shower?" I called to my mom, who was hanging up Emma's towel.

"Sure, but can I talk to you for a moment?"

I joined my mom in the small bathroom with the flimsy door. She closed it with one shoulder. Our eyes met in the mirror.

"I'm sorry," she said. She put both palms on my cheeks and held my face so I could look in her eyes. I nodded and felt a lump squeeze my throat. "I know you wanted to stay. You really liked Alina and Ruthie. And I'm sorry about your blankie. I would do anything to be able to go back and get it." She folded her arms, gripping the sides of her cardigan. "This is a lot to ask."

My heart relented at her apology. "It's okay," I said. I moved forward to hug her tight.

"We've stayed together so long."

"We'll always be together," I said. I couldn't imagine being apart from her. That seemed to cheer her up, and I felt her smile spread against my hair.

When I'd turned fifteen, my parents said their biggest accomplishment was having almost raised me. They'd said it with relief, like they'd crossed an imaginary finish line. But they still had Emma.

When I was so small that I'd had only a preunderstanding of our situation, I'd asked, "Mommy, if you go to jail, where will I get food?" I wasn't sure how old I'd been. Young enough that my blanket was tucked against my cheek and I was in her lap. My mom wore a tan suede skirt and tall boots. One of her legs jittered nervously up and down. We were in a stark lobby with marble floors, waiting for my dad to pick up our mail. I'd overheard my parents discussing how my mom and I should stay farther away in case the police grabbed my dad at the wall of gold postboxes. I was young enough that they were still speaking freely in front of me.

I most likely recalled the moment because of my mother's reaction—how frightened her eyes were. Her pupils did a crazy thing—widening and then contracting. In hindsight, I wondered if she had that reaction at the thought of leaving me and going to prison or because I'd surprised her with how much I knew.

She'd removed me from her lap, then stooped down in front of me so we were face-to-face. "Dad and I aren't going any-where."

Instead of being comforted, what I learned from the con-versation was that there was no one else. She didn't name anyone else who could take care of me. My parents were all I had between me and the big frightening world.

There was an abrupt rap of knuckles on the bathroom door, snapping me back from the memory. My mom reached across me to open it. My dad filled the doorway. He stood barefoot on the dark shag carpet.

"The IDs are ready." He held up his flip phone to show her where he'd heard this news. I knew not to ask questions.

Later that night in the motel room, I overheard my parents whisper-arguing through the bathroom door.

"No." It was a word I didn't often hear my dad say to my mom. "I've looked at it from every angle. It's not a good plan. We can't go. It was always dangerous, but now it's just stupid."

"We have to." There was a pleading note in her voice. Since she picked me up from school and all through the drive, she'd seemed slightly manic. Almost excited.

"You aren't thinking straight. You're in shock. We both were. But now I've thought it through."

Whatever it was, I knew she'd get it. Usually I saw the fire in my dad's eyes—the next-stop look—and the resignation in my mom's that we had to keep moving. But he always looked for her approval before any big moves, like he was waiting on her because she was subtly the real boss. The emotional boss. He was operations.

"No, I'm okay. I promise you. I'm not in shock. I'm oddly clear," she said.

Shock about what?

I looked over at my sister in bed next to me to see if she was listening, too—the two of us like owls with our eyes wide open—but she was asleep. Warm and snuggly. I moved closer and pretended she was still the baby it seemed she was just a second ago.

"We're all letting emotion get in the way. It's clouding our judgment," my dad said, continuing their conversation. "Everything's happening too fast."

"I doubt it's been fast. This plan has probably been months in the making. We just didn't know! Besides, what other choice do we have? It's the last house. This is about money. For our family." There was a pause. "Even you know it's a good plan," my mom said.

What the hell was she talking about? Last house? I heard mumbling from my dad. It sounded like *belly of the beast,* but his voice was so low, I wasn't sure. My mind was bouncing from word to word, trying to make meaning.

"I love you. I love the girls. I'd never do anything stupid, if that's what you're worried about. You know that," she assured him. "I'm making a promise right now: I won't break our rules." There was silence. I took it as the start of him eventually giving in.

"You think they're holding up?" My mom changed the subject.

I heard my dad's loud exhale. "I think it hasn't hit them yet. Or maybe they're so used to it. Poppy is getting hard. Emma is starting to get it."

"You think this is wrong?" she asked.

"Of course. But we get to raise them ourselves. That was our goal. One million times over, we've decided that's everything. They know us. And look at them."

"I know."

There was a longer silence.

"I wish we could stay there."

"We can't," my dad said. He sounded stern.

I heard my mom sigh, then cough as if to cover it. I pictured her resting her head on my dad's shoulder.

My sister was so warm she was burning me up. I rolled as far away as I could until there was no room left to go.

CHAPTER FOUR

Girls, we need to go."

I was so tired, I couldn't even open my eyes. My mom shook me very gently. "Poppy."

"Just go in your pajamas." My dad's voice came from the other side of the bed, coaxing my sister. Finally, "I'll just carry her, Maze."

Maze? What had he called her? I was so bleary-eyed and exhausted that maybe I'd misheard.

When I was in the truck, I saw it was 3 A.M.

An hour later, unable to sleep, I asked, "What happened?"

"What do you mean?" my dad asked. He was driving and seemed more like himself again, back in charge. The truck traveled down the lonely freeway.

In the dark, it felt easier to push. "How did they find us? I mean, we were in rural Illinois. Why haven't the authorities given up? Whatever happened was eighteen years ago."

I knew better than to ask questions. They wouldn't tell me.

My mother's face was illuminated by the oncoming glare of a semi's headlights. In the rearview mirror, I saw her eyes dart warily from what must be my confused face to my sister's sleeping one.

"It's a cold case that still matters to some people," my dad said.

Why?

I told myself to trust them, that there were things I didn't need to know.

But just because I didn't know the secrets, it didn't mean they didn't exist, no matter how hard my parents willed them away.

Some days, when we'd lived somewhere for months, I could get lulled into a routine. But in these in-between, anxiety-ridden pauses, I examined our situation all over again.

What I had to go on was this:

"We fell in love and I was pregnant with you. For your protection, the less you know, the better."

I understood their reasoning. Mostly.

But I didn't know who my parents were. Their "real" names were even fake. They weren't "Allie" and "Dan." And our last name wasn't really Winslow.

For years, I'd told myself it didn't matter.

Why did I need to know? Why was it so hard for me to quit wondering?

Because I lived in the dark. If I didn't know who they were, I didn't know who I was.

And as I got older, it was getting harder for me to accept. Every time my parents refused to answer my questions, it felt like I couldn't let them into my heart as fully as I used to.

Consciously and unconsciously, I always quietly watched my parents. I'd looked for key words, clues, anything I could google at a school library before swiftly clearing the search. But they had been careful to give me zero, because they knew that was exactly what I would do sooner or later.

Why couldn't they trust me? I'd asked them. They told me there were so many tiny ways to get caught. Ways an extremely smart person could be careless. We all made mistakes. And they'd gone almost eighteen years without making them because they were so insanely careful. They also said there were ways we didn't even know we could get caught, ways technology got ahead of us and we were just catching up, that it made the world too small. They'd had to adjust to the internet. There could be new technologies we weren't even aware of.

Sometimes I looked at my parents and I made up stories or best theories.

Both of my parents seemed college educated. I guessed that my mom was now in her early forties, old enough to have made it through college by the time she ran.

My dad was more mysterious. He seemed younger than my mom. Maybe as many as five years younger. I wondered what part he had played in their crime, because he seemed like the knight in shining armor, a protector type, crisp and straight, while she was bohemian and relaxed. Opposites attract. Maybe my mother had been the influence. The reformed bad girl to his Boy Scout. I could see her being rebellious. She was so calm, but her eyes spoke of experience and stories.

While my dad liked order, my mom loved bending rules. She'd get flashes of sparkle in her eyes that hinted at how fun and daring she must have been as a girl. She'd make up things like "Free-for-All-Friday," on which we could eat as much ice cream as we wanted. She'd let us stay up all night, cuddled up next to her, when there was a movie marathon on TV. Once, she decided we'd take over the entire living room with a fort we built out of refrigerator boxes she'd asked my dad bring home when he briefly worked as a mover. For about a month, she let Emma and me sleep in it. My dad usually just laughed and shook his head.

When I'd asked how they'd met, they were ready for my question, like they'd come up with a party line years before.

"Through a friend," they'd answered. They had both looked sad, like they missed their friend.

The other thing: they were both beautiful.

In a library in Dayton, I'd googled "modern-day Bonnie and Clyde." Nothing came up.

Whenever we started fresh, my parents had fake driver's licenses, new Social Security numbers, and new housing ready and waiting for us. Maybe they had help from an underground organization? Maybe it was as simple as finding these relocation services on the dark web. But there were definitely third parties helping us, and they were so good, their services couldn't be cheap.

We were poor because my dad could only take jobs that paid under the table. He mostly worked construction. My mother always stayed home.

I saw the look of strain and stress on both of their faces. We never did any after-school activities like other kids. We couldn't go on class trips to DC or with the French teacher to Paris. College wasn't a possibility. I didn't have any consistent records. Just different names in different school-district databases that showed I got straight A's and near-perfect test scores.

College had never been discussed, though I was coming to the end of high school. Only one more year, then kids my age would be moving into adulthood while I was still hiding, unable to lay down roots and build on something. For that I'd need a real identity.

I wanted to ask my parents what kind of future they pictured for me. I knew it was time and I was working up the nerve. Would there be more education beyond high school level? Some kind of work beside odd jobs? But in my heart, I was scared it was obvious. If I wanted more, I'd lose my family. This would finally end.

CHAPTER FIVE

We were still going west.

Keep driving, I thought, feeling more and more hopeful as the hours passed. I'd never seen the ocean.

"Can we get a dog?" Emma asked. She had a red indentation on one cheek from nodding off against the seat belt and her hair was matted in the back.

"No, honey." Fidgeting, my mom gathered her hair up into a bun before releasing it to wash down over her shoulders. Her brand-new black hair had left stains on her clothes. She'd finally quit trying to color mine, since hair dye, even the most expensive kind, made my skin break out in an angry rash.

The silver truck had been abandoned in a crowded Walmart parking lot, where litter blew like tumbleweeds, half a day's drive from the first night's stay at the Comfort Inn. The new car was a minivan and nicer than what we were accustomed to. Emma and I luxuriated in our own separate rows.

My mom angled to look at us in the back. "Why so quiet?" she asked me. I could have asked the same about her, about both my parents. Every so often, I'd watch my dad watch my mother. I couldn't tell if it was concern. He seemed to be searching her, waiting for something.

"I was thinking about some science work I didn't finish." My voice had sadness in it and an edge, like I didn't know which to choose. We were all tired and testy.

"Hey, I'm sorry about the science project," my mom said.

I brushed away a film of dust on the window ledge.

My sister grabbed the back of my gray leather seat and moved closer, straining to hear.

"Emma! Sit back. That's not safe." My dad had to call out extra loud to the wayback.

"Poppy." My mom's tone was all sympathy. "I know it's tough, dipping in and out like that. But I'm glad you can have most things—music, sports, meet kids your own age. It's important that you have them. That's why we made the conscious choice to send you to school."

"But we can only have things to a point."

"Well, I promise, it's better than me trying to homeschool you. We'd have a grand old time, but we'd get nothing done." My mom laughed and began to fidget with the radio. Sound exploded from the speakers. She was trying to lighten the mood.

I didn't say the thing that had formed in my head when I was not much older than Emma and I began to understand. I had never once said it out loud. *Why are we being punished for something we didn't do?*

Something on the side of the road caught my mom's eye.

She turned her head to keep watching even after we'd passed. I spotted the white corrections bus with grated windows parked on the access road. Prisoners in orange jumpsuits picked up trash from the brown grasses along the freeway. That put an immediate end to my internal rant.

"It doesn't matter, anyway. We can't have friends if we don't have real phones," Emma said.

A moment later, my mom would build her argument, gathering steam as she went, lecturing Emma on everything flawed about this reasoning. Overpasses, signage for fast food and gas, nondescript chain stores all passed outside my window while I tried to tune out my mom's favorite subject. In addition to the obvious dangers of us using technology, being antitechnology was also part of her parenting philosophy: *Real friendships are about human connection. Social media isn't a replacement.* They said they wanted to raise us away from screens so we had a chance to live naturally, in a way that was better for our development and happiness.

But, for a second, three of us sat in stunned silence. Emma had nailed it. She and I would always stand apart from other kids as long as we were off-line. She already knew this at age eight.

Hours blended together and then so did the days. I wasn't sure if it was Thursday or Friday by the time my dad stopped at a gas station in Nevada.

While fuel streamed into the tank with a rush, my dad pulled fruit from a wrinkled paper sack.

"We need to eat these here."

"Why?" my mom asked. The three of us had been stretching

our legs outside the car and now stared at the bruised green apple and two brownish bananas in my dad's hands.

"Agriculture inspection at the border."

"What border?" I asked.

"California," he said.

I turned away so they wouldn't see my smile.

"Eat up," he said and tried to hand off the fruit. "They don't want insects hitchhiking into the state."

My dad hated waste. It seemed deeply ingrained, like he'd been raised without much. Or maybe it was because we couldn't afford more.

I took the grossest banana, since I knew my mom and Emma would resist and I ate it quickly, washing down the flavorless mush with a swig from my water bottle. It didn't dampen my good mood. I was ready to go and see what was on the other side.

But first, we had to pass Go. We didn't have far to drive before we saw the border station. The building looked like a toll stop, topped by a silver corrugated roof that slanted up to the cloudless sky. Only two lanes were open, which caused a small backup. We watched an official in a khaki uniform and full-brimmed hat loom at the window of the car in front of us. Once the driver's window was rolled down, the inspector braced both hands on either side of the open window. Ten seconds later, the car drove off without incident.

"It's fine," my mom said to no one in particular.

"Why wouldn't it be?" I asked. "We ate our fruit."

The officer waved my dad up.

"Good afternoon. Any fruits, vegetables?"

"No, sir." I expected a quick exchange and then my glorious

arrival over the border. But the inspector bent at the waist and peered into the car. My mom shifted and reached for her purse.

"Anything inside your bag, ma'am?"

I expected my mom's automatic answer, but when it didn't come, I looked over at her. She seemed suddenly, uncharacteristically, tongue-tied.

"Honey?" my dad prompted.

She cleared her throat but only shook her head. Her purse was open on her lap and she withdrew a lipstick. She took off the cap and quickly streaked it across her lips. What was she doing? I had never, ever seen her freeze up like that before.

The inspector glanced deeper into the car at me and my sister and our scattered bags. Then he straightened and gave the top of our car a clap. "You're good to go."

My dad rolled away slowly, then rapidly picked up speed. As soon as his window was closed, his eyes flicked to my mother. He started to speak, then just shook his head. It looked like *I told you so.*

"You don't need to say anything," my mom said to him.

The car crossed over the border. *Welcome to California.*

CHAPTER SIX

Where were we going? We stayed in a terrible, dirty hotel in Vacaville, California, that had seen better days and was out of a different era. It was called the Camelot Motel. The neon sign—a knight with a lance—was sun bleached and no longer worked.

There was the vibe that we were holed up until we got the go-ahead. My dad would then leave for a shipping store to pick up a package with our new IDs. Hopefully we could purchase a few more clothes at the brand-new outlet stores that were next door in a sprawling one-story mall. Then we would drive to our next apartment and figure out if we were starting school on Monday.

"I'm going to get some air," I said. My family was playing a heated game of poker, trying to keep the bedspread as flat as possible. Oddly, poker was our constant. My dad always set up a game when he wanted to remind us we were safe, we were a family.

"You don't want to play this hand?" My dad sat cross-legged on the bed, his cards close to his face in one hand as if he were farsighted. He smiled, lines by his eyes crinkling. It was good to see him happy again, momentarily lost in the game and teasing his family as he outplayed my mom while patiently teaching my sister. It helped that he had a naturally good poker face. My mom jokingly swayed toward him to look at his cards. He grabbed her neck with his free hand and kissed the spot below her ear. Always a bit of a princess, my mom must have temporarily lost her fear of bedbugs because she was sitting directly on top of the bedspread.

"Nah. It's too dark in here. I'm going to walk to the pool."

"Hey, why don't you take your sister," my mom said.

"Sure."

She flipped her hair over her shoulder. "Stay close, okay?"

"Of course. Come on, Em," I said. There was an underlying fear that if the law ever did catch up to us, we'd be apart when it happened. Then we'd have no way of getting back to one another.

The sunlight was a surprise after mostly staying in the dark motel room for two days. Recently, I'd discovered how much I loved running when I'd set out by myself on the country roads this spring. It was a way to be by myself for once, though often my dad wanted to join. But here, there was nothing around us except for freeways. I was trapped. In the room, we weren't allowed to watch TV, and we could never get on our only device—my dad's laptop—unless we were on public Wi-Fi miles and miles away from where we were staying. If I was with him when he was using his computer in a public space and I asked, he'd let me look something up. But he always wanted to know what I wanted to see, and he was always right there while I searched.

So I'd been reading and writing and sketching. And sleeping. Sleeping a great depressed sleep. It helped block out the losses. And thinking about what everyone I'd made friends with might be saying by now. *Is Katie sick?* Then: *Where the hell is she?* Then: *I think she's gone.* That is, if the authorities weren't poking around the day after we left. I couldn't ask my parents if they had read anything in the news, if there was some kind of alert out for us. It didn't seem like it. It seemed like my parents were only tense about where we were headed.

Emma and I leaned over the second-story splintered-wood railing and looked down at the deserted pool. A paperback romance novel I'd picked up at the grocery store near Salt Lake City dangled at my side, and I quickly trotted down the cement stairs, taking note of the broken glass littering the steps. The light fixture above had been smashed.

There was a small swing set outside the pool fence. Emma headed in that direction without asking.

"No! We have to stay here," I barked.

"I want to go on the swings." A hot gust of wind tousled our clothing.

"Emma, no," I said firmly. As firmly as my dad would say it.

Emma eyed me but didn't remove her hand from the gate latch. I crossed over to her and she quickly dropped her hand to her side.

She squinted. "You always follow the rules." For a beat, her expression seemed a little too old for eight and hinted at how rebellious she would be by the time she was my age.

Unnerved, I ignored her and settled with my book in the

lounge chair, the plastic bands worn and brittle. I angled the chair away from the sun so I could see the print.

A shadow crossed the pages. "Honey, you and your sister need some sunscreen, I don't mind telling you." The woman who checked us into the motel two days ago stood over me.

"Oh, thanks. We put some on." Lie.

"I had your coloring and never wore hats or sunscreen, and the wrinkles poured in at age forty." She let out a phlegmy smoker's cough and continued to study me.

"You're right. I'll sit in the shade." Maybe she'd move along if I did.

"Did anyone ever tell you that you look like . . . Damn, what was her name? Well, you're probably too young to have heard of her anyway."

"Who was she?" I was polite, but my heart began beating uncomfortably fast with the unwanted attention. Emma was by the fence, too far away.

"I can't remember if she was a model. Or socialite. Well, aren't they kind of both these days?"

"You okay down there?" My dad appeared at the upstairs railing. Thank god. I could always count on him to know when something strange was going on. He seemed to feel it.

"All good, Dad! I'll be there in a minute." I smiled tightly up at him, letting him know we needed to get out of here.

He nodded and backed out of sight.

The motel woman was looking to where my dad had just stood. She turned back to me and lowered her voice. "Are you okay, hon?" I could feel her drinking in my details. I knew my clothes looked dirty.

"Oh yes," I said. "I'm good."

Five minutes later, we were in the minivan.

"It's in Marin," my dad informed us, referring to the package he needed to retrieve. I had no idea where Marin was.

The message came while we were down at the pool. Perfect timing. We would have had to leave anyway because of the way the woman noticed me. It wasn't just that she'd studied me. It was that she'd concluded I might be a girl in trouble. Who she needed to save.

"Won't it look weird that we just disappeared?" I asked my dad.

"We're paid up. I went down and told her we got the clearance to go home after the terrible house fire."

"Ah."

"Hey, Pops?" my dad said. "Be leery of people who are curious and bored."

CHAPTER SEVEN

n Marin County, we stopped in the most picturesque little town I'd ever seen. The downtown streets were lined with olive trees, and wooden barrel planters overflowed with impatiens. A woman with a hand trowel worked on replacing tulips with magenta-colored flowers from black plastic flats at her feet. Gentle green hills rolled in the background, and we'd passed signs for Muir Woods National Monument.

My dad threw an arm around the back of my mom's seat and expertly parallel parked the long minivan into a very narrow space between two shiny cars.

"What kind of car is *that*?" Emma piped up, peering out the rear window. "It's hooked up to something."

"A Tesla. It's plugged into a charging station because it's battery operated," my mom said. She turned to my dad. "Well?"

I hated this part.

He looked to my mom. "Stay here with the car. Give me thirty minutes exactly. After that, you leave. No waiting."

We were supposed to sit tight while he walked a distance away to pick up the package at the local pack-and-ship store. It was always our most vulnerable spot—the likeliest place to get traced, then caught. The package contained cash, driver's licenses for my parents, Social Security cards, an address, and keys for the new home. The amount of cash fluctuated. Sometimes my dad didn't need to worry about getting a job immediately. At other stops, I saw instant stress at the corners of his eyes.

My mom took a deep breath, then caught my dad's face and put her forehead against his. In profile, I saw my dad close his eyes, but she kept hers open. My dad pulled back and kissed my mom softly on the lips. Even with the uneven haircut he'd given himself in the bathroom and even with her cheaply dyed black hair and even though I was their daughter, I could see how striking they were together and how much they loved each other.

"I'll be back in thirty minutes," he said. "I promise."

"Don't promise," she said. I didn't like it that they were more jittery than usual.

My dad got out of the van. The side door automatically parted, and he stood in the opening, his back to the road. "Girls, come here."

I undid my seat belt and reached for him. He held me tight and I felt how solid he was. How safe. I rested my head on his shoulder for just a second. I wanted to fix whatever was worrying him this past week. When I'd watched him watching my mother, at times, he seemed almost sad.

"I love you," he whispered to me.

"I love you, too."

"Em, come here." I thought I heard his voice crack.

Emma scrambled over the top of my seat, her legs behind her like she was sledding downhill. "My girl," my dad said.

"You're squeezing too tight," she yelped.

"I'm sorry, baby. You are just so squeezy." Then my dad abruptly gave us his back and began walking. My mom kept her eyes trained on him and then watched the empty space for a long moment, even after he'd rounded the corner.

When she took a deep breath, it caught in the middle. She dug in her old red purse that had faded to the color of cranberries. "Girls, here's five dollars. Go into the coffee shop and buy a snack. I'll wait right here." She pointed to a Starbucks on the corner that blended into the setting with its Spanish-style red roof and fig ivy–covered facade. It wasn't the time to tell her that probably not much inside cost less than five dollars. She popped on her large sunglasses, a cheap plastic pair that made her look glamorous and also covered half her face.

"You're staying in the car?" I asked.

"I'll be right here. I promise I'm not moving. Keep an eye out. If I start the car, come back."

I took my parents' cue, raising my antenna more than normal. But I knew my parents must have things under control. They always did.

I guided Emma down the street, avoiding eye contact with strangers. You'd think I'd get used to it because it always worked out, but I hated the ritual of saying goodbye before my dad went to the pack-and-ship store. And then the stress of the timer. We were only allowed to wait for him for thirty minutes.

The coffee shop was a long, narrow space and crowded even

in midafternoon. Most tables held a laptop. First, both Emma and I had to use the restroom. I calculated that that would kill five minutes. Emma went into the single bathroom alone and forgot to lock the door, but I waited vigilantly outside. When it was my turn, I made her wait inside the bathroom with me despite her complaints. Emma put both palms on the sink, leaned close to the mirror, and made funny faces.

"Gross. Don't touch the sink! Wash your hands."

"I already did," she whined.

I doubted that. "Do it again." I was taking it out on Emma, which I sometimes did when my parents were stressed, and therefore I was stressed.

When we were done, we got into the long line. My old-school digital watch said we had twenty-three more minutes. At this point, I hoped my dad had reached the store.

I was tempted to ask Emma to wait by herself while I peeked out the front door to check on my mom. The thought of looking out and seeing police made me reach for Emma's hand. Emma shook it off. She was staring hard, fascinated by the two girls in front of us in line. They were about my age, blond, both wearing pastel-colored Lululemon tennis skirts. They were sharing what was on their phones and giggling madly.

It was going to kill Emma when she couldn't be one of those girls as she got older—popular, with thousands of social media followers. At age eight, it was already easy to tell Emma was born to be a queen bee. I'd bet anything my mom had been one once. "Come on." I nudged Emma when a gap formed in the line in front of us.

"Stop it, Poppy!"

The girls turned their heads. Emma had just used my name in public like an idiot. I wanted to smack her.

Emma knew what she'd done. At least she had the decency to stare at the ground and listen to me. She inched forward as the girls took in our scraggly appearances, mine especially—the vintage T-shirt and dirty jeans—and quickly lost interest. My cheeks grew hot.

"What can I get you?" a barista asked when it was finally our turn to order.

Emma spoke first. "I'll have a grande lemonade." Emma pronounced it "grand."

"And for you?"

"That's all." I knew there wouldn't be money left over. Emma fingered a package of chocolate-covered graham crackers, and I put my hand over hers. The last thing we needed was for her to pocket the cookies and get caught, and a manager demand to speak to our parents.

"Don't you want something?" Emma looked up at me, concerned.

"That will be $4.77." I handed over the crumpled five-dollar bill, then dropped the change in the clear plastic bucket. "Your name?"

I paused. I didn't have my new name yet and I couldn't use my old one.

The barista was watching me, Sharpie poised in one hand at the lip of Emma's plastic cup. "Name?" she encouraged.

"Sorry. It's Eleanor." Emma snickered. I wanted to grab her elbow hard and leave so she wouldn't get her expensive drink.

Instead, I acted like everything was just fine so Emma wouldn't act out. When the family got tense, I'd noticed she found ways to turn the attention to herself. I knew it was because she was scared, even if she didn't know it. I consulted my watch while we waited for her lemonade. Twenty more minutes.

We hovered in a corner and looked at different mugs for a long ten minutes. Finally, a two-person table opened up next to the large square window at the front of the coffee shop. I leaned forward and peeked down the block at our car. I sensed my mother's presence inside, still as a cat, tensed but unmoving.

I brushed scone crumbs off the table with a discarded newspaper. I was about to start a conversation with Emma to distract myself, but I took one look at her leaning back in her chair and gnawing on her straw and I had to look away. Right when I was thinking that she was completely oblivious, she spoke up.

"Hey?"

"What?" I massaged my temples. The two pretty girls from a different universe settled right next to us, talking loudly.

"You won't leave me, right?"

I glanced up at Emma. Her eyes were shiny like she was holding back tears. Immediately, I reached for her, awkwardly leaning around the table. "Oh my god, no. Never. Never, ever." I circled my arm around her small shoulders and hugged her to me, not caring that the girls were watching. Emma let me crush her against me. She could do that—completely undo me when I least expected it. Her baby-soft hair smelled like strawberries.

Emma pulled away first and went back to her lemonade like nothing had happened. I locked eyes with one of the pretty girls. She stared, fingering a delicate gold chain at her neck. I looked away, glancing down at my watch. Five more minutes. We'd never come this close to the time limit before.

I noticed my knees had begun to knock together beneath the table. At three minutes to go, I trained my eyes on the car.

One more minute. I stared out the window. My eyes darted back and forth between the street and the minivan.

"Sis?" Emma was saying. My eyes were glued to the minivan. "Sis!" Emma insisted.

For the first time in my life, time was up.

"Come on, we need to go," I said to Emma.

I knew I had to appear calm. As I stood up from the table, I saw the minivan start just like it was supposed to. Then the police car slid into my vision. It double-parked across the street and left its motor running.

I watched as the minivan jerkily pulled out of the parking spot and drove away fast.

Oh my god. Oh my god!

The blood left my face. I looked at Emma with my mouth open.

I knew Emma was saying my name, but I couldn't move.

She and I were alone.

When I wouldn't answer her, Emma collapsed her face into her arms on the table and started to cry.

I didn't have any money. I didn't know where to go. I didn't know what to do. I was responsible for Emma.

My instinct was to run after my mom. "Come on!" I grabbed Emma's hand and walked-ran from the coffee shop, losing my cool.

Out on the street, I listened for the sirens of more police

cars that were surely after my mom. But all was calm. Just people walking past, going about their business. I saw a big sign for the farmers market on Saturday.

"Where's Mom?" Emma's voice climbed.

"Oh, she had to move the car. The time ran out on the meter. Come on. Let's find her." I walked to the corner and then broke into a run, pulling Emma behind me.

Her hand slipped from mine. "Sis!" she wailed. When I twisted around, Emma was splayed on the pavement. An older couple passing on the sidewalk stopped in their tracks. "Oh dear!" I heard the woman say. The man crouched to help Emma up.

"Did you trip?" My voice was loud and high. Emma was sitting on her bottom in the middle of the sidewalk, hugging her two scraped knees to her chest, bawling. "I've got her. Thanks," I said to the couple. "Come on. Let's go, okay?" I said to Emma, as sweetly as I could manage. I eased her up and slowed our pace. We walked hand in hand, without a direction, no place to go. We rounded the corner.

Far in the distance, I saw a plume of exhaust first and then my eyes landed on the minivan. It was parked in a paid city lot and the engine was running. Later, I realized I was so scared, so messed up by those few minutes when I thought we'd been left behind, that I wasn't even relieved when I saw it.

"Why did you drive off without us?" I screamed as soon as the van door closed.

"I saw the police car and decided to get off the street."

I expected my mom to gratefully greet us or to bark out a plan. Instead, she was white as a ghost and her hands were visibly shaking where she gripped the steering wheel.

I glanced at Emma, who was busy settling herself in the back seat with her stuffed animals. "Mom?"

She didn't respond.

"Mom?" I swiftly moved to the empty front seat. "Where are we supposed to go?" I lowered my voice.

She shook her head. "This has never happened before."

"Come on. Where are we supposed to go?"

She faced me then, and it was like looking into my own eyes. "I don't remember. The Holiday Inn or the Hyatt Place? It's running together."

She was panicking.

Things got scary clear. "Hey. It's okay," I said. "But we need to go. Now." I stared at her and my heart rate seemed to slow. I looked away from her to temporarily escape.

Staring mindlessly out the windshield, I didn't believe my eyes when I saw my dad's familiar tall figure come sauntering down the street. He turned one woman's head as he passed by. I exhaled long, in jagged stairsteps. Then, for a second, I rested my face in my hands. It was too much.

My dad approached our car. My mom had the wherewithal to roll down the window.

"Move over," was all he said. His voice was flat. He wouldn't look at her.

I moved to the back and my mom took the passenger seat. My dad shut the door hard.

"Where were you?" Emma accused.

"There was confusion," my dad said.

Jesus.

My dad turned to my mom. His voice was eerily controlled. "This won't work if we're not on the same page." It was strange—even though he was quiet, I had never seen him angrier.

My mom was looking out her window, tapping her collarbone. "It worked out."

He touched her leg. My dad did that sometimes—touched my mom to get her attention instead of saying her name. He rarely used her name.

My mom reluctantly met his eyes. His were dead serious. "If time is up, you leave, no question." She tried to look away, but he gently caught her chin, making her listen. "If you don't follow our rules, this all falls apart."

"I know!" she said sharply.

My dad started the car and no one spoke. I could barely believe the four of us were in the same physical space. Still together.

I trusted my parents less than I had an hour ago.

For long minutes, I had no coherent thoughts as shock ran its course through my system.

I'd had no idea what to do if they left us, only that I was responsible for Emma.

I looked over my shoulder at Emma, who was licking chocolate from the fingers of one hand. In her other, she held a pack of stolen cookies.

CHAPTER EIGHT

Poppy! Look up!"

"Hold on," I said, turning a page, immersing myself in the safety of my book.

"How many of those can she read? She's probably reading a sex scene."

"Mom! I'm not." The mood in the car had loosened up, my parents actively trying to recover and pretend they hadn't dropped their masks and unraveled in front of us. The child in me almost wanted to let them.

I put down my romance novel and popped back into the real world. I expected a return to the realm of mini malls, big box stores, freeways. Instead, I was surrounded by water.

I saw the most incredible vistas—cliffs and islands connected by bridges. It was like a fairy tale in which we'd finally reached the magic city on a hill. And the day itself was sparkling. White diamonds dappled the water.

"See? We're getting on the Golden Gate Bridge, girls.

Where the Pacific meets the bay." For a second, we were just another family on a road trip, seeing the devastatingly beautiful sights of the country. Not one basking in the relief of another fake ID retrieval. I'd decided not to say anything to my parents about Emma's theft. They had enough on their plate. I'd deal with Emma later.

"Oh my gosh." My face practically pressed to the glass to stare at the San Francisco Bay and smaller islands dotting the water.

"I know, huh?" my mom said. When I turned my head to look out the ocean side of the car, I caught an expression on her face I'd never seen before. Pure happiness. It made her look younger.

"Have you been here before?" I asked her. It slipped out, because I knew better than to ask her a question like that. They would never tell me even that much.

Her expression closed off. My heart closed off in response. Maybe I'd thought she'd take pity on me and tell me something about herself after what she'd just put me through. Instead, I'd just spoiled the moment.

My mom simply shook her head at my question. It was politely noncommittal. Not a no, not a yes, just a *Let's glide over this before your dad comes down hard on the rules.*

My dad stared straight ahead, navigating over what seemed like one of the wonders of the world.

Finally.

The word popped into my head. I'd never felt so happy to arrive anywhere. But that was why this bridge was famous: it displayed all this natural and man-made beauty that floored weary travelers.

I'd noted the thick cocoon of gray mist surrounding the city, but I was still surprised when we went from sunny and bright to dark and cold in mere seconds, as though we were now entering this fairy tale's mysterious second act.

Once we exited the bridge, we landed at the edge of a park that led to a boulevard that was dank and busy. We sat in traffic for a good half hour.

My fragile good mood was quickly wearing off.

"We're making our way south to the Peninsula. It will take a while, but we'll get there," my dad said.

"What's the Peninsula?" Emma asked, bored and frustrated, her coloring book all used up.

"Silicon Valley?" I asked. My dad pursed his lips and they went white and bloodless. He nodded. I couldn't stop the beginnings of a smile.

"It's an area south of San Francisco known for high-tech companies, like Apple and Facebook," I said, turning to Emma, aware that I sounded like an excited tour guide. "It's the technology hub for the whole world." I'd always been fascinated by computer science, and now we would soon be in the heart of it. To this day, my mom still proudly exclaimed about my second-grade devotion to a picture book about Ada Lovelace, the first computer programmer. I read it so many times my mom had to glue pages back in while I anxiously hovered, worried about getting in trouble with the school librarian.

"But isn't it super expensive here?" I asked my parents. We'd briefly lived in Idaho, where the natives griped that Californians were invading because the cost of living had become too high. "How long can we stay? A week? A month? Summer?"

Neither of my parents said anything. My dad stared at the

road ahead with a stony expression, clearly pissed that we were even here. Maybe because it was so expensive. Or maybe it had something to do with the look on my mom's face, the tension in the car, the reason we'd left Illinois so fast.

Just when I figured my question would go unanswered, my mom said, "Maybe we can stay a little longer than usual." Then, more softly, "I don't think I can go through that again for a bit."

"We'll see," my dad said under his breath.

Around the time I saw signs for the San Francisco International Airport, the fog miraculously lifted and all was bright blue sky and crystal clear. Eventually we exited the scenic freeway bordered by rolling hills and lined with a ridge of mountains to the west. A wide boulevard led downhill, traveling east, and soon after I saw a sign that read SLAC NATIONAL LINEAR ACCELERATOR and in smaller lettering, OPERATED BY STANFORD UNIVERSITY.

"We're near Stanford?" I asked. It had always stuck out in my head—a university that produced scientists, engineers, and mathematicians who walked right out the front steps into the heart of it all, where they could easily find work or start their own companies.

"Yep," my dad said. I was surprised he didn't say, "Don't get too excited." He didn't need to worry. How many STEM opportunities had I turned down? LEGO Leagues I'd said no to? I hadn't even asked my parents if I *could* join. I hadn't even asked them that one time a math teacher said he could get the entry fee waived in case I was really interested. That had been after he saw me reading the poster tacked up in his classroom. And again after he saw me lingering to watch the kids build a robot.

I knew my dreams about college, my blurry impressions of me in a white lab coat and eventually having a PhD were just that—dreams. And not even well-defined ones.

If I ever got mad, I managed to quash the flames as soon as I went home to my family. They were my real life, I reminded myself as my mom made me laugh and both of my parents listened to every word I had to say about my day. The work I did or didn't do wasn't important.

After a drive through a small, incredibly cute downtown, similar to the picturesque one in Marin, the houses began to get farther apart and the fences higher, big houses shrouded in privacy. I waited for the scenery to change to apartment complexes, cracked sidewalks, telephone poles. If we planted ourselves in an urban area, that was usually the type of section where we stayed.

We drove for a couple of miles and then took a right into a neighborhood behind a grand stone gate. Inside the gate, the streets were quiet and shaded with the tallest trees—palms, redwoods, and pines.

"In California, there was a period when tree collecting was a hobby. Rich railroad or gold or silver magnates would show off by bringing trees from around the world."

I looked at my mom, wondering how she knew this.

"It's what Dad told me about this neighborhood," she said and shrugged. But she seemed on the edge of her seat, ready to burst out of the car so she could take a closer look.

My dad eyed her, then added, "This used to be the summer estate of a San Francisco silver baron, once said to be the richest man in California, but it was sold to developers in the fifties."

There weren't any apartment buildings around here. That

was for sure. Driving just two blocks, I already saw that there was a smattering of new and old: ultramodern mansions right next door to traditional, California ranch houses.

As we drove deeper into the neighborhood, it reminded me of Beatrix Potter illustrations: green and lush and forestlike. Perfect for long runs by myself. The neighborhood filled me with a delight I quickly tamped down. But I could tell this was a good place for us—lots of privacy. I doubted there was much of a community. There were no sidewalks, and I didn't see any people walking on the street. The bigger houses were gated. Over time, I'd learned that small to midsize apartment buildings were the worst. They always seemed to come equipped with a nosy neighbor.

I noticed an ornate urn on a street corner, nestled in a giant bush of white oleander. It was an artifact from a different century, just like the exotic trees. My dad turned into a driveway bordered by more tall oleander bushes, but these were unmanaged and overgrown. The house wasn't visible from the street. At the end of the long narrow driveway, there was a house painted beige that definitely fell into the category of aged California ranch.

In fact, it had a bit of a ranch-y theme. White boards crisscrossed the exterior, signifying barn, like we were at an actual ranch. It reminded me of the California vibe that came through in an old photo I'd once seen of Ronald and Nancy Reagan, side by side on horses at their gold and dusty Santa Barbara ranch.

The only landscaping was a large lawn, parched by the sun, and towering oak trees. The property appeared a little desolate and neglected, but someone had recently come with blowers. There wasn't a stray, prickly oak leaf anywhere.

"Don't get out of the car. Let's unload in the garage," my dad said. He hopped out and punched a code into an old plastic panel.

The rickety garage door groaned so loudly as it folded up that my dad glanced around. I hadn't seen anybody except for three trucks belonging to a landscape company parked in the hard-packed dirt at the side of the road.

My dad eased the minivan into the center of the empty garage. One dusty window that looked out on the backyard had a long, diagonal crack in it. The garage was detached from the rest of the house.

There was so little to unload it was comical. Before we'd picked up the packet, we'd stopped at a Target between Vacaville and the Bay Area. My dad sparingly used the cash he'd had on hand to pay for toiletries, a pair of larger tennis shoes for Emma, and groceries for one dinner.

My dad opened a door onto a courtyard that connected the garage to the house. The courtyard had a clothesline, old rotting wood planter boxes, and yellow grasses that poked through uneven cement pavers. A straw sunshine ornament hung in the half window of the back door to the house.

My dad checked his pocket for a key. He was about to unlock the door when my mom said, "Wait. Let me."

She turned the key in the tarnished knob, and the door opened easily. We walked into a laundry room with ancient appliances and then into a kitchen. It was amazing, like nothing had been touched since the house had been built. The kitchen tile was vintage, a washed-out baby blue. The kitchen faucet was also original. The refrigerator and dishwasher were avocado green.

After hefting the Target bags onto the tiled, L-shaped kitchen counter, my sister and I broke away to explore the house. It was generous: a wood-paneled den with an ancient TV tucked into the bookcase, a living room with a plaid couch, a bedroom wing down a long hallway lined with three windows looking out onto a patch of lawn, where bone-white birch trees with dancing green leaves and hanging baskets overflowed with short pink flowers. The back was much prettier than the dried-out front.

It was old and weird, but I loved it.

I explored the master bedroom first. It was located all the way in the back and had a huge storage closet that smelled like mothballs. There was a narrow dressing area and a pink-tiled bathroom. The shower head was built in low, as though people from past generations had been much shorter. Oddly, one wall in the bedroom was freshly painted, but only half of it, as though the project had come to an abrupt halt.

I was kneeling on the dusty cushion of a large window seat, looking out at the birch trees and the neighbors' mansion at the fence line, when Emma exclaimed, "No way!"

When I joined her down the hall, I saw a small bedroom that was newly decorated, specifically for a little girl. It smelled like fresh glue. There was brand-new wallpaper with little pink stars and bedding that matched—expensive-looking bedding. A stuffed badger rested against two pink-and-gold oversized pillows on the white canopied twin bed. Emma's favorite animal.

I walked down the hall to the next bedroom. The blue room. In my head, that's what I named it the second I saw it. The entire room was decorated in shades of blue, creating an ombré effect. I gently picked up the throw draped across the foot of the queen-size bed and touched it to my cheek. The tag read: 100 PERCENT CASHMERE.

When I noticed the small painting of a field of orange and gold poppies, it was like the person who'd prepared this room said hello. To me.

Someone knew about me and my sister. And it seemed like they quite possibly cared.

My mom walked through the doorway. She shoved her hands in the pockets of her jeans as she took in the room, turning in a slow circle. She froze when she saw the painting.

She wouldn't give me answers. But, for the first time, I had a clue. If I looked hard enough, if I could figure out who this person was, they might be someone who could help me and Emma if it came to that.

I gave my mom my back and turned toward the painting.

CHAPTER NINE

searched the house for clues. I pulled open cabinets and drawers, examining odds and ends—like a small pot holder that looked like it was made on a loom by a child, or a heavy pink hair dryer I'd found in a musty bathroom cabinet that let out a few sparks, then died. There were china plates in a cabinet—delicate bone-white and painted with pastel flowers. I guessed they had once belonged to an older woman, most likely not the person who'd carefully decorated our rooms in a more current style.

But though the house was furnished, it had been swept of most personal items and anything with a name on it. I looked for old mail and any scraps of paper anywhere. When I picked up a decades-old magazine featuring Big Sur on the cover, I noticed the address label had been peeled off. I quickly brought down a tall stack of home-and-garden magazines from a high shelf. Each and every address label had been painstakingly peeled off. My parents, and whoever had helped them, were that good.

I watched them carefully.

Since we'd arrived, my dad was his usual self—serious, getting down to business by setting up his work space in the shed outdoors. My mom, on the other hand, was behaving differently.

Typically, when we arrived somewhere new, she would be more quiet than usual. She would survey our new surroundings, her shoulders creeping to her ears, as if she hated it but had learned long ago that it was useless to complain. But here, she immediately relaxed in the sprawling old house—using food-stained place mats, flopping down on dusty sofas, wrapping herself up in ancient wool blankets. She seemed totally comfortable instead of hovering tentatively the way she would have until we'd lived somewhere for weeks, as if the ground weren't quite solid beneath her feet. I wondered if it was because the house had the stamp of the person who had decorated it for us, like they made it okay.

I worried constantly. I was trying to piece together why we'd arrived at a house decorated specifically with us in mind and what it meant. I'd always thought a dark, shadowy network helped us. But maybe it was a single person. A relative? An old friend? Would they knock on the door any moment now? Or what if I was wrong and this was a threat—someone my parents owed?

For the first time in all my years running, something had shifted. It ground me down, being so close to discovering something new but getting nowhere. Secrets swirled around me, but

I couldn't grasp even one of them, no matter how hard I tried. Those first couple of nights, I woke up hot and scared. I could almost remember what I'd dreamed but not quite, like the memory was just on the other side of a gauzy screen.

I felt the same way about the person or persons who had readied the house for us. I could almost feel them. Their presence had been in the house recently. I was dying to know who they were. I'd never had contact with an outsider who knew about us. There were only three other people in the world who knew the real me, but now there was a fourth. It was a brand-new idea. And I was surprised by how much I needed it.

"Poker?" My dad had carried a low, squat coffee table from the living room into the wood-paneled den, a tighter, darker space. I knew he wanted to bring us together and help us feel like ourselves after the scary, out-of-control–seeming move.

My dad sat impressively cross-legged on the shag carpet with me and my sister. "Watch this." He showed off by flicking chips with his thumb into the center pot, one at a time, and of course they landed exactly where he aimed them, each one perfectly hitting the same spot. He had to make up games within the game to keep himself occupied while my sister struggled with her hand.

"Did you see that, babe?" he asked my mom. It always cracked me up that the only time my dad acted cocky was when we played family games. He won almost every single time. Even in games of chance. I imagined this was what he'd been like in high school, when he'd hung out with his friends. Or maybe he'd had brothers and they'd fiercely competed in all kinds of games.

"I saw," my mom said dryly. She sat on the small sofa behind Emma.

Usually my mom played, but tonight she'd declined, even after we'd begged her. From her position on the sofa, she was distracted, absentmindedly yanking on the curtain pull. The white cord was old and brittle, and she was going to break it any second.

"Are you okay?" I asked her.

"What?" she asked, lifting her eyes to mine. "Oh yeah, I'm fine," she said.

"You ready, Pops?" my dad asked, pulling my attention back to him.

"Shuffle up and deal!" I smiled.

Once I saw my crappy cards, I rearranged my face. It wasn't a great hand, but it wasn't the worst, either. I searched my dad's expression. I dragged my fingers through the rug, noticing specs of black that the old wheezing vacuum cleaner didn't have the strength to suction.

"I'm going to find that book with the shark," Emma said and dropped her cards. That was her way of folding, apparently. She went to search for *Jaws* in the bookshelves.

My mom perked up. "Emma, don't. Not before bed."

Emma didn't listen, found the yellowed copy, and once again studied the cover art of the girl swimming atop the water and the shark below.

Now I had all of my dad's focus. "It's just you and me, Pops. What's it going to be?"

Why not? "All in," I said.

He studied me as I tried to bluff.

I could see in my peripheral vision that my mom was yanking the paperback out of Emma's clutch. But my dad remained laser focused, looking for my tells. He said I had them, but he wouldn't say what they were. My only defense was to be as blank as possible—relax, not move a muscle, think other thoughts, listen to Emma whine. Look to my dad for his tells. If he had them, I couldn't figure them out. When he wasn't trash-talking, he exuded pure confidence.

"I'm going to call," he finally said.

I showed my cards. My dad displayed his; he had two pairs. With cupped hands, he pulled the pile of chips toward him like King Midas.

"How do you do that?" Of course I had wanted to win, but it made me laugh that he always knew when I was bluffing, that he knew me that well.

"That's why I don't like playing poker with him: he can read anyone," my mom said humorlessly. "You can't hide anything from your dad."

CHAPTER TEN

It was the last week of May. Whispered conversations took place behind closed doors. It didn't matter how carefully I watched and listened—I was learning nothing. One time, I crept close enough to eavesdrop and made out the words "too generous," "risky," and my dad's repeated "no." I retreated when they stopped speaking suddenly, maybe sensing my presence.

Summer was officially in the air, and it was hard not to want to be part of it. Or at least see other people getting ready for it—more kids out in the streets, the opening of public pools, and, soon, Fourth of July decorations.

Emma and I spent most of our days walking the acre of property. It was fascinating to both of us. There was an old chicken coop, a dog run, massively tall pine trees, a small orchard of pomegranate and plum trees. In the course of one week, the plums turned ripe, fell to the ground, and were carried off by black squirrels.

With the ones we rescued, my mom and Emma made fruit leather, drying it on wax paper they'd placed on the wooden picnic table. The project was taken out of a *Sunset* magazine from 1977. My mother even looked straight out of the 1970s in one of her long, printed skirts, a tube top, and a gold bangle on her wrist. She spent hours looking through the old magazines. When I flipped through them myself, I saw stunning photos of places like Stinson Beach, Half Dome, Carmel.

Initially, I was happy to recover from the adrenaline of the move. I wanted to be as close to my dad as possible and keep him in my sight.

But then I relaxed, grew restless, and wanted to explore.

"I'm going to take a run. Is there a library downtown I can check out?" The day started out gorgeous, warmer than the past week, which had required a light sweater until the gray mist burned off midmorning.

I expected an easy yes, but my parents were silent for a beat too long. Then, reluctantly, my dad said, "I'd rather you stay here, honey."

I pushed back from the kitchen table. "You can't keep us cooped up all summer! Emma can't handle that." They had never hesitated about letting me out before. I loved my family, but I couldn't spend the summer lying on the carpet, staring at the ceiling, the day marked only by breakfast, lunch, and dinner. The dark side of summer was the boredom—the longest days of the year and life taking place in an outside world that wasn't touching mine.

"That's fine," my mom said. She wore her hair in an ex-

hausted topknot and was still in her silk pajama pants decorated with a peacock print.

"Babe," my dad said to her now in a warning tone. "Let me
talk to your mom for a second."

My mom stared after him, then wearily followed him from
the room.

My mom wasn't herself. When we'd initially arrived at
the house, she'd had a burst of energy—crafting with Emma,
paging through the old magazines, harvesting fruit from the
backyard. I'd thought it was nice for her to have more land
to roam, just like in Illinois, since she could never leave the
property. But, in recent days, she'd abruptly checked out. She
mostly stayed in bed, like she'd crashed down from her high
and needed the sleep.

I made myself a peanut-butter-and-jelly sandwich so I
could listen to what they were saying in the den.

"We can't shut them in," my mom said.

"She looks like you," I heard my dad say.

They had never worried about my visibility. That suddenly
seemed to matter—in this area, specifically.

If my mom was so recognizable here that even I would be
recognizable, then why had we come? I remembered the muttered *belly of the beast*. I wavered, wondering if maybe I'd heard
correctly after all. But I knew my parents—my dad especially—
would never bring us somewhere dangerous.

My dad relented. An hour later, I rode with him to the grocery
store, looking all around.

We stopped at the most gorgeous, gourmet grocery store

I'd ever seen. I knew we wouldn't be returning after seeing the prices, but it gave me a view of the cute downtown again and the little park that advertised a summer concert series. We drove to a different section of town and scouted out the tiny library near a quaint train station, a post office, and a police station. All housed in beautiful old buildings under the shade of redwoods. The little enclave seemed from a different era compared to the polished downtown.

Next, we drove to Palo Alto. "Can we see the Stanford campus? Look! It's right there." I pointed to the street sign.

"Another time. I have a stop to make."

My dad navigated the streets of downtown Palo Alto, searching in vain for a parking spot. Palo Alto looked different from where we were staying. It had taller, older buildings and a more urban feel on the main street, University Avenue. There were chain stores and restaurants and lots of traffic. Sweet bungalows and Victorian houses dotted the side streets.

Frustrated, my dad finally pulled into a no-parking zone, smacked on the hazards, and ordered, "Stay here." Before I could protest, he was jogging up the block. I watched him go into a convenience store, which was odd, because we'd just gone to the grocery store.

Every minute felt like ten. I was jolted by a tapping sound. A police officer stood framed in the window.

The car was off so I couldn't even lower the window. Uncertain of what to do or say, I shakily cracked open my door. My dad saved the day. He appeared at the car door and placed himself between me and the officer. He backed against the car, subtly crunching my door closed again.

"I'm sorry. It won't happen again," he said politely. We were in California, otherwise he might have added, "sir." My dad's posture was ramrod straight. I saw the police officer take an automatic step back and nod almost deferentially. My dad looped the car and was in his seat with the car started in seconds. Before he pulled out, he touched the back pocket of his jeans, double-checking that his wallet was still there.

"Dad," I started.

"I know. Like I said, it won't happen again. I got impatient and made a stupid mistake." His voice was even, but I noticed rivulets of sweat trickling down his tan neck, disappearing into the collar of his crisp T-shirt.

We rode home in silence. Had he been buying something? Meeting someone? As we drew closer to our quiet neighborhood, the main street narrowed to one lane. I loved the house, but my body grew heavy at the thought of returning and not knowing when I'd get to leave again.

We stopped at a red light next to the local high school, a rickety-looking series of beige one-story buildings connected by covered walkways. From the run-down high school, you couldn't tell that tech millionaires were a dime a dozen in the zip code.

"Stanford University Program for Accelerated Youth," I read aloud from a tight banner suspended on the chain-link fence. "Summer STEM Institute." My brain went into overdrive, memorizing every bit of information on the signage before the light turned green. I twisted my body to face him. "Dad, please?"

CHAPTER ELEVEN

My mom deserved the credit for making summer school happen.

She was out of bed and staring into a cup of black coffee while my dad was gently, regretfully, letting me down. "What are you talking about?" she asked, looking up.

"A STEM summer school thing down at the high school."

"Online payments are tough," my dad said simply.

My mom took him aside by the elbow, leading him to the small laundry room. She didn't bother to close the door. "We had to give up everything. I don't want her to."

"Shh," my dad whispered soothingly.

I knew she was trying to make things right with me, knowing she'd scared me badly in Marin. It was working. Sometimes I forgot how well she understood me.

My dad's primary concern was keeping us safe, but my mom pushed the issue of Emma and me having a more typical life when we could. Maybe because she was stuck at home while my dad moved more easily through the world, she dreamed of possibilities for me and Emma. I just didn't know what the possibilities could add up to since no one spoke about the future.

I was told I'd been signed up for a class called Introduction to Number Theory. Mainly because it still had spots open. There was also a genetics class offered at the same nearby high school, but that was full.

My dad made it sound like registering me was easy, though I knew it was a giant pain and typically he didn't use his credit card unless it was necessary. He'd disappeared for hours, probably driving a good distance away so he could do it online. Just the anxiety of getting a library card had been a lot. After my dad filled out the form with false information, the librarian did something we'd never seen before: she scanned my dad's forged driver's license, his picture going into their system. Too late, I understood the stress I'd put him through.

"Thank you so much," I said over and over again on the first morning of class. They both seemed a little disturbed by how grateful I was.

When I thanked them for the third time as I finished my toast, my mom said midsentence, "Poppy, it's fine. I know how much you love math."

She did know. When I was little, I'd excitedly quiz my mom to see if she knew the answer to what I'd learned in school that day. She'd get it wrong on purpose, making a big show of how six-year-old me knew more than she did. I knew she was joking, but she had made me feel so smart.

At first, what drew me to math was that the curriculum stayed the same from school to school, which made it easier to fit in. Then I grew to love how it was always clear, logical, and concrete—the opposite of absolutely everything else around me.

Unlike the rest of the gigantic campus, C-Wing was buzzing with people in the few minutes before the first class of summer school. I consulted the yellow scrap paper my dad had handed me. In his precise print, it had the the time of the class, the wing and the room number.

When I entered the classroom, I saw a woman, maybe around thirty, standing in front of a whiteboard. Written on the board was PROF. MARINA ALEXIEV and the title of the class: INTRODUCTION TO NUMBER THEORY. It was supposedly an advanced math course, and most of the class description had gone over my head, but I'd been encouraged by the word "Introduction."

When I'd read the course description online at the library, I had just started to grasp that there was more to this Program for Accelerated Youth than a regular summer school. There were repeated mentions of "talented" and "eligibility."

Professor Alexiev nodded to me, and I scanned the room for where to sit. There were about twelve kids in the class and, from the loud conversations, they seemed to know one another. A few of the kids looked up but didn't smile, and when their gazes lingered on me, I automatically got the pain in my stomach. I hated it. The anxiety started when I was Emma's age, when the puzzle pieces began to fit together. It was another reason I'd been happy at Lincoln West High School: I'd finally gotten over it.

I gave the other kids, and myself, plenty of space, taking a seat in the back.

When I noticed the array of laptops, I got really nervous. I'd mostly gone to schools that didn't have computers for each student. This level of preparedness was intimidating, and I knew I didn't belong.

I decided to ask the teacher if I was allowed to take the class if I didn't own a computer. Maybe it had been a prerequisite and my family was too out of touch and unsophisticated to understand.

I approached tentatively, waiting for Professor Alexiev to glance up from her phone. Her hair was cut in a jet-black bob with thick bangs straight across her forehead. Her eyeglasses had clear plastic frames.

"Hello!" she greeted me.

She was friendly, thank god. I thought I detected a slight accent. "Hi, I don't have a—

"Can you speak up? I can't hear you."

Heat rose to my cheeks. "I don't have a computer or iPad. Is that a problem for taking this class?"

Professor Alexiev scanned the classroom with its sudden sea of technology. "I don't think so. But I will be sharing reading and some independent problem sets online on a shared drive. Do you have access to a computer at home?"

I'd been down this road since most schools had moved their communications online. "I don't, unfortunately. I'm homeschooled and my parents have strict beliefs." I hated that my parents made me say this.

"Oh." I could almost feel Professor Alexiev lean away from me. My clothes from the thrift store took on a new meaning. They weren't intentional, worn because I was trying to be cool. I was different. Poor.

It was amazing how saying I was homeschooled was the perfect cover. I didn't need to produce records, and any outsiders could read into it however they wanted. But there was always the subtle distancing that came with it. Also perfect for my parents' purposes. But always painful.

"You've had calculus?" she asked, furrowing her brow.

"Some," I said. That wasn't really true. But I wanted to stay. I was too intrigued by the course description, and I couldn't go back to the long, unbroken stretches at the house. Maybe they weren't friendly, but here there were other kids my age.

Professor Alexiev glanced at the wall clock. Class was already one minute late getting started. "Most of these kids have completed AP Calculus and Differential Equations. Why don't you sit in for the first class and see if you can follow? You tested in, so you should be fine."

Oh no. I had not tested in. I wasn't sure how my dad had managed to register me without this piece.

I was thinking, at the very least, even if it was just for one day before they figured me out, I would get to spend a few hours outside of the house, when Professor Alexiev asked, "What's your name?"

"Poppy."

It just slipped out.

I'd had to explain to Professor Alexiev that it was my nickname, which was why it didn't match "Emily" on the roster. My mind turned the mistake over and over, trying to figure out exactly why it was so bad. I didn't have a searchable name in any database. I wasn't sure what my birth certificate said—if I even had one—but it probably wasn't "Poppy." The last name used to register me for the class wasn't one my parents had ever used before.

I decided I didn't need to tell my parents. We'd be leaving soon. I hated that it was true, because I loved it here, but there was a little relief that I'd never have to admit my mistake. Just last night, my dad had quizzed me on my new name. They did everything to make sure I was invisible, and they counted on me to do the same for them—to keep our family safe and together.

But it was okay. Nothing that happened inside this class-room would ever follow me out anyway.

"Is this seat taken?"

I looked up to meet the most bored-looking doe eyes.

Skinny was my first impression. I'd never seen a boy so tall and skinny, his raw denim jeans hanging off him. At first glance, he looked tired and bedraggled, but it quickly became evident that he was attractive and his wrinkled clothing was expensive and brand-new.

He stood out from the others by making direct eye contact, but his dull, uninterested look conveyed that he was used to being stared at, used to being important. Most likely a rich kid who still thought the world was all for him.

"It's free." I yanked the strap of my old black backpack and it plopped down with a thud onto the tan linoleum floor.

"I don't think he's *that* cute," a girl sitting three rows in front of me loud-whispered to her friend. The two of them appeared to be the only other female students taking the class besides me.

"Shhhh!" the other girl said and guiltily looked over her shoulder in the boy's direction.

Wow. If I could hear them, so could he. But he pretended

not to. He shut his eyes for a moment, like he was wishing he was somewhere else or like he was trying to nap. Then I noticed other kids in the class were either sneaking looks at him or watching him with open interest. *Who was this guy?*

He was well over six feet with short black hair, hazel eyes— tiger eyes, my mom would say—and angular cheekbones. Unlike the other students, whose spines seemed to curl into a C, overburdened by heavy backpacks, this guy moved assuredly, athletically, swinging his graffiti-covered backpack off his shoulder in one smooth move. He had impressive road rash on his forearm, like he'd fallen off a bike.

He must have felt me studying him, too hard, for too long, because he rested the side of his head on his palm, using his hand to block my view of his face.

"Mr. Addison, you're late," our teacher said.

He nodded and didn't bother with an excuse, though he quickly swiped at the sweat on his forehead and upper lip. I wondered if maybe he was nervous.

But once class started, "Mr. Addison" barely penetrated my consciousness. Every second of class took intense concentration so I wouldn't get lost.

I hung on every word in an attempt to keep up. It quickly became discouraging. Right when I grasped what was going on, I got lost again, and Professor Alexiev moved on too quickly.

I didn't dare ask if we could go back. This class belonged to the other kids. It was the first time I'd ever been faced with the kind of disparity that existed between their educations and mine. The thought made me feel bitter because I just hadn't had the access. That's what happened when you started and stopped and were pulled out of school so many times. In addition to that, some of the schools I'd attended hadn't offered honors classes.

I switched my energy to praying that I wouldn't be called on. I busied myself copying everything into my notebook so I could try to make sense of it all when I was alone.

Toward the end of class, Professor Alexiev said, "Last thing for today—we're going to discuss a fundamental result in number theory, deriving a formula for the sum of consecutive cubes of the set of natural numbers. As we did previously, I'll write down a formula for the sum, which I'll then prove by induction." She turned toward the whiteboard and began to write a series of equations. I made an attempt to work things out in my notebook.

I raised my hand, my brain moving faster than my self-consciousness. Professor Alexiev looked to me, one eyebrow raised.

"Why do we need to use induction when we can work out the formula as the area of a square? Shouldn't the sum be equal to the square of the sum of natural numbers?" I waited for a response. Professor Alexiev just stood looking at me, so I held up my notebook and showed her the square grid I'd drawn with sequentially larger blocks, shaded along its diagonal.

Just then, the classroom door opened and two students loudly burst in, ready for the next class. They took one look at us still in session, quickly apologized, and closed the door.

"You said you'd only had some calc, right?" Professor Alexiev asked.

"Yes," I said, angry I'd opened my mouth, wanting to disappear. She had to know I was far below level for the class. I shouldn't have blurted out my question. I just honestly wanted to know.

"I'm curious." She narrowed her eyes as if trying to peg me. "What is this homeschool program you're doing?"

The entire class waited for my answer, all eyes on me.

I put my sweaty hands in the pockets of my skirt and gripped the sides of my legs hard. "Not really one in particular. Just what my parents decide. But it's sporadic." I needed to stop talking about our nonexistent homeschool schedule. *Never tell a lie when you don't have to.*

"You just made a leap to thinking about math analytically. Most of you here," she said, surveying the array of faces looking up at her, "are still striving to make that jump." I felt the other students prickle at her pointed remark. "We've gone over. Let's end there, shall we? Poppy's right, but I'll have her explain her thinking tomorrow."

Just as I was about to leave, Professor Alexiev called after me, "Poppy." She broke away from the group of kids who'd circled her like she was a math celebrity. She was in our textbook—it turned out she was an assistant professor in the math department at Stanford.

"Hey. I wanted to make sure you're coming back tomorrow." Professor Alexiev rocked back and forth on her toes just like she did when she was teaching.

"Is that okay?" I asked. My throat immediately tightened like I was eight and getting a pity invite to a birthday party.

"Are your parents aware that you can do this kind of high-level math?"

"Um. I don't know."

"They must be, or you wouldn't be taking this course."

"It was my idea."

"Well, that contribution was impressive," she said, grinning wide. "I'm excited for the next eight weeks. As one of my best teachers used to say: 'You showed deep thinking today.'" She gave my shoulder a light pat and turned back to the other students.

It was clear and warm now, and I struggled out of my sweatshirt and tied it around my waist. I couldn't remember the last time I'd felt happy like this. Fulfilled. It was different than the usual hopeless feeling that time was passing but I was running in place.

I was on a high from that last moment of class. I liked Professor Alexiev. And, for better or worse, I'd just been exposed to what existed beyond the high school math I'd taken. Some of the other kids in the class had mentioned the different types of math they knew. One kid, Cliff, even had a tutor who taught him Russian math on the weekends.

My smile dimmed when I remembered I'd used my real name. But for three hours, as uncomfortable as it had been, I'd seen something brand-new.

I cared about this—far more than the science fair—and I wanted to hang in for the full eight weeks, to learn what I could before I had to leave. My parents must think we'd stay in the area that long, right? Otherwise they wouldn't have let me sign up. And I knew the class wasn't cheap.

But they had yanked me out of schools so many times, I knew this was wishful thinking.

From outside the classroom, I saw the changeover that was about to happen, a dozen or so students milling at the door. The teacher for the next class came in and shook hands with

Professor Alexiev. They chitchatted, then the teacher wrote on the whiteboard in all caps: GENETICS.

I made my way off the school grounds to take a path that would lead back to my hushed neighborhood. Some kids from my class were getting into parents' cars—seemingly one Tesla after another. I saw Mr. Addison climb into a black Porsche parked in a spot marked STAFF ONLY. The car was so shiny it looked like a mirror. It was another reminder that I was now located in one of the wealthiest parts of the world.

As I passed through the opening in the chain-link fence, I looked over my shoulder at him. I wouldn't have been curious except that we seemed to be the two misfits in class. He was so quiet. Maybe he'd been pushed into summer school by high-achieving parents, though he'd answered his one question competently. The only time I'd heard him speak again was when he muttered "Ow," and jolted upright, placing a hand over the nasty scrapes on his forearm as if he'd unintentionally brushed against it.

What also made me curious was that Professor Alexiev had seemed so aware of him. And also careful with him. But I didn't get the sense that they'd met before.

I'd spent my entire life observing and assessing by necessity. Nobody talked to him, but everyone seemed to know who he was. Professor Alexiev hadn't even asked his name.

CHAPTER TWELVE

Rain poured the next morning, large drops plopping in puddles while I watched from the kitchen window. Emma left kitchen cupboards open in her search for cereal, and the window was cranked open to let in fresh air. A small trail of ants marched across the sill. The clock told me I had five minutes until I needed to start the journey to day two of summer school.

"Pops." My dad kissed the top of my head and came to stand at the window next to me. We were silent for a moment, observing the summer rain.

"You like it here?" he asked. The hot-water heater kicked to life in the utility closet behind us as my mom turned on the shower at the back of the house. I took it as a sign that maybe she'd be back to her normal self today.

"I love it here," I said.

I expected a gentle warning about not growing too attached. But instead my dad put an arm around me. I rested my head on his shoulder. We stood for another moment in companionable silence. I relaxed more when it was just the two of us. I might look like my mom, but I was so much more like my dad in temperament—serious, watchful, quiet. My mom and Emma were fiery and funny with boundless energy. Usually.

"Library after summer school? I can drive you and Emma."

"Sure." I was sick of the library and frustrated at spending long afternoon hours indoors. The pale-yellow train station lay just outside the library doors, and I'd see the silver Caltrans whip past on its way north to San Francisco and south to San Jose. Depending on my mood, the jangle of the train crossing was either an excited sound or a mournful warning.

I wanted to see the San Francisco Bay Area. The Exploratorium, the Tech Interactive, the Stanford Linear Accelerator tour, Alcatraz, not to mention the ocean. It was like everything was at my fingertips but I couldn't touch it. What if we left and I never saw any of it? I couldn't drive, and my parents were worried about their own visibility and money, of course. I didn't want to ask them for any.

"How are you?" I asked my dad. He'd been busy, spending a lot of time in the shed outside.

He took a step away from me, rubbing his hands over his face and through his hair. "I'm fine."

"What about Mom? What's wrong with her?" She was usually such a hands-on mom, playing with Emma and hanging out with me. She'd suddenly withdrawn from the three of us, spending a lot of time in her bedroom and acting preoccupied when she did haunt the house in her silk pajamas. If things were normal, she would have new paints and be working on a canvas. Yesterday, her eyes were red like she'd been crying.

"She's recuperating from the move. She's fine," my dad said.

"Are you sure? Dad? This is different for us. This big house. What's going on?"

My dad placed both palms on the countertop and stared at the space between them. *Please*, I thought. "Pops," he finally said. "You know—"

The disappointment was a black hole. "'There are things we can't tell you.' I know. Don't you want my help? I won't mess up." I thought of how my class now called me by my real name. The kind of one-second slipup I'd been warned about.

"It's not that we don't trust you," my dad said. "We don't want to burden you. It's human to make mistakes."

"But I'll be eighteen soon." And there it was: I suddenly saw an opening to ask about the future. "What about Emma? I'll need to take care of her if something happens," I said.

"Poppy—" My dad pushed away from the counter. I'd hit a sensitive spot.

I wanted to keep pressing, to finally ask him outright who we were and what he pictured for me when I got older, but then I saw a rare expression of exhaustion and dread on his face. I noticed the lines around his eyes that showed the toll this journey had taken on my dad maybe most of all.

I backed down, not wanting to add to his stress. At the same time, I was so frustrated by how powerless I felt.

My dad sighed heavily. "Want a ride?" he asked. "I have an errand to run."

The second class passed in a blur, in which the gaps in my knowledge were embarrassingly brought to light for all the kids to pity. I could almost feel Professor Alexiev's frustration radiating across the room, which hurt more than the opinions of all my classmates, especially after the praise she had given me.

Just like the first day, class was interrupted by kids from the genetics class barging in. Also, like the first day, Professor Alexiev caught up with me after class.

"I wish I had the time to bring you up to speed. What about a tutor?" she asked loudly as the kids filed by, obviously listening.

"The expense . . ." I said in a soft voice with the hope she would lower hers. Mr. Addison, as I now permanently thought of him, was tying his shoe on the grass outside the classroom, only about five feet away. I knew he could hear every word.

"Can you get some kind of job? Offer to help with the expense?" Professor Alexiev asked. She crossed her arms in concern.

"Maybe?" I responded only because I couldn't flat out say no.

"This is important," she said, intense, bringing her face a little too close to mine. "If you want a future in math or engineering, if you want to get into a school like Stanford, you need to catch up."

When had I said I wanted to go to Stanford? Even if I could go, why would she think I had a chance of getting into a school like that? It was probably Professor Alexiev's assumption that every single kid who spent their summer taking Intro to Number Theory wanted to go to an elite college. Still, I was flattered.

Mr. Addison walked by, making eye contact as he passed, a skateboard pasted with stickers tucked under his arm. I wondered if he carried it around just to look cool, since his Porsche was probably waiting for him in the parking lot. I was sure he looked down on me now that he could figure out that every twenty dollars must mean something to my family.

At that moment, I was so jealous of him. Not just because he was rich. But because he was on the other side of the invisible line that divided me from every kid in that class. They lived in sunshine and I was in shadows. Worse, Mr. Addison probably didn't even want to be here like the others. I was so mad I forgot my usual shyness—automatically looking down, like I had something to apologize for. I matched his eye contact and he looked away first.

The next day, I came back to class, dreading further embarrassment. After pouring through my notes the night before, I spent the third class fighting to stay with it, to stay engaged, a part of me wondering if there was any use.

Over and over again, some writing in the corner of the whiteboard caught my eye, left over from yesterday's genetics class:

Inheritance: a basic principle of genetics that explains how characteristics are passed from one generation to the next.

Who was the person who had readied the house for us? What if that person *was* a relative? Could they have copper hair like mine?

"I have an important announcement to make!" Professor Alexiev called out.

She set her marker in the tray of the dry-erase board and placed her hands in the pockets of her trendy black pantsuit. Next to me, Mr. Addison raised his hand, asking to use the restroom. Oddly, Professor Alexiev nodded. Apparently, he had immunity from special announcements.

"A student told me about the summer internship program at Admara and thought I should announce it." When she said the last part, the class laughed, but I didn't get it. I'd never heard of the company, but Professor Alexiev said it like everyone knew it. "It's for a female student interested in the field of mathematics who will receive an introduction to data analysis. It's part-time so it doesn't interfere with this class. And it pays well!"

"Girls!" In an exaggerated manner, Professor Alexiev looked at each of us three girls in the class individually. "This is an amazing opportunity at one of the most prestigious search-engine companies in the world. This could alter your path forward." Professor Alexiev locked eyes with me. She wanted me to apply.

When Mr. Addison returned to the classroom, Professor Alexiev gestured him in like it was safe to come back. "Harrison, take your seat."

CHAPTER THIRTEEN

'm sorry," my mom said.

We lay on her bed facing each other. I'd entered the bedroom uninvited, wanting my mom. I ran my fingers inside the wooden curlicues on the headboard, playing off my disappointment.

"Of course. No, I know." I kept my voice casual. "Dad already said no. I just thought I'd tell you. It's interesting, at the very least." In an alternate universe, I watched a wholesome, normal version of myself get the job. I'd give a Social Security number, receive a badge, and then enter the world of Admara. Just hearing about the internship, I couldn't believe I'd even come this close to it.

She wasn't fooled. She never was. "Poppy. I'm sorry."

I was forming the words to ask her if there was a plan for me down the line. But right now, I couldn't handle her answer. Especially after she repeated herself.

"I'm so sorry."

It reminded me that one thing was worse for me than never getting what I wanted—it was hurting the people I loved most. It was harder to bear my parents' pain on top of my own when I forced them to say no.

During a long afternoon sojourn at the library, I watched over Emma distractedly. She plucked picture books much too young for her off shelves, discarded them on the floor, and I studiously placed them back in the proper spots while pretending to listen to her endless chatter about Dad and coins and 7-Eleven. Then, as usual, she went off to make friends with other kids. I knew I should monitor her interactions—my parents expected me to—but my mind was full of disappointment about the internship. It wasn't going away, even though I didn't want to want anything.

There had been so many missed opportunities, but this one was the hardest. My heart was full of *I want*. I wanted the internship, I wanted to be at the level of the other kids in the class, I wanted to know what they planned to do with their lives. I was working hard, staying up until all hours to study, trying to catch up to the class. But to what end? I couldn't have what they had. I would lose the thing that mattered most.

For the first time, my dad had dropped us off at the library and left. He said he wasn't positive what time he'd be back. I wondered if he was going on one of his recent, mysterious errands. Sometimes he'd be gone for only twenty minutes. Other times, it was hours. When he returned, he'd go directly to his bedroom and close the door.

I knew he wouldn't like it if he came back and saw me using a library computer. He'd want to know what I was searching for.

For fifteen minutes, I waited impatiently for the computer-skills class to be dismissed. As soon as an elderly man stood up, I nabbed the seat at his station, which earned me a disapproving glance. Wary, I looked to the door, then quickly typed "156 Foxglove Drive, Atherton, California." It was all I could think of to search. The *A* key kept sticking and I had to retry, jamming it three times.

There was plentiful information about houses on Foxglove Drive—the bedroom count, the acreage, what a house had sold for and when. But nothing for 156. I hit return to reload the search.

Nothing. It gave me the chills that there was information about every house on Foxglove except the one we were staying in, like it had been intentionally scrubbed.

Dejected, I looked to Emma and then back to the empty doorway.

I looked up more detail about some of the colleges that kept coming up in class: Berkeley, UCLA, Columbia, Penn.

What the hell. I probably had one more minute. I typed "Harrison Addison." People must make fun of how it rhymed.

I'd expected a social media hit. Instead, the top search result read: FORMER DISTRICT ATTORNEY MAYA KUMAR ANNOUNCES RUN FOR GOVERNOR. I clicked the link.

At the top of the article from the *Chronicle,* there was a photo of Maya Kumar and her son, Harrison Addison, who stood next to his mother at the announcement for her candidacy. It was a great action shot. In the photo, Harrison was smiling, which I'd never seen. His eyes danced as he leaned toward his mother, obviously saying something that made her laugh.

Oh god.

An unexpected smile curled one corner of my mouth. It was so ironic, it was almost funny. In a random summer math class, the daughter of fugitives sat next to the son of one of the most high-profile politicians in the state.

CHAPTER FOURTEEN

I t seemed appropriate the next morning when class began with Professor Alexiev energetically wiping away an elaborate family tree on the whiteboard. It was an illustration of dominant and recessive traits. She left words above her reach: *Guest Speakers: Representatives from AncestoryNow on the information age and at-home genetic testing.*

Once Professor Alexiev began class, it cheered me after a long night in my room, avoiding my family and telling myself to let my regret over the internship go. One of the other girls would have gotten it anyway.

I was entirely different in class than at home. The heaviness disappeared. I felt like I could eat, drink, and sleep what we were doing. I was now grasping maybe 80 percent of what was being taught. I dreaded the end of class.

I'm living for this.

In class, I'd assumed Harrison was good-looking deadweight. Now it made sense why he was called on so much less:

he was a celebrity kid and he was to be left alone. Maybe pre-arrangements had been made. When I'd read deeper, it turned out his mother's ex-husband, Harrison's father, was one of the founders of Admara. He was one of the original gods of Silicon Valley. A billionaire.

Today, I was up at the whiteboard, stuck. But not mortified anymore, because at this point, the entire class, minus Harrison, was used to being mortified at the whiteboard, having to ask if the whole class agreed or disagreed with your work at each step. Professor Alexiev had begun shouting out everyone else's names to come on up. It had been jarring hearing "Poppy! Poppy!" over and over again. But there was the sense of all of us being in it together. Except for him.

"Anyone want to help Poppy out?" Professor Alexiev asked in her style of enunciating every word as if to show off her perfect English.

A sea of quiet and confused faces stared back, making me feel justified that I was stuck on this line of the proof.

One hand tentatively went up. Harrison's.

"Mr. Addison. Go ahead."

He joined me at the whiteboard and held out his hand for the marker. I clumsily dropped it and he quickly bent to swipe it up. Then he took a long breath, sized up the board, and began solving the problem, going down a path I hadn't seen. Then *he* got stuck. But because of his path, I saw a way through.

"Oh, actually, I think I see it. Can I?" I automatically held out my hand for the marker.

Our eyes met. He wore a different expression than the flat one I'd seen up until now. His quiet eyes were curious and alive.

Our hands touched when he handed me the pen.

After class, Professor Alexiev called me over. "You applied for the internship?"

I'd become her cause. My parents would kill me if they knew.

"No. I can't." The less said the better.

Her eyes widened in surprise. *"Why?"*

Harrison was gathering his things, zipping up his backpack just to our right.

I needed Professor Alexiev to lose interest in me. "It's not a good fit." I hated saying it.

Instead of shaking her head at what an idiot kid I was, Professor Alexiev put her face close to mine. Her black bangs were partially in her eyes, grazing the top of her glasses. I didn't dare back away.

Her voice was low and urgent. "You need to grab hold of these rare opportunities. That's the only way you pull yourself out. If I hadn't, I'd still be in Bulgaria, unemployed." Up close, she looked even younger and her eyes wanted to penetrate mine, to make me listen.

I wasn't sure what she thought I needed to pull myself out of—if she was referring to poverty, to overprotective and anti-technology parents who wanted to live off the grid. It didn't matter that she didn't know my real circumstances. Her words scared me.

Her expression softened and she asked again, trying to help. "You really didn't want it?"

I could do this. "No," I lied to her face.

Her eyes dimmed. I wished I could go back to one minute before, when she still liked me. Professor Alexiev shook her head with no small amount of disgust.

"That was a gift," she said pointedly, and looked over at Harrison, who was typing on his phone. Then she turned her back on me.

Pissed off—about never having a shot at the internship, about being forced once again to lie to someone I respected—I violently heaved my backpack from the floor. Harrison glanced up. I looked for Professor Alexiev one more time, wishing I could tell her this wasn't my choice.

But I couldn't. I had to choose sides. And I would always choose my family.

Professor Alexiev had disappeared, anyway. The genetics class was piling in. Midday June sunlight slanted through the windows, bits of dust suspended and sparkling in the rays. Representatives from AncestoryNow had walked in—lanyards around necks—preparing to present to the class. One of them was setting up a PowerPoint entitled: CHOOSE A FUTURE IN BIO ENGINEERING. Another employee displayed their product on a table: DNA test kits.

I drew closer. The outside of the white box read: UNLOCK YOUR FAMILY STORY.

Later, I'd look back, amazed by how lightning fast the idea formed. How I recognized that it was information. A bit of light let into my airtight container. I plucked a kit off the table and kept on going.

You need to grab hold of these rare opportunities.

I had a few minutes to spare before my parents would wonder where I was. I pushed into the girls' bathroom, which smelled sharply of cleanser, closed a stall door, and in the dim pink light took apart the test. I read the instructions quickly but carefully, with a clinical remove from the task at hand.

I spit into the tube. I slipped it into the envelope. I carefully printed an email address I prayed was available: annakarenina0704@gmail.com, named for the classic I read over and over because it was mostly available in every library of every new town we ran to.

I didn't think. I left the bathroom and headed straight for the front of the school, then to an opening in the chain-link fence. Every day, I passed the pollen-coated blue mailbox just off school grounds.

I heard a cough behind me. Harrison Addison held an identical package in his hand. He reached in front of me and grasped the mailbox lever.

I glanced up at Harrison and gave him a questioning look.

"After you," he said, his voice rough. He cleared his throat and gestured with his chin for me to go first.

I turned back to the mailbox and wavered, doubt gathering strength. I watched the kit in my hand near the opening. Feeling outside of myself, I wondered what decision I would make.

The box dropped into the mailbox.

Harrison's tumbled just behind mine, down into the dark mouth.

CHAPTER FIFTEEN

When I arrived home, I followed the tinkling of laughter. Through the living room window, I saw Emma with my dad, planting some vegetables in a half-rotted-out raised bed. My mom reclined on an old chaise lounge, an open book in her lap, staring off into space. I knocked lightly on the window and waved. She startled, then looked up from under a giant straw sun hat and waved back.

All was good. I should have been at peace because they seemed at peace. Instead, I went to my room and softly locked the door.

It was just a DNA test. An untraceable kit assigned an anonymous number. It would tell me my cultural background, which didn't even really matter. So why did I want to take back what I'd just done?

Because I'd learned not to want anything for myself. Because I'd learned that what I wanted could hurt my parents.

I crawled into bed and followed the strange primal urge to pull the covers over my head and hide.

I remembered doing that after what happened in Des Moines.

The memory sickened me, but sometimes I relived it as a reminder and maybe even a punishment.

In fourth grade, I wanted to fit in. At the elementary school in the suburbs of Des Moines, I was unexpectedly a big deal. For once, I'd arrived on the first day of school, which made me seem a little more normal than if I'd shown up on a random Wednesday in March. It was the last moment my mom had any say over how my hair and my clothes looked, and now, looking back on it, I should have let her continue. My hair had been in elaborate fishtail braids, and I remembered wearing a pair of used skinny jeans and a sweatshirt that was soft and vintage with old-fashioned Disneyland lettering. Maybe no one quite knew how to place me.

As a result, I fell in with the popular group for the first two weeks of school—not enough time for any of my big differences to become apparent. No one had asked me to her house or to a birthday party yet, only to have me repeatedly say no. Most importantly, most of the girls didn't have phones yet, so that was when I still stood a chance.

One girl, named Dorothy after her grandmother, took me under her wing. She was sweet with big green eyes, and she was the one who extended the first invitation. Could I join the group of girls going to the latest Marvel movie? Absolutely everyone in the grade seemed to be going that weekend.

I asked my parents if I could go. I could still picture them sitting low to the ground on a stained tan couch telling me no. It was the same couch where only a few weeks before they'd sat side by side to tell me my mom was having a baby, fake smiles pasted on their pale faces.

But you can drop me off around the corner! You can pick me up early. Please. I've never been to a movie!

My mom, bare legs draped over my dad's lap, did a sit-up and swung her legs to the floor. She ran both hands through her hair, something she always did when she was thinking.

"No," my dad said firmly and quietly.

I ran to my tiny room, made into a private space by a dividing curtain, and threw myself onto the cot. I raged, muffling a scream into my pillow. I wanted them to pay for what they were doing to me. First, I cried, then I flipped onto my back, stared at the mold in the corners of the ceiling, and came up with a plan. I could say I already had plans to see the movie with my parents. That way, I'd save face. I'd fit in if I could at least talk about the movie.

My dad was working nights at that point—a construction job repaving roads all through the suburbs. I began my campaign on my mom for three days straight. Please could she take me to the movie? Dad didn't have to know. I understood I couldn't go with the girls because it was too complicated with drop-offs and pickups and potential parental interactions, but couldn't she and I go? We could sit in the back. I explained to her how everyone in the fourth grade was seeing it and I would look so stupid if I didn't.

It took all three days of begging. I was sincere about how much I wanted to go, but it was also the first time I'd ever been consciously manipulative. I knew my mom cared whether I had friends.

She caved. On a Thursday night, just after my dad left on foot for the nearby construction site, wearing a hard hat, clutching a neon vest and brown-bag dinner in one hand, we piled into the old green Buick we drove at the time.

My mom's mood was jubilant at first, like she'd been let out of prison. We sang loudly as we headed into the city to the massive Cineplex with reclining seats. I remembered realizing that I couldn't recall the last time she'd driven anywhere or the last time she'd been out in public. Maybe that's when it came into focus that she was the one who always stayed behind, mostly indoors.

Her mood shifted. She was singing Taylor Swift one moment and then white-knuckling the steering wheel as we hit city traffic. She was always confident and self-assured, so I became uneasy when I saw this new side of her. I'd never seen her scared. I began to feel worried about her driving, as though she were a teenager who had barely driven before and didn't know exactly what she was doing.

When we made it to the movie theater, my mom was jubilant again, like she'd just completed a herculean task. She wore her sunglasses indoors, at night, while we stood in a long, snaking line for tickets. That drew some looks so she removed them, placed them in her purse, and shook out her ponytail to shield her face with her hair.

We weren't paranoid. People were glancing at her. But in hindsight, they were looking because she was pretty. Really pretty. I grasped her hand as we slowly moved up the line. I noticed her hand was shaking. If I had been too stupid to feel guilty during the drive, at that moment, I began to feel terrible for what I'd asked of her.

"Two for the Marvel movie?" my mom asked when we reached the ticket counter. She was breathless. She looked to me for help and I quickly supplied the title.

"You'll be in theater twelve to the left, but the doors haven't opened yet."

"Shit," my mom muttered. I led her to a bench in a quiet corner of the Cineplex, where we waited until we could enter the theater. I chatted nervously.

My mom scanned the crowd while pretending to listen. She laughed at all the right places and kept saying, "No way," or "Really?" but added nothing to the conversation. But I knew if I stopped talking, she'd get more scared.

I was telling my mom everything I knew about the film to get her excited and focused on the fun that lay ahead—that would make this ordeal worth it, I hoped—when I saw her interest had been caught by a woman in our proximity, gathering straws and napkins at a kiosk. The woman was Asian, maybe my mom's age, and wearing leather pants, a white T-shirt, and holding a designer tote. My mom was checking out her outfit. The woman glanced up and caught and held my mom's eye. After a long moment, she moved on, carrying her teetering cardboard tray over to a tall blond man and two young boys. To this day, I didn't know if that woman was the one who made the phone call, but she was my best guess.

I wasn't sure how my mom sensed something was off. Maybe she had that same hair-raising sensation I'd developed over time. We had entered the theater and settled in the middle row when she abruptly whispered that she was changing seats. Then she grabbed my upper arm and drew close.

"When it's over, meet me behind the building. At the dumpsters. There have to be dumpsters back there," she said.

"Mom?"

But she was already walking up the aisle. I saw her slither into an empty seat in the last row by the exit. Thank god for that open seat.

I'd been looking forward to going to a movie theater for years, but when the show began, I found it too loud and overwhelming. I was regretting ever asking my mom for this giant favor, and I just wanted to go home. A romance in the story finally piqued my interest, and I was slightly engrossed when three or so people walked into my peripheral vision. Annoyed, I wanted them to take their seats. But they marched to the front and then slowly back up the aisle again. I couldn't see them well. Then a voice crackled through a radio. The audience's heads swiveled, and the person grabbed at his belt, adjusting the volume.

I whipped my head around and squinted in the dark at the seat my mom had taken. It was empty. I counted methodically to one hundred, waiting to see if I'd imagined the whole thing, that maybe I'd wake up and this would have all been just a nightmare. I remembered thinking how odd it was that I could no longer hear the movie.

I looked to the ceiling, at the speakers in the corners. Then, suddenly, I was out of my body. Floating above, I saw a young girl enveloped in the red armchair, terrorized and small. And I felt so sad for her.

Adrenaline must have kicked in, because my brain became suddenly, beautifully crystal clear. In my head, I heard my dad's voice telling me to focus. I quickly stood and calmly walked down the aisle. I breezed past the two cops stationed outside the theater door and the one at the entrance to the women's bathroom. I didn't make eye contact. I kept walking.

From the multiplex exit, I took a right, homing in on the back of the building.

There were three dumpsters. I stood freezing cold next to them for what I later learned was two hours. At first, I saw flashing lights from a few police cars. Then all was pitch-black beside the spurts of headlights streaming in packs from the theater lot as movies let out, one at a time. The smell was horrendous. But I focused on it. I couldn't allow myself any thought. Not *the* thought: that I was lost. That there was no way my dad would safely find me since he didn't know where I was.

It's okay, it's okay. I kept the mantra going so I wouldn't crack. When a rat passed inches from my foot, a squeak slipped from my throat. I was seconds away from losing it, from breaking open, when I heard a *Psst!*

I made out my mom's figure, backlit, illuminating her like an angel. An angel I also fiercely hated for scaring me like that. All wrapped in one.

She led me to the Buick. We got in silently. The moment we safely blended in with freeway traffic, we both started bawling.

It turned out that being in the know about the latest movie didn't matter: we left Des Moines by 10 A.M. the next morning.

That's how I knew not to want anything. My family's safety was one hundred times more important than what I, a stupid girl, thought I needed.

. . .

I shouldn't have taken that test.

I was going to back off my search. For their sake.

It was okay. I loved them. This was enough. I didn't need to know more.

I rolled over onto my back and folded down the covers so I could breathe again. I wiped the beads of sweat from my forehead.

That was a long time ago. We were okay now.

It was just a DNA test.

CHAPTER SIXTEEN

The next day, I was unfocused and hot. There was a heat wave and the California school didn't have AC.

Uncharacteristically, Harrison had arrived to class before me. My eyes swept over his long legs kicked out in front of him. Today he wore flip-flops instead of Vans and jiggled one shoe half off his foot, revealing tan lines. He had nice legs. Of course he had nice legs. I imagined a modeling scout at a skate park spotting Harrison—all sharp angles and perfect skin—and handing him a business card. His mother was lucky: Harrison delivered great optics for her campaign. Sitting next to him made me aware of my own old clothes and ragged fingernails.

I held my peasant blouse away from my body, wafting it to cool down. I'd avoided eye contact with Harrison for no other reason than our strange interaction the day before. If we got into a conversation about our dual DNA tests, I had the feeling he would be one of those mocking boys—the kind who seemed nice for a second and then said something cutting before walking away.

I shifted and played with the tassels on my shirt. I'd worn shorts, and my thighs were uncomfortably stuck to the plastic chair. From the corner of my eye, I saw Harrison furiously shading something in his notebook with the side of a pencil.

Later, after a break, Harrison and I both returned to the classroom at the same time. Harrison made an *after you* gesture, so I stepped in front of him into the narrow alleyway leading to our desks. In an uncoordinated move, my hip bumped against his desk. His spiral notebook hit the floor with a *splat,* and I bent to scoop it up.

"I've got it!" he said quickly and practically dove in front of me to retrieve it. But not before I saw the professional-looking sketch splayed at my feet. It was of a girl who looked a lot like me. Harrison quickly placed it facedown on his desk. We settled in our seats for the last half hour of class, palpable tension between us.

I had to get the sketch. That's what my dad would tell me to do if he knew someone had spent time studying my face. He'd taught me that even if someone's interest seemed innocent, you still needed to take care of the problem. Always careful—more like paranoid—he'd made us move locations based on harmless, minor incidents like this.

That meant I had to talk to Harrison after class.

Goddammit.

"Hey."

Harrison surprised me. He was the one waiting several feet from the classroom door, backpack hooked over one shoulder.

"Hi?" Why did I sound like such an idiot? It wasn't a question.

"I just like to draw. I promise you I'm not a stalker." He actually seemed nervous.

So the sketch *was* of me. "I liked it," I said. "Can I have it?"

Harrison hesitated. "Sure." We stood in the dappled shade under a tall birch. He paged through the notebook until he found the drawing.

Harrison looked up at me, almost accusingly, as if he really didn't want to give up his drawing. But he ripped it out and handed me the thick page.

"Thanks," I said, examining the picture. It was me in profile, and it made me look better, prettier than I really was. I loved the expression he'd drawn: there was a brightness he'd captured, like I was ready and eager to answer Professor Alexiev's questions. He'd captured a specific moment when he'd been watching me.

"Wow. You are a great artist."

"Nah. I just mess around. Sorry I didn't ask beforehand."

"No worries," I murmured. Harrison made no move to leave. I had the pleaser's urge to rush to fill the silence. God, why couldn't I think of anything to say? "What's your name?" I asked.

From the lightning-quick widening of his eyes, Mr. Addison looked really and truly surprised, like he couldn't believe I didn't know.

"I mean, I know you're *Mr. Addison* in there," I prattled on. Silence.

Did he not hear my question? He was studying me.

"What?" I asked. "Is that a weird question?"

"Nah," he finally said. "It's Harrison. Harry."

"Harrison Addison." Why had I just said it out loud?

He smiled once again. "Yeah, yeah. I've heard it all before. So call me Harry."

"You got it." I smiled back.

"Poppy."

"Yeah?" I asked warily. So he knew *my* name.

"No, I'm just saying it because I like it. Like the state flower."

"What?"

"You know—the California poppy is the state flower?"

"Oh. I didn't know."

"I remember that from elementary school," he said. "What high school do you go to?"

"I just moved here," I said.

"From where?"

"Florida. What about you?" I deflected. "Where do you go to high school?"

"St. Stephen's," he supplied.

That meant nothing to me, but I assumed it was private.

Harry picked up his backpack, and automatically we began to slowly walk to the school entrance together. "Why did you steal one of those DNA kits?" he asked abruptly. I stiffened. "Don't worry. I don't think anyone saw us. No one was watching."

"Why did *you* take one?"

"To see if the asshole who says he's my father is really my father," Harry said, stone-faced. Then, "Nah. I'm kidding. I don't know. I'm curious. My mom's a politician and her ethnicity comes up, so I guess it's been on my mind. People want to label her. Is she Black, white, Southeast Asian? But at the end of the day, the DNA test is just going to give me more labels." Harry raised his face to the sky. "There's the added benefit of pissing off my father about privacy. It's everything he hates."

I wanted to ask Harry what he meant by that, but then he asked, "What about you?"

"Same thing. I'm just curious." I noted the plaques on the redbrick walls indicating every graduating class. We were walking along the 1970s.

"My dad's girlfriend did one for her dog." Harry shook his head ruefully.

"Really?" I found myself laughing for the first time in I didn't know how long.

Harry grinned at my reaction, his face relaxing and his eyes taking on such a warmth, such a light, just like they had in the photo of him with his mom. It was like he shed a layer and I glimpsed the real Harry. "Oh yeah. The results are taped up on the fridge," he said dryly. "Chihuahua/pit bull mix. I could have told her that." He leaped ahead and held the heavy exit door open for me. We paused awkwardly for a moment on the walkway in front of the school. I found I didn't want the conversation to end yet. Harry looked at his Apple Watch. "Damn, I gotta go," he said, almost apologetically.

"See you tomorrow," I said. I blushed. For no apparent reason.

I didn't want Harry to see me walking while he zipped by in his car, so I stood in the driveway and acted like someone was coming to pick me up.

When Harry started the car, deafening music blared. All four windows rolled down in unison, and Harry backed out swiftly. His profile zipped by, and I thought I caught him look for me in his rearview mirror.

CHAPTER SEVENTEEN

Pops, help me move these barrels?" My dad led me to the utility part of the yard where an old clothesline stood, the aged lines sagging. I grabbed a trash can and followed him down the long driveway that was quickly becoming overgrown, towering bushes slapping my arm as I proceeded down the side.

My dad flipped open the lid of the black rubber trash can and took in the small pile of white plastic bags. He opened one, jostled it, and held the bag wide for me. "Can you take a look?"

Ah. This was a lesson. I half-heartedly peered in, but I didn't see anything to worry about—nothing personal, nothing that would identify us. I wasn't even sure why we checked or what we were checking for, exactly. It wasn't like our real names, or fake ones for that matter, were on pieces of mail.

My mom's sudden appearance was unexpected. My dad

released the bag back onto the pile below and shut the lid. It came down hard on my hand and I held in a squeak, clutching my fingers behind my back. I didn't want him to feel bad.

"Hey," he said to my mom. It sounded like *Can I help you?* They were eye to eye, the same height.

"Hi. I'm going on a walk." My mom rarely left the house, even in rural areas. But now here she stood, in clear view of the street. The buzz of a tree trimmer sounded from farther down the block. My mom brushed past us, like this was nothing and entirely her prerogative.

"Babe—"

"I need a quick break from playing *Battleship*!" she tossed over her shoulder.

"She's leaving the house," I stated dumbly.

My dad watched her back as she took a left around the leafy corner.

I had an exciting interaction at the library. I couldn't take the internship, but I could take the part-time babysitting job offered by a harried mother at story hour.

Rebecca Klosky approached me while I was helping Emma pick out chapter books. She jiggled a baby in a front carrier while she clutched a toddler by the wrist.

"I see you here every week. You're so good with your sister. Do you happen to babysit?" She said it all in a rush, like she feared being interrupted any moment. "I really need help at the pool. I have a nanny, but she just had knee surgery, so she's out for weeks."

When Mrs. Klosky mentioned that the nearby country club

was within walking distance of the library, I grew more interested. Then she mentioned the astronomical amount she'd pay me per hour.

I cautiously asked my dad when I got home. "It's cash under the table. I told her I don't have a bank account so I can't do any kind of online payment thing."

"We don't know them." My dad's voice carried a note of finality.

My dad wasn't even considering it fully, because he hadn't bothered to look up from sanding the outdoor picnic table. In the back of my head, I knew he was prepping the table for the Fourth of July, also my birthday. My family would make a big deal of the celebration—every holiday just the four of us. It was funny how he said, "We don't know them," because we didn't know anyone.

"Dad, you saw her when you picked us up. She was the mom with the baby and the toddler. You know, the kid who was crying and then he burped really loudly? And we laughed when we got in the car? She just needs help for a few hours every afternoon."

"Every afternoon?"

"Monday through Friday. One to four o'clock."

"Honey." My dad looked up at the sound of my mom's velvet voice. "It's fine," she said to him, as though her word was always the final one.

My dad didn't answer me. He was distracted by the sight of my mom, who leaned casually against the sliding glass doorframe, arms loosely crossed. She was out of her pajamas. She was wearing my Converses.

"You going somewhere?" my dad asked.

"Walk."

He swallowed but bit back words. We were making our resident guard dog very, very anxious. All he did was work to protect us, and now my mom was bending the rules. And here I was asking to do the same.

I rushed in to make him feel better. "Dad, she's looking for help at the pool until her nanny recovers from knee surgery. The country club is within walking distance! She's paying thirty dollars an hour."

It was almost imperceptible, but my dad stiffened when I said the amount. I wished I could take it back. I guessed he'd never made that much from his odd jobs.

"Why do you want money?" my mom asked. She struck me as a former rich girl by how clueless she sounded about money and other people wanting it. I was getting irritated with her. I wanted my mom back. She'd stopped braiding Emma's hair and reading her bedtime stories. She'd stopped showing up to breakfast.

"So I can help out," I answered. Maybe take more classes. Visit the sites that were so close by.

"Poppy." My dad's voice was a warning. I wasn't sure if I'd gotten ahead of myself with plans or if I'd inadvertently insulted him by inferring that he couldn't provide for us.

The sound of a hollow *thud* put an abrupt end to the conversation. My dad shot up from the bench. My mom and I followed him. I was annoyed by the interruption and that every single noise was treated like a threat. It put me on constant edge, and I wanted to tell him that we were safe. Sometimes I wondered if the paranoia was blown out of proportion.

In the side yard, my sister hung from the top of the sagging wooden fence, kicking at it to try to heave herself to the top. In a flash, my dad was holding her waist and gently prying her off. He scanned over the fence, into the backyard of the wedding-cake white mansion in the distance.

"What are you doing, Em?" My dad lightly brushed the hair from her sweaty forehead.

"I'm trying to look at the fountain. Yesterday, Mom lifted me up so I could see it."

How had my mom known about a fountain? Her face was carefully blank.

Now that I was looking for it, you could make out the top of a statue in the distance. I stood on my tiptoes.

My mom said, "Here, Poppy, if you step up, you can see over. Like this."

I followed her lead and stepped up on the lowest rung of the fence. The fountain was spectacular—at least twenty feet tall and twenty feet in diameter. A gleaming water nymph stood on the top tier, spouting water above four seated mermaids below.

"Guys. Come on," my dad said abruptly.

"That is incredible," I said.

"Come inside. I'll make everyone lunch," he urged, like he didn't like me up there. "Poppy."

"Okay. Got it. I'm coming."

We walked past the grove of lemon trees, along the cracked cement pathway to the main backyard. My dad gave Emma a piggyback ride. I wanted to point out that Emma was getting too big for that.

When my dad and I were alone in the kitchen, I tentatively

asked, "Dad?" My voice was a reminder. "Mrs. Klosky is a tired mom, not a police officer, I promise. Some things are actually the way they look."

My dad halted taking sandwich makings from the fridge. He made the point of gluing his eyes to mine, the refrigerator door gaping open behind him.

"Never forget: nothing is the way it looks."

I didn't want to feel guilty when I texted Mrs. Klosky that I was taking the job. In addition to wanting to keep me close, I knew my dad would have appreciated my continued help at home with Emma, who was acting up this summer. She wanted my mom's attention. Where was the mom who would light up the room? Who would engulf us in giant hugs that made us feel so incredibly loved? Emma was waking up regularly, crying in the middle of the night.

When class ended the next day, I started out on the two-mile walk to the country club for my first day of babysitting. When I agreed to the job, the walk had seemed like nothing, but I hadn't accounted for the heat wave and heavy backpack. I knew I looked like a drowned rat by the time I turned down the long drive flanked by palm trees and approached the circular entrance of the country club marked with an understated bronze plaque and white shutters.

A bald man with a neat beard and an earpiece barely glanced at me when he opened the club door for me to enter.

"That's okay. Um, I'll wait for my . . . I'll wait out here." He gave a slight nod. The parking lot was stacked with shiny cars. Women arrived in mostly black SUVs, while silver-haired men climbed out of sports cars and boys my age dashed over to help them collect their golf clubs from trunks and back seats. I sat on a bench under a trellis of wisteria and waited, surprised at my growing nerves and suddenly wishing I were at home, eating lunch with my family. My stomach growled angrily, and when I wiped a trickle of sweat from my forehead, the back of my hand was streaked light brown from the dusty walk.

Mrs. Klosky turned up fifteen minutes late. Luckily, I recognized her Audi station wagon when it drove past, and I walked quickly, following it down a short hill to a separate parking lot.

"Emily!" Mrs. Klosky greeted me. "Don't look at the inside of my car!" She laughed. Her car was pristine on the outside, but inside the floorboards were covered with dried fruit and snack bags. I liked her. To be a member of the club, she had to be uber-privileged, but she seemed down-to-earth.

Immediately, I reached out for the baby. I'd never babysat, but I was so used to mothering my sister that it turned out I was excellent at anticipating what Mrs. Klosky—*Call me Rebecca*—wanted. It became clear pretty quickly that where Rebecca needed the most help was with the more difficult toddler, Frank.

Rebecca pointed out the women's locker room, a kelly-green and blond-wood affair. After I'd changed in a cramped bathroom stall, I stuffed the bath towel I'd brought from home back into my backpack, on top of my soggy sandwich. I felt like a fool for bringing the towel once I saw the stacks of yellow-and-white-striped towels uniformly lining the chaise lounges poolside. Then, thankfully, I spied how an older woman in pink culottes operated the keypad for a locker. I followed her lead and shoved my backpack into narrow number 10.

Rebecca bought me lunch at the snack bar. I ate a chicken-Caesar wrap and drank ginger lemonade while successfully enticing Frank to eat his pig in a blanket. From the poolside dining area, I looked out on the shimmering baby-blue Olympic-size pool and wondered what world I had just walked into. We were surrounded by the lush green grass of polo fields. No joke. Polo fields. In the distance, ponies thundered past, their riders leaning low, elegantly sweeping their polo sticks. It could have been the present day or fifty years ago.

Lunch lasted all of five minutes before Frank grew restless and began tossing his fries to the ground, laughing at his mother's reprimands while Steller's jays lurked at the perimeter. She whisked him from his booster seat, and I trailed them with the stroller to a spot by the pool. We took over three chaise lounges and exploded the contents of Rebecca's bags onto them to search for diapers and pool toys.

Besides nannies and a few moms who rocked triangle bikinis, the crowd was mostly kids eating lots and lots of junk food. One after another, they ran to the snack bar. The lifeguards weren't much older than me, maybe college age. Besides the occasional half-hearted whistle, it was an unsupervised kid paradise.

It was hard not to enjoy myself. It was the epitome of a summer day in a beautiful place—the kind that seemed, up until this point, only something I'd read about in books. I took Frank into the pool and pushed him on a tiny floaty. I dunked under and popped up like a fish, spraying Frank, who laughed like that was the funniest thing he'd ever encountered. The pure chuckle made me smile, and I remembered how good smiling felt. It had been a bit.

I slicked back my hair and listened to the sound of the diving-board spring and the answering splash, the kids' voices echoing off the water, and low-volume rock classics playing over the sound system. It was overtaken by the burst of a noisy crowd entering through the gate.

It was a large group of teens. Some were dressed in golf clothes, some wore the tiniest bikinis. My navy-blue tank suit made me feel like a Girl Scout by comparison.

Two of the girls came to lounge in the four inches of water on the wide shelf near me and Frank. A few boys began whipping off their shirts and jumping into the pool in their golf shorts.

"Whoa," I heard one girl say to another.

"What?"

"I'm looking at Harry fucking Addison."

I stopped pushing Frank.

"Where?"

"In the corner. With Aviv." I brought up my hand to shade my eyes and, sure enough, Harry was sprawled in a chair, a skinny girl seated next to him at the table. She was of Asian descent, with bleached blond hair and a stunningly gorgeous face. Harry suddenly sat up, and I wondered if he could see me from so far away.

"I thought he wasn't allowed out of the house after what happened." One of the girls gave a snort of laughter.

The sun reflected off the white pavement, so bright I had to close my eyes. Then there was a darkening against my eyelids, like a cloud passing. When I opened them, Harrison Addison was at the side of the pool in front of me, blocking the sun, and now he was the one removing his shirt. Just as he grasped the hem, our eyes met. Harry paused when he saw me. Then, barely missing a beat, he whipped his shirt over his head. I saw his muscled abs, his broad chest, and every rib of his rib cage.

Frank made a scared sound as the floaty wavered and he almost fell backward. I steadied him just before he tipped over and prayed his mother hadn't just seen my negligence. But Rebecca was chatting with friends while the baby slept in the stroller parked in the shade.

Of course I had to be at Harry's country club. I'd briefly relaxed for the first time in ages.

I tried to look busy by taking Frank in my arms, and I began spinning him around. When I got dizzy, I closed my eyes to let the world settle.

"Sleeping on the job?" Harry waded over to me in the waist-high clear water.

"What are you doing here?" I asked. It came out all wrong and weirdly aggressive.

Harry didn't seem to take offense. "Swimming," he answered pleasantly. My eyes fell to the expanse of smooth skin, then flicked quickly back up. "You checking me out?" he asked.

"No!" I hoped my freckles hid how red my cheeks were. I saw myself reflected in the shine of Harry's sunglasses: no makeup, wet hair in a matted French braid, and I could even make out my darkening freckles.

Frank began trying to splash him, but Harry simply dodged it, moving side to side.

I untwisted the strap of my bathing suit. "I just wasn't expecting to go from talking with you about public-key cryptography to seeing you half-naked." *Please tell me I didn't say that.* I was such a nerd.

"Ha-ha. Well, I'm supposed to be at my summer job, but they said I can go in this weekend. As long as I get my work done . . ."

The sun was directly in my face again, and it hurt to look at Harry. I widened my stance, shifted Frank from his floaty to my hip, and shielded my eyes.

"Here." Harry offered his sunglasses to me. "I can't stand watching you look into the sun."

"Thanks," I said, carefully taking the black Ray-Bans. They were way too wide and loose. "How do they look? Ginormous?"

"They look good on you," Harry said.

My eyes relaxed and I could now see his angular, pretty face. "So is this your brother?" Harry asked.

"Oh no! I'm babysitting."

"That's cool." This time Frank splashed Harry in the face. "Hey!" Harry laughed.

"Emily," Frank whined, and squirmed for me to let him go.

Oh no. "That's my real name," I said, quickly covering. "Poppy is my nickname, and it just kind of came out in class."

"Oh. Can I keep calling you Poppy?"

"Of course." I'd never planned on seeing anyone outside of class. But I couldn't say I was sad to see Harrison Addison. Goose bumps rolled across my skin in the breeze. As if he sensed it, Harry automatically glanced down. I conveniently moved a restless Frank to cover my cleavage.

"Poppy," Harry said.

"Yes?" I asked, giving him a confused side-eye.

"Just saying your name."

"Harrison," I said right back.

"Harry," he corrected.

I became aware of eyes on us and realized we were ignoring the recalcitrant toddler between us, who was now pushing against me, and we were just standing across from each other in the shallow water, smiling.

It felt like we were flirting.

Rebecca glanced up from her phone. I may have been making it up, but it felt like the entire pool had quieted down and Harry and I were the focus. My goose bumps became something else altogether. The eyes on me made my skin crawl.

"What are you doing after—"

"I better get him out," I said at the exact same time. One of the girls exaggeratedly leaned away as Frank and I moved past her and exited the pool. To my intense self-consciousness, Harry let me walk up the steps in front of him.

If I could guess what Harry saw when he looked at me: a girl with an eager STEM-student vibe, in a one-piece bathing suit, who babysat in her free time. The French braid didn't help matters. My mom was really, really pretty. We looked alike, but I carried myself totally differently. My mom always said I looked so fresh-faced and sweet with my freckles. If we were cast in a movie, she'd be the glamorous protagonist while I'd be cast as an all-American girl who played volleyball in the background.

But then again, why would I even assume Harry cared enough to look? He was just being nice to me—the only other outsider in our math class. Harry *seemed* nice. The jury was out on whether he actually was.

I didn't like the way I felt around him—sort of excited. After taking my place back at the chaise lounges, I made my world small, doing my job and focusing solely on Frank.

At the next lull—Frank gnawing on an ice cream sandwich—I inadvertently looked for Harry. He was seated at a corner table, holding a paperback in one hand. But he'd been joined by a group of friends who'd just played golf: boys in visors, girls in polo shirts and short shorts. He was sitting next to the girl he'd been with at the table originally—Aviv, I remembered. Her bleached hair was twisted into a topknot. I watched as she languorously undid her hair and let it fall around her. She let her shoulder touch Harry's. My mood dampened.

A few minutes later, Rebecca began to pack up. When I bent to help, the sunglasses almost fell from my face. I'd totally forgotten I was wearing them. Harry hadn't said a word. I briefly debated sending Frank to return the glasses.

When I approached Harry's table, I heard one of his friends say, "Thanks for lunch, Harry." He—or his parents, more accurately—had bought eight people lunch. I noticed Harry was drinking a beer. Apparently no one at the country club said no to him.

Harry looked up at me, and it suddenly felt as if I were getting an audience with the king, courtiers at his elbows. Just then, a server delivered a huge basket of fries for the table. I didn't make it up—everyone seated looked to Harry. Harry absentmindedly picked up a fry and ate it. Only at that point did his friends help themselves.

I'd changed back into my shorts and ratty T-shirt with a rainbow and the logo for an ice cream shop. The girls appraised me, and I was aware that I looked like a completely different creature from them.

I carefully held out the sunglasses to Harry. He leaned forward to quickly take them back.

"Thanks," I whispered hoarsely.

"No problem," he mumbled.

Well, what had I expected? Actually, maybe a *See you tomor-row*. But he seemed different around his friends. Aloof.

When I walked away, I heard, "Nice shirt," and a "Friend of yours?" and "She kind of looks like Alix." I didn't catch Harry's response.

I hated my disappointment that he'd treated me like a stranger, like he cared what his friends thought.

What had Harry been about to ask me in the pool? *What are you doing after . . . ?* What are you doing after *this*? Yeah, right. There was no way he'd been about to ask me out.

CHAPTER EIGHTEEN

L ater, I thought again about how Harry had behaved with his friends at the country club—distant, snobby.

"You okay?" my dad asked the next day as I was finishing breakfast.

"Fine," I said.

"You seem distracted. Anything more about yesterday?" My dad was so scarily perceptive.

The night before, I'd given him the blow-by-blow of my first afternoon babysitting. It was what we did when we started something new—painted a picture for my dad of the people, the new environment, and accounted for our time. Emma still didn't understand that she was reporting in to my dad. She still thought he was simply interested in every detail of her time at the library. My dad wanted to know how long our lunch had lasted, roughly how many people had been in the pool, what questions Rebecca had asked me.

Only . . . I hadn't mentioned Harry.

"All good," I said now. I met my dad's eyes while I fidgeted with the drawer inset on my side of the rickety wooden table, pulling it in and out.

When it suddenly wouldn't slide back in, I pulled hard to unstick it. I yanked and it flew open. While Emma danced around the room, flapping her arms like a bird, I leaned down and peered in. There was something bent in half and jammed in the back. I sat up and felt with my hand until I removed the culprit—a photograph.

It was a faded photo of a group of five kids standing in this backyard, recognizable by the fence and the willow tree hanging over our side from the neighbor's yard. The photo had been taken from far enough away that you couldn't make out distinct features, but I could see bowl haircuts and striped T-shirts, and two of the kids were holding plump white chickens. They looked like a motley pack of happy kids from decades ago. The overexposed light of the photo was golden and green.

"What's that?" my dad asked. He was still standing in the doorway of the kitchen.

"An old photograph." I tried to tell myself I hadn't done anything wrong.

My dad took long strides over to the table, but his expression was even. I handed him the photo. He examined it, then all he said was, "Ah." He placed it faceup on the table, like they hadn't missed something, like he hadn't done anything wrong, either. There really wasn't anything to see except the fact that once upon a time, kids had lived here.

"You're going to be late, Pops," he said.

I was perfectly on time. I pushed away from the table, taking one long, last look at the happy old photograph. I had the feeling I wouldn't see it again.

I was leaving, my hand on the rickety doorknob that would make my palm smell like metal, when I saw my new flip phone sitting out on the kitchen counter.

Had I put it there, or had my dad taken it from my backpack to look at it without my knowing? I stepped back into the kitchen and swiped it off the counter.

"Emergencies only." My dad's tone was low. For a moment, I was brought back to this past icy March in Illinois, when my dad saw my profusion of texts from Alina and Ruthie. Even though they were so innocent—99 percent of them were about our science-fair project—he'd gently told me he didn't want me using the phone that way. I'd watched a snowflake stick to the window and apologized.

Today, though, I felt a pinprick of anger. "Of course," I said. In the guilty aftermath of taking the DNA test, I had decided to give my parents—my dad—the benefit of the doubt and trust him.

Yet it seemed like he didn't trust me. Even though I did everything he asked.

When I arrived at summer school, I expected to see Harry. At first, I thought he was simply late, like he often was. Ten minutes into her lesson, Professor Alexiev must have seen me glance at the entrance one too many times, because she called out in her careful, clipped voice, "Poppy." I whipped face forward. "Your friend is away. Why don't you join the rest of us at the front of the room?"

The thought of no Harry made me uncomfortably panicked. What did "away" mean? Was he coming back? I swept up my things and moved front and center to a seat unoccupied by the village of eager learners.

The rest of the week was different without Harry. Not that we'd spoken much, but I'd liked our quiet vibe in the back. We worked really well together the times we'd had to, and we seemed to laugh at the same things that no one else in the class found funny—mainly Professor Alexiev's sense of humor, which would come out in her quirky explanations.

By Tuesday of the second week, I gave up on him. That made it safe to admit that I missed him. I thought about him. A lot.

On Wednesday morning, Professor Alexiev glanced up from her tangle of notes when I took my new seat up front. "Your partner in crime will be back from Paris at the end of the week."

It felt like sunlight poured back into my dark, boxed-in room.

On Thursday, Harry sauntered in with his skateboard the second before class began.

He sat by himself in the back, since I had a new seat, so I only got a glimpse of him. He had dark rings under his eyes and looked like he had just rolled out of bed.

The moment we stopped midway for a ten-minute recess, I stretched and, eyes downcast, surreptitiously looked for him over my shoulder. Harry bolted out of the classroom in his boy way—like a horse whose muscles were completely relaxed— then exploded into action in one motion.

After the break, Professor Alexiev told us to partner up. In a split second, it felt like everyone had someone to work with. I slowly approached Harry. He was also partner-less, but instead of looking around, apprehensive, he sat quietly, beginning to work on the assignment by himself.

The side of his mouth went up when I slid into my old seat.

"You moved out on me?" he said dryly.

"I was ordered to move to the front."

"Well, thanks for sitting here. It makes me feel less conspicuously shunned by the crew." He tipped his chin toward the rest of the class.

I cocked my head. "I don't think they're shunning you."

"No. I didn't mean that. You know what I mean. They are the math whizzes."

"So are you."

"Ha! I wouldn't go that far. But you are. You're the teacher's pet. Feel free to move back up there when we're done."

"I am not the teacher's pet. I don't know what I'm doing."

"That's what's all the more impressive. You're picking this shit up so easily. Most of us have had tutors since the day we were born."

Professor Alexiev walked over. "Is there a problem?"

"No, I'm convincing Poppy she's brilliant."

"That goes without saying," Professor Alexiev said and I tried not to glow. Then she nervously wiped her palms down the sides of her jeans and said to Harry, "Can I chat with you for a moment?"

Harry reluctantly followed her to a corner, but they were only a few feet away. Professor Alexiev seemed to have a habit of doing that. She wasn't big on discretion.

"Your father emailed me last night."

In my peripheral vision, I thought I saw Harry swallow. I could tell the moment he knew I was looking at him, and I quickly glanced away.

"He wants a status report on how you're doing. He's basically my boss, so I'll respond, but I wanted to tell you so you don't think I'm communicating with him behind your back."

"Thanks for letting me know," Harry said. Then: "He's not your boss."

"He's a major donor and a Stanford math PhD. I'm a new professor. Let's just say he gets a large measure of respect from my department. He's not happy you went on vacation."

"Yeah, my mom wanted me and my cousin to take my grandma; she couldn't go because of the campaign."

"Don't worry—I'll tell him that you're catching up. But we both know that's not true. Do the work I sent with you."

I acted absorbed in rifling through my backpack for my cherry-flavored ChapStick. As I glided it on, Harry's gaze dropped to my lips. Then we locked eyes for a long moment.

"Poppy!" Professor Alexiev called loudly, even though I was right there. "If Mr. Addison has any questions, can you bring him up to speed?"

I paused.

"No, that's okay," Harry said. "Really, I can do a lot on my own and—"

I just didn't have the heart to leave the poor guy hanging. "Absolutely," I heard myself say. Why I had a bleeding heart for a wealthy, smart boy who made me feel slightly inadequate, I didn't know.

Professor Alexiev seemed satisfied and moved on to supervise the other partner groups.

Harry took a dramatic intake of breath and sat slowly back down.

I started in on the assigned work, "So, she asked us to define—"

"Sorry about that. You don't have to tutor me. I promise."

"Don't apologize! It's fine. If you have any problem, just ask."

He etched his fingernail into the desk. "Can I get your number?" he asked and looked up at me, slightly vulnerable.

Silence. What did I do? "I usually have a few minutes after class before I need to get to my babysitting job."

Harry nodded like he got the message and started to turn away.

"It's 415-555-7878."

Harry took out his phone and saved my contact information. He didn't even need me to repeat the number.

I shouldn't have told him. I looked down to reset, automatically about to turn things businesslike again. But I had one more thing to say to him before I put the curtain up.

"Hey, you know why they don't talk to you, right?"

"What?" Then he remembered where we left off, discussing the other kids. Harry sat back, and his expression closed off. "No, it's fine."

"It's because they're scared of you."

His face relaxed. "That is funny. Why in the world would they be afraid of me?"

"Because you're a celebrity. That's intimidating. Would you sit down right next to Steve Jobs's children?"

"My parents are the celebrities. And not even cool ones. They're nerd celebrities. Not me. I haven't done anything."

"Well, it's not like you laze around like some spoiled brat.

You have a summer job. That's impressive." Except for the day I'd seen him at the country club, and his vacation to Paris, but I kept that to myself.

"I tried to tell you about that internship."

My stomach curdled.

"Why are you looking at me like that?" Harry asked after a moment.

"I guess I should have realized . . ." But I hadn't. God, I was slow. That's why Professor Alexiev had called it a gift.

"I thought you might want to apply, that it would get you away from your obviously strict parents, and it would have given you your own money . . . not to mention it would look good on a college application."

"Don't worry about me," I said quickly, uncomfortable with what he'd picked up on.

"Sorry. It was interfering. And it didn't even work."

"You didn't even know me then." Not that he really knew me now, but we didn't even speak back then.

Harry shrugged.

"Thanks for trying," I said.

"Why didn't you apply? I'm just curious. Alexiev was pissed at you."

"I'd already agreed to babysitting," I lied. He held my eyes, like he was waiting for me to be honest. I imagined telling him how my parents wouldn't let me. How I didn't have a bank account or a real name.

Thankfully, he finally shrugged and we moved on to the work.

"How did you find out, by the way?" Harry asked about fifteen minutes later. He chewed a nail and studied me.

"What?"

"About who my parents are? You said you just moved here, and I was under the impression that you didn't know."

"I didn't."

"Then how did you find out?"

Oh no.

When I paused, Harry said, "I knew the day you found out."

"How?" I looked at him askance.

"You acted normal around me, then the next class, a little different."

"How can you tell something like that?"

"It's just a vibe. I don't know."

Again, I had the thought that he had to be more perceptive than most boys his age.

"So?" Harry prompted. His eyes sparkled.

"What?" I asked, widening my eyes, playing dumb.

"Did you google me?" he teased.

I opened my mouth, but nothing came out.

"You googled me." He sat back, crossed his arms, and smiled that crazy high-wattage smile.

CHAPTER NINETEEN

Hey, can I show you something?"

I'd looked up to find my dad watching me closely. I'd been staring out the window, a math book and small chalkboard forgotten in my lap. "Come with me," he said.

My dad led me to the back shed. He swiftly used his thumbs to arrange the correct combination on the lock, released it, and let us in. There was a tiny, dirty window at the top of the wall that let in just enough light so you could see the makeshift desk my dad had constructed from lumber scraps.

Newspapers were neatly stacked on top, all pages from the stock market section. My dad's one hobby was day trading. Or fake day trading. He didn't actually have any money to invest, but he pretended by keeping elaborate records of his "trades." My mom liked to joke about the millions he'd made. I'd always thought it was cool that he was that smart and savvy and so clever, and if the world only knew. But today, for the first time, seeing the desk stuffed into a toolshed, mostly in the dark, it struck me as sad.

"Let me show you something." He moved the lone chair aside and lifted a floorboard. Then he stretched out on his belly and reached almost his entire arm beneath. He felt around and then slid out the large rectangular lockbox I'd seen only once before in my life.

"The code is your birthday," he said simply.

He sat back on his heels. I towered above him. "Pops, if something happens, this is here. You can come back for it. There's money if we get separated."

"Separated?"

"If I'm not here and you need money."

"If you're not here? What's happening?" My voice sounded like a six-year-old's.

"Nothing! Nothing new." My dad sighed and ran his hand through his hair. "You know I'm running a lot of errands. It's for a good reason, but risk is higher while I'm doing it." He seemed to be choosing his words carefully.

"Is this about Mom? All of a sudden she's taking these long walks. You didn't even want me going on runs when we first got here." Did he think we were about to get caught?

He paused. "This isn't about her."

"She never left the house before," I said. "She never wanted to."

"We decided it's okay. There's barely anyone out on the streets here."

That explanation seemed too easy. "Well, can I run these errands for you?"

"No. Look, this is only in case of an emergency. Everything is going to work out. I'm confident."

My dad peeled back the metal casing and showed a few neat stacks of cash. He closed the case.

"Is it stolen?" I asked.

"No!" He sounded offended.

On top of the cash, there were separate manila envelopes. One was labeled CA.

"Can I see?" I asked. My dad wavered, then handed me the envelope. I extracted the fake IDs. They looked so authentic, perfect. There was even a driver's license in there for me. I found a Social Security card with my current name—Emily.

"Who does all of this?"

"Someone who charges a lot of money," my dad scoffed. "You don't need to know."

"But what if I do? Someday. For me and Emma?" I hadn't meant to push. It was part of my penance for the DNA test: I'd promised myself I'd be good.

My dad gave me a strange look. Like *Do you really not know?*

"What?" I said.

"You wouldn't need anything except cash. You aren't wanted by the police, honey."

When I stepped out of the shed, I drew up short. My mother was standing by herself in the middle of the backyard, unmoving, waiting on us. Through the windows, I could see Emma playing with dolls on the living room floor.

"What's going on?" she asked my dad.

"I showed Poppy where everything is." My dad's voice was cold. He continued to lock the shed door.

"Why?" My mom's light eyes shone.

I broke away and walked to the house. This was between them.

"In case she needs it," my dad answered with dead calm.

"Why would she need it?"

I muffled their words with the swish of the sliding glass door. Through the last-inch gap, I heard my dad say, "Then get your shit together. Stop leaving the house. You promised you could handle this. That was the reason I said okay, we could come here." I stopped short of closing the door all the way. They rarely fought.

"Dan—"

Handle what?

"Poppy!" my dad called. "Can you close the door, please?"

CHAPTER TWENTY

Summer was in full swing. The roads were clearer, the schools empty. American flags making their appearance for the upcoming holiday. It was almost my birthday.

"Poppy."

I turned toward Harry's voice and raised an eyebrow. My eyelids felt weighted to half-mast.

"You're falling asleep," Harry said.

I smiled tiredly and sat up straighter. "I didn't sleep well last night." I'd been thinking about my parents' fight. What was my mother not handling well?

"You okay?" he asked.

"I'm okay," I said. He seemed serious and studied me for a second before he glanced away. "How are you?" I asked, a beat too late.

"I'm fine." There was something in the way he'd looked at me that was familiar. It seemed heavy. Weary. For a short moment, I thought Harry was going to say more. But he suddenly scrubbed hard at his arms, as if to remind himself where he was, to snap out of it. He redirected his attention from me to Professor Alexiev.

We were down to our last five minutes of class, so I wasn't too worried about drifting. Professor Alexiev was involved in a boisterous conversation with the kids up front.

"What about you two?" she called to us.

Harry was paying better attention than I was. "Brown," he replied.

I was completely confused. "You, Poppy?" the professor asked.

Were we choosing colors? "Excuse me?"

She squinted her eyes at me and folded her arms.

"What colleges are you applying to?" Harry prompted under his breath.

"Oh! I don't know," I said. It came out weak and startled. Professor Alexiev cocked her head like she was confused.

When class ended, I sensed she wanted to press me on my response, so I kept moving. I edged to the side of the building to finish zipping up my backpack.

"Hey, can I give you a ride?" I heard Harry's voice and looked up. He'd seen me go around to the side of the building?

I bit my lip.

"Are you babysitting today?"

"I am."

"Were you going to walk?"

"How'd you know?"

"I always see you walking."

"I like to walk."

"You must, because the club isn't that close. You don't drive?"

"No. Not yet. I haven't gotten around to getting my license here." Lie. I kicked the toe of my too-narrow white tennis shoes on the concrete. They gave me blisters when I walked long distances. I was facing another long walk before they healed. I'd thought about telling my mom, but I hadn't wanted to approach her when she seemed lost in thought, sitting on the patio by herself after one of her walks.

Harry shoved his hands in his pockets. "Well, in that case, it's easy for me to drop you off. I have an hour. My job is at Intel, but I don't have to be there until one."

I stilled. I wasn't supposed to. I wasn't allowed to go to people's homes, so why would I be allowed to ride in their cars?

"No worries," Harry was saying.

I glanced around, as though my dad were going to materialize at any moment. But all I saw was the quintessential California summer day. Plums weighed down the boughs of trees just outside classroom doors. "Okay, sure," I said. "Thank you."

It was a ride. Not a betrayal.

Harry and I crossed to his glossy car. Beads of water from the sprinklers sat on the perfect, mirrorlike surface.

"Hop in," Harry said. I climbed in the passenger's side and was greeted with the smell of boy sweat and leather. But the sweat didn't smell bad. Of course it didn't. There wasn't anything unappealing about Harry, as far as I could tell. The stereo came on with a jolt. The song was like a perfect soundtrack to complement Harry's movie star persona.

Harry lowered the volume. "Do you mind passing me my sunglasses?" he asked. "They're in the glove compartment."

I obediently opened the glove compartment and saw a black box of condoms partially crushed, wedged in next to the tan sunglasses case. I removed the heavy case with Italian scrawled on the top. Our hands brushed when I passed it.

"Sorry about that," he mumbled. I wasn't sure if he was referring to the condoms, the burst of loud music, or our hands touching. I was aware once again of how different our lives were.

"I like this song," I said. I was only used to pop music on the radio. "What's it called?"

"'Kick, Push.'"

I looked over and, in the small space, every detail of him came into focus—his eyelashes, his long fingers wrapped around the steering wheel, the hole in his jeans, the scent of soap when he shifted.

"Are you on Spotify?" Harry asked.

I didn't even know what that was. "No."

"What do you subscribe to?" Harry asked. "Apple Music?"

At that moment, Harry's entire car started ringing. On the dashboard, the words AVIV CELL passed over the screen. Harry jabbed at a red box that said IGNORE.

I hadn't known phones rang in cars, through speakers.

Harry was about to say something when the phone bleated again. This time it was PAUL CELL.

"They're looking for me, I guess." Harry kept his eyes on the road.

The drive was short, and I knew I'd be close to half an hour early. Seeming to echo my thoughts, Harry began to drive more slowly, winding his way through the quiet tree-lined lanes. The houses grew more and more enormous with more space between them. Tudor, modern, French chateau–style—a mash-up that seemed right for California, a place with a history of people starting fresh and trying on something new.

"My dad's house is right there," Harry was saying.

"Where?" I asked, looking from right to left.

"On your side."

"I just see a wall." A tall, white, concrete wall covered with fig ivy bordered the street. And the wall went on and on. And on.

Harry cracked the windows, as if that would help me see better. "Yeah, that's it. Behind the wall. Never mind. You can't see the house from the road."

"Wait, everything behind the wall is his house? We've driven about a block."

"That's an exaggeration." He seemed to be getting a little embarrassed.

"Jesus, Harry."

That made him laugh. Too soon, Harry turned into the country club driveway.

"Thanks for driving me," I said, slowly unbuckling my seat belt. Maybe in the back of my mind I knew Harry had extra minutes to spare also. *What are you doing, Poppy?*

Harry angled his body to face me but was awkwardly stopped by the seat belt.

"Ow!" He unclipped the seat belt. I couldn't help but laugh. "Hey! Don't laugh. I was trying to be smooth about that." Maybe it was my first hint that he was as curious about me as I was about him.

Right then, another call came in from Aviv. He pressed IGNORE.

"Is she your girlfriend?" I asked.

"Who?" Harry asked.

"The person who keeps calling."

Harry took a breath, like he was thinking carefully about what to say. "No. We've known each other forever. She's a family friend."

Maybe she thought they were a couple. They'd looked like a couple.

"So," Harry said.

"So." I smiled. Harry smiled back and laughter bubbled up, making his eyes dance and his face light up. "What?" I asked.

"I don't know! There's something about you that makes me smile. Maybe it's your freckles or something. And how your voice goes up at the end of every sentence—like you're always excited."

I automatically looked out my window and put my hand on the door to open it. Was he making fun of me?

"I'm not making fun of you at all!" he said, like he'd just read my mind.

I gave him a *really?* look.

"Whatever. It's just fun to watch you talk. In math. Now." Harry looked out his window, and I thought I heard him swear under his breath. He tiredly ran a hand through his hair. Was he actually nervous?

"How was Paris?" I asked, wanting out of the awkwardness.

"Oh man. It was great." Harry put his hand on his flat stomach. "Croissants every day. Smoking cigarettes at cafés. Oh, and museums. And biking around Versailles."

I liked picturing that scene. I was sure Harry fit right into Paris. I imagined he was at ease wherever he went, since he'd probably already seen the world. "That sounds amazing. Except for the cigarette part," I said and laughed. I turned my one ring—silver and turquoise, found on the ground at a gas station in New Mexico—around and around on my finger, remembering that I'd never be able to fly.

"Yeah, well, when in France. We always stay at the same hotel. It's our spot. My grandmother even bought a pack of Gauloises and we would sit out on the balcony and look over the Seine." Harry tensed.

"Was it just you? You and your grandma, I mean?"

"And my cousin," Harry mumbled. I wondered why he'd closed off abruptly.

"Do you have any siblings?" I asked.

"No. Only child," he said brusquely. Why was he being cagey? Then I recognized it: he wasn't supposed to talk about his family. He was just worse at hiding it than I was.

Restless, Harry cracked the windows again, and a light breeze entered the car. "What about you? Do you have any siblings?" Classic move. Turning the questions on me.

I wondered if I should lie. "A younger sister."

"How old?" Harry rested his cheek against the leather headrest. He had a small dark mole above his upper lip—a beauty mark. Looking at his lips, I wondered how well he kissed, how practiced he was. Very. All I knew about kissing was from books.

"How old?" Harry asked again, raising his head.

"She's eight."

"So, half sister?"

"No, full."

"Wow. That's young. Are your parents still together?"

"Yeah."

"That's cool." Harry glanced at his watch.

"You must need to get going," I said quickly. I was sad to see the conversation end. I hadn't realized how lonely I was without someone my age to talk to.

"I guess," Harry said, sounding reluctant, which made me feel great. He was about to say more, but something caught his eye outside my window. Then he slid a few inches lower in his seat.

I turned to see where he was looking. It was some of the girls who were fixtures at the pool, the ones who knew Harry. I realized he didn't want to be seen. He didn't want to be seen with *me*.

Harry didn't even look at me, and there was the vibe that he'd moved on or I was suddenly boring him. I'd seen it at the pool that day. He could flip a switch.

"Thanks for the ride," I said. Harry only nodded. Then he started the car. I was being dismissed. I attempted to gracefully exit the low-slung car while holding my skirt in place with one fist.

It's his problem; it's not you. I knew that, but still. The whole experience had been a painful reminder of how useless it was to want something new.

CHAPTER TWENTY-ONE

Thankfully, there was no need for Harry and me to speak during class the next morning. We didn't have any partner work. We'd gotten off track so much that now Professor Alexiev was trying to cover ground quickly for our upcoming assessment. Usually everything else in my life melted away during the three hours, but today class fell flat.

In the last ten minutes, a light patter of rain began. Worried, I kept one eye on the windows. Rebecca had given me her home address in case we were rained out of the pool. Now I had to walk all the way to her house. I didn't even own an umbrella. I thought about canceling, but I didn't want to inconvenience Rebecca.

Steller's jays squawked, swooped down, and fought over the plums, bringing me back to the room. It was a relief that class had just ended.

"Did you get all that?" Harry addressed me, as he slowly stood from his desk. There was a tentativeness to his hovering above me. During the break, I'd walked quickly to the bath-room to avoid him.

"I think so." I began to pack away my notes.

"You babysitting today?" Harry asked. I nodded.

"Do you need a ride?"

"Oh no. That's okay," I said.

"But it's raining."

"No, it's fine."

"Poppy!" Harry's voice was frustrated. Heads turned our way. "Let me drive you."

I stared out the window. I didn't know what to do. It was raining steadily now. I could say that my dad was driving me. But he wasn't.

"I'm not going to your club. I'm going to their house, so don't worry about it," I said.

"I can drive you. That's fine!"

"Okay!" I matched his tone.

"Here, let me get that." When we got to the car, Harry chival-rously opened my door for me.

"Thanks."

"Oh, shit. Here, let me move this stuff." Harry threw a stiff indigo jean jacket and a pair of running shoes into the empty leather back seat.

Harry gently closed my door. At least the ride would be short.

"Rebecca, who I babysit for, lives right near the country club."

Thankfully, loud music spared us from having to make conversation.

I stared at the familiar sites that marked the trip I usually took on foot—the huge palm on the corner, the Tudor mansion with stained-glass windows and wrought iron fence with decorative axes spiking up at the corners, and the long, shaded avenue where the same cop car always waited in the bushes.

I prayed we'd get the green light. If Harry sailed through, he'd shave a few minutes off the drive.

We didn't make the light. I stared at the real estate company on the corner, trying to make out the listings posted in the windows. There were multimillion-dollar properties on the Peninsula, and beach houses in Santa Cruz.

"Where is this place?" Harry asked.

For safekeeping, I'd entered the address on my flip phone. I had no choice but to bring it out. I slowly unzipped my backpack.

Harry burst out with a big laugh when he saw it. "What is *that*?"

"It's my phone," I said. Too quietly. I'd meant to sound matter-of-fact and cool, but it came off as small.

Harry squinted. He braked at another red light. Then he looked at my lap as I scrolled through to find the number.

"Two fifty-one Deerfoot," I said. I pretended there was something fascinating on my screen so I didn't have to look at him. I was so out of my element. It took under two minutes to relearn that, increasingly, every passing year—no, *month*—I lived on a different planet. I was out of step with the rest of the world, in my little pod of four.

Harry was staring at my bright-red profile.

I'd hated his surprised, mocking laugh. I waited for more questions. But none came.

"Hey," he said softly.

"Yes?"

"I think it's cool you don't have a phone. I mean, you have a phone, but you know what I mean."

"Yeah, but it makes a lot of things more difficult. Actually, everything more difficult."

"Hey," he said again. "Look at me."

"Yes?"

"I'm not making fun of you." His hazel eyes penetrated mine, like he wanted me to know he meant it.

"Thanks." I looked out the window to distract myself from the painful silence.

Harry took a few more turns, then slowed his car in front of a white, modern farmhouse-style home. "It's this one," he said.

I planned to quickly thank him and jump out of the car, but Harry crept forward until he stopped next to a tall hedge between Rebecca's and the neighbors. He turned off the ignition.

"Thanks for the ride," I said.

"Can you hold up a sec?"

"Sure." *What did he want?* I reluctantly closed the door again against the rain. We sat in the quiet car. Gentle drops pattered the windshield.

"I'm not a douchebag."

I gave a startled laugh. "What?"

"I know I acted like a total asshole yesterday when I dropped you off at the club."

I didn't argue with that.

"I didn't want anyone to see us together."

"That was pretty clear," I said. I wanted to automatically say *Don't worry about it,* but this time I couldn't let myself.

Harry played with the string from his black hoodie, pulling it long on one side. "I lived here before my parents divorced, so I grew up with a lot of those people. Our families go way back. Our social circles are intertwined. Down here, up in San Francisco. So after what happened, I don't want them gossiping. Word will get back to my parents."

"After *what* happened? I don't know what you mean."

Harry looked at me askance. Then: "You really don't know?"

"No! Why would I know anything?"

"It's all people know about me. It's on, like, page one if you google my name, even though my dad did everything to have it scrubbed."

"Well, I didn't get that far when I searched you."

Harry's face relaxed. "Oh."

"So, what are you talking about?"

Harry smiled, but it didn't meet his eyes. "Hold on, let me just enjoy this one second before you know."

I rolled my eyes, pretend-exasperated, but I was steeling myself for Harry's admission. I was guessing rehab or a drunk-driving accident or maybe something so bad I couldn't even imagine.

Harry spoke woodenly, like he was recounting old news. "I had a serious girlfriend. Well, I thought it was serious." He shrugged.

I leaned forward so I wouldn't miss a word.

"She sold nude photographs of us."

"You mean, pornography?" My eyebrows shot up.

"No, no." Harry held up a hand. "We were sunbathing on the beach. But then, on top of that, she sued my family."

"For what?"

"Actually, she sued my dad specifically. For mental damages after he screamed at her."

"Did she win?"

"He settled."

Harry seemed years older than me suddenly. "When was this?" I asked.

"This past winter. Also, she's older than me. Twenty-one. So that added to the mess."

"Twenty-one?" I tried to keep my voice even.

"Twenty-one."

"How old are you?"

"Eighteen," Harry said.

"How did you even meet her?"

"In Saint Barts, where I go on vacation with my dad. She was a little famous at the time. Now she's a lot more famous." Harry scoffed. "Anyway, I almost derailed my mom's career. WILD ONE-PERCENTER SON. She tries to be the everywoman. She doesn't want to remind voters that she was married to my dad." Harry said the last sentence lightly, but it was clear: the effect on his mother had been the worst part of what went down.

"Wow. What is she famous for? Your ex-girlfriend." I just kept thinking to myself, *twenty-one.* I waited to feel different about Harry—turned off, overwhelmed, judgmental—but I found I didn't. Maybe because he seemed so deeply upset, even though he did his best to hide it, especially when he'd mentioned his mom.

I heard him mumble, "Model." Harry cleared his throat. "Yeah. I was an idiot. So now I'm down here at my dad's, far away from my mother's campaign. She asked me to stay off the radar, to not date anyone. Anyway, that's why I was weird. I have to be careful about what gets out. I just have to be careful in general." Harry paused. "So now tell me about you."

"What?" It was a whiplash change of subject.

"Who are you?"

"What do you mean?"

"I mean, I've looked into you, too. Emily Morgan doesn't exist."

I stilled.

"You're nowhere on social media. Nowhere on the internet. That's almost impossible."

I moved my hand to the door. "It's my parents. They're really private people."

"Sounds familiar," Harry said.

"Yeah. They're super strict. They hate technology." I opened the door to get out.

"Wait! So you don't post anything? Or look at other people's posts?"

I shook my head. "Nothing. I don't even have access to a computer except when I go to the library."

"That's kind of cool." Harry smiled.

I shrugged and relaxed slightly. "Yes and no. It's really isolating."

"Yeah," Harry said, agreeing, even though he had no idea.

I reached for my things at my feet, ready to go.

"Can you hold on one more sec?" Harry asked.

I nodded and slowly released the strap of my backpack.

"Look, I like hanging out with you," Harry said, sounding almost defensive.

"Oh."

Harry seemed to wait for me to say more. When I didn't,

he looked away and said in a rush, "I don't know if you want to hang out with me, but in my case, I'd like to do it more." He drew a long breath. Then his eyes came to rest on mine.

"I like talking to you, too." Saying it was surprisingly easy.

Harry continued to hold eye contact, as if he wanted to emphasize what he said next. "The thing is, it's probably better if we kept it—our friendship, hanging out, whatever it is—low-key. I just want to be honest. I can't get close to someone right now. And I know I'm guarded about all kinds of subjects, which is a pain. So"—Harry was rambling now—"I don't know if you have any interest in spending time together when there are all these weird parameters . . ."

I'd read him wrong. Which was strange, because reading people was what I did. He kept surprising me.

Maybe Harry wasn't ashamed to be seen with me, like I'd thought. I believed him. It stung when he told me it could never lead to anything, but this was wild. I'd found the one person who didn't want me asking questions and wanted to keep our friendship under wraps. It was incredibly convenient.

"That sounds perfect," I said.

"Really?" Harry asked, like he didn't trust me.

"Yeah. Sure."

I got that smile. Harry's entire body relaxed.

In response, mine felt like it was going to float with joy above these unspeakably beautiful streets where I didn't belong.

CHAPTER TWENTY-TWO

When I got home, my dad seemed to be waiting for me, stationed near the back door. "How was your day?" he asked.

"Good."

My dad didn't even know about the change of venue for babysitting to Rebecca's house. It occurred to me that, for the first time in my life, he didn't know exactly where I'd been.

He waited for me to say more. I was going to. But then I didn't.

My dad was watching me. I expected him to press, but after a moment he asked, "Poker after dinner?"

"Sure." I nodded quickly.

Did he know something was different about me? Did he want to play so he could observe me? I set my stuff down on a kitchen chair and watched his broad back as he left the room.

I made my way down the bedroom hallway, passing Emma's

room. The door was closed and she was singing to herself, just like she had been when I left for class in the morning.

Was it really possible? I could leave the house and have an experience my family knew nothing about?

At dinner, Emma showed off some dance moves she'd been practicing in her room, and my dad indulged her, allowing her to leave the table several times.

"When's Mom getting back?" Emma asked as she settled into her chair. "She said she'd be here for dinner."

When Emma asked my mom about her long walks, I overheard my mom tell her that the neighborhood was so different from where we'd lived before that she loved to explore it. When Emma asked if she could join, the answer was a roundabout no.

"Soon. It must be a long one. It's such a pretty night." My dad checked his watch. Then he saw me watching him. "It's fine," he said.

"I know." I didn't know, but, if anything, he seemed annoyed my mom still wasn't listening to him, not afraid. Although, it wasn't often I could tell what he was feeling.

With his mind on my mother, I thought he'd forgotten about poker, but after dinner, my dad herded me and Emma into the den.

We started the game, and after about a half hour of back-and-forth, I finally had a good hand. I raised conservatively but consistently, and my dad stayed in.

And then I got a full house on the river. I steeled myself, neutralizing my body language, feeling my dad's eyes on me even when he wasn't looking at me directly.

My sister knocked most of her chips on the floor, so that created a diversion. I thought I was showing nothing, tricking him, hiding any tells.

I made a small, weak bet. I was sure he would raise me, then I would surprise him and go all in.

I waited for him to bet, but he was still helping Emma collect her chips.

Then he turned back to me, his brown eyes direct, seeing through me. "You're trying to trap me. You got the nuts, don't you? I fold," he said. He flipped over a flush.

I raked in my chips and racked my brain, wondering how he knew I had that full house.

My dad could always read me. Tonight, it annoyed the hell out of me.

"Want a ride?" Harry brushed his shoulder up against mine as we walked out together after class.

Behind me, I heard someone clear her throat. It was Professor Alexiev. She gave me a small, approving smile. For some reason, it meant something that she was fond of "Mr. Addison." And she was. She seemed to have his back, as if she understood something about him I didn't know. Sometimes I'd see them conferencing at the side of the classroom.

But there was a world of that in this classroom—Professor Alexiev conferencing with people and I couldn't guess at what they were discussing. Grants? Scholarships? Internships? College math departments? Sometimes it seemed like there was an unspoken language and culture—an entire fabric—in the classroom that I could feel but I wasn't a part of. And if I wasn't too shy to ask, I didn't even know what my questions would be. It was the definition of being an outsider. But this time I really wanted to belong.

Even this—having a new friend like Harry—I didn't quite understand. He opened the passenger door for me, and I gave him a smile in thanks. He gently closed my door for me.

"Country club?" Harry asked, starting the car. It had sprinkled earlier, so I checked my small phone to see if Rebecca planned on swimming. Just like Harry, she'd asked for my phone number and I hadn't said no.

"Wait. Oh no. Babysitting is canceled," I said, disappointed. I couldn't accept a ride from Harry anywhere near my house. And I didn't want to go home yet. At home, there was only worry about my mom, who was acting like a different person.

Harry gave me a slow, lazy smile. "How long are you free?"

Understanding dawned.

"Three hours."

CHAPTER TWENTY-THREE

M y house?" Harry proposed.

I hesitated.

"We won't be alone. There are about a million people there at all times," Harry said quickly.

"Like who?"

"Staff. And you have a bathing suit, right? There's a pool at my dad's. I can drive you home later."

"I'll need to walk home. I told you how strict my parents are. I'm going to have to look like I walked home from babysitting." I was really going to do this.

"Can I drop you off at the school?" Harry negotiated.

"Maybe."

When Harry swung into his driveway, curiosity overtook my nerves. A section of unmarked wall slowly peeled back. To say that I entered a different world would be an understatement.

Set deep on the property was a white, Spanish-style mansion

with a red tile roof. Plumes of bougainvillea draped the length of a second-story balcony. An expanse of emerald-green lawn carpeted the front yard. The only interruption was a spectacular water feature set in front of the horseshoe driveway.

"It's incredible."

"My mom calls it the Four Seasons. Not her style. It's too big."

Harry pulled into a large building that turned out to be the garage. The floor was so clean and shiny it squeaked when Harry walked over it in his flip-flops. The space age–looking sports cars on either side of Harry's car made his Porsche look modest.

Harry led us through a back door into a foyer. He stashed his flip-flops, so I did the same. Each wooden cubby had an electrical outlet and what looked like various chargers. Harry jogged up some stairs, and then we passed through a small living room. Oddly, I noticed a silver-and-yellow can of Lysol on a shelf positioned next to every doorway, sticking out like sore thumbs.

The exterior of the house was traditional, but the inside was modern. The floor was covered in Moroccan tile in white, gray, and black. I noticed the entire house was white, gray, and black. We entered the largest, most sleek-looking kitchen I'd ever seen.

"Hi, Kat," Harry said to a woman with her head in the refrigerator.

"Harry!" Kat was maybe in her thirties and wore a chef's coat. Staff.

"This is Poppy."

"It's nice to meet you." Kat seemed very surprised to see me.

Just then, another woman, also wearing a chef's coat,

entered. She carried a stack of plastic quart containers. She stopped short when she saw me, like she was also surprised. "Debra, this is Harry's friend Poppy," Kat quickly supplied.

"Hi. Nice to meet you," I said. "Sorry to interrupt."

Debra said, "No, no, you're not interrupting. Kat and I are just getting lunch together. But let us make you something!"

"Oh no. That's okay," Harry said quickly.

"We would love to! You never bring friends to the house," Kat said. I could feel Harry stiffen in embarrassment.

"What can we get you?" Debra asked.

Harry turned to me. "What can we get you? You know what? I can get it. We have . . . I'm sure we have a lot," he said, sounding flustered. "Maybe we'll look in the pantry. It's over there?"

"Harry, I love you, but let me look in the pantry," Kat said. "Where are you headed? We'll bring you something."

"My room."

His room? I was getting in over my head.

"Don't you want to swim?" I asked lamely.

Harry instantly realized why I was hesitating. "We can swim. I just want to set my stuff down."

I suddenly felt so presumptuous. I didn't even know if he saw me in the same light as someone like an Aviv. And I'd temporarily forgotten about the model. Harry was so guarded—we were both so guarded—it was a miracle we were even hanging out as friends.

"It's this way," Harry said. He surprised me when he gently laid his hand on the small of my back.

His hand fell away as soon as I began to follow. I missed everything we passed, stuck on the feel of his hand on my back.

I had a vague awareness of expansive rooms with orchids and tile, artwork packed into every available space. I had a glimpse of a museum-like room with a display of ancient-looking computers.

Harry led me up a back staircase, his hand grazing the handrail.

"This is my room." Harry opened the door into a den with a small buttery leather sofa, two armchairs and a gigantic TV on one wall. He kept walking, going down a small hallway. I saw a large bathroom to my left with more Moroccan tile in royal blue and white. The hallway opened up to a generous bedroom.

The room was extremely dark except for a slim seam of sunlight beaming between the curtains. Harry waved at a panel and the curtains parted, revealing a balcony with a fireplace. Wicker chairs hung from the ceiling and looked like cocoons, begging you to sit and take in the stunning view of the Santa Cruz Mountains.

Harry opened the balcony doors, and I joined him at the railing. We looked out over acres.

"What are those?" I asked. In the distance, among olive and citrus trees, were three smaller houses and a massive black-bottom pool. A lone figure skimmed the surface with a net.

"Guest casitas."

I laughed in sheer amazement.

"It's not mine," Harry said quickly, a little defensively. "It's my dad's. I'm just here for the summer."

I had to let him know I wasn't scoffing at him. I slid my hand close to his. I saw our hands together on the railing, my pale freckled one next to his long tan fingers wrapped around the black metal.

Harry moved his hand and it touched mine. We didn't look at each other. We just stood side by side, watching over the sprawling backyard. I tried to breathe, so focused on our point of contact.

After a moment, Harry pushed off from the railing and we drifted back inside. The bedroom even smelled wonderful: clean and citrusy.

Still so overly aware of him in the room with me, I began examining the only area that held Harry's personal items. In an office nook with bookshelves and a built-in desk that held a laptop and printer, Harry had taped up photos ripped from a skateboarding magazine and some sketches he'd done, also of skateboarding. There was a newspaper clipping from *The New York Times* of his dad as a young man posing with another man in front of an office park.

There was only one framed photo. It was of Harry and his mom. In the picture, Harry had a cigarette dangling from his lips. My uneasiness crept in again. Harry's life seemed so adult.

Harry came up behind me. His arm brushed my shoulder when he reached past me to adjust the frame. He didn't move away after he'd shifted it. We stayed like that, pretending to look at the photo. I could hear the rise and fall of his breath.

"Your mom's impressive," I finally said. I tried not to feel disappointed when Harry stepped away. It seemed like he was consciously finding ways to touch me, but maybe I was imagining it.

"I'm proud of her," Harry said. "My dad said he'd divorce her if she ran for office. So she chose running for office. She works really hard."

I loved how sweet and supportive he was of his mom.

"Ready to swim?" Harry backed up to the middle of the room, like he wanted to lead me away from his personal life.

"Can I try your chair first?" I grinned. It was the coolest-looking desk chair—a white ergonomic masterpiece.

"Absolutely. Take a seat."

I sank into the springy mesh and rested my head. "Ahh."

Harry collapsed into a soft armchair and put his feet up on the ottoman. He'd left the door to his room open, and Debra suddenly appeared with a large tray. On it were ten small square dishes filled with olives, fruit, cheese, nuts, salami.

"Thank you!" I said to Debra. When she left, neither Harry nor I touched the tray, even though I was starving. It was about the time I usually had my enormous BLT at the country club. I was getting nervous, wondering what we were going to talk about. Looming behind him was his giant king-size bed, which had a tall, ornately carved wooden headboard and was blanketed in a pure white comforter. It looked very sophisticated for a teenage boy.

"You said you're eighteen—when was your birthday?" I asked.

"December twenty-sixth. I'm old for my grade. You?"

"July fourth."

"You're a Fourth of July baby?"

"I am."

"You'll be eighteen?" Harry asked.

"Yep."

"A younger woman."

"Not as old as your usual," I joked.

"Yeah, well." Harry glanced at the tray of food for a second, as if he were about to pick at it, but then changed his mind.

"How much trouble would you be in if your parents knew you were here?" He reached forward, pretending to brush something off his ankle.

"A lot." It was less about me getting in trouble than the potential for me to get everyone in trouble. I was letting in too many variables, as my dad would say. I wouldn't be able to manage them. For a moment, I felt both guilty and sad that my extremely intelligent father believed babysitting was an airtight plan. I wasn't used to feeling sorry for him.

"They're just strict because they're protective? Religious?" Harry asked. He placed one foot over his opposite knee.

"Protective."

"So you've never dated anyone?" Harry picked up a mini basketball off the floor and squeezed it with both hands, acting nonchalant.

I thought about lying—telling him I'd managed to sneak behind my parents' backs. I suddenly felt the weight of all the lies I had told, and there was no reason to tell this one.

"No."

Harry raised his eyebrows. "Never?"

"Nope."

"Did you ever come close, at least?" he asked.

I shrugged. I thought about the few times I'd had crushes. After the scare in Des Moines, I'd punished myself by staying on the outskirts of any boy-girl groups. There had been some boys who'd noticed me—making up excuses to sit near me or talk to me. But I knew I'd be leaving soon, so what was the point? I also knew my parents wouldn't like it.

I wasn't sure why I was behaving differently with Harry. Maybe because I could tell Harry tried to disappear like me. But for him, it was harder.

"What's your type?" Harry asked.

I shrugged a shoulder and played with the strap of my tank top. I couldn't tell if he was flirting. "Actually, I don't know. Definitely smart. What about you?" I steeled myself for criteria he was about to list that I wouldn't like.

"I would have said extroverted and someone who's known me for a long time, but maybe quiet and someone who doesn't know my family. And smart. Definitely smart."

I could almost physically see Harry calculating in his head whether he wanted to open himself up to this—whatever this was. Friendship? More? We were dancing around it. It reminded me of the romance novels I'd read, when the profligate hero didn't know if he was a good enough man to take on the responsibility of loving someone. *That's right, Harry,* I thought. *While you were having your sex weekend on a private island, I was playing Yahtzee with my family.*

I turned away from Harry and toyed with the computer mouse.

"You registered your DNA test?" Harry asked.

"No." I shook my head. "I didn't end up doing it."

"Why? We were partners in crime. You have to."

"I haven't had the time."

"Oh, that's bullshit."

"The library is the only place I can sneak onto a computer, but I've been busy babysitting Frank."

"Is the library where you googled me?" Harry asked, teasing.

"Shut up." I smiled. Why was it easy for me to flirt with him?

"I googled you at the skate park," Harry said, his eyes dancing.

Harry stood and brushed off his shorts. "Here. It's easy." He picked up the ottoman as if it were light as a feather and set it down next to me. He put an elbow on the armrest of my chair. I tilted slightly closer to him. He did the same, and suddenly our shoulders were touching.

"Okay, what email did you use?"

"Don't worry about this. I wasn't serious about it. I wrote down an email address I don't even have." I tried to sound casual and waved it away.

"But what if that email isn't available?"

I shrugged one shoulder.

Harry just looked at me. "You wanted to take that test."

For some reason, I didn't say anything.

"What email did you give?" Harry's hands hovered over the keyboard.

The email address would be taken, and that would put an end to this. "Annakarenina0704@gmail.com."

Harry typed for a bit, spelling it correctly the first time. Then, "It's yours." He sat back and grinned.

Oh, shit.

Harry asked for my kit number. "You still have it, right? You need to register it on the testing website."

I dug the number out of my backpack. It was written on the back of the yellow piece of paper where my dad had scribbled my summer school directions. I'd made sure to toss all other evidence of the kit.

Harry went to the DNA testing site and clicked REGISTER KIT. "I'm going to lie about your date of birth. Backdate it a few months. You need to be over eighteen. See? It's almost done. Do you want to click through the agreement?" When he asked the question, he casually picked up the end of my braid. He smoothed it through two fingers.

"Sure," I said. It came out a little husky.

With Harry right at my elbow, touching my hair, I scrolled through a long, brain-numbing page of legalese and series of boxes that were already checked. I began to sense his impatience. He moved away and reached up to a shelf, taking down a piece of pottery, then inspecting it. I saw the initials HE scratched in the bottom.

Harry looked back at the screen. "Okay, now put in a password."

At every step, I'd planned to sabotage this process. But then I hadn't. This was my last chance. I stared at the password and was about to pick autofill—a jumble of numbers and letters I'd never remember. *Just because I complete this doesn't mean I ever log on again.*

I typed in a simple password: "Emma" and her date of birth. I hit REGISTER.

The status of my kit immediately popped up on the screen. A line graph showed my sample had made it to the CLIA-certified lab.

"Three to five weeks from the time it's mailed, so we should hear soon," Harry said.

I wanted to shake off my uneasiness. I felt like I needed to go somewhere to think.

"I love sticking it to my dad," Harry was saying. "Sharing

my DNA like that. The guy doesn't even want me on Insta-gram or any social media, even though he's on some of their boards."

"Wait, what?" I asked.

"I sound like a jerk," Harry said. "Never mind. It's nothing."

I didn't quite understand what he'd meant, but I didn't want to sound totally naive. "Did you make that?" I changed the subject, pointing to the pottery in his hands.

"This? Yeah. My mom and I took a pottery class together."

I looked at the coding book on the desk, open to a page of complicated instructions. "Are you learning coding?"

Harry coughed. "My dad has made me learn it since before I could talk. I've had a tutor forever. Instead of religion on Sundays, in this family, it's coding."

I swiveled in the chair and saw the guitar in the corner. And the basketball. Pottery, guitar, coding. I thought of how bored I was, how Emma and I had been known to fight over a free catalog because it was something to look at. I would have loved to do all these cool activities. I liked to read and go on long runs, but that was all I had.

"What about skateboarding?" I said, thinking of the photos and drawings.

"Oh. Yeah, it's something I like to do."

The way Harry grew embarrassed—and also like he was proud—made me instantly more interested.

"Are you really good?" I asked.

"I don't know. Not like other people."

"Wait, you're good, aren't you?" I broke into a smile.

"I don't get out often enough with all of this college-prep bullshit and classes and the summer internship. Then in the fall, sports start again." Harry looked at his watch. "Hey, I'll go change. And then you can change? And then we swim?"

A voice suddenly came through a small speaker. "Harry? Your dad is on his way home. He called just now about dinner." I couldn't tell if it was Kat or Debra, but the tone was a little urgent, like they wanted to forewarn him.

Harry's eyes instantly looked stressed. "Got it," Harry told the speaker.

"Are you getting the heads-up because you're not allowed to have . . . a friend . . . up here?"

"Yes, I'm allowed to have a *friend* up here," Harry teased. Then his smile dropped. "My dad's moody, is all. Actually, let's go somewhere else if you don't mind. Get out of here."

So everyone in the house gave each other advance warning before Harry's dad arrived?

"Okay." My eyes landed on his collage of skateboarding photos. "What about taking me to the skate park? The place where you googled me."

"Oh my god, no."

"Why?" I asked, intrigued by his knee-jerk response.

"I don't know. It's a world away from all this." Harry looked around the room. "I go to the skate park and it's my escape. No one I know goes with me. It's so different from here."

"I'm so different from here."

CHAPTER TWENTY-FOUR

The air was light and bright, and it was still early, and my mind was on Harry's arm resting an inch from mine on the car console.

I was relieved to leave Harry's bedroom. Being there was like being suspended on a cloud; you could forget about the earth below and get lost. That was how it felt when I saw the 7-Eleven on the corner—a reminder that I was still tethered to the ground. When we passed a Starbucks, I was less grateful, not wanting to think about the family's latest designated meeting spot—the Starbucks that was located closest to the house. In fact, any thought of my family made me angry, like it was intruding on my dreamlike, fantasy day. What I was doing this afternoon didn't exist in the same world where I lived, and I didn't want a reminder that would burst the bubble.

Harry wound through the congestion of Palo Alto. I noticed the luxury cars were far fewer the moment we crossed the freeway.

We were getting too far from home. Before I spoke up, Harry pulled into a shady, half-filled parking lot.

"I found this park not too long ago," Harry said. "I go to this other spot in San Francisco, but this place is great. Everyone is friendly and welcoming to strangers. And it's in perfect shape." Harry suddenly seemed self-conscious. "We don't have to stay. Sorry, I should have had a better plan for the day."

The park was all concrete. At the edges was some patchy grass littered with trash. My eyes were glued to the vast concrete bowls and swirls of skateboarders. "No, I'd love to see this place."

Harry grabbed his skateboard from the back seat. He had parked in a distant spot, possibly so no one could see what he drove.

"I feel weird that I brought a girl to watch me," Harry said. "Like I want applause." Harry was reticent, but he also seemed lighter and different. Happy to be here. Excited.

"I just thought it would be cool. I'm curious."

"Fine. Okay. But I get to do your thing next time. What do you like to do? Beside math, that is."

"I love to run. Sometimes my dad goes with me, but I like taking long runs by myself."

"Cool. Maybe you'll let me go with you sometime?"

"Maybe." I imagined him trying to keep up, and smiled.

"Alright. Now I'm kind of embarrassed, but okay. It will be quick."

I took a seat on a metal bench while Harry strolled over to the center of the action. Looking around, I saw little kids, middle-aged men, and a handful of people, mostly male, in their late teens or early twenties. They were the ones not wearing any protective gear. Like Harry.

Harry went right up to the professional-looking group, and they greeted him. With his scuffed skateboard and faded band T-shirt, Harry didn't stand out as a rich kid here. Or as anyone special. His body language was different. He usually kept his gaze downcast when he walked, but here, his head was high and he stood up straight. He seemed open instead of wanting everyone's eyes to bounce off him.

I pulled a knee to my chest. Harry was laughing with the small group that was now smoking a joint. When they passed it to Harry, he shook his head and glanced over at me. I quickly looked away, but there wasn't much else to look at except skaters who hovered at the fringes and on the coping of the giant, interconnecting cement bowls.

Harry suddenly broke away from the group and smacked his skateboard down at the lip of the bowl. His back was square to me. Then he disappeared over the edge.

I could never—it was too scary. I tried not to tense up as I watched Harry appear and disappear, rise and fall up the walls of the steep concrete. Right when I finally relaxed, mesmerized by the up-and-down, Harry became more aggressive, his skateboard spitting out from under him. He landed hard. God—so that was why he had so many cuts and scrapes. He popped right back up like it was nothing.

When Harry's friends started skating, it was clear he was on their level, following them as they made crazy transitions to the other connected bowls. The little kids stopped to watch them. At one point, Harry turned to face me and smiled, hand on a hip, as in *How do you like me now?* I couldn't help returning his huge, joyful, and definitely cocky smile.

This was the Harry from the photo I'd seen in the

newspaper—the one that captured his joy. He was entirely happy.

Once I'd watched my dad put a one-year-old Emma in a swing for the first time, and the smile that broke across her face was different from all the smiles before. Her surprise and delight was the purest thing I'd ever seen.

I couldn't blame myself. Watching Harry, it would have been hard for anyone not to fall for him right then. Without knowing much about him, I knew this was who he really was. Beneath the layers, beneath the trappings. Most of the time, like in all of us, this pure part of him would stay buried. But I wanted to know this person I was seeing.

Eventually, Harry drifted away from his friends. In one upward motion, he came up and over the side and caught his skateboard with one hand. He walked slowly over and sat down next to me without a word. I smiled and bumped his shoulder with mine.

In relaxed silence, we watched the small groups of people, the dads and kids, some girls but mostly boys, younger ones watching the oldest. Our hands came to touch between us on the bench.

Finally, Harry took my hand, flexing, then intertwining his fingers with mine.

"Well?" Harry asked lightly, joking.

I turned to face him, and he was looking at me, expectant. I leaned forward. Harry quickly met me halfway.

The sound of sprinklers, the roll of wheels on pavement and pops of happy laughter—everything contracted into that one moment when Harry's lips touched mine.

CHAPTER TWENTY-FIVE

My arms were intertwined behind his neck. Every time I was about to get out of the car, we came back together and kissed again, unable to stop.

"Okay, I have to go," I said. Harry kissed his way down my neck. "What are we doing?" I laughed. It was 4:52 P.M. and Harry had parked under the shade of some elm trees on a side street by the high school.

Harry pulled back. "I don't know. What are we doing?" he asked. "I'm only down here for the summer."

Maybe he wanted assurances that this was nothing. I wanted assurance this would last that long.

"You're so . . . I don't know. Sweet," he said.

"You don't know me, Harry." It came out like a warning.

"That sounds ominous and mysterious."

"You know what I mean. No one is what they seem on the outside."

Harry seemed to relax. He tucked a strand of hair behind my ear.

"What?" I asked.

"I don't know. You cut through so much bullshit. You've been raised right, I can tell."

I wanted to laugh at that. At the reminder of my parents, I grabbed my stuff, knowing I was about to be late, making my dad worry, which was something I couldn't let myself do. He was worried enough about my mom, who refused to stay on the property. I could tell they were in a standoff. My mom didn't seem exhausted anymore. If anything, she seemed agitated, sometimes pacing like she felt caged in.

"I need to go," I said to Harry.

Harry leaned in to drop a last kiss on my lips. I almost reached for him again. I'd never had the feeling of wanting to be near someone, wanting to touch them constantly. Harry seemed to be the same way—never taking a hand away from me after our first kiss. On the drive to the high school, he'd held my hand, run his hand over the back of my hair, leaned over to kiss me at stoplights.

"Okay. Now. I've got to stop."

"Okay." Harry put up his hands and gave me a crooked smile.

"Bye. Thanks for today."

"You too."

I closed the door behind me, not looking back.

I walked fifty feet, smiling at the ground, wondering where to even start remembering the afternoon on my short walk to the house, my bridge from my pretend life to my real one.

"Pops!"

My dad was on an old brown bicycle with my sister scrunched into a cracked leather child's seat on the back.

My breath caught in my chest.

"Sorry, honey, I didn't mean to scare you. We needed an outing, so Em and I here decided to try out this bicycle and meet you."

Was he checking on me?

My dad got off the bike and began to walk next to me on the trail home. Emma remained on the bike, now looking over her shoulder intently.

They had come within thirty seconds of seeing me get out of Harry's car.

It took everything I had to resist looking over my shoulder to confirm what I already knew. Harry was still parked, watching my family.

Later that night, the four of us were summoned to the living room by Emma. All I wanted after dinner was to escape to my room, to slip under the crisp blue duvet and hit replay on the memory of me and Harry.

But I caught what happened only because of Emma's demands.

In the living room, she'd found the record player, CD player, and cassette deck in a large cabinet. Each component was a different age but had been lovingly added. I'd seen it during my first days in the house, when I'd snooped in every crack and crevice. But Emma's excited find today was the bench below the bay window, which doubled as a storage space stuffed with records, cassette tapes, and many fewer CDs.

The records were mostly musicals and classical composers.

The CDs were pop music from the nineties, as if a young person had lived here but grown up and left the house at that point in time.

I had to admit it was cool. Once there'd been a guitar in a house somewhere in Minnesota, and my dad had taught me some chords. Once there was a clock radio. But mostly, we listened to music in cars. We didn't do small things like that—buying music to help make a home wherever we went, putting our stamp on our surroundings. It was like we were always too scared to relax and enjoy music.

"Let me do it! Let me show Poppy!" Emma slipped under my dad's arm and began pushing buttons. Speakers came alive with a hum. "I want that one. *My Fair Lady*!" Immediately, a crisp scratch came through the speakers.

"Careful," my dad cautioned gently.

A massive orchestra belted a rousing introduction, and Emma began dancing and prancing around the room. My dad and I looked at each other and laughed. Emma was just so Emma. She twirled and curtsied and skipped.

But then I began to see a pattern in her dance. It wasn't just freestyle dancing. She'd actually choreographed what she was doing, and it was long and complicated. And kind of sophisticated. She was only eight. My smile faltered.

What a waste was my automatic thought. It would have been easier for Emma if she didn't have any natural talents. And I suddenly knew that it was going to be harder to witness Emma waste her talents than it was to waste my own. Right when she'd begin to fly, the three of us would pull her back down from the sky.

"What's going on?" My mom sauntered in. She wore a

cross-body purse, presumably about to head out for her evening walk. My dad stared at her for a beat and then gave his
attention to the stereo, not answering her question. I was mad
at my mom for slowly making my dad crazy with her insis-
tence on leaving the house.

"What are you guys doing?" my mom asked. All three of
us ignored her. "Hey, kiddo," she said to Emma. My mom
crouched next to Emma, who had stopped dancing, like she
didn't want to give my mom the privilege of seeing her show.
"Em, what are you listening to?"

Emma still didn't answer her. I knew she was mad that my
mom had been so absent lately. Uncharacteristically, my dad
and I did nothing.

"Em, come on. Why aren't you talking to me?" My mom
kissed the top of Emma's head. Emma jerked away. My mom
stared after her. Usually, she was Emma's light.

"It's music," Emma muttered.

"Oh my god!" my mom said in delight. "No way."

My annoyance with my mom morphed into utter fascina-
tion as she walked to the bench, opened it, rifled through the
stack of cassettes and, after a mere moment, seemed to find
what she was looking for.

Very carefully, I looked out of the corner of my eye to my
dad, to see if he'd picked up that my mother had just messed up
for the first time ever and dropped a potential clue. I'd guessed
she was from California. But she had just inadvertently shown
that she'd been here, in this house, before.

I could feel my dad watching me. It suddenly felt like poker.
I didn't want to him to know how lightning fast I'd picked up
on what my mother had just done—the woman whose tells

were perhaps harder to read than my dad's. My loving, generous, and funny mom was, at the end of the day, a cipher. Which was maybe part of her appeal to my dad, who believed he could read everyone.

My mom nudged Emma aside and took over the stereo system. The tape deck opened with a soft sigh. At the decisive push of a large square button, a male voice boomed from the speakers.

"Jesus. I haven't heard Jeff Buckley in so many years. Oh, girls. Oh man. This album . . . it was like my soundtrack one summer—"

My dad reached over and put his finger to her lips, reminding her gently: *shhh*.

"I don't want to listen to this!" Emma growled.

My mom acted like she didn't hear a thing. Maybe she didn't.

I was debating whether she'd really made a mistake, when that focus gave way to watching her face. Tension I hadn't even known she was carrying in her shoulders and face vanished, like years fell away from her and she was suddenly young. I was sure this was what my mom had looked like back when she was free.

In her diaphanous blouse and jeans and bare feet, she walked a few steps away from our small family grouping and lay down in the middle of the living room carpet, staring at the ceiling.

"Dan! Come here." My mom patted the space next to her. "Lie down." My dad watched her and he was as swept away as I was, reeled in, wanting to be close to her now. I wondered if, for him, this was also like touching the past.

My dad settled next to her and he began singing and even laughing. They knew every single lyric to songs on the album. They didn't include us. They forgot about us, but in a good way. I imagined them on long road trips, windows rolled down, singing at the top of their lungs. Carefree. Maybe not much older than me. Fueled by their righteousness and intelligence. And love.

"Oh. 'Lover, You Should've Come Over.' This song," my mom said.

"It's my turn!" Emma didn't like being left out.

"Come on, Em. I'll play a game with you." I wanted to lead her out and let my parents have this moment.

"No! Dad said I could do my dances to any record I wanted."

I took a deep breath, gathering my patience to persuade Emma and not lose my temper, getting frustrated that so many things were happening in one afternoon, in one moment even, and I couldn't keep up. Then I looked back to my parents lying together on the floor. My dad's expression had shifted. I listened to the lyrics:

I feel too young to hold on
I'm much too old to break free and run

He stood, brushed off his jeans, and left the room.

CHAPTER TWENTY-SIX

That weekend, I saw the neighborhood through a different lens—the fountains, pomegranate trees, tallest pines, and sagging ranch houses. Older mansions. Maybe this had been my mother's home? I dismissed that idea. They would never come back to such an obvious place. But it seemed like my mother had a connection to it. Had she been one of the children in the photograph I'd found in the drawer? It would have been too hard to tell, because the picture was taken from a distance and it had also faded. Still, I went to look for it, but it was gone.

If she *had* been here before, what was it like returning to a place where she'd lived a different life, where she'd left off?

It would be impossible not to remember better times, the "before." It would be hard not to wish she could hit rewind. But that negated the three of us . . .

And my dad—the look on his face during the song. Had he

ever wanted to break free from her? Was this where he had met her and gone along for the ride?

When I went on a run early one morning, I saw a pillow from their bed on the couch.

What was most disturbing: *If* this was a location where my mother had memories, where maybe people knew her, why would she risk leaving the house? What reason was good enough for her to endanger us all?

Maybe we'd always lived closer to the edge than I'd realized.

Leaving the house on Monday morning was a relief.

On the walk to school, my palms sweat—nerves at what it would be like between me and Harry when I saw him. Three days had passed since what had happened at the skate park, not to mention in the car.

Harry was late and he gave me a half smile, which could have meant anything.

"Hi," I whispered softly when he took his seat next to me. I was all raw nerves and excitement, happy to be in a space that firmly existed in the present day. My eyes landed on whiteboard scrawl left over from Friday's genetics class: *Forensic Genealogy.*

Harry gently kicked my foot while pretending he didn't notice Professor Alexiev's glare.

"Should we be honored by your lateness?" she asked Harry in a clipped tone.

"You just quoted Kanye West!" one of the kids let out delightedly.

Professor Alexiev said, "Come on, Harrison. Pull it together." Next to me, Harry sat up straighter.

"Speaking of, I know some of you are trying to see if you can get college credit for this course. You can't. No matter what kind of letter I write." Professor Alexiev twirled a pencil like a mini baton between her fingers. "But, of course, it will look good that you're taking my class." She smiled wryly, like she knew how arrogant that sounded. "Just focus on the test. Doing well on this test, in this program—that's the gateway. If you show mastery of this material, you'll be invited to our Fall Scholar Weekend, where you can attend classes taught by members of the Stanford math department and visiting professors from other universities. It's a really nice chance for professors to meet you as you're applying to colleges. You'll also be eligible for college scholarships through the Silicon Valley Community Foundation. I have meetings set up with some of you so we can go over your assessment. Poppy, you're today after class."

I shifted in my seat, irritated by all the benefits available to these kids, part of my brain still parsing "forensic genealogy." It sounded ominous, like it had to do with solving crimes. I glanced over at Harry, who shrugged one shoulder. "I'll wait," he whispered.

After class, I met Professor Alexiev in the quiet high school library for my midsession conference. It felt like more attention than I'd received from any previous teachers. Maybe because of her relatively young age, not to mention her position down the road at Stanford, many of the students in our class wanted to use Professor Alexiev as a counselor. She kind of let them.

"Hi there!" Professor Alexiev slid into the seat next to me.

We hadn't really talked since her annoyance with me over the internship. I worried that I'd embarrassed myself with the assessment. Moments like these, I wanted to keep studying on my own so I could remain clueless about how much my education was lacking.

Professor Alexiev pulled out my assessment. I felt a heaviness when I saw it was covered with red pencil.

"Okay, the highlights: you've gained so much ground," she said. "Here you got lost on this one proof. I could see your reasoning and strategies in the work on the side of your paper, and it does show that you deeply understand some of these concepts. Like early on in class, I can see you have a knack for analysis. That's a course you can take later."

"What? Seriously?" I hadn't thought I'd done well at all.

"I want you to know—kids who test like this get the scholarships."

When I didn't respond, Professor Alexiev held the assessment in the air. "Top universities know about this program," she said. She waved the assessment to the room at large. "That's why these kids are here this summer. Or why their parents sent them, anyway." She crossed her arms and sat back. "Get excited! So the good news is you can catch up to all the students once you have a really decent grounding in algebra. Once you fill in the blanks you have, you'll go on to hold your own in any college math course. Maybe you won't test out of the intro classes, but who cares about that? Universities want to train you in their style, anyway."

I'd thought she was just going to show me my test and I'd attempt to understand where I'd gone wrong. "I'm so surprised," I said.

In true Professor Alexiev fashion, she rolled her eyes. "Why? You're taking this class. You were aware of this accelerated summer institute. You know you have a strength in this area. Not to mention, I can tell you like it."

I nodded, vigorously agreeing with her.

I'd never had a teacher take an interest in me or give me any indication of my capabilities—of who I could be in a world I knew only a little about. I didn't even know the choices, because I didn't have the information. It was a total accident that I'd stumbled into meeting her.

"I can go through these with you, but I'm curious about your plans. With your parents and homeschooling, the next step is college? Yeah?"

I stared at the tip of my flip-flop that was wearing thin. The lie was on the tip of my tongue. If I said yes, Professor Alexiev would smile because I was taken care of, send me on my way, and meet with the next student, who was hovering obnoxiously.

Instead I said, "I don't know."

By saying it, I was asking for help, trying to pull her to my side. Almost immediately, I prayed Professor Alexiev wouldn't recognize it as such.

Professor Alexiev paused for a long time, studying my face. "It's important to have options."

I left the library with another appointment: Professor Alexiev and I were going to meet again to discuss different ways I could catch up to my classmates. I wasn't sure if she meant mathwise or in terms of applying for college.

Maybe Professor Alexiev was only being kind in the moment and she'd forget her promise to meet with me. But I was so curious to hear how she saw me fitting into the bigger world. For just a moment, I could pretend I would become this other me.

I was almost late for babysitting. Outside the library, I looked for Harry but didn't see him. I'd thought he was going to give me a ride. But, per his rules, maybe he was waiting in his car so no one would see us. I walked to the parking lot, part of me assuming his car would be nowhere in sight. I didn't know how this worked, how Harry worked. We'd kissed, but maybe he would distance himself now. I'd observed boys—and girls—do that at every school I'd gone to.

My shoulders were stiff and my backpack heavy.

Suddenly it was gently being pulled from my back and sliding down my arms, Harry taking the weight. I spun to look at him and, in the broad daylight, he leaned in and kissed me.

I was late again. Every day, I was a couple more minutes late for babysitting.

We'd been making out, parked under a willow tree a block away from the country club, our hands seemingly everywhere. Harry ran his palms over my shoulders, down my back; I sifted my fingers through his short hair. Harry pressed a hand to my lower back to bring me closer.

Life was better than any romance novel I'd ever read.

I kissed his neck and smelled expensive soap that was probably wasted on a teenager. But I'd spent enough time around Harry to know he liked these luxuries. Maybe he was uneasy with who he was in relation to his parents, but he was at ease in his own skin, whether he knew it or not.

Harry lowered his head so he could kiss the spot above the

first button on my blouse. I half-laughed to cover my gasp of surprise. Then he began kissing my collarbone while he gently held me still. I tipped my head back, loving it. This wasn't me, after all. It was me in this life that wouldn't last.

Harry started to undo the next button, and I instantly sat up straight. I drew in my breath. Harry rested his forehead against my shoulder, regretting that he'd done that or regretting that I'd stopped us.

Then Harry sat back in his seat. For a long minute, neither of us spoke. I checked my watch. I was two minutes late for my job. "I have to go," I said. It was lunchtime and it seemed like Range Rover after Range Rover, Tesla after Tesla drove past us, no doubt turning into the country club entrance.

Harry finally looked at me. He nodded.

I felt like a prude with my braids and my blouse, and so out of my league.

But then Harry said, "You're so beautiful."

We shared a long look. We were so different, but somehow, we just fit together.

"We need more time," he said.

"I know."

I would have to lie to get it.

CHAPTER TWENTY-SEVEN

July 4. My favorite day of the year. I brushed aside guilt that Harry and I had found a way to spend some of it together.

I basked in bed, listening to Emma's happy chatter in the kitchen and the clatter of dishes as she set the table for my birthday breakfast. I heard my dad's footsteps, then he knocked lightly on my door.

"Happy birthday, my oldest girl." My dad stood framed by the dim, low-ceilinged hallway behind him. He was wearing jeans, an old T-shirt, and a denim jacket because it was always chilly in the house.

"Thanks, Dad."

"How are you eighteen?"

To me, this birthday had always loomed large because of the inevitable questions that came with it. I'd thought if I was patient, those questions would be answered. But they hadn't been, and eighteen was here.

"I can picture you at two when we put your hair in two pigtails every day. God, I wish we had photos." He smiled a little wistfully, then shook his head as if warding away the sadness. "But it's committed to memory forever."

When I thought about baby Emma, it was weird that all I had were snapshots from my mind's eye. And I found the images lost their crispness over time.

I had a terrible thought: As the years went by, would it still feel right to have my dad greet me on my birthday and talk about me in pigtails? I knew I'd always be his little girl, but—

My dad cleared his throat. "You slept until almost nine. Come on, get up! It's birthday breakfast!"

Birthdays in my family were a big deal. The person celebrating their birthday got to decide what the family would do for the entire day. I always chose board games—which grew more advanced the older I got and could take hours. I had loved getting my parents' focus for that amount of time.

"Is Mom here?"

My dad's smile slipped. "Of course."

I sensed I'd hurt his feelings a bit. I'd heard him mutter under his breath once, asking why Emma and I always wanted Mom.

"I'll be out in just a second!" I said, hoping I could convince my dad of my typical birthday excitement.

"Okay, sweet girl." My dad gazed at me silently for a moment, then crossed the room and bent low to kiss my forehead. Without a word, he left the room and gently closed my door.

I got up and went to the window, lifting the shade. It was

clear blue skies and sunshine already. No mosquitos, humidity, thunderstorms, oppressive heat. My first Fourth of July in California.

Under the guise of babysitting, I was going to meet Harry at the club.

Opening my bottom dresser drawer, I pulled out my bathing suit and cutoffs and then searched for a tank top. Because of the holiday there was no class, so I'd offered to help Rebecca at the pool.

Amid protests from my dad and Emma, I'd finally secured permission to disappear for a few hours to babysit. My excuse was that it would be fun for me to see the celebration. From the instant look of pure jealousy on Emma's face, it had been the wrong thing to say. From the immediate stoic expression on my dad's face, I knew I'd hurt him, too.

"Sis!" I heard Emma holler. "Hurry!"

When I took a seat at the wooden table in the small dining room, my whole family was waiting for me.

"Happy birthday!" my mom greeted me. She wore a bathrobe, and her hair was loose and messy. She leaned over to kiss me, and her lips felt dry against my cheek. When she pulled back, I saw hollows beneath her eyes.

"Are you okay?" I asked.

"Couldn't be better," she said. I couldn't tell if she was being sarcastic. "Hey, I thought maybe we'd change it up this year? Maybe we'd give you your present tonight?"

We'd never once done it that way. And we lived by our traditions because that was all we had.

I knew she didn't have my present yet or the idea for my

present. Which hurt. I understood she was going through something, maybe because she was here and that reminded her of her past, but it didn't change the facts. She'd made her bed. She couldn't go back in time and erase me.

"Wait, I have something I want Poppy to open now," my dad intervened. "Em, will you go grab it? I left it on the kitchen counter." Emma scooted away from the table, knocking her chair over in the process. My mom sighed, adding a sudden tense undercurrent to the birthday breakfast.

"Here you go! It's from me and Dad." Emma grinned. God, she was a mean girl, needling my mom by saying that.

"Hey, I had something to do with it," my mom said.

"Thanks, guys," I said and started unwrapping the package that was clearly a book. The corners of the wrapping paper were tucked perfectly—my dad's precise work.

It was a blank notebook with an elephant on the front. Because I received something with elephants every year. Because I'd once been obsessed with elephants and my family somehow still thought I was eight.

I pasted on my best fake smile. "Thank you. I love it. I can add it to my collection." Most of which had been left behind at various places when we'd had to move.

Luckily, my dad missed my delivery because the oven timer went off, alarmingly loud. He got up to go to the kitchen, and a second later, my mom followed.

"I have a gift for you. Just from me," Emma said. She handed me the children's book *The Giving Tree*. It was an old copy but in almost perfect shape.

"I love this book!" I said. "Thanks, Emma. Where'd you get it?"

"I found it in the bookshelf."

So she was giving me a book that wasn't even hers to give. Okay. It was still sweet, I supposed.

"It reminded me of a birthday, because look at the inside," Emma said.

I opened the still-shiny lime-green cover.

"Look," Emma said.

On the title page an adult had neatly handwritten a poem in black felt-tip pen: *Now We Are Six by A. A. Milne*

Then below the poem: *Happy Sixth Birthday, Gregory! Thank you for inviting A and M to celebrate your special day.*

"That's so nice," I said. "Look, the inscription was from so long ago. 1983." I ran my thumb over the boxy black lettering, almost expecting it to smear.

"Well, that makes ol' Gregory—" Emma tilted her head side to side while she calculated. "Forty-three!"

I smiled. "You're right!"

"Who are A and M? Who was Gregory, I wonder?" Emma asked.

"Me too, Emma." I wished there was more to go on, but I loved how the book only added a wistful flavor to this already beautiful place where time seemed to hold still.

My dad called from the kitchen, "More bagels. Poppy, I got you *poppy*seed."

"Ha-ha-ha," I said.

Another tradition that didn't seem as magical this year.

At 11:55 A.M., my dad dropped me five blocks from the country club.

"You sure about this? You won't even see the fireworks," he

said, fiddling with the radio. The rule was I needed to be home by 5 P.M.

"I know. I just thought it would be fun to go to this barbecue, and Rebecca needs the help. Babysitting is perfect. I get to be a fly on the wall."

My dad's hand stilled. "What do you mean, 'a fly on the wall'?"

"I mean, I get to see the normal things people do. Or the things normal people do. I don't know. It's interesting."

My dad's eyes dimmed a little, and I was sorry I'd said it. I hadn't known I wanted to subtly jab him until it was out of my mouth. What was wrong with me? It was my birthday, and I didn't know why I felt suffocated by my family. Instantly, I couldn't stand what I'd done. It wasn't me.

"Dad, I can't wait to come home. Trust me. It's cool to get to go swimming and all that, but I'm so excited for tonight. Can we play *Catan*?"

His shoulders relaxed. "Of course."

I grabbed my tote containing my wallet (which had elephants on it), water bottle, and change of clothes. "Hey, Dad?"

"Yes?"

"You are the best dad." I couldn't remember the last time I'd said it, but I had the sudden feeling that I had to let him know. It was the job he'd given up everything else to do. And he was really, really good at it.

My dad half-laughed, but I saw that I'd cheered him up. Looking at him now, it felt wrong to ever want anything more than the life he'd made for me, because no one would ever love me more than him.

. . .

The crowd at the pool was much larger than normal. At the small playground off to one side, I loomed over Frank while he played with his Matchbox cars in the sandbox, and kept one eye out for Harry. I could hardly wait.

I expected Harry to arrive at his friends' table any moment. They were stationed in their usual spot, a corner with partial shade amid an array of birds-of-paradise. The friends had an intimidating vibe, closed off to everyone else, not unlike the various adult cliques that had formed poolside.

When I babysat Frank at the pool, I pretended I didn't see Harry's friends. And, after the girls looked me up and down and didn't smile, they pretended—or they didn't have to pretend, they just believed—I didn't exist.

There was always the disappointing reminder that these were Harry's people. Maybe they were nice if you grew up with them? How they sensed their own was amazing. Even I could tell the difference between the club establishment and the nerds who had made heaps of money in Silicon Valley. The latter were Rebecca's peers.

Frank punched me in the back for no apparent reason. Right in the spot left exposed by my bathing suit. "Hey!" I exclaimed.

"That might leave a bruise." Just as I heard Harry's voice behind me, I felt a hand on my lower back where Frank had socked me. I whipped around. Harry was giving Frank a very direct stare. Harry was standing close enough that no one could see his hand on my bare skin.

I looked around surreptitiously, thinking of Harry's rules about being together in public.

"You ready? You asked if you could leave early?" Harry asked.

"I did and Rebecca was sweet about it, but, ugh, I hate asking for things."

"That's no good. You deserve to ask for things, Pops."

I didn't know if it was strange or right that Harry had landed on my dad's nickname for me.

Harry's friends spotted him. He drifted away from me.

While I signed off with Rebecca, Harry said hellos to his friends but didn't get too comfortable.

Harry left first. I gathered my belongings, said goodbye to Frank, and watched out the corner of my eye as Harry did the same from his side of the pool.

One friend called after him, "See you in the city!"

Unfortunately, the group was still watching Harry's exit when it was time to make mine.

I gently unlatched the gate, wishing Harry could have just held it open for me, and I tried not to look awkward with my bulky tote bag. As I squeezed out, I heard, for the second time this summer, "Doesn't she look like Alix?"

I'd expected worse. I glanced up, thinking it was the same person. But it was another girl I'd never seen at the pool before today. I watched Harry's friends for a second longer, curious, wondering if they would talk to me and maybe show me a picture of this Alix. Then I heard the sound of a car engine revving. I tried not to smile, not a doubt in my mind who was telling me they were impatient and ready to go.

Two minutes later, I was in Harry's car, flip-flops kicked off and my feet on the dashboard. Free. The second Harry pulled out of the country club, he turned up the volume on the stereo, rolled down all four windows in tandem, and let the music blast.

Talk about living in the moment. I'd never had a better one.

Harry brought me to his house. As soon as we got out of the car, we reached for each other, unable to wait another second. Our lips met, and Harry leaned me back against the car with his body, flattening his palms on either side of my head.

"Come with me," he said, a little breathless. There were ten steps to the back door of the kitchen area, but we stopped in the middle to kiss again, this time laughing at not being able to get enough.

"I have to get home by five o'clock. And I have to walk. I can't be late."

"It will be fine. I promise. I'll take care of you." I wasn't sure if I was comfortable with the sentiment at all—I was taken care of on a level Harry would never understand—but it was so sweet.

"Where is everyone?" I asked when we reached the kitchen.

"Most people have the day off. I was supposed to be in San Francisco. My dad is at a party. We're alone." My heart began to pound a little harder. "This way," Harry said, leading me through many rooms. He stopped me under an arched door-way. "Okay. Close your eyes. Count to thirty. No, fifty." He held my shoulders and waited for me to close my eyes, then he kissed my forehead.

"Fine." I began to count. "One, two . . ."

"Slower."

"Okay!" I obliged, laughing. I reached fifty. "Ready?" I asked, excited and impatient.

"Yes," Harry said, sounding more serious.

I opened my eyes. In a vast living room, an enormous white birthday cake sat atop a low glass coffee table. The cake was covered with eighteen lit candles.

Harry took a seat on the floor. I crossed the large room and sat crisscross as well, facing Harry across my birthday cake. The candles glimmered between us, the moment suspended in time.

"Happy birthday, Poppy."

will never eat cake again." Harry threw one hand over his stomach.

Feeling my face burn, I propped myself on my elbows. "I can't believe you ate half of it. I didn't know that was possible." I looked down at him, self-satisfied and stretched out in the sun. We lay on soft green grass that ran directly to the pool, creating a seamless edge.

"Oh, that was nothing. When I don't take my Adderall, I can eat a house."

"You are the skinniest person I've ever met, so I don't know where you put it. Your jeans hang off you," I teased.

"Hey, are you making fun of my personal style?" He laughed, eyes still closed.

"Not one bit. I have to admit, I like it."

Harry squinted up at me, shielding his eyes. He seemed like he wanted to say something, but instead, he curved a hand behind my shoulder, drawing me down to him. He leaned up, meeting me halfway.

Our lips touched, but I pulled away. "What? What were you going to say?" I asked.

Harry sighed at the unexpected break in the kiss and flopped down on his back. "Nothing. I just like that you like me. Maybe you even think I'm cute."

"You are cute and you know it." I rested my nose against his. He tilted his face up and our lips met.

As the kiss deepened, Harry's hand moved beneath my shirt, traveling up and down my back slowly.

Harry surprised me by ending the kiss. He stayed close and we were still face-to-face. "I like your style," Harry said, continuing the conversation I'd almost forgotten.

"What? Vintage chic?" I was distracted, wondering why he'd stopped.

Harry leaned back a little, appraising me. "You own it. You're not like other girls I've met."

"That's sort of a compliment."

"What part isn't?" he asked.

"I don't like being different from other girls."

My comment hung in the air, and I was so annoyed with myself for being weirdly vulnerable.

"Why?" Harry asked.

I didn't want to be honest with him. But I'd been alone for so long. "Being homeschooled, you miss out on a lot. Sometimes it's like I live in a different world. A bubble, I guess. I can see everyone doing things, but I can't do them." When had homeschooling become a substitute for living underground?

"Yes, you can. Look, you're in the class."

"Yeah, it's like I get to touch some stuff, but then it's taken away."

"What do you mean, taken away? How strict are your parents?"

I sat up, knowing I needed to downplay this fast. But before I could speak, Harry said, "But you'll go to college soon and start your own life. It'll be a fresh start. Right?"

"Of course," I lied to get out of the conversation.

"Where are you applying?" Harry seemed to relax, assured that everything in the world was how he believed it was. He began playing with my hair, sifting it through his fingers.

"I'm still figuring it out. What about you?"

"Hmmm. Somewhere far away. Maybe the East Coast. Just to get away from some of this shit. I don't know. I really want to go to Brown." I noticed how Harry started by saying he didn't know and didn't care and then ended by telling me the truth of what mattered to him.

"Brown would be so lucky to have you," I said. "Maybe no one would know who you are there."

"They would know in about two seconds. As soon as they looked me up online. But probably no one would care."

"I don't know. You have a pretty sexy backstory," I said. I tried hard not to feel a pinch of jealousy when Harry talked about college. My eighteenth birthday took on an uncomfortable weight again. Soon, I'd no longer be even with my peers. They were all about to pass me by. Go to college, have careers, start building lives. For me, the years would fly by. I'd be the same at nineteen, twenty-five, thirty-two.

"What about your backstory?" Harry was asking.

"What?" I asked, not following the conversation, feeling agitated by my rabbit hole of thoughts.

"You're mysterious. Tell me about your parents. What are their jobs?"

"You're breaking your own rule. If you won't talk about your family, I don't have to," I said.

"It's getting harder and harder not to ask personal questions. I want to know more about you. Come on, tell me more about your family! Do you guys—"

I cut Harry off midsentence. "I need to get going soon." I was all too aware that it came off sounding too abrupt, a little harsh.

"Okay," Harry said slowly, sensing he'd crossed a line. "Let's get you out of the sun. You probably burn."

I wanted to go back to how we'd been together thirty seconds before, so I could continue what had been the most perfect birthday I'd ever had. As we walked to the house, I caught Harry's hand and didn't let go, wanting him to know we were good.

"Do you know someone named Alix?" I asked.

"Alix who?"

"I don't know. I've now heard two of your friends at the pool say I look like her."

"Ah. Alix Bell. That's funny. You totally do." He whipped his phone from his back pocket and shaded it with his hand. "I'm finding her on Instagram."

Harry showed me a close-up of a girl with luxurious brown hair and light eyes offset with long, lush eyelashes that had about five coats of mascara. Her pink lips looked bee-stung and pouty.

"Sorry. She sort of looks like a porn star in this picture. I don't know why she's posing like that. She's cool. Alix runs in that San Francisco crowd I know. She comes down here, too, sometimes."

We had the same unique eye color, but other than that, I couldn't see any resemblance.

"Here's another picture. This is what she posted yesterday."

This photo showed Alix on an elaborate parade float. She stood arm in arm with a handsome, fit, middle-aged man in aviator sunglasses. They had big white smiles as they waved to the crowd. Both wore black T-shirts with rainbow lettering. Hers said PRIDE. His said LOVE IS LOVE. Alix's caption read:

TBT last year's Pride Parade with @ABellSF. #bestday-ever #activist #inspiration #dappercousin #loveislove

Alix Bell looked like she had a fun, full life. With loads of privilege and proximity to powerful people, if riding a parade float through San Francisco was any indication.

Harry consulted his phone before replacing it in his back pocket. "You have ten more minutes before we have to go."

"Thanks for my birthday cake," I said. I tugged on his hand so he'd look at me and know I meant it.

He shrugged one shoulder like it was nothing, but he quickly kissed the back of my hand.

"Come inside. I need to make out with you," Harry stated, matter-of-fact.

"Oh my god. Harry!" I started to laugh.

"Poppy!" he mimicked me, laughing.

"Fine," I said.

. . .

We had to stop. I was about to be late. Harry pulled away, catching his breath. He had led me inside, then lowered me down onto the soft sofa, our bodies flush. "Tell me again why you have to leave?"

"I'm not allowed to date."

"You're eighteen now." Harry rolled to his side and curved his body around mine. Without thinking about it, I melted against him. He tightened his arm around me. We were actually cuddling. His lips brushed my neck.

"Harry," I said, my voice dead serious, "if we want to keep doing this, I have to be careful. The second they know, you'll never see me again." It was as close to the truth as I could ever tell Harry.

"Okay," Harry said slowly. He was leaning back, eyeing me, maybe realizing this was a bigger deal than I'd let on. *Please don't ask questions.* "I'll drive you to the school?" he finally said.

I exhaled. "Thank you."

Harry left to use the bathroom and I wandered to the kitchen. I rested my elbows on the dark stone counter, cradling my chin, and stared out into the backyard. I was so happy. When I stayed in the present moment, with Harry, in class, even in the old house on the beautiful plot of land with my family, my life was exactly how I wanted it. I felt like who I was supposed to be.

I just couldn't think below the surface.

Two tall men suddenly appeared at the glass door outside the kitchen. I startled and straightened.

One of the men slid the door open wide, then stood aside

as the other brushed past him. My eyes couldn't decide where to land. The man holding the door open reminded me of an off-duty police officer in his polo shirt, slacks, and cell phone clipped at his waist. The other man carried all the authority. I instantly guessed: Harry's father.

He was white, wore sparkling clean tennis shoes, and was well over six feet—as tall as Harry. He wore crisp jeans, an untucked dress shirt, and trendy eyeglasses. It was hard to tell he was Harry's father except for the height and maybe something about his eyes.

I opened my mouth to say hello, tell them I was a friend of Harry's. Maybe because I glanced over my shoulder for Harry, willing him to magically appear, I showed my nervousness and that I could be intimidated. Harry's father crossed his arms and stared at me, dead air between us.

"Hi. I'm, um, a friend of Harry's."

"You don't have a name?"

Harry sauntered into the room and drew up short when he saw them. He stayed where he was, several feet away from me. For a split second, there was a look of fear on his face. I saw it. Then he covered it with the same look I saw on Emma's face every day: obstinance.

"What the fuck are you doing here?" His dad's voice was so cold, it was completely jarring. I'd never heard a parent speak that way to their child.

"Living my best life," Harry said dryly.

"You told me you were going to your mother's."

"I'm leaving in a minute."

"Are you wearing shoes in the house?" Harry's dad's voice

was incredulous, mean. Harry wasn't wearing shoes. I was. I'd just put them back on.

Harry didn't say anything. His father grabbed the can of Lysol stationed by the door.

I looked over to the other witness—the man in the polo shirt still standing in the doorway. He held his arms behind his back and stared at his now-shoeless feet. He didn't seem surprised like me.

"Send your friend home. Then you spray down this floor and every single room where you've been."

"I'll do it after I drop off—

Swiftly, Harry's dad crossed over to him and grabbed his upper arm. I held my breath, watching Harry refuse to flinch. The grip had to hurt.

"Okay. Got it," Harry quickly said, standing down.

Harry's dad released him and stepped back. "Who's this?" he asked. He didn't look at me.

"My friend from class."

Harry eased away and came to my side. Behind my back, out of view, I reached for his hand. Harry didn't take it. Instead, he stepped away. "I'll drive you home," he said, not meeting my eyes.

"What did I just say?" Harry's father said.

"It's fine!" I said. "I can leave from here. Really, it's fine."

Once I was down the block, I broke into a run. I was late, yes, but I ran because I wanted to get away. As fast and as far away as I could from that eerie situation.

I listened to my flip-flops slap the pavement, my bag bouncing up and down uncomfortably on my shoulder. I couldn't shake off the bad feeling in that room. Or the expression on Harry's face. I'd never seen someone deaden themselves, mentally exiting the space.

I was sweaty and dirty and I'd slowed outside our neighborhood gates to catch my breath so I'd appear calm by the time I walked down the long, overgrown driveway. I was so, so late.

From the mailbox, I saw my family—all three of them—gathered in front of the house, awaiting my return. I saw my dad glance at his watch. As soon as she saw me, Emma yelled, "Now!"

Even my mom looked happy as she lit their sparklers and cheered, "Happy Birthday!" and met me halfway to hand me one of my own.

My dad hung back and looked at me questioningly.

Sorry, I mouthed. My dad opened his mouth, and I tensed up, but Emma shouted, "Let the party begin!" He seemed to let it go. For now.

Through the bouquets of sparklers, I watched my family. I wanted to fall into their arms, I was so relieved to be home. I saw their closeness and their happiness and what they were doing for my birthday because they loved me so much.

After cake and cards and laughter and the beautiful gift of a drawing by my mom of me at every age from her and my dad's memories, I closed the door to my room, still feeling like I'd woken up from a bad dream. My sheer relief to be home hadn't worn off yet.

It was only when I unpacked my soggy bag, still damp with sweat from my frightened run home, that I let Harry rise from my thoughts, where I'd abandoned him.

CHAPTER TWENTY-NINE

The day after my birthday, Harry came to class a full fifteen minutes late.

When he passed down the aisle, I said a soft "Hey" under my breath, which earned me only a cursory nod and zero eye contact.

Oh, I thought. It was clear what was happening—after I'd witnessed that messed-up tableau, Harry never wanted to talk to me again. He was more horribly embarrassed than I'd thought.

At break, Harry took off without speaking to me. I heard him tell Professor Alexiev he needed to leave five minutes before class ended to get to work.

He tried to go without saying goodbye.

"Excuse me," I blurted to Professor Alexiev. Without explanation, I followed Harry.

"Hey, can I talk to you?"

Harry paused then reluctantly turned around, unable to be rude enough to pretend he hadn't heard me.

"What's going on?" I asked.

"Nothing's going on," Harry said defensively, his entire skinny body going into his shrug. "You got home okay? You knew how to get home?"

"I did. Thanks. Hey, I just wanted to say, don't worry about it. Bad things happen to families. Bad things happen *in* families. We don't have to talk about it. Ever." This was something I knew all about.

Harry's eyes widened like I'd slapped him. Then they became dead and blank, as if he didn't want to hear. "I don't know how to . . ." He stopped. "Sorry, I've got to get to work." Without waiting for my response, he left.

I knew I was paying a price for what I'd seen. It almost wasn't personal.

It's good, I told myself. Our relationship had become too risky and we'd gotten too close.

What Harry didn't know was that I had a lot of practice with this—with closing myself off to disappointment from friendships that weren't meant to be. It was what happened when nothing could ever truly be real.

But it was too bad, because I'd really liked him. So much.

I walked the long walk to babysit.

It was the worst comedown in history. Even the day was gloomy and overcast.

The pool was busy because of the holiday week. Behind huge black sunglasses I'd borrowed from home, I hated Harry's friends across the pool. Harry would go back to them. He'd be the Harry I'd first known—closed off, staying in his lane.

A group of men lingered at the snack bar. Men who came from the golf course were always an unwelcome sight. With their loud voices and attitude of owning the place, they felt like interlopers on the kid-, teen-, and female-dominated pool scene.

First, I recognized the security guard from Harry's house. He had to be a security guard. He stood off to one side, not speaking to anyone, blending in with a golf shirt. Then I spotted Harry's dad, surrounded by three well-groomed men with heavy watches. And, like Harry, it was clear he was the center—the focal point. It took thirty seconds of observing to see that he looked bored while the other men rushed to please him with their conversation. That's where Harry got it.

Harry's dad sensed someone staring at him and looked up. I pleaded internally he wouldn't recognize me.

From what I'd seen, he seemed mentally ill. Definitely a germophobe. I was guessing controlling. Maybe abusive. At least verbally.

I hated him. For how he'd treated Harry. For how he'd treated me. For ruining my relationship with his son. For trying to ruin Harry. In Harry, of all people, I'd seen a world of shame.

It was amazing what parents could do. Whether they tried to hurt or tried so hard to protect, they ended up doing damage in their own way.

A strong breeze suddenly ruffled the Uno cards, blowing a stack of them under the table. Frank dove to collect them.

"Emily?"

I carefully leaned down, the baby in one arm, picking up a few cards within my reach.

"Emily? Emily!"

Oh my god. "Yes! Sorry." I looked over to Rebecca.

"Hey, honey." Rebecca held up her phone. "I just got the news that my nanny will be back on Monday. She's off her crutches."

"Oh."

"And then this weekend we're leaving for Pajaro Dunes, so Friday is our last day together. We've loved having you so much. I hate that we won't see you all the time."

I'd forgotten this day was coming. When I'd taken this job, their nanny's recovery seemed so far in the future.

"I'll pass along your name to my friends? Spread the word?" Rebecca looked truly sorry.

"No, that's okay. I need to use the rest of the summer to study and babysit my sister."

"Okay." Rebecca gave me a wan, small smile. "We'll miss you."

"I'll miss you guys, too."

The swim-team pace clock ticked off my remaining time with Rebecca and her family. Two more days, then I'd exit from this world.

I couldn't eat and I could barely hold a conversation. When I arrived home and my dad grilled me about my day, I thought the news of my babysitting job ending would come out. But it didn't.

CHAPTER THIRTY

I n class, I took Harry's lead. I didn't look his way.

"Poppy! You! Come on up. Determine whether there is a nontrivial integer solution of this equation. Show us."

Of all days. I wasn't in the mood.

I had no choice but to stand when Professor Alexiev called on me. When I was next to her, she handed me the black marker. I uncapped it, cleared my throat, and grabbed my ponytail, bringing the end to my lips while I studied the board, waiting for the numbers to speak to me. The long string of numbers swam and then crisped into focus, finally becoming the most important thing in the room.

Everyone was waiting. "Complete the square?" I asked Professor Alexiev.

"You know. You don't need to ask permission."

I nodded thoughtfully. I did know it. "I'll complete the square in x and y with a change of variables." I began to work through the algebra, getting more excited as the solution came together. "So we end up with this expression, which is the standard form for a conic selection."

"Remember Legendre's theorem?"

"Yep."

"So, use it to characterize the solution."

I worked my way through but had a few roadblocks. I was getting impatient with myself about what I didn't know. "Don't get frustrated!" Professor Alexiev said. But then, after some prompts from the class, I had it. It felt like magic when it clicked. By the end I was openly smiling.

"Good job." Professor Alexiev gave me an actual pat on the back, and a couple of kids gave gentle claps. I headed down the row to my desk, happy, my mind still on the small victory, when I glanced up. I caught Harry looking at me before he quickly averted his gaze. As he absorbed himself in whatever was on his laptop screen, I noticed he was blushing. I looked down at what I was wearing and self-consciously tugged at the hem of my shorts.

I'd forgotten all about him and how much it hurt while I'd been working out the problem on the board. Harry had been watching me, on display, for the past five minutes. He'd had to face the fact that I existed.

The way he'd been looking at me, like he didn't know what he wanted, messed with my mind.

When we finished for the day, one of the class superstars, Crosby, caught me on my way out the door.

"Good job today."

"Oh. Thanks," I said.

"Have you started studying for the test?" Crosby scratched his nose. He wore a light-blue polo shirt and khaki pants. He was handsome and ultra earnest.

"Yes. A little bit. I need to do more." I tucked a strand of hair behind my ear.

"Ah. Well, let me know if you ever want to get together to study. Let me give you my number," Crosby said.

"Excuse me," Harry said. He needed to get through to the exit. He had his skateboard tucked under his arm. Crosby and I separated so Harry could pass. Granted, we were blocking the path to the door, but for someone who had been dashing out of the classroom to avoid me, Harry seemed to take his sweet time walking between us.

I took Crosby's number, knowing I would never use it.

I was surprised when I saw Harry lingering on the patch of lawn outside.

"Hey," he said, walking a few steps to meet me. He sounded calm, but he nervously turned his watch around and around on his wrist. He wore sunglasses so I couldn't see his expression. Today I wasn't in the mood to be excited by his mere presence.

"Hi," I said. I kept walking. Why was he talking to me again? Was it because Crosby gave me his number? I hated that I felt a sudden excited anticipation.

I heard him clear his throat. "I got my results."

"What?" I glanced over my shoulder.

"I got my DNA results." Harry held up his phone. "Did you?"

I was supposed to forget about the DNA test. I'd tried. I mostly had.

"No. I haven't checked that email," I said.

"It's a bad interface. Do you want me to show you how to get around the site?"

Harry didn't wait for an answer and drew near. He typed in his passcode to unlock his phone and angled it toward me so I could see the screen. We weren't touching, but he was so close, I remembered exactly what he felt like.

Even in the shade, it was a bit hard to see. Harry leaned in and our shoulders touched. He didn't move away.

"The first thing you'll probably want to look at is the ethnicity report. Click on the *DNA* tab and then *DNA Story*."

Wait, this is going too fast.

"There're pretty cool details about where your family is from. See? My ancestors are from Jamaica and Kerala, India. And Europe. You get a big location and then smaller regions and the percentage of your DNA you share with that ethnicity."

I had no idea there would be this level of detail. This was years ahead of where I thought it would be. I couldn't take my eyes from his results. "How do they know you share seventeen percent of your DNA with ancestors from Germanic Europe who moved to North Dakota?"

"Enough people have taken the test at this point." Harry nodded to some kids from class who trailed by. "Do you want to look at your results real quick? A friend is meeting me, but he's not here yet."

Harry had already thought about how I didn't have a smartphone or computer. This was what I had loved about Harry—how surprisingly considerate he was. Even though Harry and I were seemingly over, he wanted to finish helping me with the DNA test.

Harry held out his phone, expecting me to take it.

I don't know. I don't know.

"Sure. Thanks."

"I'll be right there," Harry said reassuringly, almost like he was picking up on my nerves.

I nodded. I tried to look poised, though my heart had started a hard, consistent beat. Harry grabbed his skateboard and walked across patches of yellowing grass a distance away. Without his phone, he busied himself by balancing on his skateboard while he casually hopped it off and on a cement curb.

I logged Harry out. Then I paused. This was a Pandora's box, results at my fingertips once I signed in.

I'd promised to stop looking.

I didn't hesitate for another second. I filled in the blank boxes of username and password. Enter.

The ethnicity for ANONYMOUS loaded.

I was Irish. Lots of Irish. My region was Southwest Cork. There was also England, more specifically Dorset in central southern England, and Wales and northwestern Europe. I was also European Jewish from Germany. And some French and Finnish.

I squeezed my eyes shut for a moment, filling in the blanks with watercolors, beginning to give my parents definition and shade. I guessed my mom was European Jewish and my dad was Irish. I didn't know who was French or Finnish.

The funny thing was, none of it surprised me. It just made me happy, like getting to know someone you loved even better.

Including myself. I knew I was white but I felt like an outsider to the point where I could have been from outer space. That was how different I felt from everyone beside my family. It was an isolating weight. And now, it was a little thing, but it gave me some sense of belonging.

So far the DNA test had been a positive, if this feeling of lightness was any indication. After years of murkiness, secrecy, and emotion, I adored this straightforward data.

This was so simple.

Harry paced just outside the open library doors. I heard his skateboard hit the ground and roll, and one of the librarians made a show of closing the door on Harry's surprised puppy-dog expression.

Unfocused, I watched while he toyed with his skateboard and did his small tricks. He unexpectedly came down hard on one hand. For a moment, he bundled his hand in his T-shirt, revealing his tan stomach. I dropped the phone to my side and was about to start toward him, but Harry shook it off.

My mind was still on Harry's injury when I clicked the DNA MATCH tab.

Then all was the sound of squawking jays and the distant thrum of skateboard as my focus telescoped in on a name: CGhumming.

I had a match.

Multiple categories were highlighted as possible ways we were related: FIRST COUSIN, ONCE REMOVED; GREAT-AUNT/UN-CLE; GREAT-GRANDCHILD. I shared 902 "cMs" with her. Below the graph, cMs were defined as centimorgans, a unit of measurement for genetic linkage.

I clicked on CGhumming.

There was a family tree with only one name on it: Carol. Filled in under MOTHER.

Carol Ghumming. I looked up. Harry once again smacked to the ground hard before jumping lightly to his feet.

Carol.

"Enough, man! You're giving yourself a beatdown," a boy called out as he approached Harry. He matched Harry with his nice clothes and shades.

Harry turned around. He said something I couldn't hear. He would have to explain to his friend why this weird girl had his phone.

I had to wait until next time. I didn't know when that would be. In my last second of opportunity, I searched "CGhuming." I retyped as fast as I could, adding the extra *m*. Adding quotation marks.

Harry had started toward me with his long, loose strides.

When I hit return, I saw one result for a username "CGhumming" on a site called Pinterest. I clicked on it. Hummingbird images, dozens of them, filled the screen.

CHAPTER THIRTY-ONE

That afternoon, I said goodbye to Rebecca, Frank, and the baby. It was one more loss in a week of losses. I was unnerved from the DNA site and felt so totally strange. Something I'd internally celebrated for straightforward data had opened a door I wasn't expecting.

Then, when I got home from babysitting, the house was uncharacteristically silent.

I let myself into the kitchen, the straw ornament flapping precariously from its thin, rusty nail. The light-blue-tile countertop was sticky with syrup, and the breakfast dishes were still in the sink.

For the first hour, I loved being by myself. I couldn't remember a time when I'd ever been alone in any of our houses or apartments.

I picked the spot with the most traffic, where I would spend time if I didn't always retreat to my room—the living room. I sprawled on the floral sofa, turned on my side, cradling my head on my upper arm so I could see out the sliding glass doors into the beautiful, wild yard. I heard the distant winding gears of the oven clock. The refrigerator hummed, and I heard the call of a bird outside.

CGhumming. Carol. Somewhere out there, I was blood-related to Carol G. It was mind-blowing to think about. An actual relative. Who loved hummingbirds.

I must have drifted. I awoke suddenly, sitting bolt upright. The sun had shifted and the living room was dim.

According to my watch, I'd only been asleep for minutes, but I felt like I'd come out the other side in a wildly different mood—slightly scared.

Where was everyone? What had seemed luxurious now felt off. A little bit of fear licked at my heart—that same fear from the dumpsters in Des Moines. And from when my mom drove off in Mill Valley.

Unlike in Mill Valley, I was all alone, without Emma.

If they had to leave suddenly, they would come back for me, right? Or was I supposed to know to get myself to the closest Starbucks—the one we'd agreed upon, in the small downtown? I jumped up and went to the kitchen, unzipping my backpack and feeling for my flip phone. Nothing. No messages.

It was so silly. I was scaring myself. I should enjoy the peace.

While I was being ridiculous, I decided to check the bedrooms to make sure everyone's belongings were still in place.

In Emma's room, her new favorite stuffed badger was on its side at the end of her plush pink bedding. She loved that badger. She would have taken it.

My parents' room was at the end of the hallway, and the

door was shut. No one was home—I knew that—but I knocked softly anyway.

The air was perfumed with my mom's distinct scent of wildly fragrant Pantene shampoo. The bed was made. A blouse was folded neatly on her side of the bed, and I imagined my father picking it up off the floor to make his point.

I opened a couple of drawers in the enormous chest that matched the headboard of the king-size bed. My parents' clothes barely filled the deep drawers.

They'd be home soon. I felt like I was coming down from a fever dream. I hadn't been left behind.

I was closing a drawer with my mom's clothes when I saw the very edge of a piece of newspaper peeking out from beneath a robin's-egg-blue sweater. I carefully pulled it toward me. It was a brittle clipping from the local paper, *The Country Almanac,* announcing a Garden Guild show in 2009 and lauding the local group of master gardeners. A photo accompanied the piece. Seven well-groomed, older women were pictured, three seated in the front and four standing in the back. Behind them was the enormous fountain located next door, the nymph spouting an arc of water.

Why did my mother have this? She must have found it somewhere in the house, if not in this drawer. It had somehow escaped the cleaning. Why had she kept it? The owner of the house could be in this photo. I carefully replaced it beneath the sweater after trying to commit the names to memory.

Because I was never in this part of the house, I poked my head into the closet area of the master bedroom. I'd completely forgotten about the storage closet. Without thought, I opened the door with a big *whoosh*.

The closet was cooler than the rest of the house, and the beige tile retained the cold from the outdoors. It smelled like mothballs.

The closet was bare except for odds and ends—unused wood shelving and rolls of wallpaper. One of our black suitcases was nestled beneath a stack of sheeting coated with splatters of paint.

I lifted the unzipped lid a few inches. It was enough to see neatly ordered stacks of cash. Tons of it.

How did my dad have all this cash? He hadn't transported it from Illinois. I'd seen this suitcase, chock-full of clothing, at the motels where we'd stayed on our journey.

And he definitely hadn't picked this up at the pack-and-ship store in Marin. My parents never got as much cash as they wanted, citing the limitations of the mail because of cash-sniffing dogs.

So this was what my dad was doing: he collected cash on his "errands."

I knew, almost for sure, that this had never happened before. We'd never sat on a trove of cash. There'd been too many days in a row when Emma and I had eaten spaghetti while my parents looked on. So who was funneling it to him? The person who set up this house?

I heard a door slam and the accompanying shutter of single-pane windows. I dropped the lid, turned off the light, closed the closet door, then the bedroom door, and scurried to my room.

Thirty seconds later, I sauntered out and entered the kitchen. My dad was sweaty, and Emma, still wearing a bike helmet, was unloading library books from my dad's old blue knapsack. So many of the books had ballerinas on the cover. I'd been hoping she'd let her interest in dance go.

"Poppy! Dad's teaching me how to ride a bike!" Emma gave me a triumphant grin.

It was about time. He'd taught me when I was much younger than Emma. I had a flash of memory—my mom watching from a window of a small house. She'd had a hand shielding her eyes, like she couldn't bear to look. I remembered my dad saying, *Don't look at the window. Look ahead. Even if I'm not holding on, I've got you, Pops.*

"Dad?" At the memory, after the scary time alone at the house this afternoon, I wanted to be hugged by my dad. To feel the way I had when I was young and he was everything I needed in my small world.

But my dad was distracted, looking past me.

"Where's the car?" he asked.

The sky darkened. The three of us ate a dinner of tasteless macaroni and cheese. We were on edge, waiting for the groan and clack of the garage door.

"Emma, shouldn't you take a bath?" I asked around 9 P.M. My dad wasn't paying attention. He stood at the window, having moved aside the curtain two inches to peer into the night. Even Emma didn't dare talk to him. I imagined his eyes trained on the same spot: the end of the driveway, waiting for the sweep of headlights.

"*You* take a bath."

"Emma," I warned, lowering my voice, not wanting to interfere with my dad's concentration.

It had been hours. Where the hell was she?

"Emma, go take a bath," my dad said a full minute later. He faced us. Did he know where she may have gone? I scanned his expression, which revealed nothing. That in itself was more revealing than anything else. He was in tactical mode now. Would she get caught? Should we pack bags? Should we grab our one item? Would the sweep of headlights be police instead of my mom?

She had the car. What were we supposed to do? Take off on foot? Find a bicycle built for three?

That my dad of all people found himself in this position told me my mom must have had an incredibly compelling reason to take this risk. I wanted to believe that, instead of my other thought—that maybe she had left us.

My hands were shaking as I started the bath for Emma. While Emma was in the tub, should I pack her clothes? I was fine with taking very little, but Emma would need some comforts to get her through. I would take one thing, though: the poppy painting.

CGhumming. I briefly wondered if she was nearby and if I'd be leaving her behind, too.

"I bet I know where Mom is," Emma said. She was sitting in the tub, her skin bright pink, too pink. I felt the water. It was far too hot, but Emma was withstanding it. I quickly twisted the cold faucet and water shot into the tub.

"Where?"

"The hospital."

I thought I'd heard wrong. The water was so loud. I didn't turn it off, though, because it masked our voices. I kneeled closer to the cast-iron tub. Now I could see the secret in Emma's eyes that she was so happy to share. She knew something I didn't.

"Where?" I asked. "What do you mean?"

"She wanted the car and Dad said, 'No, that's insane.' She kept saying she'd stay very, very far away. She told Dad she has to be there. That 'he'll know I'm close by.'"

What the hell?

Emma slipped under the water to her shoulders. She was loving this power.

"How do you know this?"

"How do you think?" Emma asked, like I was stupid. Again, she surprised me with that too-adult voice that seemed to come from a different Emma. Like her babyishness was only her cover.

"I have no idea," I said.

"They thought I was napping. You were away. You're always gone," Emma said.

"Do you know who's in the hospital?" I asked. Who was *he*? *He'll know I'm close by*, Emma had said.

"No. Just *he* or *him*. They said it over and over again."

When I turned off the water, I heard voices down the hall.

"Shhhh." I put my finger to my lips and cracked the bathroom door. I couldn't see my parents, but I could hear them. I turned my ear to the opening.

My mom was bawling. Hysterically.

"*Please.* You have to go."

My dad was shushing her.

"You *have* to."

"You know I can't," my dad said. His voice was calm and reasonable. Whatever had happened, he wasn't punishing my mother. He felt bad for her.

"They're all there. That means it's the end. You of all people could figure out how to get in."

"You know I can't," my dad said sadly.

"Oh my god," she said. "He won't know."

"He knows."

"Please." I heard my mother begging from the bottom of her heart. "I'm asking you for this one thing."

"I can't," he said simply.

What she'd asked had been too much.

"The kids come first," he said. *Above you and what you want,* I filled in the blank. "I'm not taking that kind of risk. Even for you. My kids are everything."

My mom heaved a sob full of grief. Then her cries were muffled as she let them go against my father's shoulder.

CHAPTER THIRTY-TWO

'd been biding my time until I could go to the public library to use a computer. When I woke up on Saturday morning and my dad wasn't home, I saw it as my chance and used Emma as my cover, even though my dad had been refusing my offers to take her to the library recently.

On a weekend morning, it was sparsely populated except for a few elementary-age kids who'd come for the activity "Reading with Sandy!"—Sandy being a merle-colored Bernedoodle therapy dog.

"You good?" I asked Emma as she settled on a soft carpet next to three other eager children. Emma's blond hair was beginning to grow out of the hackish, pixie haircut my mom had given her early in our stay. The journey to California felt like a lifetime ago. Emma appeared like any other ordinary kid. She was intent on stroking the nonplussed dog's fur, intentionally ignoring me like she had been since I'd scolded her for running across the parking lot.

Once I could leave Emma, I beelined to the computers like I was running to a finish line, catching the edge of the carpet and nearly tripping into the small bank of desks.

Immediately, I typed in "Carol G Humming."

Then "Carol Humming."

Then I tried "CGhumming" again.

I saw the Pinterest result, but now I saw that CGhumming appeared in one other place—on offerup.com. The website said BUY AND SELL LOCALLY. I clicked on the post.

There it was. A screen name: CAROL GILBERT. Now I had a last name.

My hands paused over the keyboard. The post offered a free treadmill for pickup in San Francisco. I quickly clicked on LEARN MORE ABOUT THE PICKUP, but the link was now dead.

Carol Gilbert, Carol Gilbert. At least it was a clue to follow.

She lived in the area.

I searched "Carol Gilbert, San Francisco."

There were three.

"Emily!"

I jolted upright, audibly gasping when I heard the voice. It was Erin, a friend of Rebecca's from the club, standing three feet away, acting like she hadn't seen me in a decade instead of only yesterday. She was so expectant, I had no choice but to stand and enter her embrace.

"We're going to miss you!" Erin said. Then her daughter, Eve, who was Frank's best friend, attacked my legs and pulled me by the hand over to the big sweet dog, now lying patiently on her side.

It was almost impossible to contain my resentment. But I

did. I smiled while I knelt next to Eve by Sandy's tail. *Why do I always have to be nice?* Why did I have to go along with whatever everyone wanted me to do?

Erin pulled up a chair and took her phone out of her purse, knowing there was now another pair of eyes on Eve. When Eve scrambled into my lap, Emma gave her a small kick when she thought no one was looking. Eve was so tough, she didn't even notice. But Emma saw me notice. I narrowed my eyes at her in warning. She buried her face in Sandy's fur. I felt slightly bad for her, knowing she was jealous of the attention I was giving Eve.

I looked longingly past the group of kids on the carpet to the computer, which had my search results sitting out for anyone to see. Not that there was much there. Just three listings for a common name.

I silently let out every expletive I could think of.

It was Emma's turn to read to the dog.

There were some *ooh*s and *ahh*s, and I heard a "How old is she?" Emma was reading in such a show-off voice, knowing she was reading far above grade level. I leaned down to see the cover of the book: *The Phantom Tollbooth.*

Emma was eating up the attention over her brilliance. But more than being annoyed, I had the surprise emotion of being sorry for Emma. It was much simpler when she was a sweet baby whose only need was us. It was hard being understimulated, easy to get depressed. I knew that from experience. All the days felt the same.

Someone's stare pulled at me. I glanced up. My dad hovered in the entryway of the small library, not wanting to take off his sunglasses or come all the way in. I gave him a quick nod.

That was too close of a call: I'd had no idea he was coming. Emma and I had walked and I'd assumed we'd make our own way home. I hadn't been looking out for my dad when I was on the computer. Now it mattered that the results were on the screen.

I saw that Emma had half of a dense page left until the chapter's end. I surreptitiously held my finger up to my dad: *one minute.* Erin happened to look up from her phone and over to where my dad was standing. An *Oh!* expression lit her face, putting two and two together that this relatively young, handsome man was my father.

My dad must have seen this woman's look of recognition that he belonged to us, because he backed away and slipped out the door. It was almost uncanny how quickly he could disappear.

"Sis, we have to go," I interrupted, as Emma began the next chapter. I couldn't risk him coming back inside.

The next child happily dove into reading to the dog, leaving Emma no choice but to follow my lead. She wasn't there to listen to anyone else, anyway. Trying not to create too much of a disruption, I gave Eve a kiss on the top of her head and set her on the carpet. With a few whispered, empty promises to see her again soon, I said goodbye to Erin and led Emma by the wrist to the parking lot. We loaded into the minivan parked tightly among other SUVs. Once my dad started the car, I'd breathe again.

"Hey, girls. Thought you might like a ride," my dad said.

"We literally just got there," Emma complained.

"That's what happens when you walk so slowly," I snapped.

Both my dad and Emma stilled, unused to hearing me lose my cool. "Sorry," I muttered.

The minivan pulled away from the library, my search interrupted. I tipped my head back against the seat and closed my eyes.

"Sorry, Em. I wanted to have lunch with you guys," my dad was saying. We hadn't seen him yet today. He'd left before dawn. But it wasn't like he'd been away for a week.

My dad seemed to be holding me and Emma closer since my mom's breakdown. My mom was behaving like she'd woken up and wanted to be with us again, as if my dad's gentle comment about choosing us had been a slap across her face, snapping her out of it. She'd abruptly stopped leaving the house.

But I was in a totally different headspace than my parents were. All I kept thinking was if I could just untangle myself from them, from all of the restrictions, I could find Carol Gilbert. It was shocking seeing that information on Harry's phone, but now I really wanted to know who she was. I wanted to know my family history. I'd been craving it my whole life. And now I potentially had a way to do it. Safely. From a distance.

I needed time and I needed access.

CHAPTER THIRTY-THREE

On Monday, Harry dashed into the classroom late. "Sorry. I got pulled over," he mumbled to Professor Alexiev. Possibly a made-up excuse to avoid me again. He was wearing a long-sleeved white T-shirt from a surfboard company, which made his shoulders look broad and his chest concave, like it hadn't gotten the memo that it was time to fill out.

At the end of class, Professor Alexiev asked me to wait, then lifted a heavy book from her satchel. "I brought this for you," she said. "Focus on Algebra Two for the test. Take care of it, okay? It's my only copy."

The heavy book bent back her palm. I took the book before she dropped it, but I tried to hand it right back. "I shouldn't take it. We're moving houses. I don't want it to get lost in the shuffle." There was always the chance we'd leave suddenly and I wouldn't be able to return her book.

She looked at me steadily. "Take it." Then, "Please."

The book was worn. It might have been one of her own personal textbooks. I opened my mouth to say thank you, but Professor Alexiev was already heading to the front of the classroom.

For once, Harry was still seated next to me instead of exiting at the first opportunity. Even after helping me with the DNA website, he hadn't said two words to me today, so I'd assumed we'd gone back to the new normal.

"You're moving?" he asked.

"We move around a lot," I said quickly, keeping it nonchalant.

"Out of town?" Harry seemed irritated. Or concerned. I couldn't tell.

I shrugged. It was better than lying.

He nodded to himself a few times, like he was digesting this information. Harry didn't say anything more. He just stood up from his desk and, all limbs, swiftly exited, easily parting the sea of genetics students.

As usual, I was disappointed when he was gone.

The computer screen reflected the fluorescent lighting. Two librarians sat on the floor of the ghost-town library, conducting a summer inventory. I wasn't sure they'd seen me come in or if the school library was even open, but I'd realized it was another place I could get online. My parents thought I was babysitting.

With the doors closed, the library felt sealed up like a tomb, leaving me in cool privacy to search for Carol Gilbert.

Three Carol Gilberts lived in San Francisco, and the online

white pages listed a mind-boggling amount of information: previous residences, relatives, ages. If you paid, you could see driving records, any court records or bankruptcy records.

There was so much information available I didn't know where to start.

I clicked on the Carol Gilbert listed first. Age fifty-seven, she lived in South San Francisco. She had two traffic records, two cell-phone numbers. I searched "Carol Gilbert, South San Francisco." There was a hit on Instagram.

This Carol Gilbert had a sandy-blond bob and was holding up a miniature poodle in her profile photo. Her job was listed as graphic designer.

I squinted at the screen. Did she look like my dad, maybe? If she was twenty years older than he was—I guessed since I didn't really know his exact age—how could she be related to him?

I scrolled through her few Instagram posts quickly. I was unsure of what to look for. I saw photos of Carol Gilbert's children, the family gathered around Carol, who held up a Mother's Day card. There was one of Carol in front of a snowy mountain peak. Also, lots of food photography.

I decided to quickly cover my bases, so I moved on to the next Carol Gilbert, San Francisco, age twenty-nine, related to Honey Gilbert. Thinking Honey might be easier to find, I googled "Honey Gilbert." A beekeeping business came up.

I sighed heavily, catching the attention of one of the librarians. For a moment, I wondered if they could help me if I had a specific research question, but I couldn't ask. I wasn't sure what my plan had been to begin with. I'd never had one.

"Sweetheart, the library's closed for inventory."

Both librarians watched me now, waiting for me to leave, forcing me to be done for today. I was suddenly, irrationally angry and wildly frustrated. "Oh. Okay. Sorry about that!" I said, ever polite. But for a moment I stared mutinously at the screen, at the link to the last Carol Gilbert, her white-pages phone number listed beside. I wished I'd moved a little faster.

"You on your way?"

"Yes. I'm going."

I committed the phone number to memory and then I cleared the search.

I felt incomplete without a full search on the last Carol Gilbert, but what was I supposed to do? I moved through the school parking lot toward the opening in the fence, near the mailbox where this search had all started. What was I really going to find, anyway? For all the information at my fingertips, I didn't even know what bread crumbs to follow. It would take hours of going down rabbit holes to find . . . what? How would I even recognize a clue?

I was almost next to Harry's car before I noticed it.

His driver's side door was ajar, and I saw one of his Van-clad feet resting on the floorboard. He must have seen me in his side mirror, because both feet dropped to the ground.

Harry closed the car door and leaned one shoulder against the paint. "Hey."

"Hi?" I still hadn't surfaced from the cloud of my search. I saw his cracked phone in his hand, and the idea left my mouth even as it was forming. "Do you mind if I borrow your phone? Just for a second."

I'd knocked him off his game. Harry looked surprised, but he straightened and stretched long to wordlessly hand me his phone.

"Thanks. This will just take a second." I couldn't believe I'd asked Harry for this favor. I wandered a distance away. I wasn't done with the third Carol Gilbert.

Harry had been on his Instagram account when I took his phone. I saw skateboarding photos. That was it. No captions. Nothing personal. Still, he had eight thousand followers.

I dialed the number I'd committed to memory, then brought the phone to my cheek.

"Hello?" It was a woman's voice.

"Hi. I'm looking for Carol Gilbert?" What questions could I even ask her? If she was related to a criminal runaway from eighteen years ago? I just wanted to hear her voice, which was silly. I wouldn't be able to tell a thing from the sound of someone's voice.

"This is Carol."

A pregnant pause stretched between us.

"Hello?" Carol said again.

I stayed silent. *Hang up, Poppy.*

"Hello?"

I was lowering the phone from my ear, about to end the call, when Carol Gilbert dropped her voice and whispered, "*Are you still there?*"

It was the conspiratorial tone of her voice. Hairs rose on the back of my neck. I stabbed at the phone to end the call.

Maybe she'd thought I was someone else. Maybe Carol had just wanted to know what the hell I wanted and that was why she'd stayed on the line.

Why had that felt strange?

Harry was watching me, hands shoved into the pockets of his jeans.

I was still invisible, I reminded myself. Everything was okay.

I handed Harry his phone. "Thanks for that," I said. My voice came out hoarse.

"You okay?"

"Yep. All good." Why was Harry still at the school? Had he been waiting for me?

"You're moving?" He stared at the ground before looking up and squinting at me.

"We always move."

Harry crossed his arms over his chest almost defensively, fingertips tucked tightly beneath his armpits. "When did you say you moved to California?"

"Just recently."

"Like when?"

I gave him a look like *What's your problem?*

"Can you tell me when you're moving?"

"I don't know. Soon, I'm sure."

Harry exhaled loudly. Like he was frustrated.

"What?" I asked. *Why do you care?*

"Can I drive you to babysitting?" Harry shoved the long sleeves of his white T-shirt to his elbows.

"No—" I was about to say more but stopped, fascinated by Harry's reaction. He widened his eyes and stared at the ground.

"No, you don't want a ride?" Harry was maybe embarrassed but sounded pissed off. It took everything for him to raise his eyes to meet mine.

"No, babysitting is over," I explained. "Their nanny came back."

"You need to go straight home, then?" Harry squinted at me and shoved his hands deep in his pockets again, his shoulders lifting to his ears.

I hesitated. "I forgot to tell my parents. They think I'm still babysitting."

"So, you have hours?" Harry said.

Was he asking me out? "I should help out with my sister." It would be a joke to any other person I knew. They would choose what they wanted over their family and chores.

"How often do you get free time? Maybe I'm misunderstanding, but they won't let you out except for babysitting and this class, right?"

Harry's gaze dropped to my lips, and I realized I was biting my lower lip hard.

"Why are you suddenly talking to me now, Harry?"

"Just—" Harry stared over my shoulder. "Can I take you to the beach? I know you said you wanted to go . . ."

"What about your job?"

"I was supposed to be at a funeral today with my mom. But then I didn't end up going. Come on. It's your chance, Poppy. Why do I feel like you don't get many of them?" he asked.

I really wanted to go to the beach. I also wanted to hear what the hell Harry could possibly have to say to me. I knew it was weak—I shouldn't want that after he'd mostly ignored me for days.

I was torn. Choosing myself over my family never ended well. I'd never been that physically far away from them before. I was about to say no when Harry said, "Please?"

It was so vulnerable, so un-Harry. "It's okay," I said quietly, almost to myself.

Harry prompted, "Like, no, it's okay, you're not coming with me?"

"No. What I meant is, it's okay. Just for today." I sounded like I was reassuring myself. If I was honest with myself, I had started lying to my parents, bit by bit, when I'd accepted Harry's rides and then a lot that day at Harry's house and on the Fourth of July.

I saw Harry try not to smile. I'd just made him happy.

It was wrong and I was almost ashamed, but there was nothing I'd ever experienced like the rush I felt at the prospect of time with Harry—a clear stretch of it ahead.

CHAPTER THIRTY-FOUR

We drove up, up, up, on curvy switchback-style roads, entering a new dark and foggy microclimate enclosed by California redwoods. A motorcycle passed us, the woman on the back holding tightly to the driver, who wore a red bandana. Maggie Rogers was on the stereo—so Harry had told me when I'd asked.

He played the music loud enough that we couldn't talk. It could end up being a field trip where we barely spoke. But I refused to be the one to open up first.

At one point, as we climbed the tight, curvy roads, Harry asked me if I felt okay, if I was getting carsick. I just shook my head, indicating I was fine. I wanted to tell him I was too busy to feel sick, that I was taking in the scenery. It looked straight out of a storybook.

There was a brief clearing in the woods allowing rays of sun to slant through. Just as we passed a rundown café teeming with motorcycles parked out front, Harry abruptly turned off the music.

"I just wanted to make sure you know my dad isn't physically abusive."

I looked over at him in surprise. Was this why he'd asked me to come with him, so he could clear things up? Was he worried about what I thought? Or just about what information might get out?

"These bruises are from skateboarding, not him. Skateboarding is where I can pound it out. Sometimes I go overboard, I know."

I remembered watching Harry skate, and a moment when he seemed to leave his body and not react to pain.

Harry kept his eyes on the road. "I'm sorry for the way I've acted. I got a lecture from my dad about not embarrassing him or my mother this summer. I'm supposed to work and go to school. It's just a tense time. Obviously, it's not worth it to fuck it up. You saw that," he added.

He'd finally referred to what happened.

"I'm fucking it up?"

"You're a girl. I don't have a good track record lately."

"Is it because I'm a girl who's not from a good family? Who's already approved?"

"I don't care about that," Harry scoffed.

"You do, Harry."

"Look, I'm supposed to stay quiet this summer. If my dad's not happy, it's not quiet."

"Okay, then." The hugest lump filled my throat. I looked out my side of the car.

"Poppy."

"What?"

Harry hesitated for so long, I didn't think he would say more. Then words began pouring out.

"Only my cousin has seen the worst once. He saw me on my hands and knees picking through the carpet to clean it, per my dad's orders." Harry kept his voice neutral. "But my cousin was a witness on the inside. You're the first real outsider. My dad usually hides his psychosis in front of strangers. But it's why I don't like to invite friends over."

Harry drew a breath and tightened one hand on the steering wheel, dropping the other to his lap. "I've heard all the excuses: *It's only when he's off his medication. He's the son of an alcoholic drill sergeant.* And the worst one: *But he's brilliant.* Well, he might be a genius, but he is for sure a miserable dick."

It was true. All I'd ever seen online was great press—Robert Addison's company, his philanthropy. Even Professor Alexiev seemed to have a good impression and had referred to him deferentially as her "boss."

"Your mom knows?" I asked evenly. I wanted to let him know I was listening closely and I wasn't scared or judgmental, but I didn't want him to think I felt sorry for him. Even though I did.

Harry nodded. "My mom moved us out in the middle of the night when I was five, because his"—Harry held up one hand in an air quote—"'control issues' got out of hand. But sometimes, when I was younger, she'd give in to needing his help and she'd send me back to the lion's den. I tried to forgive her for it. This summer I was all too willing to accept the punishment of living with him. My mom said she wasn't mad at me for the bad press and embarrassment, but she wasn't that convincing. And she was grateful to my dad for quickly settling the lawsuit. He always asks for me. So, she gave him back his son for the summer."

"Ugh, Harry. I'm sorry." I couldn't help it. I had to say it. I was sorry for him.

Harry gave a small shake of his head. "I'm okay. I just want to explain."

I didn't want to scare him off. I pretended to adjust the knot on my blouse above the top of my jeans. "How often is he like that?"

"He's been bad this summer. Like maybe he's gone off some medication. He finds ways to catch up with me and tell me my faults, how I've earned nothing. But, I mean, he's right. When my shitty friends clapped me on the back because of those naked photos, deep down I was so sorry it had happened and that I'd upset my mom. I was suddenly—maybe I've always been— sick of myself. I knew I could have anything I wanted—drugs, girlfriends, vacations, admission to any school. Maybe when I was fourteen, fifteen, that was exciting, but now it's just . . ." Harry shrugged and trailed off.

"So, this summer, I've tried to stay in my lane, keep my head down, take this math class because my dad thought it would give me that extra edge for Stanford, just in case his name doesn't do the trick. Then I walked in and took a seat next to you, who, like everyone else, stared too hard and too long. I was like, *Who is this girl who won't stop looking at me? Do I have something on my face?*"

I laughed. "I didn't stare!"

For a second, his eyes sparkled. "Yes, you did. But pretty

soon I began to think of you as my ally in the back of the class. It was us and then everyone else. Me and the freckled girl with French braids who I couldn't place." Harry's smile fell away. "First, it was easy to tell you were genuinely nice. And brilliant. It's pretty heartbreaking to watch how your brain works. You're so quick and you don't miss a moment of what's being taught, but then you get lost. I see you going inward, being so hard on yourself, and thinking *Why don't I know this?*"

Now my smile fell and I wanted to melt away into the redwood forest.

"When I found out you were homeschooled, and I listened in on your conversation with Professor Alexiev, I knew how badly you wanted to stay in the class and how frustrated you were that you couldn't keep up. I was worried. I imagined you trying to get out from under controlling parents like me and I wanted to throw you a line. I knew my dad's company had that internship. That Allison from class now has."

I half-laughed, trying to keep things light, but I wished he would stop talking about his impression of me.

Harry nervously flipped the console up and down a few times. "I've been thinking I need to distance myself. That it doesn't matter how soft your voice is or how you become more and more gorgeous every single day, how sexy you are with your summer tan and even darker freckles." Surprised, I looked over at him. "How you're so multilayered and textured and smart. And how you seem to just get it. To get me. And how fucking lonely everything can be when you make yourself unknowable."

My eyes welled up. What he'd said was so nice. And he was right—I did get it. I knew the loneliness. I knew exactly.

Harry shifted in his seat. "I know you don't want to hear it, but everything about you makes me want to keep you safe. When you said those words about bad things happening in families? It made *me* feel safe. But how's it going to work, Poppy? I don't know if you still want to be with me after the way I've acted. And after what you saw. And know. I'm fucked up," he said.

"You have no idea how fucked up *I* am," I said. An unexpected tear slid from the corner of my eye.

"I'm sorry you saw my dad like that. The sight of me has been setting him off all summer."

"It's not your fault, Harry."

"Why does it feel like it?"

"That's the shitty thing about shame," I said.

At that, Harry looked exhausted but so much lighter. As he'd spoken, a weight seemed to come off him, his secret easing off his shoulders. It was a beautiful thing to see. It must have taken so much to expose your deepest shame and then say what Harry did next.

"It's never worked out when I've gotten close to people. Still, I really want this." He looked at me, finally.

At that moment, the car crested the tree line and plateaued. The Pacific Ocean stretched to infinity.

CHAPTER THIRTY-FIVE

The Pacific was a gray-blue, and the beach was quiet and pristine. I saw four surfers in wet suits, two older women strolling the long expanse of state beach, and a couple about our age as they ventured into the water to their shins. Harry and I stared out at the powerful waves, the couple getting sprayed and laughing with surprise, then glee.

Am I really here? For years—while living in the crappiest apartments with leaking roofs, skittering roaches, and broken heaters—I'd stared at my mother's painting of the ocean. I remembered arriving at one dirty apartment, sitting on the very edge of a ripped-up sofa, afraid but holding it in. I'd looked to the painting for some kind of hope. Now here I was. It felt like I'd finally arrived. That inexplicable feeling that I'd come home.

"Why is the beach so empty?" I asked.

"It's the middle of the day on a Monday. And Northern

California surf is rougher and colder than Southern California's. I used to go to boogie-boarding camp in Malibu."

"Of course you did," I teased.

"Yeah, yeah." Harry got a little embarrassed. I was reminded that he wasn't who I'd thought he was. Before, it was thrilling enough that he was interested in me, that he'd made my birthday special before things went off the rails. But part of my old impression of him had stuck with me: that he was shallow because he could afford to be, that I was summer entertainment, that he would move on to the next thing soon. Maybe because of that, I'd thought he was safe. I'd labeled him as my infatuation, too cool for me, a rich kid with fine everything: fine features, clothes, stuff.

But I had never shaken the feeling that I couldn't quite pinpoint him. And he had kept surprising me. He was more broken than I could have guessed, but also deeper and far more kind. Still playing in my mind was his surprising vulnerability in the car.

Wind whipped through my hair. I grabbed it into a ponytail, then held on to it with one hand.

"You cold?" Harry asked.

"Only a little."

I was surprised when, in response, Harry moved behind me and slowly enveloped me in his arms, like he was giving me plenty of opportunity to say no. He was scared that I'd changed my mind about him. But when I leaned back against him, I felt his muscles relax. He was relieved I still wanted him to touch me after I'd seen a part of him kept carefully hidden.

The two older women passed us on their walk and one of

them smiled. "God, what was it like to be that young?" I over-heard her say to her friend.

"Heaven."

My shirt came off and I was sitting in Harry's front seat in a bra and skirt. We'd escaped the cold wind and we needed to start driving back. But one thing had led to another and well . . .

Harry's shirt came off, too.

"No one can see us. These windows have tinting," he said.

"But I can sometimes see you when you drive away."

"Shhhh," Harry murmured against my lips, laughing.

I pulled away and scanned the parking lot. There were only two other cars and an honor-system pay station made of splin-tering wood.

"One more minute and then we *have* to go," I said. I reached for him again, wanting the skin-to-skin contact. The way Harry kissed me now seemed different. Almost more inti-mate rather than just dazzling me with his skills.

I ran my palms down his chest, feeling the delineation of the six-pack on his stomach with my fingertips. "How do you have so much muscle? You're so skinny!"

"That tickles. I don't know," Harry said, catching my hands when they moved to his sides, over his jutting ribs.

I could not stop touching Harry. I was so attracted to him. Not only when I was half-naked with him. Always. Sitting next to him in summer school, in the car, watching him tear into the classroom late.

"You're so pale here. You even have freckles on your chest," Harry said and leaned back to look.

"Stop staring!" I was only sort of joking.

"Why? I love it. I love you," he said.

I wasn't sure I'd heard right. Before I could react, Harry's lips were on mine and he was kissing me intensely to distract from what he'd accidentally said. He didn't mean it. He'd been talking about how I looked.

But even in the one hour since Harry had told me about his family, he seemed happier, more fully himself because he'd let go of his secret.

I'd had a lot of time to think about what it takes to keep a secret. You have to suppress parts of yourself. You have to compartmentalize in order to keep a secret safe.

Witnessing Harry's happiness made me wish I could let go and be myself, too.

Harry stroked my knee while he drove on the freeway home, avoiding the curvy roads.

I scooted closer. My shirt was unbuttoned a button too low, the hem of my denim skirt was a few inches too high, and Harry's hand traced over the bare skin. My hair was tangled from the wind and loose around my shoulders. In the side mirror, I saw that it had lightened and reddened to a strawberry blond.

It's okay, I told myself. *Enjoy your time with him while you can.*

"What are you doing after this?" I asked.

"Skate park," Harry said decisively. "It's better if I go."

"What do you mean?"

"I stay out late. Stay out of the way. And I go insane if I don't skate."

"Because you love it that much?"

Harry didn't even skip a beat. "That, and I need it."

"You need it?"

"I feel free. I have some control. I don't know, that's where I get calm."

"You also get hurt a lot," I said.

"But I love it," Harry said.

Like you love your dad, I thought. *And he also hurts you.* I'd seen the magazine clipping of his father taped above Harry's computer. Whether or not he said it, Harry was proud.

"You can love and hate the same thing. Sometimes at the same time," I said, worrying for Harry.

Harry's eyes became guarded, knowing from my tone exactly what I was suddenly referring to. "You sound like you're speaking from experience."

"What?"

"You're not pissed off?" Harry asked.

"About what?" I edged my shoulder closer to my window.

"That you don't have any freedom? Look, we have to get you home by four o'clock. The look in your eyes when you tell me that, I don't mess with it. I know you mean it."

I didn't have a response. I inhaled long, relieved at the cool air circulating through Harry's car.

I hadn't been talking about myself.

Then why, in my heart, did I so completely understand Harry's complicated emotions?

CHAPTER THIRTY-SIX

P oppy? This Friday? After class, I have time to meet," Professor Alexiev said, looming over me and consulting the calendar on her phone.

I'd thought the promised meeting had slipped Professor Alexiev's mind, and I'd been a little sad about it. When we'd sat down to discuss my assessment, she'd mentioned discussing what classes I could take after ours ended. It was all for nothing, but I was excited for her extra attention. I liked seeing myself through Professor Alexiev's eyes, hearing what she thought I was capable of.

"Yes!" I said a little too enthusiastically. So much for acting cool about it.

"Wait, why are you meeting with Professor Alexiev? Didn't you already have your conference?" a kid named Cliff asked. Harry gestured with a tilt of his head that he'd meet me outside. The next three hours were ours.

"We're going over some things?" I said, not sure how to answer. Cliff looked from me to the professor's back, wondering how he could get an extra meeting. Harry had told me how so many kids and their parents were after a teacher recommendation from Professor Alexiev for college applications. They believed that a recommendation from her would help differentiate them from the competition. I was on the outskirts, but over the past weeks, I grasped the pressure my classmates felt. The scent of overachieving was practically in the air.

Outside the classroom, I saw Harry sitting crisscross-style on the lawn and laughing to himself at something on his phone. When he laughed, his entire body shook and his eyes sparkled, even at the dumbest things.

"What was up with Cliff?" Harry asked. He grabbed my hand in full sight of the rest of the class as they trickled out of the room. Harry had been doing that today—acting far more affectionate in public.

"Oh, he's wondering why I get extra time with Professor Alexiev on Friday."

"You're going over test stuff?" Harry asked.

"I don't know. She mentioned advising me on what I need to complete in order to apply to colleges. Since I don't have all my grades because of homeschooling."

Harry looked at me. "Wait, you don't?"

"Don't what?"

"I guess I thought you were doing some master homeschooling program that colleges accept."

"It's a little more haphazard than that."

"But you know a lot of math, so it's not that haphazard.

Are you mostly self-taught, then?" Harry was distracted by his phone buzzing and pulled it from his pocket to check.

"I've been to some schools."

Harry replaced his phone in his pocket. "You never told me that. Where?"

"It doesn't matter."

"It does! I want to know you better." Harry walked backward a few steps, facing me. He caught my waist to stop me, then leaned in. I gently held his cheekbones with my fingertips while we kissed right in front of the school entrance.

A shadow passed over us as someone walked by. Harry pulled back.

It was Allison from class. Her eyes were wide from witnessing Harry's and my make-out session. Harry surprised me by giving a little smirk, then moving in to continue the kiss.

"I thought you wanted to be secret about this."

Harry simply shrugged one shoulder.

"You'll get me back on time?" I asked Harry.

"Have we been late yet?"

"Almost," I said. My foot was tapping incessantly, my knee bouncing up and down. I didn't even realize until Harry placed a hand on my knee to still it, then intertwined his fingers with mine.

Harry said he was starving so he wanted to take me to a café where I could "work" and he could eat. My continuously aborted search for Carol was hanging over me.

I'd been close to letting it go. It was beyond stressful. Also, leading nowhere.

But then, before I'd left for class that morning, my dad asked to see my phone. I'd obediently handed it over, biting my tongue. He'd scrolled through, then handed it back to me without a word of explanation. In a way that made me feel . . . helpless.

"Your hand is ice-cold. I can turn off the AC." At a stoplight, Harry turned down the air, then enclosed my hand in both of his to warm it up.

It was weird how my body seemed to register my uneasiness about the search before my mind. I felt fine, but my hands were cold and I could feel my pulse in the backs of my legs.

"I saw your family that day," Harry was saying. "They seemed nice. I mean, that was your dad, right? With your sister on the back of his bike?"

I'd been worried about my dad seeing Harry. I hadn't given much thought to what Harry saw. I assumed he'd driven off, uninterested in my family.

"That was your dad, right?" Harry asked again.

"Yeah."

"What's his job? I mean, it's cool that he's free in the middle of the day to pick you up and to ride around with your sister. Did he sell a company or cash out his options like seemingly everyone else who lives around here?"

I settled on: "He has a pretty flexible schedule," hoping that would end it.

But Harry kept talking. And talking. He'd told me earlier that he was hungry because he'd forgotten to take his ADD meds that morning. "It was nice. Your dad was so happy to see you. He looked proud of you. And he looked psyched to be a dad and looking after your sister in the middle of the day. Damn, he's in great shape and about a million years younger than my dad. You run together, right?"

"Uh-huh," I said, fiddling with the air vent.

"Well, he seemed really cool and normal. I imagined this oppressive dude with all of your rules, but you looked excited to see him. It was nice how your dad got off the bike so he could walk next to you. And your sister was sitting on the seat in the back and singing. You guys could have been a portrait from the seventies with that old bike." Harry smiled to himself, and I thought he was off the subject when he turned his head to glance at the juice bar on the corner. But then he asked, "He's your real dad?"

"What?"

"I mean, the DNA test. I just thought maybe . . ."

I didn't answer, hoping Harry would get the message and back off. Harry was asking more questions. Like he'd said— wanting to know me better.

I'd been hurt when Harry said he preferred to keep things secret and low-key. But in hindsight, that made sense. Harry had wanted to protect himself. Keeping things casual was where he felt okay. In Harry's experience, trust equaled pain. That was the case in his relationship with his father, with the girl he had recently dated. Even to a lesser extent with his mother, when she left him to fend for himself with his dad.

I felt myself falling for Harry all over again when I realized how big a deal it was that he was letting me in and trusting me. Me of all people. The one person who would never be honest with him.

The thing about our agreement . . . it had worked for me too. Now Harry was holding my hand in public, and today he'd kissed me out in the open.

A darker, more mature part of me was beginning to sound warning bells. Harry was making me nervous with his questions. It was a problem that he wanted more.

CHAPTER THIRTY-SEVEN

Without a word, Harry slid his laptop across the small round table in the café. It was the lunch rush and the place was packed. I looked longingly outdoors at the fountain, dogs tied beneath tables, children meandering with food in hand. Harry had planted us in a corner inside and I hadn't spoken up.

"I'm buying you lunch. What do you want?" Harry asked directly, nonchalantly, as if we always went to restaurants together.

"No. Let me buy you lunch. As thanks for letting me use your laptop," I said quickly, shaking my head.

"Some other time. I'll get in line. You probably want to get started on your research. The passcode is my birthday—1226. There's Wi-Fi here. What do you want to eat?"

I looked at the slate menu board and couldn't even focus. "That's nice of you. Surprise me. I like everything." Harry turned toward the line. "Harry," I called. "Thank you." He nodded and gave me a small smile.

I'd learned that every second I had by myself counted. I made sure Harry was in line and back on his phone, as usual, before I opened the laptop. It was so new, the hinge was stiff when I folded it back. I entered 1226. It took a moment to connect to the Wi-Fi, and then I was off. Alone with Carol Gilbert.

Finally, I could click on the third Carol Gilbert listed on the white pages.

Age: 75; Lives in: San Francisco; Related to: Joseph P. Connelly, Jr., Harold Gilbert, Julie Gilbert; Used to live in: Pacifica, Redwood City.

My heart drummed as my fingers hovered above the keyboard. Now what? Harry was talking on the phone and looking around outside the restaurant, searching for something. The line was still long ahead of him.

If Carol Gilbert was seventy-five, could this Carol Gilbert be my great-aunt? Or a cousin? For having a mathematical brain, I was confused by how we might fit together if she was the one.

I typed in one of her known relatives—"Joseph P. Connelly, Jr."—thinking maybe the name was more unique than Carol Gilbert. Mainly because I didn't know what to do next.

A short obituary came up. But for a Joseph P. Connelly, no "Jr."

Joseph P. Connelly, born at home in Manhattan on October 1, 1917, died peacefully at Sequoia Hospital in Redwood City on December 21, 2002. Joseph is preceded in death by his wife, Emma, and grandson, Joseph III. He is survived by his daughter Carol Gilbert (Harold Gilbert) of San Francisco, son Peter (Frances) of Hayward, and son Joseph Jr. (Maryann) of Redwood City, five grandchildren, and one great-grandchild on the way.

Emma. My sister's name.

It was probably a coincidence.

I scanned the long obituary, feeling like I was taking a left turn, a step too far away from Carol Gilbert.

Skimming the obituary, I learned that after a decorated military career, Joseph P. Connelly had moved with his wife, Emma, to the then-sleepy Northern California coastal town Pacifica. He began an electrician business carried on by his son, Joseph Jr., after the senior Joseph's retirement. *Blah, blah, blah.* I scanned through his volunteer work with veterans, his hobbies—deep-sea fishing and spending time with his grandchildren. I was about to click off when my eye caught on two words, deep in the text: Navy SEAL.

I slowed down, reading more carefully.

It was about Joseph's grandson, Joseph III. He had carried on his grandfather's commitment to military service, making his grandfather exceedingly proud. He'd just completed SEAL training before his untimely death.

Untimely death. That there was no elaboration made me curious. Wouldn't they have said if he died in the line of duty, serving his country?

My fingers flew, almost of their own accord. My body knew it before my mind. "Joseph Connelly III Pacifica." Enter.

I blinked. That was it. That was all the time it took for the computer to load a screen full of hits and a collage of images.

One of the images was my mother. She stared back at me. She looked like a girl. Maybe twenty years old.

She wore fatigues and posed with a rifle, a tiny, all-knowing smile on her face. The iconic San Francisco Coit Tower appeared in the background behind her.

"Poppy? There's someone I want you to meet."

No! In the split second between taking my eyes from the screen and meeting Harry's, I had to somehow not go insane.

"This is my mom."

In one motion, I closed the laptop, stood, and faced Harry's elegant mother, Maya Kumar, standing arm in arm with her son.

"I'm Maya," she said, leaning slightly forward while she grasped my hand in both of hers. She was so warm, a consummate politician, a pro at connecting.

"I'm Poppy. It's so nice to meet you." It was the oddest sensation—floating away from my body. From some distance above, I watched this other Poppy carry on.

"Here, Mom, take a seat."

I crashed back down. The story of my life was right in front of me, but I couldn't get to it.

Harry asked the table behind us if he could borrow an empty chair. He gestured for his mother to sit, wanting to make everything nice for her.

Harry's mom's voice was rich and smoky. "Thanks for your patience; I didn't know if I'd be able to make it. I was down the road at Apple, and after the service yesterday, I really wanted to see my son. But things always run long and . . ." Maya unwound a lightweight scarf from her neck.

"How was the service?" Harry asked.

"It was really sad," Maya said.

From seemingly out of nowhere, a young woman with a large leather tote over her shoulder took the scarf and handed Maya a cup of coffee. Maya nodded her thanks but otherwise, Harry and Maya ignored the assistant.

Harry scooted his chair as close to me as he could get and put his arm around me so we were facing his mother. It was like he was presenting me to her. He'd thoughtfully placed his mother's chair so her back was to the restaurant. A few people had noticed her, and an excited current was traveling through the restaurant.

"Sorry I didn't tell you my mom was coming. I wasn't sure she was going to be able to make it." Harry's eyes were doing their sparkly, dancing thing that happened when he was happy or exhilarated. So were his mother's. They were the exact same pretty eyes. Their fondness for each other was palpable.

"So, Poppy, you and Harry met in math class?" Her gaze was direct, making me feel like the only person in the room.

"That's right." I nodded, hoping the smile on my face was convincing. My eye was on the laptop, sitting like a bomb between us. I wanted to scream at everyone to leave me alone, to go away.

Meanwhile, Harry was in his own movie. It was suddenly clear to me why he wanted his mom to meet me: he wanted her approval. And I was perfect mom material. He'd met me in math class, not at some clothing-optional rooftop pool party.

In reality, I made his past girlfriends look awesome.

I was sitting across from a serious politician with the highest aspirations, and I had one parent quite possibly wanted in her state. The other was supposed to be dead. My mom with a rifle, San Francisco cityscape in the background. Joseph Connelly III, somehow tied to that young, young woman in the photo.

I shouldn't even be in Maya's presence.

"Harry, see, why did you resist summer school?" Maya joked, smiling at me.

"Um, because it's one more thing you guys are making me do so I'll get into an Ivy League school?" Harry joked back.

"But wasn't I right that you'd like it? Aren't I always right?" She laughed and threw an arm around the back of her chair, giving us the illusion that she had all the time in the world. Her silk blouse was peach colored and complemented her luxurious hair and glowing skin. I wondered what she was really like beneath the facade.

Harry pulled me closer, actually kissing my temple, branding me as his girlfriend in front of his mother. Maya appraised us, giving Harry an amazed look, but they carried on their joking banter about summer school.

"So, Poppy, tell me about your family. Do you have any siblings?"

"Yes. One sister," I heard myself say.

"Ahhh. Sisters are the best. I have one also. Older? Younger?"

"Younger."

"Much younger. Isn't she, like, eight?" Harry added.

I nodded. I saw a middle-aged couple taking photos of our

table with their phones. I quickly shifted left. I couldn't be in those pictures.

"That's quite a big age difference. Different marriages?" Maya stirred her iced coffee. Trails of cream swirled down the tall drink.

"Yes. Different marriages," I said.

"I thought you said you had the same parents," Harry said.

"Oh, what? Yes, sorry. Same marriage. Just a big gap." I picked up my water to sip. The ice cubes rattled. My hand was shaking.

Harry gave me a strange look.

"That's lovely. Your parents must love having a little one around the house."

"Unless she's having a tantrum or making them sleep with her," I said. I moved away from Harry and placed the laptop on top of my backpack, beneath the table.

"I forgot about those days. Harrison used to come to my room with his little bear every night for years and tell me his bear needed to sleep with me. Mr. Ruffles."

"Mr. Riffles," Harry said, slightly embarrassed.

Amazingly, I could feel that touch my heart. The rest of me felt numb.

"Then you saw your father's sleep-apnea mask and you never came back again!"

"That scared the shit out of me. I still remember. God, it feels like a long time ago when you two were married."

"Yeah, well. I had to give up so much, but I'm happy with where I landed." Maya glanced up. "I had to be my full self," she said, looking directly at me.

The assistant reappeared. Maya placed both hands on the table and stood. *Please leave,* I pleaded. I was having trouble with the shaking.

"Are you cold?" Harry asked me.

"Would you like my scarf?" Maya asked, holding it out to me.

"Oh, I'm fine. Thank you, though."

Maya rewound the delicate scarf around her neck. "Next up, Facebook. I'm so sorry to run. I had a funeral yesterday, so today's schedule is packed. Let's find a time for you to bring Poppy to the city."

"I thought you were campaigning nonstop for the rest of summer?" Harry said.

"It's tight, but we can figure something out. By the way, I need you on the twenty-fifth for a breakfast. It's the San Francisco Big Brothers Big Sisters of the Bay Area. Your new Little Brother will be there. I'll need the perfect son for two hours. Can you bring him?" She was joking/not joking. Obviously still a little pissed off at Harry about the lawsuit and embarrassing publicity.

I saw Harry tip his chin back at the slight. "I thought I was excommunicated for the summer," he said.

"Not if you can be the Harrison Addison we know and love."

Harry laughed humorlessly but dutifully took out his phone. "That's the day we have our final test. It's only offered that day." He looked up at his mother. She looked right back. Harry replaced his phone. "I'll figure it out," he mumbled.

"Like your father says, everything is negotiable. I can't wait until you're back at home, Harry. It's not the same without you. We both need someone to tell us to put down our phones."

Harry stood and hugged his mom. She held Harry tight, her eyes squeezed shut for just a moment. "I love you," I heard her whisper.

"I'll be back from exile soon," he joked.

"Very funny. You're fine with your father, Harry. You know how to handle him. And he loves you." Harry stiffened ever so slightly at her words, pulling away first, left to deal on his own.

"Poppy, so nice to meet you. Thanks for keeping my son out of trouble."

CHAPTER THIRTY-EIGHT

Maya left the scent of bergamot in her wake.

Harry returned his mother's chair to the table behind us. He hadn't said a word to me yet, maybe wondering when I was going to compliment his mother.

"You changed the agreement," I said. I should shut the hell up and play along. Then disappear.

"What?" Harry moved his chair so he was facing me again.

"This isn't what we agreed on. You said we had to be a secret, that your family couldn't know about me and that you couldn't date anyone."

Harry was about to take a sip of water, but his hand froze midair. Then he took a long drink. It had never occurred to him that I wouldn't want to meet his mother. That it wasn't some big gift.

Harry's expression closed off. "I'm sorry. I didn't mean to bombard you."

Our food arrived: baguettes, butter, ham, salad, soup, chocolate cake. Harry began to help the server make it all fit like puzzle pieces on the small tabletop.

I didn't want to eat a thing. I didn't want to make conversation. I wanted to get back to the computer. I didn't know how I was going to get through any of the minutes I had to spend eating.

I forced myself to pick up some bread and begin the charade.

"What's wrong?" Harry asked.

"Nothing."

"What the fuck, Poppy? Why are you breathing like that?"

"Like what?"

"You're hyperventilating."

"No, I'm not."

"What do you call those rapid breaths?"

I shook my head, as in *I'm fine*.

"Come on. Let's go outside." Harry grabbed my hand to help me stand. I resisted, sweeping my hand under the chair, searching for the laptop. "I've got it," Harry said curtly.

"No, I've got it." *She was holding a rifle*. Right there for Harry to see if he opened the screen. And that half smirk. I'd never seen my mother so self-satisfied. I held the computer tightly to my chest. Harry and I stared at each other, in a sort of face-off.

"Follow me," he finally said. He led me past the long line of people snaking through the restaurant doors. We sat in the shade on a low concrete bench near the fountain. "You need a paper bag. Hold on." Harry came back a moment later with a white paper bag. "Breathe," he ordered. He gently pried the laptop away and set it between us.

"No! Why would I breathe into a bag?"

"Because you're having a fucking panic attack. Just listen to me."

It was so stupid, but I took the bag and began to breathe in and out. Harry rubbed my back and wouldn't let me stop. "You don't have enough carbon dioxide. You'll feel okay in a minute."

Sure enough, the feeling that I was having a heart attack at age eighteen receded. I stopped, then covered my face with my hands, trying to get a grip, trying to reset.

Harry, who I'd been a jerk to moments before, was still rubbing slow circles on my back.

"What happened?" Then it dawned on him. "Your DNA test?"

I shrugged.

"What do you need, Poppy?"

I was so spent. I dropped my hands to my lap. "I need time with that computer."

"Done."

Our stuff was splayed on the table where we'd left it. Harry began moving plates of uneaten food to a newly empty table behind us. I placed the laptop down.

"Sorry. I knew you were in the middle of something. Bad timing," Harry said.

"No, I'm fine. Sorry about that." I wiped my nose with the back of my forearm, catching some of the wetness from my cheeks. I wasn't sure if it was rivulets of sweat or tears.

"Take as long as you need. I can go next door to the bookstore."

"I'm sorry," I said. It was unclear what I was apologizing

for—my reaction to his sweet introduction to his mother, my meltdown, or for everything. For being me.

"You always apologize. You don't need to apologize. You've seen me worse." Harry kissed my temple.

Harry gallantly pulled out my chair for me. My backpack weighed it down and it tipped backward. I leaped to catch it.

When I looked up, the laptop was already open on the table. Harry leaned down and typed in the passcode for me.

Shit.

My search lit the screen. There was my mother. My mother holding a rifle. I left my body the moment Harry saw it. This beautiful woman, girl really, posing like a model, pretending to be a militant. Though she wasn't pretending.

Maybe I thought Harry would see the arresting photo and be curious, then confused about what I was searching. That was bad. What I hadn't expected was the outpouring of enthusiasm that followed.

"Oh my god. Have you been reading the news? Maisie Bell."

I slowly sat down then leaned forward, curving my palms over my knees.

"Her brother, Andrew, just died. My mom went to the funeral. Yesterday."

"What?"

"You know this story?"

I shook my head.

"Like, I've met the family. At fundraisers. It's so crazy. They're old-school San Francisco. They own a shipping company that was the first to have routes to Hawaii. Anyway, they had this daughter, Maisie, who was kind of wild." Harry gestured to the computer screen.

"Wild?"

"Like she was in and out of Catholic boarding schools before she ran off to Amsterdam, and they had to bring her back. She got clean and started college at Santa Clara. Everything seemed fine. Then one day, some kind of neoguerrilla group who'd targeted her broke into her apartment. They beat up her roommate and they kidnapped Maisie Bell."

Harry was actually telling me my mother's story.

"Who were they?" I knew I wasn't breathing.

"Some crazies with a leader. I think they were a bunch of young white people who were anarchists and became domestic terrorists to get attention. So they kidnapped this heiress and asked for ransom." Harry's eyes glittered with the telling of a good story. "But the family refused to pay. I think they blamed her for all the shit she'd already put them through—who knows. But then months later, she resurfaces with that picture sent to the media. She had joined the cause."

"What did she do?" My voice sounded like a different person's. Low and quiet.

"They robbed banks—that's all I remember hearing. But no one could catch them even though they seemed really stupid. They had this compound up in Oregon, and the FBI or ATF or whoever organized a siege. But the leader lit the entire place on fire, so they killed themselves instead of getting caught."

A little brown bird flew through the open doors of the restaurant and distracted Harry, who followed it with his eyes as the bird soared wildly beneath the ceiling.

I waited for him to remember what he was saying. Some employees gathered in a corner, pointing and debating how to get the bird out.

I couldn't stop myself. It felt like he held my fucking life in his hands. "So what happened?"

Harry turned back to me and tried to refocus.

"Everyone died?" I pushed.

"Oh. No. Everyone thought there were no survivors, but then, sometime later, Maisie Bell waltzes into a bank in Sacramento wearing a wig. She somehow took out a shitload of her money. And she's never been caught since. Growing up, I'd hear rumors of sightings, because we sort of know the family. But it's been a long time. I'm sure she's in another country by now."

I thought of Des Moines. Maybe that sighting had made the news.

Harry laughed to himself. "It's so badass. Especially because her parents are total assholes. Andrew—Maisie's brother who just died—told my mom his parents refused to acknowledge he was gay." Harry looked satisfied with the end of his story. "Anyway, it's just been in the news again lately because of her brother passing."

Andrew was my uncle and he'd just died. "Your mom went to the funeral?"

"Yeah, I shouldn't call the family assholes, because they just lost their remaining kid. Andrew was really cool. He died of cancer. He was *maybe* forty. My mom loved him. He ran the family business and he was a huge donor. Jesus, everything is connected. My friend, Alix Bell—who we were just talking about—she's Andrew's cousin."

Harry touched my shoulder. "I'm going to run to the bathroom. You feeling better?"

I nodded.

"Cool. I'll be right back."

I was so serene. I'd never felt so serene in my life. My mind got crystal clear. It was maybe what people experienced that last moment before a bomb exploded at their feet.

I watched Harry cross the restaurant, palming his iPhone into his back pocket before rounding the corner.

My dad once said people's brains respond either fast or slow to an emergency. My dad was fast. My mom was slow. Turns out my mind was fast.

It let go of what I didn't need in order to pinpoint focus.

I danced my finger over the touch pad and the screen came alive. There she was again.

It was like looking in the mirror.

There was so much to learn. Acres and acres of information to read. But right now, Harry was in the bathroom and he had just seen this photo.

Would his brain move on to the next thing? Or would it stop for a second, nudge him. Why was his girlfriend looking at that photo, and why did she look so similar to Maisie Bell? Different hair, same face. But if he wasn't expecting a resemblance, maybe he wouldn't see it.

Alix Bell was the problem. She was the connector, the Instagram influencer Harry's friend said I resembled, whom Harry and I had inspected on his phone because I'd asked.

My young mom stared back at me with that enigmatic smile, full of power. *Whoever you are, get me through this. Please don't let him realize. We've gotten this far.*

In places on the screen, the name *Joseph Connelly III* appeared. But there wasn't time.

I cleared the search like a good girl, cautious now, the loyalty bred into me by my parents silently bringing me over to their team. Harry had been gone maybe two minutes.

In an abundance of caution, I could close this computer, leave it, and disappear. It was what my dad would want me to do.

But there was no way; Harry wouldn't figure it out. It wasn't going to register.

Harry had mentioned a funeral for my mother's brother. More pieces moved into place. My uncle may have been the one who prepared the house for us. And his illness the reason the improvements—the new wallpaper, the fresh paint— weren't quite complete. He was the person my mom had been risking everything to see. The person my mom wanted my dad to see for her. This rich brother whom I guessed had been our lifeline. But now he was gone.

A long five minutes had passed. At least. The line of customers still stretched past the door. People chatted, jostled purses, looked at their phones. A server with a tablet worked his way down the line. The sound of the fountain carried inside.

Where was Harry?

I was 99 percent sure Harry wouldn't stop to think. We just had to pass through this moment and easily move on to the next thing.

Harry appeared in the doorway.

He walked with his usual gait, head down, eyes on the floor. My shoulders relaxed. He looked completely normal. Just like he had when he left the table. It was fine.

Harry sat down across from me. First, I noticed his careful, bland expression, the same one he'd worn the first day I'd met him. Then I saw his phone in the palm of his hand.

And my brain slowed down.

• • •

"Hey, I need to get going, actually," Harry said. He coughed into his elbow, glanced up at me, lowered his eyes, and busied himself replacing his phone in his jeans pocket.

"Sure. Of course. Everything okay?" But, see, this was where I was good. My father's daughter. I could pretend nothing was out of the ordinary. I'd watched two people fade into the background my whole life.

"Yeah. It's all good. My mom's next meeting just got delayed and she wants to hang out until it's time."

"At Facebook?"

"We're going to meet at a restaurant down there." His response was so smooth.

Harry raised his eyes to mine, taking me in. *I'm a redhead with freckles.* If I thought it hard enough, maybe that's all he'd see. Then a smile split his face and his eyes danced, and I thought I saw a flash of *No, I'm imagining things* in his eyes. He leaned forward and tucked a strand of my hair behind one freckled ear.

Maybe I was crazy. It was in character for him to drop everything for his mother.

"You better go. I can walk home from here," I said.

"You sure?"

"We're two blocks from where you usually drop me off. I'm fine!"

"What are your parents going to say when you get home early?"

Was he watching me more closely again?

"It's fine. They're busy working. I'll just say Rebecca had an appointment." Now I was back to unsure. "Have fun," I said. I slid his laptop across the table. The immaculate silver glinted in the California summer light.

"Did you find what you were looking for?"

I didn't miss a beat. "Not yet."

"Bye," he said softly.

I met him halfway, expecting a kiss that would be prolonged in public as usual, hard to break away from. But it was over so fast.

I watched Harry gracefully extract himself from our tight corner table and navigate through the crowded restaurant, all rangy limbs.

He knew.

CHAPTER THIRTY-NINE

There was really only one answer. When I reached the house, I'd pull the trigger for us to go. I'd tell my parents everything. The DNA test, the boy I'd met, how he knew. How it could even help his mother's career if they found us.

My parents would immediately understand that I knew who they were. Margaret Bell. Harry had called her Maisie, which must be a nickname for Margaret. My dad had called her "Maze" in the middle of the night at our first dank hotel when we'd left Illinois. To come here. Because my mother's brother was dying.

I worried Harry might follow me to see where I lived. I also knew every second mattered. At any moment he or Maya could call the police. I ran to the neighborhood, tearing past the lush gardens and mishmash of old houses and new, sheltering me from the rest of the world with its pretend sense of what life was really like. Safe. Beautiful.

I walked swiftly down the long driveway, then through the back door. The sunshine ornament fell off its nail.

"Hey, sweet girl!" My mom smiled from the kitchen sink. "You're home early."

I couldn't make myself look at her. The image of her weird, powerful smile in that iconic photo was burned into my brain. She wasn't my mom anymore. She was a stranger. It felt so scary. *She* felt so scary.

Deep down, I knew she'd caused this—our situation. It was all her. Not my dad. She'd brought him along on her ride.

"What are you doing home?" My dad entered the kitchen. His ever-serious expression softened when he saw me. His expression only ever lightened when he looked at me and Emma. He loved Maisie Bell, but he never looked at her this way.

I carefully set down my backpack on the washed-out 1950s linoleum. *Thank you for inviting A and M to celebrate your special day*, it said inside *The Giving Tree*. Andrew and Maisie? Were they friends with the little boy who'd lived here? Maybe this was where my mom's life started out before it all went wrong.

I couldn't meet my mother's eyes, so I focused on my dad's. They told me I was the apple of his eye. I stared right back into them, knowing in minutes we'd have to leave this place. In just a moment, he'd never look at me this way again.

I opened my mouth to speak. "Rebecca had an appointment."

CHAPTER FORTY

I didn't sleep all night. I paced, edging to my window and staring out into the darkness, waiting. I'd always scared myself by thinking about how it would eventually happen. Would I see one set of headlights, followed by a stream of them? Maybe I was naive. Maybe it would be silent. We'd be surrounded—lights off, police lining the perimeter.

The two times I started for the door, assured that I had to come clean, I stopped short, internally begging for more time to think things through.

It all kept coming back to Harry.

He might not know.

He might not be sure.

If he did know, what would he do?

Harry wouldn't call the police on me. He wasn't black-and-white in his thinking. Also, he didn't trust himself. He never did. He wouldn't be sure of what he did know. Harry had a sense of himself, of other people, of what was right—but he didn't know it. He trusted few people and he might look to his mom for confirmation.

Or, before he did anything, maybe he'd look to me.

I couldn't sleep, but reality blurred into small waking dreams as I stood sentry by my drafty window. Of Maisie Bell and Joseph P. Connelly III. Another reason I didn't leave my room—I was leery of the people just outside my bedroom door.

The next morning, I mumbled my goodbyes through a piece of toast, pretending to be frantic and bogged down as I collected my things. My entire family was unhurriedly eating breakfast and reading at the kitchen table. They looked like a perfect family, the kind you would see on a cereal box. *Get me out of here.* At the same time, I was scared to leave them.

It was the longest short walk of my life.

If you don't know your opponent's hand and the risk is too great, you fold. I could turn around, give up Harry, give up Professor Alexiev, give up this golden state, and do what I was supposed to do. We were never supposed to take risks. If my dad had hedged his bets like this, we wouldn't have made it as far as we had. Maybe I was as reckless as Maisie Bell.

The moment I opened the door, I saw Professor Alexiev and the sun cascading at a slant over half the classroom.

But no Harry.

Harry was always late. That was his thing. But soon he was ten minutes late.

If he had guessed the truth, Harry might take mercy on

me and simply decide to never see me again and let it go. That choice would protect him from the wrath of his parents and ensuing humiliation.

Or—

There could be a lone officer waiting to speak with me after class.

There was still a chance that he was only late.

Come on, Harry.

If he didn't show, I had to go home. Tell my family. Take the essentials. We had potentially lost precious hours.

I'll wait until 9:15.

At 9:15, I gave myself five more minutes.

Professor Alexiev boomed, "Alright. I'm going to have everyone pair up at the start of class today."

The students began the bustle of pairing off, but I couldn't move.

"Poppy?" Professor Alexiev waved a hand to get my focus. "You and Cliff work together."

"I think I need to go. I don't feel well."

Cliff scratched behind his ear with his pencil. Professor Alexiev squinted at me. "You don't look well. Go on, go ahead. Rest. I have our meeting on my calendar."

"Yes, I'll hopefully see you tomorrow."

"Poppy?"

"Yes?"

"You forgot your things."

"Oh. Thank you." I grabbed everything. When I was out of sight, I would start running.

The halls were silent. I rounded a corner too swiftly, my

feet almost slipping out from under me. When I swung into the new wing, I saw Harry.

He glanced up from his pacing.

I would never forget the look he gave me. So freaked out.

I caught sight of my reflection in the circular glass window of a classroom door. I looked shockingly wholesome and expectant with my freckles and hair loose from its braid.

I could have said, "What are you doing out here?" and played dumb. I wanted to gear up, to do this again. But when I tried to climb that mountain, the one I forced myself up and over every time I lied—to people like Alina and Ruthie—this time I slid back down.

I had been alone and undercover for so long. I guessed my cover was blown. I didn't know what that would feel like.

It felt like unzipping a costume and stepping out of a lifetime of pretending.

His eyes were bright and shiny. He was scared. He swayed backward when I took a step closer.

A stray kid entered the end of the hallway. "Do you want to go somewhere? Your car?" I asked.

"Aren't you going to ask me what's wrong?"

I didn't know what to say, where to start. I'm sure I looked the way I felt—terrified but also sorry. Just so sorry.

We were standing near the double doors to the auditorium. "Let's go in here," I finally said.

At first, I didn't think he'd follow, go behind closed doors with me. We entered a room full of theater seats and an empty stage. The new carpet fumes were strong.

"What were you looking at on the computer? I thought you were searching your DNA results." Harry accidentally bumped hard into the edge of an armrest. He was jumpy, which was making me even more jumpy.

"I was."

"Why were you researching Maisie Bell, and later, when I googled her, why were there photos of the guy who picked you up that day? The guy on the bike with the little girl. You said he was your *dad*."

"I messed up." I held my hands high in surrender.

"Who are you?"

The theater lights dimmed and flickered, then pulsed brighter than before.

"I know my name is Poppy, but everything else changes."

"Because your mother is Maisie Bell." Harry was getting a little loud.

"I didn't know who she was! We've been on the run my whole life, but I've never known why."

Maybe Harry heard in my voice how upset I was. He perched on the back of a chair, his palms flat against the hard metal.

"My parents wouldn't tell me their real names. As a precaution, they said. But it felt so hard not knowing the basic facts of who I am." Saying it, I felt every moment of how hard it had been. "After thinking about it most hours of every single day and getting nowhere, turns out all I had to do was take that DNA test. That's it. It was right there. I had the username of a match, then I discovered her real name because she once posted an ad to sell her treadmill. That led me down the right path. After all this time, it was that easy. Yesterday, I found out who my mother really is, right when yours walked up."

I saw the click in Harry's eyes when he remembered the timeline of my crazed reaction and desperation to get back to the search.

"Look at me. Have you told anyone?" I asked. Harry shook his head slightly. I needed to hear him say it. "Harry! Have you told anyone?"

"No," he said.

Then Harry started laughing as some sort of stress response. "Only I would do this. The girl I'm in love with has parents wanted by the law."

In the back of my mind, I heard *in love*. But mostly, I felt shame. "But *I'm* not wanted by the law." Saying it out loud for the first time, I realized how much I shouldered living like a criminal, even though I wasn't one.

The moment seemed to calm, like a balloon losing air and drifting to the floor. We stared at each other.

A door flapped open, letting in sunlight. A man with a clipboard entered, followed by a three-person crew. He pointed up to the lights.

Harry surprised me when he said, "Let's get out of here."

Harry wouldn't look at me at first. He didn't even speak until we'd driven far from the school.

"So what's been real and what's been a lie?" His voice was politely cold, but I knew he was nervous, because he wiped his palms on his jeans over and over again so he could hold on to the steering wheel.

I had to put myself in his shoes. This was so strange for him. Strange wasn't the right word. He knew something no one else knew. He knew where criminals were hiding. Criminals who had been at large for almost two decades. And he'd accidentally let us into his life.

"I've tried not to lie to you," I said. "I liked that you didn't want to talk about our families, so I didn't have to."

Harry stated, as if he was confirming the information to himself, "Your parents are strict because you're in hiding. That's why you're so secretive. And why you're homeschooled."

"We move around constantly. But I've been in and out of schools."

"How?"

"We get new Social Security numbers. Probably from dead people."

Harry's eyes widened and he leaned closer, like he wasn't sure he'd heard right. Then he was silent for about a mile.

"I'm still me," I said.

Harry ignored that. He tore down another Atherton street and took a sharp right into a driveway, pulling up to a gate. "We can be alone here." Harry punched in a code, and we drove onto a property that was mostly gardens. It was at least two acres. A section had a rolling lawn, and there was an enormous pool, a volleyball net, an outdoor kitchen, and two small modern houses.

"Where are we?" I asked.

"My dad has this property for events," Harry said.

"It's just for parties?"

"Yep. The caretaker moved out, so I know it's empty. In fact, I was going to take you here."

"Why here?"

"Romantic date? King-size bed, house all to ourselves," he

said. "That was the plan." His tone was mocking. Mocking himself for ever sweetly, intentionally, planning that for us.

Harry led me to a seating area around a firepit looking out over a massive aqua swimming pool.

Harry lowered himself into a plush chair. I caught sight of his hands shaking before he grasped the arms tight.

"I'm sorry," I said. I was always sorry.

"I can't believe I'm still talking to you. I shouldn't be anywhere near you. The fact that you're here—"

Harry shot out of his chair. A man was walking into the backyard. He held up a hand in greeting.

"Jesus, Mark. You scared me," Harry called. It was his dad's security guard.

Mark walked toward us. "I got the notification that someone entered." He held up his phone. "The cameras aren't working."

Harry moved in front of me, then met Mark halfway.

They talked for a second, but I couldn't hear what they were saying.

"I'll be right back," Harry tossed over his shoulder to me. Then he and Mark went inside one of the houses.

The birds called out. The pool motor kicked in. I sat perfectly still with my hands on my knees.

What were Harry and Mark discussing? Maybe Harry had told him about me last night and they had a plan. I wouldn't blame him. What Harry had learned was upsetting. Even horrifying.

Should I run? I unzipped my backpack and felt for my phone at the bottom. I couldn't find it. I started scrambling, shifting textbooks, searching beneath with my hand. I was closer to the meeting place than to home.

I froze when Harry exited the white house and crossed to me. I sat up and watched for any signs that he was acting suspicious.

He raked a hand through his hair. "Jesus, what does it take to be alone? He left out the front."

"What's going on?"

"Mark reset the cameras. He's being cautious, but this is dumb. He's worried just because there were a lot of cars parked on my dad's street last night."

"He's your dad's security guard?"

"He's head of security. Basically, in charge of keeping us from getting kidnapped." Harry laughed humorlessly. "But I guess we know that actually happens," he said to me. "It happened to your mother."

My heart was racing, but I tried to act like everything was fine. So much trust was involved at this point, I almost couldn't take it.

"Did you tell him?" I asked, referring to Mark.

"No." Harry looked almost insulted.

"Are you going to tell anyone?"

"No. If my mom finds out . . . the fact that she met you face-to-face . . ." He brushed a hand over his face.

Again, the shame was sharp. "It's my fault. Not yours."

"It doesn't matter."

"I'm sorry. I'm not supposed to get close to anyone," I said. Harry stared at two squirrels fighting in a distant leafy tree. "I'm sorry," I said again. "I thought you were safe. That we'd never get that involved because you're not very available—you have lots of friends, a job; you're only down here for the summer. So I accepted that first ride. And then more. And then I thought we were going to keep things secret and casual. But . . ."

"This whole time, I thought you were searching for a birth parent," Harry said. "I wanted to help you."

"Not quite. But you did help me. I wasn't even going to register my DNA test."

Finally, Harry looked me in the eye. "You've lived with your parents your whole life. How could you not know who they were?"

I slowly shook my head. "They are so good. They never slip up."

"You knew they were hiding—that you were hiding—but you didn't know why?"

"Yep. I didn't have anything to go on. When I could, I searched the internet with random key words."

"You've lived like that? That's why they keep you away from technology? Because they don't want you digging?" I saw the dawning of understanding. Maybe a spark of protectiveness.

"Mainly," I said.

"And to keep you disconnected. Nice," Harry said disgusted. I knew he believed me now, that I didn't know who my parents were.

"They said they were keeping us together, that they wanted to be able to raise us themselves."

"But you're raised," Harry stated.

"What do you mean?"

"You're eighteen now."

I tried to form an immediate response. I found I didn't have one. That wasn't not how it worked in my family.

I glimpsed Harry's watch. I was always running out of time. I lowered my voice. "I still don't know what they did. I got as far as that photo yesterday."

Harry dug his thumbnail into his jeans. He comprehended that I knew close to nothing. He knew everything. Maybe it was too bad to say.

It's not your fault, I told myself. *Whatever they did, you didn't do it. It doesn't reflect on you.* But I knew that wasn't the case. Harry's mom had told him as much about his stupid mistakes.

"What about my dad?" I asked him.

At the mention of my dad, Harry's eyes lifted to mine. He wanted to tell me something about him. His expression was different; it wasn't scandalized or mildly disgusted, the way it was when he spoke of Maisie Bell.

"I shouldn't be the one to tell you. Here." He wrenched around and slid his laptop from his backpack. "I'll give you some privacy."

I watched Harry head to the gate, walking across pavers surrounded by clover, his white T-shirt clinging to the sweat between his shoulder blades. He unlatched the gate.

"Harry!" I half-stood, catching Harry's laptop before it fell to the ground. He paused, turning his face in profile.

"Will you stay?" Maybe Harry could have been anyone, just someone to hold my hand when I knew the plane was going down. But I was too scared to be alone right then. That was the only reason I took the risk and asked.

Harry paused briefly. Then he simply closed the gate and came back.

I finally knew what it was about Harry that I hadn't been able to put my finger on.

Harry had so much empathy. He could easily pick up on other people's emotions, put himself in their shoes. Maybe he'd been born with it. Or maybe it was from being careful to sense his father's moods. Sometimes he tried not to have it. It was maybe why he was only half-present much of the time. He avoided situations and people because he could read a room. When he hadn't even known me, he'd wanted to help me.

Only later, I realized I'd asked him to decide between his family and his friend. He wanted to protect his mother. He'd been asked to. It was something I understood. We'd both been bred not to trust other people.

Harry silently pulled a chair close to mine.

CHAPTER FORTY-ONE

inhaled the words.

*Margaret Bell (born May 8, 1977) is the granddaughter of shipping magnate **William Scott Bell**. She became internationally famous following the events of her 2001 kidnapping by the domestic terrorist group **The United Freedom Army**, who declared themselves the enemy of the US government and wanted to "fight for the freedom of all people oppressed by the fascist capitalist state." Margaret Bell was discovered eleven months after her abduction, by which time she was a fugitive wanted for crimes committed with the group—most notably the fatal shooting of a police officer during a botched robbery. In a widely publicized government siege, members of the group were killed in an apparent mass suicide by fire at their Oregon compound. **Joseph Connelly,** a Navy SEAL privately aiding the Bell family, died in the fire. It became known that Bell was the lone survivor when she was seen* *on security cameras withdrawing funds from a Sacramento bank in November 2002. It is widely speculated that her family's resources have enabled her to remain at large.*

"She killed a police officer?" I asked Harry.

"She drove the getaway car."

Joseph Connelly. I clicked on his highlighted name.

***Joseph Connelly III** (January 2, 1979–March 24, 2002) was a Navy SEAL who died during the siege of a compound belonging to the domestic terrorist group **The United Freedom Army**. The siege was carried out by American federal and Oregon State law enforcement, though Connelly was there in an unofficial capacity. The Bell family of San Francisco requested his aid in the safe extraction of their daughter, Margaret, kidnapped a year prior by The United Freedom Army from her apartment in Santa Clara, California. Connelly's association with the Bell family began when he attended Saint Francis High School in San Francisco with Margaret Bell's younger brother, Andrew. The Bell family came under criticism for their role in Connelly's death, though a civil suit brought by the Connelly family was later dismissed.*

The text blurred. "I don't understand," I said. I moved the computer off my lap to Harry's and caught tears with the inside of my wrist.

"Which part?" Harry asked, unsure. Harry's hand moved to the back of my chair.

"My dad. All of it. People think he died?" I couldn't stop the tears. Harry briefly left and came back with tissues. "Thanks," I mumbled, and pressed my face into the white. "Can you tell me what you know? There's too much and not enough time."

"You're overwhelmed. Maybe now isn't good. Do you want to stop?"

"And go where?" I pressed the tissue into my eyes. "I'm so sorry," I said again.

When I refocused on Harry, his eyes weren't scared anymore. They were sad. "You don't have to apologize. It's not your fault, Poppy."

I held Harry's gaze, wanting to grab onto someone sane. "Why does it feel like it?"

I repeated Harry's words from the car, the day we'd driven to the beach.

He repeated mine back to me. "That's the shitty thing about shame.

"What do you want to know? I don't know if I'll have the answers, but I can find out. Whatever you need," Harry said. That sealed it. Harry was the kindest person I knew.

"You said you read about it all last night?"

"For hours."

I waited for Harry to say more.

"Come on." He placed the laptop down on a chaise lounge next to him and stood. "Let's walk."

We walked the straight blocks. This area was sunnier with fewer, shorter trees than my neighborhood and more urban. The cute downtown was only blocks away. I told myself chances were low that my dad would drive by. I looked again at Harry's watch. He obliged me by holding up his wrist so I could see.

"I don't know if what I read is *Us Weekly*–style information or *New York Times* information," Harry started.

"What did it say about my dad?" I took note of each crack in the pavement, feeling every second until Harry spoke.

"I guess he was Andrew Bell's best friend. They went to my rival school—the other super-fancy all-boys' school in San Francisco. I think Joe was much less privileged than the Bells, because that was part of the controversy—that they asked this young, shining-star Navy SEAL to do them a favor and fetch their daughter. And then he was killed. Or, Jesus, he wasn't." Harry turned his head to look at me. "Why would he run with her?"

I realized I'd been holding my breath. This was the only part of the story I knew. "My mom was pregnant with me."

A dog walker with five dogs on various leashes came toward us, and we remained quiet until she passed. "Why would she have gone to jail for the rest of her life? She drove a car. What else did she do?" I asked.

"That was enough. A police officer was killed."

I looked to the sky and could see it all. My dad becoming entangled with this convincing girl.

"Hey, what would you do if you were pregnant, facing twenty years in prison, and had the means to run? They must have known there was a way. Your dad's a noble guy for sticking with her."

"He threw his life out because of me."

"I don't see you as throwing his life out. Look at how you

turned out," Harry said. "They did something right." I looked over at him like he was crazy. "Are they good parents?" he asked.

"They've devoted their lives to being parents."

"So that's a yes?" Harry asked. We passed a small fern garden decorated with gnomes for pedestrians on the sidewalk to admire.

I nodded. No question, they had been devoted parents. My dad's background proved he was everything I'd guessed at and more—heroic, capable, a leader. But what about *her*? Who was she really?

How did she feel about the police officer being murdered? How did she feel about not paying for the crime like she should have? I tried to reconcile the mother I knew with Maisie Bell, a girl who joined up with a half-baked mission replete with guerrilla violence to "fight for the freedom of all people oppressed by the fascist capitalist state." Could I picture it?

Maybe. How she bent the rules and hunted fun. Her charisma.

"Why was he even involved with her after what she did?" I asked, as if Harry would have a clue.

"I read about the kidnapping. Her roommate was tied up, beaten, then thrown in a closet. Who the fuck knows what they did to your mother and why she helped them. And your dad knew her from before all that."

I pictured my mom's sometimes-faraway expression, how she wasn't totally knowable. Not in the same way as my dad. Maybe because she'd lived through traumas he hadn't.

"Who was this group?" I asked Harry.

"Something about September Eleventh and the antiwar

movement. I don't think they really knew. Just a lot of quasi-political talk, and somehow they had money. From robberies. Maybe from your mom, though not from her family. The group wanted to exchange her for a prisoner in San Quentin, and of course they wanted tons of ransom, but her family refused to even communicate. Maybe that's why she became one of them. She thought her family abandoned her."

Harry led me down a wooded path to a dry creek bed. Down in the ditch, there were remains of a homeless encampment. Just beyond the creek, on the other side of the tall redwood tree border, there was a parking lot for the upscale mall.

Harry broke away and walked over to a tin can. He kicked it hard and it sailed down the tunnel of dried-up creek.

"Why did you come to school this morning?" I asked. "What were you planning on doing?"

Harry slowly faced me, intertwining his fingers on the top of his head. "I was never going to call the police. But I was sure I'd guessed right. You look so much like her—your mom. Then I thought of all the times you made excuses or didn't answer questions, the homeschooling and strict parents . . . It fit together perfectly. I almost didn't come to school. One plan was to look the other way, break all contact, and do everything I could to move back to San Francisco early."

"When I saw you in the hall, you looked like you didn't know whether you were coming or going," I said.

"I don't think I could have left," he said.

"Because you needed to know for sure?" I asked.

"No, because I wanted to see you."

"To confront me?"

"You know why," was all he said. Then, "Once I guessed

who you were, I didn't stop to think about why you took a DNA test."

I heard the distant clamor of the train crossing. "My dad is a hero and my mom is . . ." I didn't have words to describe it. Private, sometimes apart from the rest of us.

"California royalty," Harry said.

It explained so much about my mom. Her refinement.

Harry half-laughed. "All my mom wants, and my dad, too, is to get in with people like the Bells. San Francisco elite." He pulled out his phone. "Look at this," he said after a moment of typing. He came closer so I could see, slanting the screen out of the sunlight, allowing his shoulder to touch mine. I wasn't sure if he noticed, but it made me feel better, like I wasn't gross.

It was the Margaret Bell Wikipedia page—the segment under "Personal Life." There was an old black-and-white photo of an unsmiling couple, the Bells, Margaret's great-great grandparents who'd settled in San Francisco, invested in the railroad, then successfully established a shipping company. Then there was one from 1981 of a tall, older woman with faded red hair. She crouched gamely between two young children dressed in Sunday best, Easter baskets clutched in their small hands. They posed in front of the very same fountain located directly over our fence.

The caption read: Lindsay Cashen Bell, with her grandchildren, Margaret and Andrew, on her Atherton estate.

I remembered the newspaper clipping I'd found in my mother's drawer. Lindsay Bell had been in the photo. I had a flash of my mother, earlier this summer, standing on the bottom rung of the fence, yearning to see over. So she could see her grandmother's house.

It blew my mind to think that, had I researched every name in that photo, there was a good chance I would have found the truth. It could have been that easy. Like my dad always said, all it took was one small mistake.

Harry was typing something else into his phone. "Your father's mother—her name is Maryann Connelly—lives close by," Harry said. "She's in Redwood City." He held up his phone to prove it was as easy as that. "Her house is right by the train station. 123 Scarlett Drive. Easy to remember."

I was surrounded by family.

CHAPTER FORTY-TWO

was late and Harry was driving like a maniac. "What I don't understand," he was saying, "is why would your parents risk coming back?"

Harry hit the brakes hard and simultaneously threw out his arm to keep me from flying forward. "I'm guessing they came back because her brother got sick," I said, holding tightly to the door.

"But what are they still doing here?"

I remembered my parents' fight behind closed doors, hearing the words *It's the last house.*

Now I knew what that probably meant. My uncle had procured it. Maybe the way he'd procured everything for us. He was gone now and there wouldn't be more safe houses. Was our only option to remain in this house? *Could we?* Even thinking it felt too good to be true.

Harry slammed on his brakes again when the car in front

of him stopped to allow a pack of bikers to cross. "Damn, I'm sorry. What's going to happen if you're really late?"

"My dad will be at the window, waiting. He doesn't even move when he gets like that—on guard. If you met him, it would make perfect sense that he was a Navy SEAL."

"He looked like a really nice guy. And young. So much younger than my dad. Is he even forty?"

I thought of his dates in the obituary. "Barely. Yeah, he's a really good dad."

The slow car in front of us, now in a silent war with Harry, dawdled into the left turn lane, and Harry showily accelerated past before taking the tight turn into the gates, much too fast, a hair away from scraping the side of his car.

"Want me to get a little closer in?" he asked, slowing, waiting on my answer.

"Just a bit." I couldn't afford another ten minutes of walking.

"Nice," Harry muttered, as he turned into the black wrought iron gates of the neighborhood. "I didn't know what was back here."

I tried to hide how nervous I was about the time. "Ha. Yeah, these houses are only six million dollars instead of twenty."

"I mean, this is the wrong side of the tracks in our zip code, you know," he joked. "I like thinking of you here," he said, more seriously. "It's pretty. It's hidden."

Harry navigated blind curve after blind curve through the lush neighborhood with its exotic mix of trees and statuary.

"Take this street—Theodora—and then stop midblock and I'll hop out." It would put me one block away, on the street behind my house. As soon as Harry was out of sight, I'd start running. My heart began a methodical, hard beat as I bent low to gather my backpack at my feet. One of the laces of my white Converse was untied. I squished down farther to tie it tight. I felt Harry slow.

When I sat up, bringing my backpack into my lap, I noticed we were past where I'd wanted Harry to pull over. "You can leave me right here," I said quickly. Harry's eyes were fixed on something in the distance. He didn't listen and kept creeping forward, like he wanted a better look. My eyes flew forward.

The giant sun hat screamed old lady, but Harry would have noticed the woman's white short-sleeved blouse and perfect faded soft jeans that flared at the hem. Her giant sunglasses rested in her collar. She replaced them, but not before automatically turning her head to look directly in the windshield of the Porsche.

"Stop the car," I said. "Stop the car!"

Harry braked and the car jerked forward, then backward. His expression was somewhere between wary and awed. When I looked back to my mother, I saw her through Harry's eyes, experiencing the eeriness of glimpsing Maisie Bell. For a moment, my mom became Other. I did something strange—I reached for Harry's hand.

Then, I snapped to. Without a word, I opened the door and leaped out. "Bye! Thank you!" I called with fake cheer before slamming the door shut without a backward glance.

I walked toward my mother, who stood at the side of the road in the ivy, in front of a ten-foot black metal fence. The bushes had been generously pruned so anyone from the street could enjoy a view of the magnificent fountain on my grand-mother's former property. I was aware that Harry still hadn't moved. The car hovered.

When I came face-to-face with my mother, she was still looking directly at Harry's car. Trying to look *into* it. Harry came to his senses and, from my peripheral vision, I saw his car flash past.

I could feel my mother's gray eyes piercing me from behind her gigantic black frames. That I couldn't see her eyes made her seem more frightening.

"Why was that kid looking at me like that?"

"Like what?" I asked, all innocence.

"Like he *recognized* me."

My mom swayed forward, like she wanted to get in closer to hear easy answers from her dutiful daughter so her life could fall back into place.

Then power shifted as I watched my silence slowly unsettle her. She took a big step backward, and her shoulders curved as she jammed her hands into her pockets. My fear took a back seat once I observed how scared my mom was. She was scared this kid knew who she was. And that I was the one who had told him.

"Who is he?"

"A boy from class," I said after a long pause.

My mom watched me closely. If I had found out, how had I done it? Had she made a misstep somewhere? Had her daugh-ter seen Maisie Bell—the photos and headlines? Did I seem different?

I could tell her I knew.

My parents' primary goal had been to stay safe on the run. But they had always had a side job—keeping their secrets from the children.

You would think it would be a relief to shed that whole separate burden.

I couldn't do it. I didn't know how to break old habits. We didn't speak openly about so many things.

"He saw me walking and offered me a ride."

My mom exhaled, visibly relaxing at the fact that we were going to continue to play this game. "You let him drop you one block away from where we live?"

"I was late."

Two women were out on a fast-walk together. They both wore visors, and one held the leashes of two small terriers. I nodded hello, and my mother subtly turned to pretend she was admiring the fountain. I joined my mother at the fence, leaving plenty of space between us.

We stood side by side and watched the fountain, fifty yards in the distance. It seemed to mock us, like it was something so beautiful that we had to hold in our hearts because we couldn't touch it. We were in exile. I held the fence in both hands and let my body sway against it.

My mom kept her eyes fixed on the fountain and the partial glimpse into her grandmother's magnificent yard. She'd been a master gardener, I'd read.

"He's your boyfriend?" my mom asked. Her breath was now an easy in and out.

I gripped the fence harder, trying to figure out what to say.

"I'll take that as a yes," my mom said. She still didn't face me. Then she spoke so softly I almost missed what she said. "You're allowed to have something, Poppy."

My mom's fingers curled around the black fencing, mirroring mine.

It turned out not to matter whether my mom would keep Harry's existence a secret. When we entered the house, something was off.

About thirty seconds passed before I identified the feeling in the air: the winds had changed. The shift that happened just before we moved.

My mom tensed and I knew she felt it, too. There were no packed bags, no panicked pacing—just my calm dad with one shoulder against the doorjamb, waiting for us.

"Dan?" My mom asked. *What's going on? What is it?*

He nodded. My mom's face fell, as in *fuck*. That was all it took—their secret language passed between them, almost twenty years of understanding, the two of them being alone in this together. I used to be jealous and want to be included on their island.

"What happened?" I knew it was a futile question and my dad wouldn't answer.

Emma, wearing a stained pink tank top that was too small and rolling up her belly, padded down the hallway. Her face was tearstained. "He pulled me out of the library." She pointed an accusing finger, wanting to tell on him to my mother, her favorite parent, the one who coddled her. "He said he didn't 'like the look' of this one guy." She glanced at me to see if I'd caught her use of air quotes.

My mom exhaled. "Oh. That's all?"

"It's a feeling."

It sounded so thin. I wondered how many other times simple paranoia had caused us to prematurely pull up stakes.

"Can you think of anything? Any small slipup . . . ?" my dad asked my mom.

"Zero. I stayed in the shadows. I would tell you if there had been anything." I felt my mom's energy radiating out, asking me that same question now that I had opened a door, letting in someone new. I waited for him to ask me next. But he didn't.

My mother opened her mouth like she was about to argue. I thought she was going to fight to stay in this place filled with her history. It surrounded her, from that fountain to the tape deck lying in wait all these years, just waiting for Maisie's index finger to push PLAY and continue where she'd left off, like she'd never missed a beat. But then her face dropped and she looked tired. Then the veil was back in place.

She crossed her arms tightly. "Do we have enough?" she asked my dad.

He shrugged one shoulder. "There's never enough."

Do we have enough? They were talking about money. I could hear Harry asking, *But what are they still doing here?*

"It is what it is," he said, matter-of-fact. "I could use more time."

My dad was picking up money. That had to be the reason my dad had allowed us to come here when it was such a dangerous thing to do. Before he died, Andrew must have arranged it. I remembered the arguing in the motel room when we'd left Illinois. *This is about money. For our family. Even you know it's a good plan.*

My dad knew my mother would be tempted to see her

brother. In the motel bathroom, my mom had assured my dad that she would never be so stupid. *I stayed in the shadows*, she just said. Had she gotten close to Andrew? Whatever she'd done, that night she'd come home almost hysterical, it was clear she couldn't take the last step to see him.

When my dad acted this way—still, quiet, like he was listening for something—we were typically days away from leaving. Sometimes hours. Anything could unsettle him, and then we'd be gone.

Was there anything I could do? Was there anything I could say to back things up, to make my dad relax again so we didn't have one foot out the door?

Like a child, I'd hoped there was a chance this was the last house, that we were here to stay. After Illinois, I'd been tired and beaten down, so how had I set myself up for this much bigger disappointment? I'd always known better.

CHAPTER FORTY-THREE

The next morning, I anxiously waited for Harry at the front of the school.

I heard the low growl of the engine just before I saw the black Porsche speed around the corner, then cut a sharp right into the high school parking lot.

I stepped forward to meet him, to tell him I was worried I'd be leaving soon, when two motorcycle cops shot out from the camouflage of bushes. In tandem, lights flashed as they tailed Harry into the lot while giving a whoop of siren.

I swiftly walked to class by myself. Poor Harry. And now there was no time to talk before class.

"Sorry I'm late. I got pulled over. Again. And I swear I wasn't speeding," Harry said, looking genuinely apologetic and like, *I know how this sounds.*

Professor Alexiev rolled her eyes.

"Maybe you need a new car?" I joked when Harry sat down.

"Jesus. Tell me about it." Because he was flustered from the police, I couldn't tell how badly seeing my mother in the flesh had thrown him. He'd seen an actual fugitive. And I was implicitly asking him to pretend he hadn't.

Class was interminable. There was no time to talk at the break. Professor Alexiev had us work through most of it, cramming in preparation for the upcoming test.

"That's it! We're almost there. Next week is already our last." Professor Alexiev finally stopped. The invisible pressure of the genetics class could be felt bearing down from behind the door.

I couldn't wait. "Harry, I need to talk to you—"

"Poppy? We meet today?" Professor Alexiev called from across the room.

I felt pressed in from all sides. "Yes!" I nodded to her.

"Excuse me." A genetics kid edged around me.

"Cool," Harry said. Then he proceeded to swim upstream, through the sea of students, leaving me behind.

Did that mean he was going to wait? For how long?

I lingered outside, impatient, kicking at some weeds. How long would this take, and would Professor Alexiev even remember why she'd wanted to meet? She'd said it was important to have options, and she was curious about my future plans. Did she want me to lead our discussion or did she have advice for me? Sometimes I believed Professor Alexiev took a special interest in me, keeping tabs on my progress. But then long stretches would go when I wasn't even called on in class.

Professor Alexiev came barreling out of the door and dropped a shopping bag. Two students from our class rushed to help her. She waved them away, pretending she didn't enjoy being our celebrity.

"Poppy!" she called to me. "You ready? Mind if we sit outside and I eat my lunch?"

"Not at all." I followed her to a nearby bench in the shade beneath a giant oak. The bench was spotted with bird poop and leaves, but I decided not to care if Professor Alexiev didn't.

"Oh my god," she said, unpacking a Tupperware container brought from home. "Never in my life have I met such stressed-out kids. Where I grew up, we smoked and listened to music. My colleague told me about the suicides—not at this high school but the other one. This area."

"But weren't you always studying?" I asked.

"Oh god, no. I was an indifferent student." Professor Alexiev pried off the stubborn Tupperware lid.

I hadn't expected that. "So, what happened? How'd you end up here?" I asked.

"Luck. It was pure luck. I took a test and did so well I was asked to take part in a national math competition. From there I met people who were applying to programs outside the country. And the programs were fully funded. My family thought I was crazy. It came down to choosing between Germany and the US. But I couldn't say no to California."

I smiled, imagining the professor enjoying this weather, coming from a cold place.

"Did you love it?" I asked.

"I couldn't believe it. It was so different. The people were so different. I had a hard time at first. But then I adapted." Professor Alexiev twirled cold pasta on a fork. "It's amazing how people can adapt. Not so many years later, I have a job and friends, a green card."

"Do you miss your family?" I opened my backpack and brought out my own sack lunch.

"Yes. My youngest sister is coming for a month to stay with me. I want her to go to university in the States, but I don't think she's interested. You need to be driven to figure out all the red tape and language barriers. You have to be brave to separate from your family and live with being so homesick. And she's more content than I was, hanging out with the same people and going to the same bars."

"I don't know if I could do it," I said.

"Be far from your family? Yeah, but what choice is there? Stick around and be half-bored forever? You can't run in place. That's not good for anyone."

"What if they had needed you?"

Professor Alexiev replaced the lid on her container, and from the pause of her hand, I saw her register that maybe that's what my deal was. Maybe I was homeschooled because I was taking care of someone.

"I can't speak for everyone, but I know in my experience, it was right. I would have died if I'd stayed. Math became more than math. It was my way out. It offered a life."

My brown bag was wrinkled and limp from where I clutched it. Her words woke me up. They made me feel like it was okay to be driven—it wasn't selfish.

Of course, Professor Alexiev was different from me, but she also came from the edges.

It was the first time I let myself realistically picture a different future than one of endless moving and stagnation.

I wasn't the same Poppy I'd been at the start of our conversation. I could never unhear what she'd said.

I walked away from my meeting with Professor Alexiev with practical information swimming in my head. Standardized tests that could bring me to the same level as my peers. Scholarships if I was guided in the right direction by the right people. Like her. Her last gentle suggestion of online college if I couldn't strike out on my own. She'd said eighteen was a natural entry point; each passing year would be doable but ever more challenging.

I thought she saw me as trying to keep up, always running a three-legged race. It thrilled me to hear what a trusted adult thought I'd be able to do. And from someone like her, who had broken out of her circumstances and should never have ended up where she did.

"How'd it go?"

My head jerked up. Harry stood at the front of the school, on the sidewalk, hands shoved in the pockets of his hoodie.

"You waited!" I hadn't meant to sound so surprised or pleased, but I was both.

Harry kicked at a rock on the pavement before meeting my eyes. His expression said, *Where else would I be?* And *I don't know what I'm doing.* "Of course I waited."

Then very slowly, Harry leaned down and touched his lips to mine, holding me gently with a hand on my lower back. It was the first time since he'd found out everything. Because of what it meant—his acceptance of who I was—I'd remember the kiss even more than our first.

Harry pulled back. He lifted his chin in greeting and held up a hand to someone in the parking lot.

In the distance, Professor Alexiev waved to both of us before lowering into a Smart car. I smiled, turned back to Harry, and felt like I had two more people.

CHAPTER FORTY-FOUR

Finally, I was able to tell Harry my worry that I would be leaving. Simply because of a small incident at the library, my dad's senses were on overdrive.

It made us both feel urgent. Harry's hand caressed my knee as he drove, while I impatiently played with his thick hair.

Harry's phone rang and the car's digital display read ALICE, CAMPAIGN.

"I always forget that you're a big deal," I said.

"I'm not a big deal. Just a rich brat," he joked. It felt like our first normal conversation in so long.

"Um, I don't think so. You're more than that. And you're so sexy." I said it like I was teasing, but it was true. I thought of him closing his eyes when I touched him, waiting for more.

"Poppy!"

I'd disappeared for a moment, so clearly picturing how Harry looked the few times we'd been able to take things beyond just making out in his car. "Oh god. Yes?" I exhaled the "yes."

Harry registered where I'd drifted. "My place okay?" he asked softly. He adjusted the strap of my tank top.

I almost asked, "Really?" but I kept my mouth shut. At that moment, I didn't want to remind him of my circumstances.

"I thought we were going to your house?" I asked when Harry took a left, driving in the opposite direction of his neighborhood.

"No. I'm taking you to a different house. It also belongs to my dad. Someone was going through our trash last night, so Mark was at the main house when I left this morning."

"Wait. What happened?"

"Someone was taking stuff out of our trash can on the street. A bearded guy with a flashlight. One of our neighbors was walking the dog late, and the guy took off as soon as he was seen."

"Maybe he was homeless and looking for food?"

"Well, he drove away."

"To be fair, you can be homeless and hungry and still have a car. Maybe he's looking for the next iPhone or something."

"Ha! Probably. And all he found was yogurt containers." Harry tilted his head into my hand.

"So where are we going?"

"My dad kept his old house in Palo Alto. No one ever uses it. I have high hopes that we'll finally be alone."

Harry hovered over me, shirtless but still wearing jeans. We were in a bedroom with pale-gray walls, a white stucco fireplace, and a four-poster bed. Harry suddenly sat back on his haunches, leaving me where I lay against the pillows. The pristine white bedding was like a cloud. But Harry checked his watch.

"We need to get going in about twenty minutes," he said.

"Nooo!" I threw an arm over my eyes. "Why is it always time?"

Harry stretched out next to me, but purposely left a few inches between us. "I like it when you're frustrated," he teased.

I stretched my hands above my head, surrendering to his decision to stop. Harry picked up a lock of my hair and twirled it around his finger. I trailed the backs of my fingers over his skateboarding bruises.

"I've read too many romance novels," I said.

"What happens in the romance novels?"

"Lots of ravishing. Bodice ripping. Swords thrown into corners. The first time is urgent; the second time is slow."

For a moment, Harry had an entranced look of *Tell me more.* Then, "I love you, Poppy." He said it like *I love how you can be,* not *I love you.* "I think I have a thing for good girls. Big time."

"But you'll get naked on the beach with the bad girls." It was meant as a joke.

"They weren't bad. Just not you. Well, maybe the last one was a little bad, since she sold photos of us."

I was suddenly bitter that he'd obviously slept with other girls—women—but not with me. "I don't want you to see me as different," I said. I picked a strand of hair from my eyelashes.

"I'm *not* not sleeping with you because you're different. I'm not having sex with you because it's going to hurt too much when you leave."

I didn't want to hear that. My instinct was to deepen things with Harry before time ran out. But, out of necessity, Harry had grown up finding ways to protect himself. He stayed where he felt okay. It was totally unlike him that he'd let things go this far.

"I don't know when we're leaving, exactly. We could be here forever." That was a fantasy I'd been entertaining. *The last house.* Hearing my wishful thinking out loud, I suddenly felt hopeless. "I don't know what's going on," I said. "I never do."

"I just don't think I can take the day when you don't show up again." Harry kissed my cheek.

I did a gigantic sit-up and began searching for my tank top amid the soft mounds of white comforter. I sat cross-legged and lowered it over my head. I was hurt but wanted to hide it.

Harry grabbed his phone off the bedside table and was looking at it when he said, "There's another way, you know. For you to stay, I mean."

"What's that?"

"You take the SAT and apply to colleges."

"But the money. The identification. The transcripts." I was beginning to come down hard from my conversation with Professor Alexiev. There were impossible hurdles that I'd ignored when Professor Alexiev preached that the sky's the limit.

"What do your parents say when you ask them?"

I didn't know what to say. I couldn't tell him I was too scared to ask because I didn't want to face the answer.

"I'm sure they've thought about how you could stay here.

You have grandparents. You could live as yourself." Harry scrolled on his phone, but he was only pretending to be preoccupied. He'd been thinking about this.

"I don't think so. I can't even imagine."

"You deserve the best, Poppy. That's all I'm saying." Harry said the kindest words while keeping his eyes fixed on his screen.

I wanted to rest my head on his shoulder, acknowledge his sweetness. "It's fine."

My answer seemed to make Harry mad. He quit pretending the conversation was casual and chucked his phone to the foot of the bed. Wary, I sat up straighter against the headboard, guessing I knew what was coming.

Harry squinted. "You understand it's not fair that they ask you to do these things. That they hold you to these standards."

"You mean like you?" I shot back. "I'm sorry," I said immediately. "It's totally different."

For a long moment, Harry watched his phone sink down into the comforter. "No, you're right," he said slowly. "I'm held to impossible standards. After I screwed up, I fell in line. I haven't pushed back."

Harry touched a hand to my waist. "I'm just saying, you were so excited when you first told me what Professor Alexiev said. Nothing is impossible. That's the one fucking thing my dad has taught me. There's a way to negotiate everything. There's always an out."

"But what if I don't want out?" I said. It was automatic and defensive, but Harry didn't get it. The finality of it.

"Then I'm sorry to say it, but that's crazy. I think you're afraid of making anyone unhappy. You're a pleaser."

"No, Harry, it's because I love them." I found I still meant it, despite their secrets that had eaten away at me and the life I had to live. I couldn't imagine leaving Emma. And I was used to being part of my family, not by myself.

"If I left, that would be it. Gone. I would never see my family again," I said. I didn't know how people did it—what kind of bravery it took to leave loved ones behind for good. Maybe I'd be fine at first, but then a whole year would pass. Then years. It was its own kind of jail sentence.

I lowered my voice. "You can't understand. I've lived every single day of my life with the threat of them being taken away from me. Do you know what that feels like when you're five years old?"

Harry stared at me for so long, I thought he wasn't going to respond. "When we're young, our family is everything. But then it becomes the most natural thing in the world to step outside the circle and choose for ourselves. Kids grow up." In a softer voice, Harry said, "What happens to your life?"

I'd live theirs.

"You would kick such ass, Poppy."

I kept my face carefully neutral but wished I could scream.

Harry took my cue and dropped the subject. Frustrated, he left the bed. "Can I get you something to drink?" he asked, suddenly formal.

"Sure. Anything."

"Cool. I'll be right back."

I didn't want my situation to get in our way. I could hope and pretend, but I felt it: we didn't have much time left.

I reached for Harry and he obliged me by coming to the side of the bed. I held his face and kissed him slowly. I let my fingers run over his chest, touching him where I knew he loved to be touched, from the way his breath became shallow. He put one knee on the bed and began to lower himself over me again.

"Okay," Harry said, laughing and groaning at the same time. "We're having sex right now, but here's the deal: I want the whole awkward first time with you. I've never had it—candles, stripping each other naked, cuddling after. But"—he paused— "only if you promise you're not going to leave." He was joking. I could tell he also wasn't.

I suddenly knew I couldn't mess with Harry. I had to respect his need to keep himself safe. I was never going to stay.

It was easiest to treat what he'd said as a joke. "I'll have a sparkling water if you have it."

I saw the hurt, then Harry covered. "That's evil. I need to stop kissing you, anyway. Your lips are puffy." He ran his thumb over my bottom lip and then backed away. On his way out, he nodded to his phone at the end of the bed. "Hey, feel free to use that. I'm sure there's more stuff you want to know," he said. "Or my laptop is in my bag."

I immediately got the now-familiar nauseous feeling. "Thanks."

I watched Harry leave the bedroom, slipping his shirt over his head, his rib cage visible. He was such a boy, but—maybe I was making it up—he looked more mature since the beginning of summer. I worried about all the cuts and scrapes on his body from skateboarding. Harry kept his issues invisible—except on his body. Except to me.

Once Harry left the room, I picked up his phone. My thumbs hovered. I finally typed "Margaret Bell and Joe Connelly."

Three photographs of my parents, together, appeared in the search.

The first was from a yearbook. ST. FRANCIS SENIOR PROM, MAY 1997. PICTURED: ANDREW BELL, JOE CONNELLY, MARGARET BELL, CYNTHIA CASWELL.

My dad looked like a teenager. He *was* a teenager. Andrew stood next to him, both boys wearing tuxes. My uncle and my mom could have been twins. Even in the photo, I could see Andrew had the same light eyes and dark hair. He was as tall as my dad, so handsome, and there was something instantly likable about him. He looked open and friendly.

My mother looked older than the boys and like she was at a different party altogether. Cynthia Caswell, my uncle's date, wore a puffy formal dress, while my mom wore a black slip dress, a strap sliding off one shoulder.

I imagined it: my mother reluctantly agreeing to go to my dad's prom. Or her brother coercing her to be his best friend's date. And yet they looked close in the picture. Maisie's fingers easily intertwined with my dad's. They were familiar with each other. Connected. I was glad she acknowledged him in public—this chic rich girl, diamond bracelet dangling from her wrist.

Another photo was a snapshot of a crowded party someone had likely submitted to the media or police. My mom was laughing as she gave the camera the finger. Her hair was in an elegant knot, cigarette in her other hand halfway to her lips. She was in her early twenties, I guessed. She sat across my dad's lap.

My young dad had a military-style haircut and was gazing at her, his lips turned up at one corner. His expression perfectly captured the sentiment of him rolling his eyes at her and be-ing in love with her. I'd seen it a million times. Her dress was scrunched up, and my dad's hand rested just below a tattoo of Roman numerals on her thigh. The tattoo was gone now. Erased. Now it made sense why she had that circle of pale, scarred skin.

I enlarged the last photo: Andrew and Margaret Bell with Joe Connelly. Graduation of SEAL qualification training class 293.

My dad was in a sailor's dress uniform at his graduation ceremony. My uncle and my mom flanked my dad, their arms tossed around him as the three of them posed for the camera. My dad was laughing, which was something I rarely saw. The three of them looked close, a unit.

Next, I searched Andrew. In a photo from the *San Francisco Chronicle*, pallbearers carried a casket covered by sprays of white lilies through a crowd of mourners. The casket was followed by a silver-haired man supporting a frail-looking woman with rounded shoulders and jet-black hair mostly cov-ered by a black lace church veil.

Mourners celebrate San Francisco's Andrew Bell, CEO, philanthropist, marriage-equality activist. Attended by civic dignitaries and mourners dressed in widow's black lace, the service was held in Grace Cathedral, the Nob Hill landmark that represents the apex of San Francisco society.

I had so many mixed emotions looking at the photos, I had to stop searching for more. I wasn't sure if I felt angry or sad. I didn't know if I felt regret for them or for myself. Andrew had been robbed of his life and I'd been robbed of ever meeting him.

I was setting down Harry's phone when I remembered Harry had put the Anna Karenina email address on his phone for me. Once I got my DNA results, the account had served its purpose and I hadn't checked it since.

"You said sparkling water?" Harry called.

"Sounds good!"

I had twelve emails. Some dated back to the AncestoryNow setup and the status of my sample. A few were additional information about the slew of services they offered. But the most recent message had the subject Looking to Connect.

Hello! My name is Carol Gilbert and I just received an email that I have a new DNA relative on the AncestoryNow site. I'm trying to place you in my family tree. The amount of cMs we share is small enough to make it tricky to figure out our connection, but large enough that you could be a fairly close relative. Are you part of Peter's branch?

I threw the phone back to the foot of the bed. It missed and landed hard on the floor.

"What's up?" Harry stood in the doorway, sipping a can of sparkling water. He squeezed the can a few times, the metallic crunch filling the silence. He handed me an unopened can that slipped through my fingers, landing on the bedding.

"Why is someone emailing me from AncestoryNow?"

Harry rested the cold can against his forehead. "Like, someone from the company?"

"No. A relative."

Harry swiped up the phone. "Can I take a look?" Harry read through the email and I waited for him to say something. Then he set his drink down by his feet and began scrolling through the phone, giving it his full attention.

When he looked up, he was a little ashen.

"What?" I asked. "What's going on?"

"It's your settings. You must have shared your information."

"No way."

"Where'd you set it up?"

"Your house!"

"I helped you." I saw him mouth *Fuck*.

I nodded. I remembered scanning so quickly, wanting to get back to Harry.

"Oh *shit*." I balled the sheet in my fist.

"It's fine," Harry said confidently, in an about-face. "We can change your settings." He sat next to me on the bed and began unchecking a slew of boxes. "It's not your fault. You have to opt out of all of these. You didn't know."

"Did you share your information?"

Harry mumbled something.

"Did you?" I asked a little more insistently.

"Nah. But I know all this stuff. My dad is in the business of getting as much user data as possible but lectures me on not sharing mine. But it's impossible."

"What's impossible?"

"Every time you use the internet you leave a footprint."

"Is she going to be able to trace me?"

"She would have to be the detective of the century. You're anonymous on there, right?"

"But how did she get my email?" My voice was getting too loud.

"She's messaging you through the platform."

"I don't know what that means."

"AncestoryNow has your email. Or, actually, no—she can see this email address. They don't use a middle messaging service." Harry wasn't making eye contact.

There was a long silence while I tried to calculate risk. But I had no idea. The internet, my digital footprint, permissions, preferences, consent, usernames, platforms—it felt like a foreign language I didn't speak.

"Harry, look, you know all of this. How badly did I fuck up?" I cleared my throat. "Why did you just smile?"

"You rarely swear. This is probably her hobby; she emails a lot of relatives. Don't worry about it. You're no longer sharing your results. No one can see you on there now. But just in case, don't log in to your email again."

I scooted farther away from Harry so I could face him. "Why? Are you worried?"

"I'm not." He played with his watch. He seemed to be wrestling with what he wanted to say next. Harry drew a deep breath, his shoulders rising to his ears. "Look, when you set this up, when you took the test, I didn't know who you were, so I didn't help you figure this out. There's stuff about these sites that's hidden in the agreements."

"Like?" I gestured with my hand for him to keep going. Cold spread through my legs.

"Some of these DNA sites share with law enforcement, including this one. But—" I came to my knees. Harry grabbed my shoulder to stop me from leaving the bed. "You're fine.

They don't know anything about you; no one is even looking for you. They think your dad is dead."

Harry took my hand and I squeezed his hard.

"No one is looking for you," he repeated. "Let's close all this shit down just in case. Okay? I'll do it now. Your profile. You can watch me do it."

"You're not worried?"

Harry looked me dead in the eye. "I'm not worried."

CHAPTER FORTY-FIVE

When I got home, my dad was at the kitchen table, intently scratching in a ledger full of calculations. He was crunching numbers, trying to make something work. Not a good sign that he was doing this during the day instead of late at night when we were asleep.

My dad looked disheveled, like he'd been in the car all day, and he smelled faintly of sweat and gasoline.

"Hi. Where is everyone?" I asked.

"Outside pressing flowers, they said. Your mom's keeping Emma out of the way while I figure something out."

"Wait, when did you get glasses?" I blurted, sounding almost offended. Because we didn't take photographs, I never noticed my dad growing older. He stayed in place, my handsome, strong dad. It felt like an affront that the glasses aged him. When you lived in a bubble, it was easy to ignore the march of time.

"I just grabbed them at the drugstore. What's up, honey?" he asked impatiently. He continued to work.

It was time to know. I had to. If I was going to ask—if there was anything next for me, if there *could* be anything next for me—I had to ask now. I tentatively took a seat at the table. He didn't look up. "I was wondering, this class is almost over and it's made me realize I can do some advanced-level stuff. The high school down the road has AP classes. Have you given any thought—"

My dad's hand paused. My life suspended over a gulf.

He understood what I was asking—that I wanted more. He had to have been the best and the brightest, all of that training poured into him because of his potential.

"I have my hands full at the moment, Poppy."

"Oh, okay. Sorry," I heard myself apologize.

My chair made a scraping noise as I pushed back.

"Pops? Start separating out your things. I need to dispose of what we're not taking."

There it was. We were leaving.

It was such a blow, it was hard to believe I was still on my feet.

And I knew. I knew in my heart I'd just caused it. Yes, he was already on high alert, but I'd just pushed him over the edge when I brought up my future. This was his response. If we kept moving, we didn't have to address it.

"Sounds good." I smiled. If he thought he didn't need to worry about me, maybe he'd lose his urgency.

On the way to my bedroom, I saw Emma and my mom seated at the picnic table outside. I paused at the window, appraising my mom as if I didn't know her. Because I didn't. She wore a short-sleeved blouse and frayed cutoffs. She sat sideways, one knee pulled to her chest, supervising Emma's activity, leaning in to Emma now and then. At that moment, it was hard to imagine her ever holding a gun.

My mom picked up a small blue flower and brought it to her nose, briefly closing her eyes and smiling. This was where she was forever young.

What on earth went through her mind? Did she think about that police officer every day? How did she live with herself for that? How did she live with herself for getting my dad swept up in this, too?

I held the dusty floral curtain in my fist, feeling nothing but resentment for her—for our situation, for making me love this place, for letting me love so many things that would be taken away. Endlessly. I hated her for all of it.

My mom spotted me. "Poppy!" she called automatically. It was muffled by the glass between us.

I was expressionless. The smile slipped from her face.

Emma saw me, and not wanting to lose my mom's attention, got up and plunked down in her lap.

My dad came up behind me and gestured for my mom to come inside. Maybe to tell her his decision. My mom lifted Emma off her lap, recentered her shorts on her hips, and started toward us.

She came through the sliding glass door and silently moved past me to follow my dad from the room. My mom had been avoiding me, scared of what I might know. But now she stopped in her tracks. Then she did our thing—silently, she reached behind her for my hand, waiting for me to take it and squeeze.

I was brought back to car rides when she gave me her hand without twisting around to look. It said, *I know you're there, I see you*, and *I love you*. It also reminded me of when it was just me and my mom, before Emma. Those long days without my dad when he found work. When it was the two of us.

I ignored the gesture.

That night, my dad was tense, clanging our ceramic bowls from cereal-for-dinner into the ancient olive-green dishwasher. He'd reiterated that if we were separated and it was time to run, we'd meet in the alley next to the Starbucks downtown.

It was Friday, which meant I had the weekend standing between me and seeing Harry in class on Monday.

Nothing could happen until then.

CHAPTER FORTY-SIX

My dad checked on me Saturday midmorning. I closed my eyes against the sun pouring through my window and slowed my breathing, hoping he would believe I was still asleep. He backed out and gently closed the door.

Loud discussions took place down the hallway, and I pieced together that my dad was headed out. Emma would play in the sprinkler my dad had found in the shed, while my mother painted her toes and kept Emma company.

I stayed frozen in bed, staring out the pollen-coated window, waiting for them to vacate the house. I must have briefly drifted. When I awoke, for one beautiful pause, I didn't know who I was.

I listened. When it was quiet, I shot out of bed. I swiftly pulled on sweats and wrapped myself in an extra-large, ancient hoodie that said CAMP TAWONGA. I laced up my shoes and didn't bother with a bra. I'd be right back. I had to make my call to Harry quickly.

I grabbed the cell phone from the bottom of my backpack and started walking. Emma was shrieking with delight, and I saw a twirl of pink bathing suit outside the sliding glass door. I kept right on going.

I wound through patches of dark and light on the nearby streets, passing old-fashioned white mansions, ranch homes, and brand-new modern fortresses. None of it—our house, this neighborhood—felt like mine anymore. I walked to the viewing spot for the fountain.

The nymph was spouting water down into the circle of maidens. I pulled my phone from the shallow pocket of my sweatshirt. If Harry didn't pick up, I could at least leave a message. I was scared I was going to disappear on him.

My phone was dead.

Of course. I hadn't used it in ages.

My dad had the charger.

I rested my head against the fencing, my fingers curling around the metal like they had before. This time it felt like I was in jail.

CHAPTER FORTY-SEVEN

One weekend felt like ten. When Monday dawned, I greeted it fully dressed. I wasn't sure if I'd ever slept, but when I slipped a yellow T-shirt over my head, I remembered a sliver of a dream—of fountains and fruit trees and a test I couldn't get to on time.

In the kitchen, I heard the familiar hiss of the coffee maker. I had to get to class. Harry wouldn't be there tomorrow. He had the breakfast in San Francisco—his first public appearance with his mother in months. But Harry had been left to deal with a pissed-off Professor Alexiev, who resented making special arrangements for him to take the test.

I squeezed my dry eyes shut. If this could just be a normal week . . . I'd sense if it would be as soon as I set foot in that kitchen. Maybe I could even take the test.

At 8:20, I shot off my bed and decided to take my chances.

"Hey! I've been waiting for you," my dad greeted me.

"Hi." I tried to sound casual and light as I bellied up to the counter and stared down into the toaster, jiggling it. The coils began to glow red. I felt like I was near a dangerous animal: I didn't want to make unpredictable moves. If I didn't rock the boat, everything would stay the same. It would be a typical day.

"Poppy, I need you to stay home today."

Please, no.

"Mom's coming with me, so I need you on Emma," he said, like it was no big deal, like he was talking about the weather.

"Dad, it's the last week. We have the final test tomorrow. If I take it, there are opportunities I could qualify for—"

"We need to survive right now." He'd raised his voice.

It was so unexpected, it felt like a slap. He'd snapped at me under three times in my life. I checked the toaster again to hide the automatic jut of my lower lip.

In my head, I heard Harry and Professor Alexiev pushing me. I forced myself to face him. "This class means everything to me."

My dad watched me, knowing I rarely asked for anything. I'd asked for the class. And now I was asking to finish it.

He stared at me. Then, "Why is it so important?"

"I just—I really love it. Please. *Let me go.*" The last sentence sounded more loaded than I'd intended.

It was the exact wrong thing to say. It made him feel threatened.

"I can't," he said.

We both knew I was asking for something more than the class. I was asking for something beyond him and the little world of our family. And he was telling me no.

"Poppy, don't cry. It's just a class."

We both knew it wasn't, but maybe he needed to keep lying to himself.

My dad didn't want to face that he was asking me to live like he did—running in place, only surviving. It was better to not speak of it and pretend that time did not exist, that Emma and I would be children forever. He wasn't guilty of my mother's original crime, but he was guilty of this.

I couldn't stop the tears. I turned away so he wouldn't see.

I was crying for the class, but also because the person I loved most had just killed something in our relationship. When my dad left the room instead of rushing to my side like he always did when something was wrong—a beesting, a stomach flu, even a scraped knee—I knew he understood that, too.

My dad backed out the entire length of the driveway, swiftly, assuredly, the car making a high-pitched *whir* as it went. My mom waved from the passenger seat. Then they were no longer visible in the tunnel of dusty oleander. They couldn't say when they'd be back. But my dad had packed sack lunches.

Emma clapped her sticky hands. "What are we going to do today?"

At any other point, the hurt in my chest would be worry for my parents. They didn't have to say it out loud: my mother was serving as lookout. But today I was angry. My cell phone sat in the console of my parents' car in case they needed two phones.

"Come look at the butterfly chart I made. I'll tell you about each one." Emma grabbed my wrist and pulled me into the house.

I'd been told to stay close to home since we didn't have a phone. Not to let Emma climb. You could tell they were paranoid; the phone had mostly sat forgotten at the bottom of my backpack, but now they were aware that Emma and I were untethered from them.

Emma ran to her room to find her project. I bit my nail. It would be a matter of hours until Harry texted that phone. He knew he wouldn't hear from me on the weekends, but if I was a no-show in class, he'd text.

I could picture my dad glancing at the phone, reading the text, and we'd be gone before dark.

"Poppy. Move your guy!" We were playing some elaborate board game Emma had spent an hour teaching me, and I hadn't listened one bit. To her credit, she patiently coached me through every move and was only now getting mad.

"Let's go," I said. I couldn't do it anymore—listen to Emma's incessant chatter, pretend I wasn't jumping out of my skin while trying to mentally communicate to Harry that I was still here, only a mile away, and to please not send me any messages. I'd told him not to use my number unless he had to, that my dad always said it wasn't mine, it belonged to the family. And I wasn't allowed to have friends.

"You don't want to play?" Emma looked crestfallen. I snapped to and saw her frustration. "But I just taught you the whole thing!" she said.

"We'll come back to it. I promise. Let's go on a walk. I need some sun."

Emma flopped onto her back and stared at the ceiling. I'd need a bribe.

"Or, I know!" I said. "What about the library?"

"Didn't they say we couldn't leave the house?"

"Maybe some of your friends will be there?" I ventured.

Emma sat up.

After loading my backpack with water, the math book Professor Alexiev had lent me, and a red apple for Emma, we hit the road. It was 10 A.M. Two hours until Harry finished class.

Emma kept up with my long strides, equally excited to break free after a long summer weekend no different from the weekdays.

"I think I have a blister," Emma said as we crossed the train tracks and descended the small hill. In one more block, we'd see the police station, town hall, library, and little yellow train stop.

"Why did you wear those shoes?" I scolded her. Emma's face changed in reaction to my tone. *And here we go,* I thought, expecting a defiant response. But I was surprised when Emma's shoulders drooped and she slowed her pace so she didn't have to walk next to me. When I turned to wait for her, I was taken aback by the sight of silent tears streaming down her cheeks, plopping to the ground. She didn't make a sound. Loud, angry crying, I could deal with. That was Emma's MO. This quiet crying scared me because it seemed to come from deep within. They were tears of utter defeat.

"Emma, what is it?"

Her nose was running. "Hold on. Let me get you a tissue." I searched my backpack for anything.

It didn't matter, because Emma used the tail of her shirt and honked her nose loudly. I watched with the usual exasperation, but then I noticed how she had grown, like she'd gone into the next stage of childhood—from little kid to big kid. She wasn't five anymore. She was eight.

Emma looked up at me. "I hate you," she said.

"Great," I said, done with her. I started walking again. Then, from the corner of my eye, I saw Emma dart across the street.

"Emma! Stop!" I waited for a car to pass and then ran to catch up with her. I caught her shoulder. "What's wrong?"

"I wish I had a friend." She said it automatically. She didn't even need to think about it.

"I know," I said. I did. I really did.

She shrugged off my hand and kept walking, more slowly now.

How did I tell her to get over it, to get used to it? Other people weren't something we could have. I'd never understood why the wanting didn't go away when I was surrounded by my family—the people I loved most.

"When I get my bit money, I'm not giving you any," I heard Emma mutter.

I thought I hadn't heard her right. *Bit money. Hit money? Sit money?* I couldn't come up with what she was talking about. "What kind of money?" I asked, just as I grasped the brass handle of the library door.

"Bit money. Bitcoin. Dad said if I do chores, he'll start giving me an allowance."

"But Bitcoin isn't real. I mean it's real, but it's not like money you hold," I said, grabbing Emma's arm and moving her aside so a woman with a stroller could pass.

Emma yanked her arm away. "I know what it is." She sneered. "And it is real. You get it in dollar bills if you go to the special

ATMs." Emma started to walk away, stepping through the rickety sensor.

"Wait. Emma." She turned and raised her eyebrows. "Did
he tell you that? About the ATMs?"

"I figured it out. That's what happens when you pretend to
be asleep in the car." She said the last part like *Aren't I clever?*

"Can we go outside a second? Just for a second. I promise."
I carefully kept my voice nice. Emma looked at me askance.
But I saw it—she liked that she had something I wanted.

She sighed theatrically and followed me halfway down the
block. We took a seat on a bench and watched a gathering of
nannies who looked like they were feeding snacks to strollers,
the babies invisible under shades.

"What else do you know?" I asked Emma, going for a tone
of one-adult-to-another.

She scooted down and rested her head on the back of the
bench. "Not much. He does one a day, but he has to do more
now. He's in a rush after he got mad at the library. When he
saw that guy here."

"You mean one ATM a day?" I asked.

Emma nodded. "When Mom was sleeping all day, he had to
take me. A couple were far away and we had to cross a bridge."

I pictured my parents crossing the bay today, stuck in
snarled traffic. "What else have you heard when you've pretended to be asleep?"

"Not much. But maybe one day I'll find out who they really
are. Like, they'll say a name out loud when they're fighting
and I'll finally know!" Emma sounded like this was a fantasy
she regularly entertained. "Hey, at least I know who you are!"
she said.

"At least I know who you are," I said back and nudged her shoulder with mine. I'd never thought of it that way—that Emma and I had each other. Only the two of us shared this same strange existence that wasn't our choice.

"Can we go inside now?" She pushed off the bench. I noticed yellow pollen had stained her white shorts. I opened my mouth but then decided to leave her alone.

"Sure. Do you mind if I work on the computer for a little?"

CHAPTER FORTY-EIGHT

n the kids' section, Emma lay on her back dangling a paperback above her head, reading quietly for once. At the moment, there were no other kids her age to befriend, so I could relax at the empty bank of computers. I put down Professor Alexiev's math book next to the computer. She'd given the clear direction that she wanted it back, and if, god forbid, I didn't make it to the test tomorrow, I planned to leave it on the hood of her car today.

I started with Bitcoin ATMs. There were five thousand, spread over ninety countries. Most of them only allowed the purchase of Bitcoin, but now there were machines that had buy-and-sell capacity. You could withdraw up to $5,000 daily. The first ATM of that kind debuted in Silicon Valley.

A flock of strollers made their way into the library. 10:55 A.M.—almost time for story hour. We'd start walking to the high school in thirty minutes so I could see Harry. Emma had perked up, ready to sit behind the gaggle of babies and listen to a read-aloud that was far too young for her. But at least it was something, some form of entertainment.

I returned to the screen feeling sort of satisfied, thanks to Emma. Harry had thought to ask the *why*. Now I had confirmation that coming here was never about saying goodbye to my mother's brother, my dad's best friend. My dad was here to collect cash, and this was how we were getting it.

Cash is king, I always heard my dad say. We couldn't have bank accounts. There had always been a limited amount of cash our support network (my uncle) could send. Before his death, Andrew must have figured out how to pass money that might sustain us without him. Not forever. There was only so much money that could be packed into a minivan.

Miss Staci, the children's librarian, started her greetings with the cat puppet. Emma was rapt.

There was a headline from a week ago in the San Jose *Mercury News* about the price of Bitcoin beginning to crash. I wondered just how much money my dad was withdrawing.

I rubbed my temples and tried to block out the tinny musical recording of "Skinny Marinky." I stared at the screen. It might be a long time before I had the opportunity to use a computer again. I had thirty whole minutes free.

My fingers flew across the keyboard. I found an older feature from a slick, gossipy national magazine about my mother's family that painted them just as Harry had said: California aristocracy. They were shipping magnates who had amassed a fortune from their routes to the Hawaiian Islands. My mother's grandmother was the beloved family matriarch, while the next generation—my mother's parents—were rumored alcoholics who squandered money. I read about a small plane crash that had killed my grandmother's brother, the scandal of my mother that came to define the family, and my uncle, who was the bright hope as the new face of the family business.

The feature was accompanied by photos: a grand San Francisco mansion, an annual Easter-egg hunt on the lawn of the Atherton house, a bevy of small cousins with ponies, the same photo of the dour couple posing—the original Bells who had staked their claim in San Francisco, first in the railroad and then in shipping. And, of course, the one of my mother holding the rifle. The article tantalizingly concluded that whispers would always overshadow the family's successes. They would always be haunted by speculation that someone in the family— maybe Andrew—funded my mother's disappearance.

I saw more photos of my uncle's funeral at Grace Cathedral in San Francisco. There wasn't an article about my uncle's death that didn't also mention my mother's crime and disappearance, putting a decades-old cold case back in the news. Another reason why we needed to leave.

Joe Connelly was mostly lost in the shadow of the Bells. I read about the futile search and rescue for my father; his obituary, which said he'd been at the top of his class at the San Francisco prep school he'd attended on scholarship; how he'd enlisted the day after 9/11. I hadn't known he was an only child.

In the past eighteen years, his father had died of complications of diabetes. His mother lived in Redwood City. Presumably alone. I could hear Harry saying it—*123 Scarlett Drive.*

I couldn't imagine my dad not being a loyal son. Didn't he feel guilty for leaving them? His mother was so close, just one train stop away.

I rolled my neck from side to side. Across the room, Emma felt my stare and looked up. I held up my hand: *five more minutes.*

Five more minutes before I lost internet access for the foreseeable future. I could check my Anna Karenina email. Harry had said not to, but this was it: I was about to disappear. I entered my password.

There were three new messages. All from Carol.

She was insistent on figuring out where this new match fit into the family tree. Her first message expressed her confusion. But now she was fixated.

I hadn't been worried about Carol placing me. I'd grown up invisible and I thought I still was. But suddenly, stupidly, I understood I should have always been very worried. This was complicated but mathematical. Only patience and legwork and other matches were required. We'd matched on my father's side. He was an only child, which made me easier to place.

And then there was the massive fact that my dad was supposed to be dead. He wasn't supposed to have a child.

It was the first time it clicked that I'd placed my father on the map. I was a genetic informant. With my DNA handed over on a silver platter, there was no more hiding.

If someone was smart enough to keep digging, they would figure out my dad had a child. I could also be matched to my mother's family, even if only a very distant relative had taken a test.

For a moment, I listened to my breathing. I covered my face with my hands. They came away wet with sweat. I just hadn't known what I was doing when I'd taken the test. I hadn't known my dad had been so much safer than my mother because everyone thought he was dead.

The only grace in leaving was that I wouldn't have to tell my parents what I'd done.

As I grabbed a reluctant Emma's hand and pulled her down the library ramp, I thought about how I had been so focused on my mother's family. Now I thought about my dad's. I couldn't believe his mother lived so close by.

"Why do we have to go home already?" Emma pulled her hand out of mine, stopping in the middle of the crosswalk.

A white sedan swept swiftly around the corner, and I yanked Emma out of the street, leading her back across the train tracks.

"Don't worry, we're not going home. Not yet."

Emma was surprised but game for adventure.

"Where to? Downtown? Do we have money to buy something? Like a treat?"

"No. We're going to the high school. We're almost there. I need to return a book to my teacher." I thought of the book and then the odd lightness of my backpack. "Oh, shhhhh . . ."

"What?" Emma twitched her nose like a rabbit.

Professor Alexiev's book was at the library, sitting next to the computer. I'd need to go back to get it after I saw Harry.

"Nothing. So, look, we need to wait for a friend from class for a second. He'll be out soon. We can stay right here in the shade."

Emma very slowly turned her head to look at me. "You're not supposed to do that."

"What?"

"Are you telling him we're leaving?"

We stopped and waited by Harry's parked car, just on the

other side of the fence. A line of cars already idled in the school driveway, ready for pickup. I leaned against the chain link, keeping an eye out for the first sign of kids trickling from the hallways.

"That's breaking the rules."

"What? No, it's fine. I need to ask him what I missed today."

Emma backed up against the fence and sagged next to me. "Yeah, right. Is he your friend?"

"No, just someone I sit next to." Harry was my best friend.

I sensed the shift: morning summer school had just ended. Harry would exit any moment.

Emma was expecting me to hold up my end of the conversation. What had she said last? "I need to be ready for the test tomorrow," I said.

"We won't be here that long."

Now I looked at her. What did she know? Emma pulled at the hem of her T-shirt. There were pinpoint holes where the shirt had rubbed against the button at her waistband. "Why do you say that?" I asked.

Loud voices erupted at the front of the school, and I straightened, eagle-eyed. Emma quit talking when she realized I'd stopped listening. She bellied up to the fence to watch the action of the kids.

Where was he? After a few minutes, the cars in the pickup line thinned out.

"Is that him?" Emma asked.

I craned my neck to see where she was pointing.

"That guy. With the black T-shirt and black jeans. Why isn't he wearing shorts?"

Harry walked with his head down, chewing his bottom lip.

He'd apparently had his hair cut over the weekend, because it was much, much shorter. He looked even better.

I was about to call Harry's name when I felt a car pull up behind us. Annoyed, I glanced over my shoulder at the minivan that had stopped in the bike lane, traffic on the busy road rushing by. It was one full second before it registered that I knew that minivan.

Oh my god. Harry's car chirped and unlocked. I slowly turned my back to Harry.

Through the window tint, I saw my mother's profile. When there was a gap in traffic, my dad got out of the car and jogged over to us. I prayed Harry wouldn't call out to me.

"What are you girls doing here? We were driving past and . . ." My dad held up both palms like *What the hell?* He wore sunglasses, so I couldn't read his expression.

"I had a math book I was supposed to return to my teacher. But I just realized I left it at the library." Behind me, I thought I felt Harry see me.

My dad clasped the back of his neck with one hand. His shoulders drooped like he was weary. "Come on, guys. Hop in the car."

Emma trotted ahead of me. As soon as my dad turned to settle her in the car, I faced Harry. He was standing stock-still, watching us.

I held one hand to my chest and waved, quietly saying goodbye.

There wasn't time to see Harry's response. My dad was waiting impatiently for me to get in. Then I saw his eyes move past me and on to Harry. My dad took him in for a beat too long.

I brushed past my dad and ducked into the minivan. When the door clicked closed, I looked out the window. Harry was smart—he'd already moved out of sight and started his car.

I wanted Harry to look up. Just in case this was it. But he kept his eyes down, and my dad drove away.

CHAPTER FORTY-NINE

The car blended into traffic and the four of us were silent. From the cave of the car, I stared at the sunlight and trees and the busy world outside of where I was trapped.

"Dad?" I moved to the edge of my seat. At my mother's feet, I saw a peanut-butter-and-jelly sandwich resting on its foil wrapper, missing only one nibble.

"Yep?" He drained the rest of a small bottle of water.

"That book at the library. Can you drive there now? I can run in. I'll be quick." I couldn't think about Harry down the road and wonder if I would see him again. But I could fixate on the math book. Because if my dad let me get it, that meant there was a chance I could return it to Professor Alexiev tomorrow.

We were ten seconds away from the neighborhood gates. *Don't turn. Please don't turn in.*

"Dad? It will just take a second." He didn't answer. I closed my eyes, waiting for the despair that would hit when the car pulled right.

I opened my eyes and saw the black gates flash past. I squeezed my eyes shut again. *Thank you.* It was a tiny bit of hope.

The car went up and over the train tracks. Then I saw the familiar little park outside the library and the modern stone sculpture near the row of redwoods. I unclipped my seat belt so I could hop out, anticipating the obstacle course of strollers rolling down the ramp.

My dad slowed but then unexpectedly kept going, passing the library and gaining speed. I opened my mouth to tell him he could pull over. But when he turned the corner, he accelerated even more.

"Wait!" I cried. The little town center receded in the rear-view mirror.

"Dan?" my mom asked, her voice rising.

"I don't know." He glanced over his shoulder quickly, then changed lanes, melding into traffic on a busy street.

"It was that car again, right?" Emma asked. "I saw it, too."

"What are you *talking* about?" It was easier to raise my voice at Emma.

"That guy drove a white car—the man who scared Dad. It was at the library again." Emma folded her arms and sat back, congratulating herself on her detective work.

"The same car was at the library twice?" I asked. That was *it*?

"Yep!" Emma said. I didn't want to hear from her.

"Dad?" I demanded.

"Something's off," he said. No other explanation.

"I need that book," I said.

"Poppy," my mom said. *Not now.*

"I need that book. I have to give it back," I said.

My dad eyed his side mirror. "It's not safe."

"Just let me out. I need that book." I flung off my seat belt, still hanging loose across me.

"Poppy!" my dad barked.

"Stop! *What are you doing?*" My mom whipped around in her seat.

"I never ask for anything!" I shouted.

The car went completely silent. I reclipped my seat belt and turned my face away from all of them. I knew my dad would never go back.

"It's just a book," my mom was saying. "It's just a book."

My dad drove aimlessly for an hour before he felt it was safe to return to the house. After I'd calmed down, I stared mutely out the car window. Emma chattered nervously. My parents didn't say a word except to give Emma cursory answers. I could feel them silently communicate. I'd never lost it on them like that.

When my dad crept the car into our garage, I was out of the van before it came to a full stop. I went directly to my room, opened my closet doors, and stared at the array of clothes.

There was a knock on the door minutes later. My mom poked her head in. "Are you okay?"

"Can we take the painting?" I asked, unemotional, tipping my head to the poppy painting. I found I couldn't look at it. It reminded me of when I'd first arrived at this house on that strange, magical day when I'd felt like I had a friend. I'd been right. The friend had been my uncle, welcoming me home for the first time.

"What are you doing?" My mom watched me pull my clothes off hangers.

"Packing. Isn't that what I'm supposed to do?"

"Yeah. I was just coming to tell you to get started on that."

"He's overreacting," I said.

"He's gotten us this far. He's smart in ways we're not."

"Are you sure this isn't how he keeps himself busy?"

"Poppy!"

I felt terrible as soon as I said it. Even now I couldn't diminish my dad of all people.

My mom stood with her hands in her pockets, tentative in the doorway, like she was scared to be alone with me. She had trouble making eye contact. "I need to go help Dad make dinner." She turned to leave.

I suddenly saw red. "Why can't you just say it?"

Leery, my mother slowly faced me, one eyebrow raised.

"Maisie Bell."

My mother shushed me wildly. She took a giant step into the room and swiftly closed the door.

"Why didn't you just tell me who you were?"

"It's too easy to make a mistake," she said, her voice low. She began shaking her head back and forth. "It takes one slip. That's it. And then someone can put all of the pieces together."

"There's nothing worse than living with secrets."

"Plenty of things are worse," she said harshly.

That only made me angrier. "Who are you? Why do people believe Dad is dead?"

Immediately, my mom's eyes got so big I almost wanted to back down. But I didn't. Since that day at the café when I'd seen her photo with that Mona Lisa smile, the bottom had fallen out of my small world.

"Why in the world would he go with you?"

Finally. There was the guilt I had hoped to see. It was written all over her face.

"Tell me!"

"Shhhh!" She quieted me with both hands. "Fine! I'll tell you. Fine. Just, shhhh."

My mom walked closer to me, deeper into the room. I backed away until my hip bone hit the windowsill.

Her voice was so soft I could barely hear her.

"Your dad and I had been together, on and off, since . . . forever, basically. I don't know what you know . . ."

"It doesn't matter what I know. I need to hear it from you. First, tell me what happened with Dad."

My mom stared mutely for a moment at a point on the carpet near my feet. Was she being stubborn? Finally, she drew a long breath and released it slowly, and then she began, surrendering after so many years of running from me.

"After I was kidnapped, he left the Navy SEALs to look for me. He was there when everyone closed in on the ranch," she said.

"What happened at the ranch? A standoff?"

Before answering, my mom paused to listen, trying to sense if someone was standing in the hallway. Emma? My dad? She walked to the door and put her ear close. After a long moment, she backed away.

Very quietly, she said, "Yeah. We were surrounded, awaiting the raid, and the leader, Jim, decided we needed to make a suicide pact. He poured out a bunch of gasoline and lit it on fire; the entire group just sat there. I thought I was willing to die but, apparently, I wasn't. I ran, got to the garage, and hid. From the windows, I could see agents streaming into the house. Then I saw your dad. I knew he would die in the fire looking for me. So I went back in."

I wanted to tell my dad to turn around, to run, right at this point in the story. "You found him?" I asked. "Obviously."

"I found him at the bottom of the stairs."

I crossed my standing legs and leaned in so I wouldn't miss a word.

"In all the chaos and smoke, we made it back to the garage, and then, later, outside. I begged him to get me out of there."

"So, just like that, he decided to run with you?" That didn't make any sense.

"No, no," she said quickly, like she'd just remembered part of the story. "I promised him I was going to turn myself in, I just needed some time. I meant it. But I kept stretching it out, negotiating with him because I was scared to go to prison. We both knew it wasn't going to be a light sentence. Weeks went by and, lo and behold, I got pregnant. That changed everything."

Her gray eyes looked tired. "We made a series of hasty decisions we couldn't—or wouldn't—come back from. In hindsight, we were in love, dumb, and young enough to believe we were invincible."

"You weren't that much older than me," I said.

"We were practically still kids," my mom said. "And then

our kids became the only thing we have—the one thing that's ours. I think we also didn't tell you because we didn't want you to look at us differently. And now you do. I see it. I could tell the moment you knew."

"Of course I'd look at you differently! You took part in a murder!"

"That wasn't supposed to happen." Her face was stoic, but I saw a sheen of sweat on her forehead. I'd never seen her so expressionless. I felt like I was waiting for a whole new person—the real Maisie Bell—to emerge and finally show her face.

"So did they force you?" I asked. "Were you brainwashed?"

At that, she said an emphatic, "No!" Then she stared at the ground again.

"If you aren't going to tell me the truth, I want you to leave my room." I was either about to start screaming or sobbing, and I didn't want her around for either. I fully expected her to go.

My mom took a seat on the very edge of my bed. She looked up at the ceiling while she spoke. "Before the shooting, I thought they were just a band of crazy, theatrical fools. I had no idea any of them were even capable of pulling a trigger."

"Who were they?"

"Only one of them was a convicted criminal. The others were a group of activists who tutored at San Quentin, where they met him. When he was released, he found them and organized them." She twisted her silver bracelets back and forth on her wrist. "Until they kidnapped me, most of what they did were stunts and performance art—things like stealing a truckful of live turkeys and delivering it to a poor neighborhood for Thanksgiving. But then the robberies got bolder. Banks, supermarkets."

"Why would you join them? Because your family didn't pay your ransom?" I kept trying to get her to look at me.

My mom smiled bitterly. "You don't know my family. Everything went to pieces when my grandmother died." She exhaled, losing some steam. "To be honest with you, I'd gotten pretty deep into drugs. My parents paid for rehab, but they were up-front that they were washing their hands of me. My dad slapped me across the face and said I'd finally embarrassed them enough. People in our family didn't do that—go to rehab. That was a few months before I was kidnapped."

Footsteps passed by my door. Emma.

We waited until the sound was faint.

"So?" I pushed. I was sure she'd jump on the interruption.

She shrugged one shoulder. "So, I was living the life of a nun, either going to school or sitting in my apartment. I had totally cleaned up my life and I was hoping your dad would speak to me again. Everything seemed pretty bleak before I was kidnapped."

"They broke into your apartment?"

"Yeah." She nodded. "The kidnapping itself was terrifying, but then they didn't know what to do with me after my family didn't respond. Weeks went by, and they were showing me their faces and chatting about the 'people's revolution.' They did convince me they were helping people in contrast to my parents, who were just sitting on their piles of money. At the very least, I wasn't thinking about drugs and how much I wanted them."

She hooked a finger in her necklace. "Then I realized, actually, there was nothing waiting for me at home. I was willing to do the propaganda photos, and I loved the chaos that ensued. Had I joined? Had I been brainwashed? The group recorded me reading their 'communiqués' and released them to the media. There was no coherent message, so I started writing them. The way I saw it, if I appeared to be a willing participant, that protected my new friends. Besides kidnapping me, they weren't doing much that was illegal."

"Armed robbery?"

She scrubbed her scalp with both hands. "Clearly, I have a habit of believing I have things under control."

"Why didn't you get out of the car that day, or drive away?"

Now she looked at me directly, piercing me with the weight of that fateful decision. "You think," she said fiercely, "I don't ask myself that question every single day?"

"What happened?" I didn't want to know, and I also had to know.

"I'm sure you read it all."

"I want to hear from you!"

My mom gave me a sad smile. Then she nodded a few times, as in, *Okay, I get why you need to know.*

She slipped her hands in her pockets. "I was supposed to be the lookout while the couple I was with—Nicole and Denny—went inside a hardware store to buy sleeping bags. Next thing I know, they're running into the street and firing shots behind them. At that point, I had so many options. I could have, should have, driven away." My mom fluttered the fingers of one hand, like a butterfly flying. She tucked it back in her pocket. "Instead, I started the engine like an idiot and they got in.

"Suddenly, a police officer was running toward us. Nicole

rolled down the window and shot him point-blank in the chest. It was like watching a movie, like there was no way this was real life. And then I was just driving. We switched cars and went to Oregon, to a ranch Nicole knew, where the group planned to meet if something went wrong. I think at some point in the night, what I'd done sunk in. I was probably going to die with this stupid group. But that was okay. I wanted to die. Once that police officer was killed, I knew that was it. The door to my old life was closed."

I didn't want to feel sorry for her. "You really thought I'd never find out any of this?" I asked.

"I didn't want you to. Ever."

"It would have been so much better if you'd told me. Instead, I feel like I don't know you. I'm scared of you."

"Poppy, you know me. Like we've always said, you know what's really important."

"That's not enough!" I whisper-shouted. "You don't get it. You had a normal life. You had a choice." I shook my head. "I want to know about Andrew."

"My brother was your dad's best friend. He was my best friend, too. As I'm sure you know, he passed away."

That immediately lowered the temperature in the room. "I'm sorry," I said.

"Thanks."

"You and Andrew grew up here?"

"Not in this house," she said. She actually smiled. "Our grandmother lived in the house behind this one, the one with the fountain. Andrew and I came down from San Francisco and spent our summers there. My grandmother was so great; she was the only stable person in our lives." My mother's face was open for a moment. "You would have loved her, Poppy. She was the best part—maybe the only good part—of being from a big family. She had these traditions for every holiday." My mom shifted on my bed, bringing a knee to her chest. "We grew up with the neighbor kids who lived here. We'd spend summers running between our houses."

"You were trying to see Andrew that night? Before he died?"

"Yeah. But I didn't." She leaned back on her arms. "It's been hard. My past is everywhere here. But lately I've been telling myself that that's a good thing. Maybe it still exists, that somewhere out there, my brother and I are still together—in this yard—picking fruit, climbing trees." She shrugged again. "That's what I tell myself, anyway."

"Tell me. How did you find out?" she asked.

Should I admit to the DNA test? I didn't want to.

"Dinner!" Emma shouted from down the hall.

We looked at each other for a long moment, knowing our time was up. We could hear Emma coming to get us. So I avoided answering her question. "Are you going to tell Dad I know?" I asked.

She allowed me to evade her question because maybe she was scared to know. "No! It would kill him. He was a hero before everything—in the eyes of his family, his friends, his mentors. All he has left are his children seeing him that way."

It would be just one moment before my mom planted her feet on the floor and returned to the present, to pretending. I stared at the crimson polish on her toes, reminded of how she'd kept me busy when I was small, painting my toes, too. It was just a glimmer, but for a second, she was my mom again instead of Maisie Bell.

My mom stood and came close. I kept my arms locked at my sides and didn't breathe when she wrapped an arm around my shoulders and kissed my temple.

"You deserve so much more than this. Believe me, I know that," she whispered. She rested her head against mine and stayed that way for long seconds, like she wanted to remember this moment before it was gone, like I was still her little girl. "I love you, Poppy. Always."

I couldn't picture a time when I would ever say it back again.

CHAPTER FIFTY

Hours later, when it was dark outside, I was hungry enough to leave my room and quietly make my way to the kitchen.

Rapid-fire, my dad was dealing silverware back into the drawer. We would leave this house the way we found it.

My mom was reaching high into the cupboard, replacing a stack of plates.

"Let me do that," my dad said, putting one hand on her waist and reaching up to take the dishes from her.

"I got it." She smiled at him, their faces inches apart. They kissed for a long moment. Even I could see they still shared attraction between them all these years later. And real love was beneath it.

I was about to leave, since the din of the utensils had covered the sound of my entrance. I didn't want to see either of them. But my dad whipped around. He brought my burner phone from the back pocket of his jeans and held it between us. "Tell me. Who is this?"

I uncrossed my arms and accepted the phone. There was a text from a 415 number—Harry's. The text read ???

Harry had known not to send an overt message, but he'd grown concerned enough to reach out.

"Someone from class wondering where I was," I said, monotone.

"Why do they have this number?" my dad asked quietly. It was a tone that would have sent me scrambling with explanations at any other moment in my life, but I was too angry to care anymore.

"We were working on an assignment together in class. Rebecca had my number. I didn't think it would be a problem if I barely used it."

My dad's face was blank, but I saw his jaw tense. "What's this person's name?" My mom's hand paused before she closed the kitchen cupboard.

I didn't answer.

"Was it the boy I saw in the parking lot?"

I exhaled loudly. Exasperated.

"I asked you a question," my dad said.

"It's nothing. He's no one." I looked my dad directly in the eye.

My dad searched my face. He looked both pissed off and confused, unsteady from my response. Usually I apologized and told him everything he wanted to know. I didn't act like a teenager.

Was he confronting me because he honestly believed the phone could be traced, or was it because I had a friend?

I'd never stonewalled him or been defiant, so I didn't know

what his response would be. Things had never not been okay between us.

The silence dragged on, getting under my skin. I tried to hand the phone back to my dad, but he shook his head. "Keep it," he said.

I turned to leave the room.

"Where are you going?" he asked.

I froze and put my hand on the doorjamb. "Mom told me to pack," I said.

"It can wait. Emma wants to play poker."

"Don't we need to get ready?"

"One last game."

My dad wanted to reset our dynamic. Go back to how things had always been. This was my dad calling a game to reestablish family order. I was formally tolerating my family.

In the golden light of the cozy den, I saw Emma's joy at being surrounded by us. Holding her cards close to her face, she rolled onto her back and kicked her striped-sock heels to the ceiling in excitement. She was eight and her family was still everything.

Would I feel that way again? That they were most important. Or at least enough? I remembered what Harry said: *It becomes the most natural thing in the world to step outside the circle and choose for ourselves.*

My dad dealt.

"Fold!" Emma tossed down her cards and began doing something resembling a painful-looking set of push-ups.

"Fold," my mom said. "Emma, keep your back flat. Why don't you put your knees down?"

It was just me and my dad. He thought he would win like he always did. He'd be one step ahead and see my tells. Tonight, maybe it was his way of expressing how well he knew me. That I couldn't hide.

I didn't used to mind it. Now it annoyed me. I wanted to be separate. To keep some things to myself.

To grow up.

My dad, blank faced as usual, kept raising.

I kept calling. At the river, I went all in.

My dad paused, considering me. I was dead serious. Usually, at this point I'd be folding.

"You've been trying to trap me," he said, smiling, his shoulders relaxing. "But I know you don't have it." Then he got the look he always had when he won—the one that made him seem cocky and boyish. "I'm calling."

In response, I fanned my hand on the carpeted floor.

My dad went quiet.

"It's a miracle! You got him!" My mom whooped.

My dad leaned forward in his limber, cross-legged position and examined my full house. Then he sat back. I'd surprised him.

I'd beaten him.

The reason I knew I'd scared him was because, later that evening, he joined me on the patio. I'd gone out to look at the dark sky for what I knew in my gut was the last night. The stars were faint, but I loved listening to the crickets and feeling held by the peace and safety of the garden.

"I'm sorry, I know you like it here."

He sat close to me on the picnic bench for a few minutes,

smart enough to know there was nothing more he could say. My growling stomach was the only noise.

I was so angry with him. Usually when it was time to move, I looked to my dad for guidance and followed his lead like a good soldier to set an example for Emma. This time, I was having trouble doing that.

"Come inside, sweet girl." He stood.

I wanted to hurt him. "You gave up your life for Mom, didn't you?"

His jaw muscles tightened beneath his skin. In the weak patio light, he opened his mouth to answer and then closed it.

The bench dipped as he sat down again. "No," he finally answered. "I gave up my life for you."

A giant weight crushed my chest, like the wind was knocked out of me. I hadn't expected his honesty to hurt. "No one asked you to," I said.

"Hey, look at me. It's okay. *Look at me.*"

I stared at the ballpoint-pen stains on my dad's faded jeans before raising my eyes to his tired but still-youthful face.

"You and Emma are the loves of my life. I would make the same decision over and over again to have this family. To be with my family. That's better than a conventional life."

I knew he wanted me to believe that, too.

"What's the plan for me? For my future?" Finally, I asked it directly.

We sat in the longest silence. "There isn't one," he said.

My dad, who always had a plan. Even when we'd left Illinois, I'd trusted his guidance implicitly. This summer I'd learned there was a limit to his abilities.

"That's not right," I said.

"It's not." His voice cracked, making him seem suddenly vulnerable. This whole time, he hadn't wanted to answer questions about my future because he was scared. Because he didn't know.

We sat in the dark garden with the hard truth resting between us. Where did we go from here? I sensed it would feel like three adults and Emma now.

My dad finally stood. He kissed the top of my head. "Poppy, why don't you take the test tomorrow?"

My unyielding dad, who always put safety above emotion, had just let my wishes override his own. Anything so I wouldn't pull away from him.

It felt strange to get what I wanted. What I'd pleaded for. For a second, I was reminded of Des Moines.

"It's only one more day."

He sounded like he was reassuring himself.

CHAPTER FIFTY-ONE

In the morning, I planned to leave early so I wouldn't waste a single last minute of freedom. I tried to walk right through the kitchen, past my dad, tossing over my shoulder, "I'm leaving now so I can study a little. The room opens up early."

"Hey, hey, stop for a second," my dad said. He backed against the counter, clutching it with two hands. "You'll be back here at noon, correct?"

I forced myself to inhale and slow down enough to answer his questions. He was wasting my time. "Twelve thirty. I need to finish, walk home."

"Make it twelve fifteen."

My dad looked worried. He shook his head quickly as if to clear it.

"What?" I asked, then regretted it in case he changed his mind about letting me go.

He seemed to be wavering, like he wasn't sure he could let

me go after all, that it was going against his every instinct. "You have your phone?"

I curled my fingers around my backpack strap. "It's in the front pocket."

"One-one-one. That's what you text me if there's anything out of the ordinary. Anything different at all. A stranger you've seen twice. Same goes for a car. *Anything*. Can you promise me that? It doesn't matter if you think I'm crazy; do it for me, okay?"

His expression was even, but his eyes held a hint of *Please* I'd never seen before.

My mom walked into the kitchen. "Good luck, Poppy," she said. I ignored her.

"I'll be back in four hours." I stepped down into the small courtyard with its clothesline where a swimsuit of Emma's hung forgotten and fading, stiff as a board. The ancient straw sunshine ornament was gone. My dad would want my mom to pack more lightly.

When I went to close the door behind me, I saw my dad had moved closer to the doorframe to watch me go.

"Pops?" he said.

"What?" I asked, unable to keep impatience out of my voice now.

He looked at me like he was remembering, like he was about to say, *When did you grow up so fast? You were just five years old.*

"Good luck on your test."

At the end of the driveway, I began to run.

Please. Please be at school. Harry was supposed to join his mother in San Francisco for the breakfast.

Half a block from the school, when I saw his familiar car in the distance, I didn't trust my eyes.

Harry paced by his car. When he saw me, he swiftly moved to meet me. As soon as I entered school grounds, he took my wrists and pulled me toward him. "I thought you'd left."

"I was scared you were in San Francisco."

Harry shook his head. "I couldn't leave in case you came back today."

The Harry I knew would have moved mountains for his mother; it had been bred into him, just like me, to put family first and outsiders second or, in my case, not place them at all. But Harry had said no. That couldn't have been easy.

I told him we were leaving, maybe as soon as class was over. I felt like I couldn't stop talking. There was too much to say.

Harry interrupted. "In that case, don't leave."

"Harry." My voice cracked. "I wish. So much."

He rested his forehead against mine and closed those beautiful eyes. When he opened them, he seemed to readjust. In a joking voice, he said, "Think of the year we would have had together. Maybe we'd get into the same college."

"Or we'd go to different colleges and fight." I liked playing this fantasy game. I was relieved we were going for light.

"Maybe break up at Thanksgiving but be sleeping together again by Christmas."

"I'd be angry that you were dating some rich family friend."

"And I'd be jealous of all the math nerds who worshipped you. But you know we'd end up together, right?"

I loved this fantasy most of all. "Oh, we definitely would."

Harry's eyes darkened and he looked off in the distance. "You're my best friend," he said.

A car eased into a nearby parking spot, forcing us to move.

"Professor Alexiev said the test wouldn't take the whole class. So at least we'll have a couple of minutes after?" Harry asked.

That cheered me up. "The test won't take me very long. I didn't study. I realized it doesn't matter."

"It does, though. It matters to you."

"Yeah, well . . . there's an upside to nothing counting, I guess."

"Until there's something you actually want." Harry grabbed my hand and we began walking to class. "Professor Alexiev was concerned about you yesterday. I told her you may have moved."

"Did she mention her book? I had a book of hers I didn't return. Was she mad?"

"She doesn't care about her book. She cares about you."

I still didn't quite know why I was lucky enough to have her care about me.

When we entered, Professor Alexiev glanced up from her phone. As soon as she saw me, she started sorting through papers and folders. She snatched up an envelope and headed over to me.

"This is for you." She took my hand and placed the envelope in it. "Harry said you aren't allowed to have email or a phone, so I printed this out for you last night."

"Thank you. What is it?" I asked.

"Just take it. Don't lose it," she said brusquely.

I walked over to my seat next to Harry and let my backpack slide down my legs to the floor. When I sat down, I peeked into the envelope beneath the cover of the desk. There were two letters. There was one that seemed like a formal college recommendation. And another to help me get into high school AP calculus. An orange Post-it was stuck to the top letter with Professor Alexiev's email and cell-phone number.

I glanced up. She was watching me.

Thank you, I mouthed. So much "currency" in one envelope. Of all the teachers I'd ever had—and I'd had many—she was the first to take an interest in what happened to me.

Professor Alexiev gave me a smile that didn't reach her eyes. "Five minutes until start time," she called to the room.

The clock said 8:55 A.M. Three hours and twenty minutes until I had to report home.

If I was leaving this area and never coming back, I couldn't spend my remaining time taking a test. One that was futile for me.

My entire life, I had never seen another family member besides my parents and Emma.

"Harry?"

"What?" He stuck out a leg and looped his ankle under mine.

"I think I need to go."

"What? Where?" He tried to sit up but then stopped because he didn't want to dislodge my leg from his, like it was a way to hold on to me.

I had to glance at the whiteboard writing that had faded over the past two months—GENETICS—like it was some sort of bookend for my time in California.

"Do you think there's time to visit 123 Scarlett Drive?"

. . .

I stood at the busy Silicon Valley train station, frozen, wishing I'd accepted Harry's offer to come with me. I'd forced him to stay, mad whispering flying between us.

"You need to take the test," I said. Out of respect for Professor Alexiev, because he needed to finish the class, because it was good for him. Harry was torn for a moment, but we both knew it was the right thing to do.

His fast brain had shifted into gear and he'd quickly shown me directions on his phone. It was only two stops, then five blocks to my paternal grandmother's house. After, I was to get back on the train and Harry would meet me at the country club. Each location was just blocks from the train station.

My hair flew behind me as the silver Caltrans rushed up to meet the station. It halted, then kept creeping, creeping, until it finally screeched to a full stop. I stood between two cars and didn't know if I should move left or right. I was scared and I hated that I felt more Emma's age than eighteen.

That feeling grew worse when I boarded and didn't know where to sit on the packed car. It was peak time on a weekday morning. I glanced upward at an unexpected second tier of seating. There were empty seats, and I shakily proceeded down the aisle, looking for the stairs.

Harry had said I had only two stops before I reached Redwood City, and I was scared I'd miss my stop if I was upstairs and away from the exit. I found a single seat across from a young man with earbuds, who glanced up briefly and then shielded his iPad away from me.

The train lurched and I inelegantly fell back into my seat. I watched out the window as we gathered speed and the familiar sights became a blur of green and pavement.

Professor Alexiev had grown annoyed when Harry and I were whispering. But when she saw me stand and gather my things, she met me at the classroom door and followed me just outside.

"I can't stay," I said to Professor Alexiev. "My family is in the middle of a move and they need my help . . . I'm sorry." I resisted the urge to close my eyes so I could ride out a tirade.

Instead she was quiet. She pulled at the hem of her Star Wars T-shirt. Then, "You would have done well on this test. You know that, right? It could have done a lot for you. I wish they would let you take it."

My throat constricted. She wasn't blaming me. "Me too." I glanced away and saw the reflection of our outlines in the windows. I hadn't realized how much shorter she was than me. In my mind, Professor Alexiev would always be a towering giant.

Professor Alexiev ruffled her fingers through her black bangs. "I'll still be here tomorrow if you change your mind. You understand that you don't need to listen to your parents?" For a second, I saw her as a young woman, not a teacher, maybe only ten years older than me.

I gave a series of small nods. She seemed to know that I was scared to speak because I was trying not to cry.

"Okay." Professor Alexiev walked back into the classroom and gently shut the door. That was our goodbye. I pictured her pacing in front of the class, lit up, lecturing on the beauty of mathematics. Professor Alexiev was the epitome of what Harry's mom had talked about: her full self.

A sharp bark brought me back to the train. "Ticket?" A

large man in a Caltrans uniform swayed easily from side to side, moving with the train, his hand resting on the back of my seat.

"Um. I only have cash."

"You have to pay more on the train. Next time buy a ticket at the station."

I fumbled in my backpack for my babysitting money in my embarrassing elephant wallet with a dirty grosgrain ribbon I'd had since I was fourteen.

I paid for the round-trip ticket and heeded the warning to get ready. We were approaching Redwood City.

CHAPTER FIFTY-TWO

With the train ride behind me, I felt steady on the flat city streets. The train depot was part of a plaza with chain retail stores that aimed to look quaint with old-fashioned streetlamps and hanging flower baskets.

I crossed a major boulevard and for the first time wondered what the hell I was doing. There hadn't been much thought—similar to when I'd taken that DNA test. Just laser focus. Maybe what Professor Alexiev had said—*You need to grab hold of these rare opportunities*—had never stopped playing in my mind. I thought about it often. It was a moment that would stay with me, probably haunt me, for the rest of my life.

This was my only chance to get a glimpse. It wasn't much, but I wanted to see where my grandmother lived so I had the memory.

Scarlett Drive. Thank god Harry and I were both good at numbers and directions, because our exchange with his phone had been lightning quick. I was midway down the quiet street with small homes and chain-link fences. I guessed it had once been a nice, well-kempt block with its faded pastel houses and vinyl siding. Some homes were still cared for, yard art on display, others spotted with debris.

My heart began pounding when I reached 123, though it was just a small pink house with roses out front. There was nothing to see, really. Just a house. And I had only a few minutes.

Mission accomplished. Silently, I stood in front of a decaying white picket fence.

There were signs of financial hardship—a gutter hanging loose from the roof, the badly peeling house paint. It was the roses that got under my skin. The rows of pink and yellow, clearly someone's passion. It said something about the widow who lived inside. The roses made it real that this was all I'd ever know about my dad's mom.

At least it was something personal. I'd felt the same way when I first saw my bedroom, then the poppy painting—and I'd had those glimpses of my uncle in photos and articles I'd managed to see. I hadn't known how badly I wanted them.

I shifted my weight and watched silently. One more minute.

A truck down the street eased over a speed bump. Standing alone, I felt like I was paying my respects to the woman inside who had lost her husband and her only child. I thought of the grand houses I'd seen in the articles about the Bells, their wealth in such stark contrast to this much more modest life. I knew my dad had to have been their pride and joy. He was my dad. He was so amazing.

Except that he had left them. Just like that. My mom had struggled being back here, wanting to rewind, wanting parts of her old life back. I sensed her regret. But I never, ever sensed that from him. Did he even think about the past?

If I were him and I saw this house, I would feel nothing but guilt.

I heard the sound of a car door closing behind me. No one had driven by, so someone had been sitting in a car. Were they going to ask me what I was doing, why I was loitering? I had to go. I wasn't ready, but it was time. I thought about boarding the next train and the relief I'd feel when I walked down the drive of the country club. I started to walk.

At first, it didn't surprise me when I saw my dad, like I'd conjured him from my thoughts.

He was across the street, parked two houses down, as though he'd wanted to watch his mother's house unseen. His hand was still resting on the handle of the door, like he might quickly get back inside the car.

I froze.

My dad drew a deep breath, his chest rising in a wave. He was standing in front of me, totally exposed for who he really was. If I'd found his mother, I knew.

Then I saw the shame. So much shame.

My dad gave one big nod and then slipped into the car, like some kind of professional spy, and peeled away swiftly. The interaction had been maybe five seconds long.

"Excuse me?" An older woman called out to me. She had snow-white hair tied back into a ponytail. She came closer. Her smile was the same as my dad's. "Is there something I can help you with? I saw you standing out front."

Despite the white hair, my grandmother's face was youthful. So were her clothes. She wore khaki shorts and a Golden

State Warriors T-shirt. For a moment she squinted at me—like maybe I was familiar—but that was probably wishful thinking. She waited, smiling expectantly at this teenage girl who appeared lost.

"I think I know where I am now," I said stupidly. "Here." I bent down and grabbed a rolled-up newspaper at my feet.

She met me at the fence. I passed her the paper, which she politely took even though it was just a flyer.

I took one last look at her, nodded, then I began jogging. It was all I could think of to do.

I fucked up. I fucked up. My backpack thumped against my sweating back.

It had always been dangerous for me to find out who my parents were. I just hadn't known there was emotional danger as well. My dad, both of my parents, had carefully constructed a mindset. It was just that—a construct, a house of cards. And I'd just pulled out the most important one.

Now I understood what my mom had meant: for his sanity, my dad needed this mindset. He wanted to be heroic, fighting for a worthy cause—our family. Not the young man who had made a series of bad decisions.

From the look on his face, I knew he and I would never be the same again.

CHAPTER FIFTY-THREE

The setting was so peaceful and serene, it almost seemed like a joke. I was the only person who got off at the tiny train station by the library. Compared to the busy Silicon Valley I'd seen just north, this place was an old-fashioned, quiet hamlet.

The train's doors slid closed behind me and, in an incredible burst of noise, the train pulled out. Seconds later, a strong wind in its wake, the train was far down the tracks, headed south to San Jose. The last car was obscured by a mirage of heat.

I knew my dad was waiting for me at home. He could hide himself again behind a flurry of action. I imagined taking one step in the driveway and seeing our scant belongings marshaled into the minivan. I'd get into the car, the door would slam shut, and we'd go to the next place. The four of us would share a ratty hotel room tonight.

My knees were shaking. I watched the green leaves quiver in the breeze.

My dad wouldn't ask me in front of Emma how I'd found out. Would he take me aside tonight? Whisper to me in front of a motel ice machine? Maybe he would never ask and it would live between us. A new weight.

I wouldn't be able to forget the raw shame on his face, shame at who he was and what he had done. He hadn't hurt anyone. What had started as a young man's misguided attempt to be a hero had gone off the rails, digging him deeper and deeper. He pretended his choice was a good one by living his life in savior mode. Joseph Connelly had hidden for years, but he'd also concealed himself from his children. I was never meant to see the real him, the man who had regrets and had allowed himself just a glimpse of his own mother.

My family waited on one side of the train tracks and Harry on the other. I was terrified of facing my dad.

I chose to say goodbye to Harry.

I was sweaty and bedraggled when I reached the brick entrance to the country club. I walked down the center of the drive. An Escalade honked at me to move, and I listed to the side like I was crazed and drunken.

It helped that I knew my way around. I let myself into the pool area like I had so many times earlier in the summer, and no one questioned a teenager with bright brown freckles and a heavy backpack.

I searched the pool deck for Harry, not holding my breath that he'd already arrived.

The pool was far less crowded than it had been earlier in the summer, August no doubt being the most popular time to leave town. I thought of Rebecca and Frank, and wished so hard that I could go back to being that clueless girl enjoying just that tiny bit of newfound freedom.

In the distance, I saw a hand raise. Harry was seated at that same table with his friends. He rose halfway from his chair, but once he knew I saw him, he sat down again, expecting me to come to him.

I stood mutely. He had to be kidding. Harry knew we needed to say goodbye. In private. I wanted to get in his car and have him drive me within a block of my house. I'd tell him how crazy that was—that I'd seen my grandmother in person—and then about what had happened with my dad, how he'd been watching his mother's house, maybe silently saying goodbye like me. *How often had he done that?* Then I'd watch Harry drive away. We'd never see each other again.

"Excuse us!" A gaggle of middle-school-age girls ran past me, bumping me with a large flamingo floaty.

Harry gestured to me again. More insistently. *Come over here.*

I took a deep breath, my nostrils flaring. I felt like I was going to jump out of my skin.

When I reached the large round table, I could barely make eye contact with the six friends tucked around Harry. Their curiosity and scrutiny were palpable as soon as I stepped beneath the shade of their umbrella. This was my nightmare. It had once been Harry's.

I edged near Harry. There was nowhere to sit since every chair was taken. The table was already crowded with Harry's fans, whom he'd been neglecting all summer.

Harry caught my wrist and pulled me down onto his lap. He smelled like his sheet spray and fancy shampoo.

"This is Poppy," Harry said to his friends.

Maybe Harry was making a show of how he'd changed. That he wanted to be public with his feelings for me. But that seemed like last week. At this point, he was well aware that I was about to run and that he should hide that he knew me.

I moved and Harry rearranged me on his lap. He was so skinny, he wasn't very comfortable. But he was strong, which was kind of comforting.

"Harry, I have to go," I said softly.

"I know," he whispered near my ear. "I just ran into Alix." Then, louder, "Alix, what were you saying?"

That was when I noticed the beautiful brunette.

She nodded. "Yeah, so, like I was saying, did you know you can just take someone's DNA? It's legal." Her voice was throaty and her hair gleamed like she'd just had a blowout before putting on a bikini.

The word "DNA" stood out to me first. Then her features sharpened into focus. It was like looking into my mother's face. Her eyes were gray, like my mother's.

Harry squeezed my waist. Then began rubbing my back.

Alix Bell. I remembered, right here in this exact spot, one of Harry's friends had cited my resemblance to her.

How the gray eyes were such a dominant feature in that family was incredible. Even more mind-blowing was that someone who was a cousin could look so similar to me and my mom. With her same dark hair and lack of freckles, Alix looked more like my mother than I did.

I knew I was staring, but so was everyone else, rapt. She seemed like as big or even bigger a draw at the table than Harry. I began to listen to what she was saying.

"So what did they tell you exactly? That's so weird," a red-headed guy to her left said.

"Not much. You know how police have started using those DNA test sites to solve cold cases? Well, I guess they had some of her DNA uploaded to a database. Then, suddenly, after all this time, they got a hit. They think it's her daughter. But they took DNA from all of us to fill out the family tree, to try to place her, make sure that's who she is." Alix rubbed her bare arms like she had goose bumps. "So, yeah, we're all on edge right now."

"Oh my god, that's insane," someone muttered.

"She logged in from Atherton, guys," Alix Bell said in a hushed tone, truly uneasy, sharing a secret with her friends.

"Logged into what?" a girl with a buzz cut asked.

"The DNA site."

Harry put his hands on my hips and gently pushed me off his lap. Then he stood up behind me and took my hand. I was floating somewhere high in the sky, miles above the pool.

"Every day, we think they'll find Maisie by the end of the night. We've been thinking that for at least two weeks."

"Shouldn't she be hiding in South America or something?"

"Yeah, but her brother just died, which maybe brought her back. It's so weird: no one would ever speak of her, and now all of a sudden . . . this is weird for my mom. They grew up together."

"Did your mom ever talk about her?"

Alix combed her fingers through one side of her hair and looked wistful. "She said she was the cool cousin, but she was always looking for trouble."

"We've got to go," I heard Harry say to the group. "Later."

"You're okay. You're okay," Harry kept repeating softly as he guided me through the blacktop parking lot. For a moment he halted, like he'd lost his car.

"Harry."

"I know. I know."

Harry held up his key and his car, one among multiple Porsches, chirped from somewhere straight ahead. He put his hand on my back and guided me, opening the car door for me when we reached it.

At my side, he leaned in and kissed me somewhere under my cheekbone. He had the foresight to know that might be the last time we touched.

When Harry started the car, I opened my backpack to find the little burner phone.

He put the car in reverse. "What are you doing?"

I held the phone in both hands, cradling it, shaking.

My dad had been right all along.

"I need to tell my dad. Message him that we have to go. Right now."

Harry drove down the long club driveway. He kept raising his eyes to the rearview mirror.

"Poppy?"

"What?"

I typed it: 111. I drew half a breath, held it, then pressed SEND. I imagined it traveling through the air, across the one mile between me and my family. Right now even one mile between us was too much.

"I don't think you should be in the car with me," Harry said.

"I'm so sorry, Harry. I know you shouldn't be with me. I have to meet at the emergency spot. The Starbucks downtown. Can you get me a little closer to it?"

"No, I mean, this is why I keep getting pulled over by the cops." Harry locked the doors. Beads of sweat were forming on his forehead. "I got pulled over two days ago by my dad's old house and then those mornings right by the school."

"Wait. What are you saying?"

"You used my laptop at those locations. Also, at my dad's house. That's where I set up your email." Harry thought for a second. "I wonder if that guy going through the trash was someone watching the house."

"Harry, I'm so sorry."

"You didn't know." Harry started laughing. "The cops must be so confused. They're looking for a girl and they keep finding me."

"I logged in yesterday. After you told me not to. At the library." I thought about what I'd believed was my dad's paranoia. Both incidents had taken place at the library. There'd been the strange man when he was there with Emma. That had triggered his desire to leave. Then yesterday he'd noticed a white sedan for a second time. My dad was the smartest person I knew.

"Poppy, if I get pulled over now—between here and Starbucks—they're going to know who you are."

The cell phone beamed red in my hand. 5 minutes was the response.

Harry glanced down at the cell phone. "I texted your phone. If they're tracing mine, they're tracing that one. It's pinging cell-phone towers, and they know where you are. Throw it out the window." Harry rolled down my window, took it from my hand, and tossed the phone like a Frisbee. It landed over the steel fence of a mansion, on private property. He fished his phone from his pocket, slowed, and hurled his after mine.

"How could I have been so stupid?" I said. "And so selfish. They told me not to go looking." My dad had always said it would be a slipup that got us. I'd pictured Emma saying the wrong thing, a surveillance camera at the pack-and-ship store. I hadn't known it would be a colossal mistake made by me, the rule follower, because I'd been living in a different century.

We were nearing the small downtown, stuck at a four-way stop with three cars ahead of us. Harry palmed the back of my head. His eyes were scared and he stared straight ahead.

"It wasn't selfish," he said. "It was selfish that they wouldn't tell you."

We slowly drifted past the fire station. A group of firemen and first responders milled in the front. One held a softball and glove in his hand.

Harry laughed.

"What?" I asked. I was thinking of what Harry had just said—about me not being the selfish one.

"I realized, if we get pulled over—right now—you didn't actually do anything."

"Yeah," I croaked. I knew exactly what was coming next.

"I have to say it one more time: you can leave them and have a normal life. You could do it right now."

"My sister."

"You would be an example. Maybe when she's your age, they would let her go to you."

"They're all I know, Harry." I couldn't not see them again. Even the thought—it felt like part of me would be cut away. To not be part of a family of four. To not be with my dad.

Harry shook his head. "They've raised you to be the amazing person you are, so you can be independent."

"They don't think that."

"Deep down, they do." Harry squeezed my hand so hard it hurt. "For all their faults, they've done the best job."

"I'm sorry," I said again. I saw the candy store on my right and the pet store on the left. Harry braked for a pedestrian, and I couldn't remember if the Starbucks was one block away or two. Each remaining second with Harry felt alive and like it passed in slow motion.

"I love you, Poppy," Harry said. For the first time, it wasn't hidden in the sentence among other words, leaving me guessing.

"I love you," I said. I stared at him until he turned his head to look at me. I wished I could convey all the facets of my love for him: appreciation and attraction and respect. "Harrison Addison." I tried to lighten the mood.

He wasn't going for it. "Poppy Connelly. That would probably be your name, right?" He pulled forward and I saw the Starbucks.

"Poppy Connelly." I'd found out who I was this summer.

I saw the minivan already idling on the small side street. It was tucked between a Mercedes SUV and a Smart car that reminded me of Professor Alexiev's.

"They're right there," I said to Harry, placing the back of

my hand against my window, showing him where they were while covering them up at the same time.

Harry slowed and we drove past. I saw my mom and dad in the front seat, but they couldn't see me. They looked like just two regular people. For a split second, I wanted to tell Harry to keep going.

"You can let me out on the corner." Harry took a right and pulled into a handicapped spot. I'd thought he would just drop me off and he would drive away, fast and far.

"Harry," I said, "go. I have to run."

"No way. I'm watching you leave. I have to. I need to."

There wasn't any more time. "Bye," I said decisively. I swung open the car door and, with my backpack hanging from my elbow, I ran across the street. At the corner, I made eye contact with my dad, who was watching in his side mirror.

I stopped running. Maybe it was the fear of seeing my dad, that he knew I saw him for who he really was. I stood on the sidewalk. It reminded me of my last day in Illinois. I'd been the only family member outside of the car. I'd known we were about to drive away from a place where I'd found some happiness. I'd felt so tired and had a glimpse of separateness from them. But last time, the thought of being apart had scared me and I'd leaped into the back seat with Emma and swiftly closed the door. I didn't feel that way anymore.

My dad got out of the car. His face was ragged. He tilted his chin up in greeting at someone past my shoulder. I turned around and saw Harry standing a few feet behind me, staring back at my dad. The expression on Harry's face was somewhere between calm and confrontational.

My dad searched my eyes. His were wary and tentative. I

saw that he believed I hated him. He said, "I made my choice, Poppy. You get to make yours."

By giving me that freedom, in one fell moment, I released all of the rules, all of the structures that had penned me in tight. He and I both knew what I needed to do.

In answer, I said, "Do you know how much I love you?" We both knew what that meant. What choice I was making.

I expected this would crush him, but I thought I saw a burden lift from him. Relief, because this was the right thing. Relief that even though I knew his real story, that I saw all of him now—his secrets, his flaws, his shame—I still loved him. He didn't need to be perfect.

"You've been the best dad," I said. "You made it. You raised me."

I had a flash of him pushing me from behind on my bike, me fighting him, not wanting him to let go. Then he'd released the bike and stayed behind. I'd been so terrified. *I've got you. I've always got you,* he'd said. But he'd let go.

I hoped it was that realization that played over his face. He'd completed what he'd set out to do. It was why he'd run in the first place. He'd raised me himself. He'd also made me ready. Because wasn't that the job? To prepare me to start my own life?

My dad began to cry openly. "Ace that test for me, Pops," he choked out. "It might not be too late." He moved quickly to hold me close, but it was over so fast. He grabbed the door handle and got back inside the car. I walked alongside it. My dad started the car and rolled down the window. I leaned forward and saw my mom in the front seat. Emma stuck her head between them.

"Go to my mom's house. I want you with her," he said.

I didn't see any belongings in the car. Only my mom's purse and Emma's stuffed badger. One thing each. I'd caught them unprepared. Because of me, the bulk of that money was lost, left behind on the closet floor.

"We're always with you, okay? Even if we're not. Got it?" My mom was bawling.

"Mom! I love you." I had to make sure she knew.

She gave me a smile I'd never seen. It was pure joy. And relief.

She raised her tearstained face to mine and gave me a bigger smile—the one that made her the indelible Maisie Bell. I couldn't help but return it.

"Emma, I'll see you later." I looked to my sister, needing her to be mature for a second and understand what I was saying.

Emma gave me an odd, preternaturally grown-up nod, us getting each other on a level no one else ever could. Then she threw herself back against the seat and tried to raise her feet up to kick the roof, a kid again. Just like that. She still needed them.

My dad rolled up his window and faced forward, steeling himself for the next challenge, ready to take care of everyone. He pulled out. I looked after the minivan until I couldn't see it any longer, watching them disappear.

Part of me would always be with them in that car, with them wherever they went.

Harry came forward and took my hand.

ACKNOWLEDGMENTS

In a year full of twists and turns, I'm so grateful I didn't have to make this journey alone. My thanks to the following people who inspired this book and made it a reality:

My beloved editor, Sarah Dotts Barley, who miraculously intuits what I want to accomplish and couldn't be more fun, supportive, and smart along the way (and who doesn't mind receiving emails with lots of exclamation points!).

Megan Lynch, for believing in this story, and the incredible, hardworking team at Flatiron Books.

My now longtime agent, Kerry Sparks, my intrepid partner, who made sure my career moved forward during a pandemic. Sylvie Rabineau, for championing this book and for all her efforts on my behalf.

Yaki Tsaig, Andre Beskrowni, Rick Redman, Diahan Southard, and Megan Frederick, for their expertise in areas where I needed guidance: mathematics, cybersecurity, life off the grid, and genetics. This book wouldn't have come together without them.

My sweet friends who listened to me put this puzzle together: Vivian Raksakulthai, Mina Kumar, Meghal Mehta, Leigh Sebastian, and Elizabeth Burns Kramer.

Amanda Ward, Shellie Faught, and Shelby Boyer, for being early readers and giving insightful editorial guidance.

May Cobb, Peternelle van Arsdale, and Tara Goedjen: I couldn't do this without author friends like you.

Joan Sanders, for sharing history of the Peninsula and especially Lindenwood, formerly the Flood estate. I'm so grateful for your and Mo's friendship, and I can't imagine my childhood without your family of five kids living over the fence.

The Wilson family, who was part of the early years and who gave me my copy of *The Giving Tree*.

My parents and my sister, Kjersti, as well as Sophy Hagey and Sandy Manley, for our years together in one of my favorite places on Earth.

My family: Jeff, Astrid, and Margot. The bulk of this book was written with everyone working in the same space, so I appreciate your patience and effort to make it work. Special thanks to both girls, who read multiple drafts of this book (maybe they were bored?) and gave me feedback and advice along the way. I think Margot knows Poppy as well as I do. I couldn't have done it without you, Margie. I'm lucky to come from a family of solid editors and beautiful writers.

ABOUT THE AUTHOR

MARIT WEISENBERG has a master's degree in cinema and media studies from UCLA and worked as a film and television executive for a number of years. She currently lives in Austin, Texas, with her husband and two daughters. She is also the author of *The Insomniacs*.

maritweisenberg.com
Instagram: maritweisenberg